EBUR`

SARASV*

Kavita Kané is the bestselling author of six novels. Today, she is considered a revolutionary force in Indian writing, mainly because she has brought in feminism where it is most needed—in mythology.

All her seven novels are based on lesser-known women in Indian mythology—*Karna's Wife* (2013); *Sita's Sister* (2014); *Menaka's Choice* (2015); *Lanka's Princess* (2016); *The Fisher Queen's Dynasty* (2017); *Ahalya's Awakening* (2019); and now *Sarasvati's Gift*.

For one who confesses that the only skill she knows is writing, her literary journey expectedly began as a journalist, with twin post-graduate degrees in English literature and mass communication and journalism from the University of Pune. With a career spanning two decades in Magna Publishing and DNA, and as assistant editor in the *Times of India*, she now devotes her time to being a full-time author.

Passionate about theatre, cinema and the arts, she is also a columnist, a screenplay writer and a motivational speaker, who has given several talks across the country's educational and research institutes, corporate and management forums and literary festivals.

Born in Mumbai, with a childhood spent largely in Patna and Delhi, she lives in Pune with Prakash, her mariner husband, two daughters, Kimaya and Amiya, two dogs, Chic and Beau, and Cotton, a not-so-curious cat.

Sarasvati's Gift

KAVITA KANÉ

EBURY
PRESS

An imprint of Penguin Random House

EBURY PRESS

USA | Canada | UK | Ireland | Australia
New Zealand | India | South Africa | China

Ebury Press is part of the Penguin Random House group of companies
whose addresses can be found at global.penguinrandomhouse.com

Published by Penguin Random House India Pvt. Ltd
4th Floor, Capital Tower 1, MG Road,
Gurugram 122 002, Haryana, India

Penguin
Random House
India

First published in Ebury Press by Penguin Random House India 2021

ISBN 9780143452560

Typeset in Adobe Caslon Pro by Manipal Technologies Limited, Manipal
Printed at Manipal Technologies Limited, Manipal

www.penguin.co.in

MIX
Paper from
responsible sources
FSC® C043100

To
Maha Sarasvati, invoking the Devi of Knowledge within

And to my parents and all my Gurus,
who tutored me with intellectual, ethical, emotional and social
instruction not typically taught at school or university

Contents

PROLOGUE

HER PROPHECY

A river is a Mystery; of distance and source,
Touch its flowing body and you touch far-off places,
You touch a story that can't stop telling itself,
A story that's always just beginning,
The song of a river ends not at her banks,
But in the hearts of those,
Who have truly loved her . . .

'Don't leave us! No, please, please don't!'

The lady in white froze and turned her head to look straight into the terrified eyes of the young sage.

'I had once become a river for you!' she drew in a slow, deep breath. 'For you, O Man, I brought the Fire of Knowledge to Earth from Heaven . . .' she whispered, the heat of the anger in her breath frosting against the icy air of the mountains. 'Today I shall return to the Heavens, never to come back . . .'

'You can't, O Sarasvati Devi!' cried the rishi. 'You are our river, our goddess, our livelihood!'

'And also your wisdom,' she added, her face unsmiling, her frosty face melting into a profound sadness. 'But one you seem to have lost. Or forgotten?'

He flinched at the cold contempt in her voice.

'If you forsake us, you will have forgotten us!' the rishi implored, his tone desperate.

'To this day, Devi Sarasvati, you refuse to be tamed, free and flowing! You are that goddess who refuses to be confined by a temple roof over her head. That is why we worship you as a river, the flow of human thought and creativity . . .'

'I prefer to remain a concept, a thought you would construct as wisdom,' Sarasvati said coldly.

'I would rather be the supreme power of *rasa*, the essential communication between mind and free thought!' she stated.

'But by free expression, I did not mean the freedom to defy the natural order, to destroy Nature. Man did. You have forgotten the essentials of Life!' she accused, her fury freezing the blood in his veins.

'In your arrogance, you forgot the gift I presented to mankind. You forgot to preserve Nature, its beings; be it the vale or the hills, the flowers or the trees, the air or the waters. You ravage all, in your blind worship of profit and power, war and violence,' her lips curled.

'You consume all, devouring everything in your greed. You are men of no faith, just monsters of fear and hate and destruction. So then, why should I wait, whom should I serve?' Sarasvati asked calmly.

'Us! All of us!' implored the sage.

'You, who are not friends to each other but fiends baying for each other's blood, ready to reduce me to a river of blood of butchered forests, exhumed earth, slaughtered animals and murdered people? I shall not!' she raged, her cold eyes gleaming in the barren whiteness.

The rishi quailed. 'Yes, we have forgotten,' he said. 'Once we venerated you out of respect and need. That's why we worshipped the water, the trees, the breeze, the sun . . . Now we worship wealth, fame, power and title. No wonder we lost your trust, no wonder you turned against us,' he drew in a shaky breath, his eyes full of unshed tears.

She looked up then, her face white and her eyes glittering. She looked beautiful, but it was a terrifying, dangerous beauty.

'You can't leave us!' he beseeched, his teeth chattering in fear. 'You are Sarasvati, born to bring life and knowledge to us . . .'

'Which you have long spurned for mindless violence and continued ignorance,' she scoffed. 'And to reckon that I once carried the Fire of Knowledge for ingrates like you!'

He couldn't meet her cold, steady gaze.

'Yes, you deigned to become a river, taking the form of cool water, to carry the heat of the monumental fire of destiny—the Vadavagni. You are Sarasvati, constantly moving, flowing. You cannot stop!'

She lifted her head and stared at him, her eyes dark with rage.

'I have to stop this madness, I have to stop you!' she announced frostily. 'I shall halt, for I am dying. I am

drying up . . .' she whispered, her voice rasping. 'A river
that is dying . . .'

'A river cannot die!' he cried.

'*You* made me die!' she lashed out. 'Man did achieve
the impossible,' she continued with a sneer, her tone ironic.
'You killed a river!'

'No, no, we will save you!' he blubbered in a frenzy.

Sarasvati paused briefly, her eyes glancing down at the
languid waters she was standing in, bubbles gasping in
strangled sighs. 'I am,' she swallowed. 'I am dying.'

He shook his head vigorously. 'No, you are the water
of plenty. You are evergreen, you are our perennial lifeline,
you are immortal!'

He noticed the slight nod of her beautiful head, and
his voice rose hysterically. 'You are our Sarasvati, our
support, our sustenance, our salvation! You have been
with us since time immemorial, vast and splendid and
bounteous, your holy waters flowing from right here,
the mighty Himalayas to the Earth and into the sea,
nourishing not just our lands but our minds, blessing us
with knowledge.'

'And I did,' she smiled grimly. 'But where is that
knowledge now? It has gone, and so shall I.'

'No, you are us, you can't abandon us. We love you,
we worship you, we need you. You are our Vedas, you are
our source of life, our Ambitame, Naditame, Devitame!'
he cried hoarsely. 'That is, the best of mothers, the best
of rivers, the best of goddesses. You are our witness to
history. On this shore, Kartikeya was grandly anointed
the commander of the Devas. Parashuram dipped himself

in these very waters to cleanse himself and the Earth of the scourge of tyranny. You encouraged the love between Pururavas and Urvashi when he first met her galloping along this very bank. Even the Mahabharata war was fought here!'

'Didn't you realize that like the Great War, it was the beginning of my end too,' she said quietly. 'That was when it finally sunk in, that my time on Earth was done.'

The rishi threw her a startled look. 'But there has been prosperity since. We are a great empire, a land of great kings and people,' he broke off, watching the expression on her pinched face.

'Prosperity, perhaps, but not peace, harmony or enlightenment,' she lashed out. 'There may be knowledge, but I see no wisdom. I see progress but no achievement, experience but no expertise,' her full lips curled in cold contempt.

'I see only pain, hate, violence, war and suffering. And I cannot live in such a land where man is against man, Man is against Nature, and Man is against animals and all living beings and creatures. I can exist only in harmony and goodwill, I cannot flourish otherwise.'

Her tone was flat and final, filling the rishi's beating heart with renewed terror.

'How can you turn your blessing into a curse?' the rishi wept. 'You can't forfeit us now, you had promised you will stay on Earth forever,' he glanced tremulously at her fading, wilting figure.

'You had made me a promise too, remember?' she asked softly, her voice a caressing reprimand.

'Yes—that we shall forever respect you and the precious gifts of Nature.'

'And what is that, pray?'

'You, the mighty river, the precious waters, the land and the skies, the trees and the animals, the birds and the beasts, the saplings and sunlight, the air and the sun,' he said, his voice faltering.

'You remember? Man seems to have forgotten it long ago in his arrogance and profound ignorance,' she observed wryly.

The rishi shuddered. 'We have erred, forgive us, O Goddess, and pardon us our mistake!'

'Mistake?' she repeated dully. 'You commit the same mistake over the years, down the centuries, through the ages?! What you have done is not a mistake, it is a colossal crime.'

'Then punish us some other way,' he said wildly. '*I* shall atone, we shall atone.'

'No, it was I who was punished,' she said sadly. 'You killed me.'

The raw rasp of pain in her voice pierced his heart.

He folded his hands. 'Be with us. We shall revere you to remind us lest we ever forget, that we remain forever blessed with the knowledge . . .'

'Not knowledge, but wisdom,' she corrected gently, but he recognized the grim undertone in her voice. 'Man has enough knowledge, in fact, so much of it, but so little wisdom.'

Her pale lips were rigid, her eyes glacial on her fair face.

'But it was through knowledge that you linked the Heavens with the Earth, the celestial with the mortal,' he implored. 'Right from the time when the devas, the asuras, the *aditya*s, the *daitya*s, the rishis and the *jana*s, all interacted freely.'

She shook her head.

'You were part of the evolved human race of seers and scholars,' she reminded him dourly. 'You were the ones responsible for bringing the Gods and Earth together, not me!' she returned with a humourless smile.

'In your perennial quest for information, you discovered the uncanny powers to travel freely between Heaven and Earth, through portals and planes, not me!' she ended with a scornful laugh. 'I was just a vessel to transport this divine knowledge to Earth.'

The derision in her voice was unmistakeable.

'Please don't mock us! It was you, not us!'

Her eyes grew wider. She appeared to hesitate, then nodded. 'That fire I carried for you with my cooling water,' she smiled sadly, her tone oddly wistful.

'Those waters still retain the heat of the fire I have carried over the centuries. That heat is still within me, I am warm even in these icy mountains,' she murmured. 'So much heat that I can feel myself drying, evaporating, vapourizing, vanishing . . .'

He shook his head vigorously. 'You have in due course, spanning over thousands of years, blessed us long. How can you evaporate from the face of the Earth?'

She regarded him with her calm, remote eyes. Her quiet calmness frightened him.

'Yes, I became a river for this world, for mankind,' she nodded. 'But was my descent from Heaven to this world worth it, was this world worthy of me?'

Her cold, flat tone sent a shudder of terror through him. 'We love you, we worship you,' he beseeched. 'Our Rig Veda hymns chant your praises as our saviour, as the life-giver of all the people residing in your river valley. You are our mighty river, the seventh river of the Sapta Sindhu, right from the Sindhu in the west to the Sarasvati in the east. You have cradled culture and civilization in your fertile river valley, our literature—again your gift to us—sing your paeans. You are our spirit, our devi, our greatest of rivers that has nurtured the people like a loving mother. A mother cannot abandon her children!'

'Then it is my children who killed me!' she exploded.

The rishi flinched. He imagined the world, a world without the mighty Sarasvati, the parched earth, the arid banks, the bleak, barren wasteland, the endless drought and wasted, withered children, too weak to weep, dying slowly of hunger, and his voice broke into a sob.

'I beg you!' he heard himself weep. 'I know we have plundered and ruined the world . . . and you. But save us. You have no feelings for us, but the children . . . what have the children done?'

Sarasvati sighed, her face grew softer, moved by his words. 'I can't stay any longer, I have no waters left, nothing to give, and hence I shall disappear underground and continue my glorious flow beneath the surface. My absence shall be a reminder, the curse of your doing, as henceforth I shall remain only a memory, the blessing you turned . . .'

The rishi fell at her feet. 'No, don't disown us, we have learnt our lesson well,' he shrieked desperately, his voice shrill in terror.

'Have you?' she whispered. 'Has Man, will he ever?' She was backing away from him, pushing him away with steady hands.

A long moment passed in silence. He heard her sigh passing over her pale lips, holding her breath to stop her inward trembling, while the rishi stood before her motionless, like a post, and looked at her in astonishment and terror. And then she was gone . . . a swift whiff of white vanished in a blink.

He heard the swirl of her last words in the chilly echoes of the mountains, in the raging pain in his heart, in the inner tumults of his churning mind. *Have you?*

He clutched his head in his hands and moaned. Have we, he wondered. He knew the answer. He and all mankind would know it sooner or later; never for the better, but for the worst, he knew. The legend of the Sarasvati shall live on, he thought to himself. Centuries will pass, but no one will be able to find where this great river was. Some will call her the lost river, the invisible river, that mysterious river kept alive in their imaginations, which still flows beneath their tired feet. Invisible to the mortal eye shall Sarasvati pass from Heaven on to Earth and into the realm of lore.

The rishi looked at the dry, cracked riverbed, the jagged, shingly shore, the sterile lands for miles, thirsting without the mighty waters of the Sarasvati, mapping a parched course of an enormous dried-up river beneath the sands of time.

She had gone. She had taken away the gift with her. But her curse was upon them.

1

THE CREATION

Thou art Brahma, thou art Vishnu, thou art Rudra Shiva,
thou art Agni, Varuna, Vayu, Indra, thou art All.

The turret rose bulkily through thirty tiers of windows before attenuating itself to a graceful dome of shining white. Then, it darted up again another hundred feet, thinning to a mere oblong tower in its last fragile aspiration towards the sky. At the highest of its high windows stood Brahma, full in the stiff breeze, gazing down at the city.

His Brahmalok.

He gazed down for a long time and retreated inside, walking slowly inside the chamber.

Brahma glanced at himself in the grand mirror on the wall. He was Brahma, the Creator, the Maker of the world. But in each of his creations, he had seen that he was manifested in every one of them, living in them as the Soul, the Brahman: the Ultimate Reality. He was the Cosmic Universal. He was that God existing within each living being he had created.

Brahma steadied his shaking breath, turning away from the reflection in the mirror. He looked down at his big, slender hands: he had been creating and moulding with these very hands and his mind, but he didn't know how he had been created. His own origins were uncertain. When did he turn from the abstract metaphysical Supreme Reality of the Brahman to become one of the masculine gods in the Trinity—in which the cosmic functions of creation, maintenance and destruction were personified as a triad, with him, Brahma, as the Creator, Vishnu as the Preserver and Shiva as the Destroyer?

An exultation filled him. As Brahma, he was omnipotent, omnipresent and omniscient, creating the metaphysical and the empirical, the Sarg and the Visarg, all in an endless cycle of cosmos and life continually created, evolved, dissolved and then re-created. But an invisible line had been crossed, and he had become aware of his own distraught emotions, his fatigue and his acute sense of isolation.

While searching for his incentive, he had found he was searching within himself. He was searching for his partner, his Shakti. Was creativity the pursuit of creation?

A miasma misted his mind: he recognized a form, a fleeting solace, a manifesting concept. *She* was his creation . . . *Sarasvati.*

He rubbed his throbbing temples. He was going mad, he surely was, he thought, steadying his quivering breath. Above all, he was an artist. And not unlike all artists, he was a little mad. But passion and creation was what were closest to his heart and mind. It was a vision he had: unique and incomparable, a vague pleasant dream, something that was going to happen to him some day . . . *Sarasvati*?

He blinked to clear his mind. As Brahma, he had created all forms in the universe, but not the primordial cosmos itself. He knew why: his creative activity depended on the power of a higher presence: he had seen her, the lady in white, of purest thought, seeing the beginning and the end of the universe: *Sarasvati* . . .

He touched the drawing lightly, his touch a soft caress, as his long fingers trailed the outline of the woman of his dreams, of his contemplations, of all his ideas. His inspiration. *Sarasvati* . . .

He gazed at the nebulous sketch he had drafted in his precious book. It was his little secret: his journal of thoughts and ideas, a little, thin leaflet with a slim compilation of sheaves held together. Brahma hardly went around anywhere without his secret diary, carrying it effortlessly in the folds of his shawl, gripping it hard or softly, holding on to it. But it had to be with him. In this book lay the seed of his anxiety, his passion, his restlessness. For this private dossier was the lifeline he could not do without. He had found, to his consternation, that he had fallen in love: that deep, steady love with an urgent passion.

He reverentially called his memoir *Sarasvati*. She was the most important book in the world, his most beautiful being: slender and slim but voluptuous in manner and word. She was essentially feminine, full-breasted in her chagrin when she argued, full-hipped as she moved forward to break down his arguments, often confrontational, contrary and challenging, stripped of the irrelevancies of notion and reason.

He spent all his time with her, pouring out his ideas, his slightest thoughts, his desires, infusing warmth and colour into the doodles he drew, each stroke deeper, richer, giving her a fulsome form, a fluid figure, supple and sinuous.

'Like a winding river, full and strong,' he murmured, his hooded eyes lighting up with trembling emotion, smiling gently as he took out a soft, silk handkerchief to wrap her gently, swathed back in the hidden folds of his shawl.

'I am going to visit Indra; I can't take you there,' he said dourly as he placed her gently on the table. 'You are, after all, a lady of knowledge and dignity. How can I carry you to irreverent places where drunk *gandharva*s pass coarse remarks?'

He recalled how he had once got worked up in an unfamiliar, ungovernable rage when she had received unwanted attention from Surya, the handsome Sun God.

'What is in this book? A treasure trove of information?' Surya had peered enquiringly, his eyes on her. 'Or secrets of your trade?'

Then there were some like Chandra, the Moon God, who took liberties with her, who, once curious, had dared to hold her and tried to browse through the open pages. Brahma had snatched her from him with a snarl.

'Don't touch it ever!' he had growled.

Shiva had cast him an enquiring look. Brahma was never violent: in thought or speech.

It had been worse when Kuber, the God of Wealth, had slapped her rudely down on the table. Brahma had caught him by the scruff of his fat neck.

'You won't ever be blessed by me or her,' he had muttered through clenched teeth, his face contorted with an expression that had left all agape.

He sighed as he recalled these incidents and rifled through the sheaves, his touch tender.

'Oh, how long can I keep you my secret?' Brahma whispered. 'I want to see you, read you, talk to you, love you as one person does another,' he sighed, wretchedly, staring into the emptiness of the darkness that swelled around him like a swirling whirlwind: *the vortex of Fate.*

'I want someone, I want *you!*' he cried, as he shook his handsome head agitatedly, his slender, delicately pointed nose aquiver with a deferred awareness: sensing something amiss, inhaling the first whiff of hope and excitement. Should he do it? Should he make Sarasvati come alive?

He allowed himself to calm down, collect his thoughts, besieged and restive. He failed. The voice rose higher and higher within him, strident and insistent, screaming at him to do the needful . . . and then he heard her: a woman's voice, soft and clear, as the sound of his thoughts knocked dully to summon her presence. Two fair, slender hands, with slim fingers and long legs, emerged from a pool of coagulated shadows in the deepest recesses of his mind.

He blinked: petals dropped from a white lotus with a faint, soft sigh and then he saw her, a flare of silk and flesh blazed as he caught the light, like a searing slice of relentless blades, carving out all that came between them . . . her silhouetted face was a glimpse of immense beauty: eyes darker than the starless night, stark against the veined, blue-stained fair lids, her parted lips, two precise laminas of scarlet between a small, imperious nose and a firm, pointed chin. Each feature on her porcelain face appeared like white hollows burning with a precarious fire, the heat of untrammelled beauty flowing down her long neck to the high swell of her breasts, covered by the swirl of her diaphanous drape that clung to her flaring hips to fall away to her slim ankles . . .

She was as stunning as he had imagined her to be, rising from the waves of his thoughts, from the crest of his ocean of desires, a soft spray of stimulation and brilliance. He had done it! He had created his inspiration! *Sarasvati!*

* * *

'I presume you would have thought of a name for me as well?' she said, tossing her head, each word enunciated crisply. The rich colour of her hair glistened in the dim twilight.

Her first words did not sound wise, but rather brusque.

Brahma furrowed his brows, as was his habit. Right now, his expression betrayed his irritation at her tone. He had expected reverence, not flippancy, considering that he had created her.

Brahma felt momentarily bemused. What he discovered so anomalous was his agitated, mystical hope of romance had actually come true. And when it had happened, with such a pleasurable confusion of impressions and emotions, he scarcely understood it at all.

Brahma could not believe what he had created. She came through the smoke haze, her head tilted, her eyes speculative, almost conceited, her manner haughty yet careless about her endowed beauty. She seemed to realize its potency, but did not care much about the power it gave her; she was almost contemptuous of it.

Brahma inhaled slowly: his breath chilled as he studied her. She was small and delicately put together, hiding her immense strength within. Each time she took a step, she walked as if she were floating. Her hair was a fine ebony wave, long and loose, as dark as her eyes were velvety black and had almost no expression when they looked at him.

She came close to him and smiled with her thin, taut lips. Her heart-shaped face was fair, stark white against her eyes, dark and fiery. Swathed in gossamer ivory, the sheerness accentuating her lithe body, she gave the impression of cool nonchalance with an immaculate instinct of beauty.

That lazy carelessness, he was soon to know, underlined a special charm, often like those who are dreamy and languid or, conversely, rapt and sharp yet quickly bored when done. But what he found fascinating was that she was exquisite even at her most casual. Her silk raiment appeared crumpled at her tiny waist; without her hair done up in a tiara, spilling wildly over her shoulders, an untamed curl came loose from it on her wide forehead. Her neck and shoulders were fair and bare, without any glittering gems to adorn their slender loveliness, the casual folds of her drapes and cascading mane suggesting an air of freedom and lazy intellect.

An undecipherable emotion flared within him: a flash that knocked him backwards and sent a flame through him that dried his mouth, made his heart pound and left him breathless . . .

But she hardly seemed aware of the effect she had on him. Or hold him in any awe as her Creator: she seemed more taken in by the swirling dimness of the garden where they were together. Through the milky mist of the Akash Ganga, she could see the silhouetted patterns of some white flowers.

Her eyes were vibrantly curious, soaking in all they could see. Brahma's garden was heavenly; bursting with flaming flora and fragrance in sharp contrast to the tall, austere man standing in front of her. Attired in gleaming white, he appeared almost frosty, his face inscrutable.

Lost in the eddying fullness of colour and cologne and looking up at him, she sighed, expelling a long, euphonious breath.

'You have just uttered the Om,' said Brahma faintly, his gaze fixed.

She smiled, a swift, dazzling smile. 'Was it how it all started? With the enunciation of Om, the sacred sound? All of your creation, even me? Was I the last?'

Brahma shifted uneasily, wondering what to say. How could he tell her why he had created her? That he had been miserably lonely, the ideas screaming inside him, bursting in the emptiness around him . . . and that was when he had decided he wanted to create the perfect woman of his mind: and it was she. And she was all and more than what he had imagined her to be; his treacherous thoughts taunted him.

He stood motionless in the semi-darkness, looking at her, aware that his blood was racing, his heart thumping, and mindful that he had never seen a woman he wanted so badly as this one . . .

His inscrutable eyes flickered, clenching his fists. *No!*

She turned her dark head to bestow him a straight, fixed look. 'Am I going to keep asking you questions that you won't answer?'

There was again a certain flippancy in her tone, which he did not appreciate. Brahma straightened his tall, heavy frame, realizing with consternation that he had been speechless and had not replied to a single question of hers.

'Sarasvati, in answer to your first question,' he replied shortly. 'Your name is Sarasvati.'

She frowned. 'Hmm, quite pretty. And why?'

He gave a start, baulking. 'That's the meaning of your name—the essence of Self. "*Sara*" means an ocean. "*Sva*" means one's own. "*Ti*" means personification. "Sarasvati" is the embodiment of one's own ocean of experience.'

'So "Sarasvati" is a portmanteau—of *saras,* meaning "pooling water", and . . . Am I from vapour?' she interrupted herself with a question, her thin, small nose flaring slightly as she inhaled the cold air.

He found the gesture strangely fascinating.

'Yes, you are from energy.'

She nodded, her loose raven hair falling forward softly on her bare, white shoulders.

'But does not *saras* also mean "speech" and *vati* meaning "she who possesses"?'

It was his turn to nod curtly. He had the uncomfortable feeling of being cross-examined.

She persisted. 'But why are water and speech accrued to me? I can speak, so can you, so what is so special about me, or my name?'

She was as exasperating as she sometimes was within those pages . . .

'You are the *sara*, the essence of knowledge, that is expressed through speech and collected in the vastness of its waters,' he clarified, mildly annoyed that he sounded so earnest in his explanation.

'Like the vastness and depth of the mind,' she added. 'From which I was created by you.'

Brahma found himself nodding again and stopped himself.

'And am I the last one?' she repeated her earlier question. 'The very last being?' she expanded, watching his expressionless face.

'No, of course not,' he said tersely. 'Look around you, it's there to see,' he said cryptically, shrugging his wide shoulders. 'My work is still incomplete . . . there's so much more to be created and that's why I . . .' he halted, wondering if he should let her know her reality.

She threw him a discerning look and he reckoned it was only now that she had first noticed him. It bothered him that he had not grasped her attention before. A tall, square-shouldered man, strong-featured, big-handed, gruff of voice, abrupt of manner—this was him. Or did she see him as an obstinate man who worked relentlessly, chasing his own demons and dreams that were beyond relief, his austerity battling the remorseless requirements of his circumstances?

But she seemed to see more than what he would like her to see: a big, trim man, with straight hair and raven eyes as remote as eyes could be. He had a narrow face with a prominent straight, strong nose and a pair of slanting, intense eyes that made his cheekbones seem higher and pointed, adding to the lean look.

His hair, framing a high forehead, was night-black, long and straight, spread richly over his heavy shoulders. There were grey streaks on his temples that augmented his severity; the high broad forehead, the dominantly aquiline nose, his thin-lipped mouth over a square chin, unhidden in the faint grey stubble, restating the formidability. His eyes were striking: deep-set, deep black and deeply piercing. He was arresting to look at without being handsome, and gave an immediate impression of a rare age-old sagacity, besides granite-hard strength.

His long-limbed frame seemed languid, but was deceptively powerful, as was seen when he moved; his motion swift and supple, his skin smooth and glistening as he moved like a man with very sound muscles.

She did not show what she saw or thought—of him. Instead, she continued in a cool and collected voice, her stare as uncurious as before. 'You are Brahma,' she said, moving slowly around him, inspecting him. '. . . Also Swayambhu—self-born from the cosmic egg; the Hiranyagarbha—the self-existent Supreme All-Being; thus viewed as *sagun*—a form—of the otherwise formless *nirgun* Brahman, the Final Reality.'

'You make me sound ancient,' he commented wryly.

She turned and looked at him. Her velvet eyes were disconcertingly frank.

'You are, aren't you? The spiritual concept of Brahman is older and you are its symbolic commencement. As Brahman, you were the uncreated creator of the universe and time itself—the cosmic cycle of *kalpa*.'

Her full, red lips curved into a swift smile that came and went so quickly he wasn't sure if she had smiled. 'It adds to your enigma!'

His face turned solemn. 'The kalpa is for real. Long time enough, isn't it?'

She nodded, her head tilting. 'Long enough to create, to preserve—and to destroy.'

Brahma frowned. 'Don't!' he said, his voice sharpening. '"Destroy" is a word I abhor.'

'But what is created, gets destroyed,' she said quietly.

He shook his head, his eyes bleak. 'No, I shan't allow what I created to be destroyed, ever.'

'But is it in your power to do so? Can you stop the destruction, if it happens?' she questioned, curiously. 'You only have the power to create.'

'That I have done. It is a solitary job,' he said gravely.

He shrugged his broad shoulders, hoping to shrug away the worrying thoughts. Creation. Preservation. But destruction? Why destroy what has been created?

'Because of Evil,' she prompted, reading his thoughts.

He looked shocked. 'I didn't create evil!"

'Consciously, no,' she said. 'But what you have created might evolve into evil. That is a possibility, isn't it?' she intimated, her hot coal eyes deepening. 'How will you know good without the bad?'

He felt an unfamiliar knot of fear in his heart, tightening his voice as he whispered, 'Yes, but the thought never struck me . . .'

'All things created cannot be wonderful and beautiful,' she said, her eyes thoughtful. 'But with that, there is also the dark and the evil.'

'But I cannot control the evil,' he protested, his frown deepening.

'You cannot,' she assented. 'But that is why Vishnu and Shiva are there—the Preserver and the Destroyer, for evil, when it becomes a threat to existence, has to be destroyed. The three of you are thus the Trinity.'

He let a chilled breath drift down his nostril as he stared at her: he had lost the argument to her. He had no power to destroy the evil he might have created in the process of making the world. Which made him what? Just a maker with no control over what he had made? Just an artist? He was the Creator, but once his deed was done and he had finished making the universe, creating life, he had to hand it all away? The onus of preserving the good and destroying the evil now lay with Vishnu and Shiva, respectively. It would be up to them . . . and then, what of him?

He was struck by an unfamiliar fear of uncertainty. Her soft laugh interrupted his thoughts and he opened his eyes.

'But yes, creation *is* the most crucial job,' she assured him, her eyes warm. 'And so you created light and darkness, water and earth, and the different species of animals from parts of your body . . .' she stopped abruptly.

'And I was from where?' she asked, her tone probing.

'From the mind, of course,' he said swiftly, obliterating any further thought. He could not tell her that she arose from all his thoughts—and emotions he had never experienced before . . . She was the loveliest thing he had ever created, he had ever seen in his life: she was young and beautiful and fresh, and everything about her was exciting—from her thick, long, glossy hair to her small bare feet.

The sight and the voice of her ignited a spark inside him that had been waiting to be triggered . . .

She continued, her voice detached. 'So let's start from the beginning. The first phase of Creation was the Mukhya Sarga, the planets with the respective geographic morphology, along with the gravity you created with the Universe. Vegetation, birds and animals were formed in the Tiryak Sarga. Then, the Deva Sarga, including all divinities—the four eternal Kumars, the ten mind-born *manas putra*s, the chosen *saptarishi*s and all the demigods. But much to your disappointment, instead of procreating—as was their purpose—all the four *Kumars*—your four eldest sons, the first beings you created from different parts of your body to aid you, chose instead to follow the path of celibacy, frustrating your great plans of propagation of humanity!' she observed, her clear, clever eyes narrowing.

Brahma stood impassive, his face severe.

'But this simmering anger and your sense of acute frustration led to the creation of the asuras, the demons—your dark side,' she pointed out.

The muscles on either side of his jaw stood out suddenly.

'But focusing your positive energy again, you reacquired your Satvik form to create the deities, the devas. You created the horse from your right eye; from the thigh, the daityas, the asuras, the *danav*s. And to counter them, the adityas and devas, where your eternal presence is reflected in the universe's nature of having no beginning and no end. That's why this process of creation repeats itself.'

'Go on,' he urged, because he wanted to go on listening to her soft, exciting voice, which made so much sense and meaning to all that he had done.

Cold clouds swirled around her, making her look paler than she was, a haze of infinite beauty. But he could feel the heat of her gaze through the chilly air as she scrutinized him.

'And then you created me,' she lilted, bestowing him her half-smile. 'Intelligence and knowledge. But I have a question for you—did you create the world with intelligence or will the world you created lead to the creation of intelligence?'

A slow, languorous smile flitted across his face, softening the craggy lines.

'The process of creation is not some random explosion in nothingness,' he replied, raising his eyebrows.

'But it questions the essence of the world's existence, the philosophy of why you created humans. Why you created me,' she again gave that knowing smile. Her fixed stare did not leave his haggard face.

'So now, after all that hard work, you have decided to take a break. Right now, in your Rajsik relaxed form, you are deliberating about all the work done . . .' Her clear, clever eyes looked enquiring. 'Is there more to be done?

This is where I need you . . .

Not waiting for his reply, she provided the answer herself. 'You still desire to create gender by dividing yourself into male and female counterparts—and you created me out of yourself.'

Something in her tone made him give her a sharp look. 'As I plan to do with all the world's creatures,' he remarked quickly.

She tugged at a loose tendril, looking thoughtful. 'In essence, you as the Prajapati, the head of the world—created all because you wanted to express yourself,' she paused, her full lips broke into a small smile.

'What did you want to express through me?'

Brahma heard the wild racing of his heart, against the ensuing silence.

'Knowledge, wisdom, insight, sagacity,' he said, his voice stilted.

She laughed. 'Prudence, acumen, intelligence, sense . . .' she added.

'I thought *you* were all this and more . . .' she peered up at him. 'Am I you?'

He looked startled. Had he created another him? *Was she he?* Was that why he was so hopelessly drawn to her, why the sound of her voice made him short of breath? For a moment, he could not reply, and he stood there motionless, his fists clenched, listening to her gentle breathing.

Her question had shocked him as she continued to fix him with her dark, velvet eyes. He slowly shook his head. 'You are not me, you are complementary to me,' he said. 'If I have the Rajas qualities of passion and action, then you as Sarasvati, have Sattva—the attributes of balance, harmony and creativeness.'

'Through you,' he reminded her gently. 'I am your first student,' he gave a small, crooked smile. 'Under your guidance, I have acquired the ability to sense, think, comprehend and communicate. Now I look upon the chaos I created with new eyes of wisdom.'

Sarasvati filled a sharp pause. 'I know. I have been constantly in your thoughts, your work.'

She hesitated and then slowly nodded her head. 'Your work defines you. As you personify birth and the absolute, you are the Creator, the foremost in the Trinity. The Tridev are responsible for the creation, maintenance and destruction of everything that takes place in the universe, represented by *guṇa*—qualities to be found in all living beings. Of these three qualities, Rajas is mapped to you. It is passion and action which drives you and so as Vedanath, you are the creator of the four Vedas—one from of each of your head and mouth—Chaturmukha. As the *saguna* Brahma, you with the representation of face and attributes are Vishnu, Shiva and the Devi, respectively, and the soul, atman, within every living being created is part of this eternal Brahman.'

'You have wonderfully defined me,' he said expressionlessly, crossing his arms across his broad chest.

'And your work too,' she smiled. 'Clearly there's still a lot of unfinished work. The universe is still perceived as sunk in sleep . . . but you willed me to exist.'

She flashed that quiet smile again. 'You must be tired?'

He was, but her easy smile seemed to quickly dissipate his weariness. He had been almost torpid with fatigue and was terrified he would err. But then he had made her . . . he hadn't erred, he had excelled.

'I shall leave you with your work,' she said, straightening her shoulders as she lithely moved away from him.

'Wait; I'll see you as far as the gate,' he said, following her out.

She continued walking, her steps not faltering. Her oval, very earnest face, chilled by the frost, her delicate black eyebrows, the swish of her slim, lithe figure, as she held the folds of her sari high to avoid stepping on the wayside flowers, oddly moved him.

They walked along the milky path, the silence between them inexplicably comforting. The clouds churned into straying wisps of mist, and they could see the star-studded sky in the luminous distance. As though covered with a veil, all nature was hidden in a transparent, colourless haze through which her beauty peeped gaily. But all he was aware of was her: *she* was there, walking close beside him, her arms folded, not swinging. Although it was dark, he could just make out the shape of her head, which she held a little on one side as she looked at him, drawing him to her, like a man into a whirlpool . . . It had to be her. It couldn't have been anyone else or he would not have felt the way he was feeling. His heart would not be pounding like this.

Brahma stooped and bowed to her. Then, in silent emotion, he straightened his shawl, shifted his bundle of books to a more comfortable position, paused and said formally, 'Your palace is down the path and up the hill to your left,' he said gruffly. 'It has the best view.'

She smiled widely. 'I am sure I shall be able to find my way from here. I won't get lost in Brahmalok!'

Brahma smiled back, breaking the solemn severity of his hooded expression. For some seconds, he stood in silence as she entered her garden through the natural archway of canopied trees, leaving him inexplicably inadequate.

For perhaps some still seconds, he stared after her, aware of her faint lingering fragrance and hearing her quick, gentle breathing as she strolled away, and in those moments, everything around him went out of focus . . .

It was a moment in his life he would never forget.

2

SHATARUPA

Brahmalok looked warmer in the daylight. The mist had thinned, and from her palace window, Sarasvati could glimpse the five peaks of the golden Mount Meru on whose summit lay the vast city of Brahmalok, encircled by a river, the Akash Ganga.

Her palace stood halfway down a steep hill and from her window, she could glimpse a narrow strip of the sea below and, opposite, the city of Brahmalok.

Sarasvati had not ventured outside the palace yet, but she intended to scour the capital city as well as the other eight cities that surrounded it. One was supposed to be of Indra, and the other seven of the other devas like Surya, Chandra and Agni.

Perhaps they were more populated than Brahmalok: this city was unusually isolated, she frowned as she absently strung at the veena, thoughtfully placed in her chamber. In a vague way, she realized that this was all for her benefit. Even the lake outside her window turned obligingly to a deep wine colour in the evenings, with the ivory swans loitering delightfully at her windowsill. It was a privileged paradise, this white little palace on the water, surrounded by woods in which she was free to do what she liked because . . . she was Sarasvati.

She was surrounded by beautiful things that breathed of taste and refinement. If you live in an atmosphere of luxury, luxury is yours whether it is yours or another's, Sarasvati decided. She would rather treat it like an educational institution.

Likewise, since the past week, the palace had kept her busy: it was well-stocked with enough books for her to stay put. She had barely browsed through half of the enormous library downstairs, and she was yet to explore the music room. Brahma was as generous as he was thoughtful; she pursed her lips, pondering.

Brahma. He was a strange person; a person of few words, and almost no presence. She had met him a few times since that first day and from what she could gather, he seemed to be a loner, or rather an intellectual hermit, always deep in work and thought. Everyone revered him, with less fear and more awe. He mixed very rarely, very little with people. In the mornings, she occasionally spotted him in the distance, strolling by the seashore, lost in his thoughts and then retiring to his palace for the day, often disappearing for weeks. He was seldom invited anywhere, as people found him daunting. Besides, he seldom accepted the invitation.

Just as she did; she preferred her own company. She vaguely strung the instrument again. She had to do something, she sighed.

'Look up,' she heard a voice command her. She turned around with a start to see Brahma standing at the doorway.

He walked in slowly, his gait guarded and careful. 'When you play music, always look up,' he said to her, pointing to the sky with his long, muscled arm. 'Look up at the sky! Even the tiniest stars are all worlds! And you are creating an entire new world yourself with the music you make—how significant you are compared to the universe!'

She was surprised to hear the vehemence in his voice, so dissimilar to his otherwise stony demeanour.

'A modest speck!' She beamed her brilliant smile, gesturing with a wide wave of her hands. 'This palace is a trove, a museum of sorts, and I haven't gone through even half of it.'

'As is Brahmalok,' he remarked, his lips pursed thin. 'You will take some time to get used to it. It's not very . . . lively, more on the quieter side. Because it is a planet composed entirely of Brahman—the highest thought.'

Sarasvati gave a knowing nod. 'The land of the abstract Supreme Soul, greater even than Svarga, or Heaven: sated with eternity, knowledge and bliss.'

As always, her words pleased him more than he thought could affect him. Brahma watched her as she gracefully stood up to greet him, her hair delectably tousled, flowing free down her shoulders, below her waist, her sari creased as she attempted to smoothen the wrinkles at the waist. Yet she looked heavenly.

And as he looked at her, he felt a thickness in his throat.

'There is no hurry, you can take all your time to study, to explore,' he said unevenly, his tone slipping to slight hesitancy.

He cleared his throat, his face an expressionless mask again.

'Er, I would not have interrupted you from your pursuits but for a reason. A certain urgency . . .' he faltered. 'I come here today, asking for a favour . . .'

'Favour?' she frowned, tilting her head sideways, appraising him with her steady stare. He flushed, feeling the heat climbing up his neck.

'Am I supposed to run some errand?' she asked bluntly.

Some could term her forthrightness rude, but he found it strangely exhilarating. He looked at her, hoping he was not staring. He saw her face turned at an angle and at the same time he was again struck by that strange thing about her which excited him. He swallowed convulsively, the thickness tight in his throat. She was oddly disconcerting.

He struggled. 'I created you as a woman so as to aid me in my work of creation. Shatarupa, a female deity in many forms . . .' he said, not moving a muscle except to speak.

She widened her eyes. 'Am I supposed to be her?'

She had this charming way of framing her views as a question, as opinionated as herself. Brahma found himself relaxing in such talks, enthralling his mind and his heart.

He raised his brows again and nodded.

His brows seem more vocal than his words, she thought irreverently.

His baritone had gone husky. 'Like your presence, your origin holds great importance in the balance and creation of the world. After creating the universe, I checked what was made and realized it was utterly lacking in concept. To help me with this monumental task of creating a form, I created you to help me out . . .'

'I know, but how?' she interrupted in an impatient, questioning tone. 'How do you want me to help you?' Her voice had a tinge of tetchiness.

He raised a brow at her unbridled display of impatience. 'I want you to be my Shatarupa,' he stated stiffly.

She looked away; she had not missed his hesitance.

'Shatarupa—the one with a hundred forms,' she explained primly, mustering an air of dignity. But her heart strangely sang, her face lighting up: they were going to work together!

'Could you elaborate on *your* definition of Shatarupa?'

'I need your help to make me create a set of new beings,' he said, the words coming out swift but sure. 'Not just that. I need to pair each one of them, the male with the female. For that you will have to help me,' he paused briefly, raising uncertain eyes to her sparkling ones.

'Er, will you?'

She turned her head and smiled at him: it was vivid, almost rapturous. 'But of course!' she exclaimed, but hearing the thrill ringing in her voice, she lingered and continued in a more measured tone. 'I've to look into what the Kumars left undone: creation and procreation.'

'Not just humans, but all beings,' he clarified quickly.

She nodded. 'Of course, you must have had it all planned. Opposites should attract, shouldn't they?' she asked.

He was bewildered by her sudden turn, her mode and manner of direct questioning he found distinctly disconcerting.

'Yes,' he agreed, puzzled. 'They often do.'

'But logic says you should get along more with those with common interests and a certain like-mindedness. So then, how can opposites attract?' she demanded, her tone vexed.

Brahma hesitated, then shrugged. 'Maybe that's not the case always.'

'You should know,' she said peremptorily.

'I frankly don't know what you mean,' he said stiffly, keeping up a pretence of formality, which he knew did not deceive.

She watched with some amusement the flush rise under his tanned skin.

'I mean, you have created so many beings. How do you plan to pair them? There has to be some attracting factor, don't you think?'

'That is what I came here to ask you,' he stated, slightly unsure now.

'It is the execution you are not sure about, aren't you? About pairing and coupling,' she said bluntly. She tilted her head again and looked searchingly at him.

His heart leapt in relief: she knew him through and through. He almost felt foolish when he nodded and muttered, 'Yes,' for the third time.

A hint of a smile came back into her glib, black eyes.

'How do we go about it?' she asked, her tone brisk and eager, the voice of an ever-curious, excited child.

'Let me first explain why I made you—what Sarasvati is to Brahma and Brahma to Sarasvati,' he said, his voice unconsciously going tender. 'When I first created the Universe, I was very pleased with myself and decided to see the whole world with my own eyes and set out on my journey. But what I saw was a beautiful world, serene— but so silent! Everything and everyone on Earth appeared lonely. I was forced to realize that what I had created was incomplete. I felt lost. After I created the cosmic Universe, I realized that it lacked form, concept and order. I knew I needed assistance to organize the Universe I had created. No other deva could help me and that was when I decided to create the very embodiment of knowledge to help me with this colossal task,' he paused, absently tapping his fingers. 'And from this state of mind emerged you— Sarasvati. My Brahmi, the energy wisdom of Brahma,' he said expansively.

She sat motionless, her hands between her knees, her eyes a little wide, listening.

'You were to help me, guide me, give me directions on how to further magnify and multiply while maintaining order in the cosmos. I discovered the melody of mantras in the cacophony of chaos. You, Sarasvati, as Vagdevi, the Goddess of Speech and Sound, uttered Om, infusing the universe with prana, the vital energy—with which things took shape. First the Sun, then the Moon, the stars, the nakshatras, the Akash Ganga were born, the oceans emerged and the seasons changed. With you guiding me, the cosmos gained structure: the sky sprinkled with stars rose to form the heavens; the sea sank into the abyss below, the earth stood in between. Gods became lords of the celestial spheres; demons ruled the nether regions, humans walked on Earth. The sun rose and set, the moon waxed and waned, the tide flowed and ebbed. Seasons changed, seeds germinated, plants bloomed and withered, animals migrated as randomness gave way to the rhythm of life. I, as Brahma, thus became the Creator of the world with you, Sarasvati, as my wisdom.'

She listened while he talked and watched her. He saw her arched brows knotted, an expression of consternation on her face.

'All the work we have been doing together till now makes me not just your colleague but also an important figure who helped you form and finalize your creations,' she wondered aloud in vehement astonishment.

'And I thought I was just a personification of your thoughts! Like the garnishing on flavoured rice to make it appear interesting and tasty?'

Her impishness, often inappropriate, he found endearing.

His lips twitched. 'No, you are the flavoured rice itself. You are the incarnation of inspiration and intellect, Sarasvati. I merely boiled the rice: created matter but finding lacking in form, I came to you to bring order and beauty and intellect to the world.'

She was strangely moved; she was in his thoughts, his mind, his consciousness, even when he was creating her, even as he created every new form and being. She had to be with him. It was almost like a breath of air to sustain life . . . that was the definition of their work, their relationship. The enormity of that responsibility was overwhelming.

Brahma stood up, and dusted his black-and-silver hair back with the flat of his big hand.

'Now, having formed the universe, I proceeded to generate a two-fold creation—the pairs and the couples—with a view to "complete" the world. And here I confess, I placed and kept you, Sarasvati, in my heart,' he said, looking at her with intent eyes she found oddly perturbing.

Though she kept on listening, she wondered what he meant. She felt his enigmatic, dark eyes were scanning her face with a dispassionate yet disconcerting attention. She had discovered already that he was sharp and she had a feeling that the relation between them excited his cynical curiosity. She found a certain amusement in baffling him. She liked him and she knew he was kindly disposed towards her.

He was oddly witty and brilliant and had a dry, incisive way of putting things which was diverting. His solemn face, all masked in a grave façade, made him look formidable but when they chatted, she saw him relax, become more casual, affording his remarks to be almost innocuous. Sometimes his frankness was brutal, but it was more out of concern than malice. He was not a malicious man at all; he was kind, clever and, most importantly for her, humble and interesting. He had created the world but he looked upon creation and life in a spirit of banter and his sardonic ridicule of it sometimes was barbed. He could not tell any story without his characteristic matter-of-fact tone, making it sound almost absurd as if the Heaven and the Earth were both bizarre and ludicrous places, not lending the sense of pride a creator often flaunts for his creations.

Fortunately, Brahma seemed unable to read her thoughts. He continued talking to her, his baritone rich and velvety.

'I created you as a woman so as to help me in my work of creation,' he confessed, with uncharacteristic self-consciousness. 'Then as I was muttering my prayers, I divided my body and gave to the half the form of a woman, and to the other half the form of a male. This female part is called Shatarupa. I didn't realize I needed a female complement until Vishnu explained the concept of the female principle to me,' he confessed. 'Shatarupa was the result—you were to take a hundred beautiful forms—but when I created you to be my female principle, I myself couldn't take my eyes off you . . .'

She realized with a sense of shock how much she meant to him.

'Everything good that comes to me, I want to share with you,' he added hastily, his eyes intense, trying to reassure her.

She felt the heat rise warmly up her neck and quickly bent her head in confusion. Her long, silky hair fell forward, hiding her face. She straightened up, then looked at him.

'I understand I am your Shatarupa,' she whispered. 'That is why as your Shatarupa, you need me now to help you,' she said in a low voice, an undecipherable emotion grabbing her throat.

'Yes, you represent the fair species of creation,' he leaned forward in his earnestness to explain, bringing his head close to hers. She did not move away, taking in his words and what they meant to her—and him.

She sat still for a long time, her hands folded in her lap, her eyes lost in thought.

'You have to take a hundred roles and as Shatarupa, keep changing her form as I cast my stare on you,' he exhaled sharply. 'You will become every creature on earth to counter my male gaze. I as Brahma, the creator, shall, however, change my form to the male version of whatever you are and thereby shall every animal community in the world be created—as pairs.'

Sarasvati continued to sit motionless, staring through Brahma, her eyes distant, yet thoughtful. His heart sank. She was going to refuse him . . .

'Are you sure you want to hear more of this?' he probed gently. 'You can always decline.'

She bristled. She felt his strained eyes on her and that made her more disconcerted.

'Obviously you are a little overcome by the enormity of what the task entails,' he said with a reassuring smile, wanting to put her at ease again, yet wondering what had upset her. He took her hand and there was something so friendly in the feel of his strong hand against hers, something so intimately affectionate, that she stifled a gasp of wonderment.

She looked away, baffled.

He waited, holding his breath for a long, fearful moment.

'I will do it,' she said finally—and firmly, a ring of defiant thrill in her voice. 'What do I have to do?'

Fearing she would change her mind and turn him down, he grinned with a forced joviality. 'So, are you ready?

I shall be there, I promise I won't put you in any danger,' he vowed solemnly.

The tenderness in his voice made her flinch.

She nodded her head, avoiding his eyes. 'I know you won't,' she said softly, twisting her fingers in her lap.

His heart melted hearing the trust in her voice. Again he felt a slight thickening in his throat as he looked at her: should they go ahead?

'Sure?' he repeated, more to assure himself than her.

She nodded. An obstinate look came into her eyes. 'Yes. I want to. "*Knowledge helps one find possibilities where once he saw problems,*"' she softly cited and threw him an assuring smile.

'I am, above all, Sarasvati, the Goddess of Knowledge. But to help you in Creation, I shall become your Shatarupa and take a hundred forms to populate the world with various animals and beings . . . First I shall take the form of a cow, you then shall follow as a bull. Then, I shall change into a mare; you will chase as a horse. Every time I turn into a bird or a beast, you will be the corresponding male equivalent. Thus, I shall be the goddess with multiple forms,' she paused, a soft smile on her trembling lips. 'The Shatarupa.'

'Not just my Shatarupa, Sarasvati,' Brahma said, a thoughtful look in his eyes. 'You as Shatarupa shall thereby personify material reality: alluring yet fleeting.'

His words thrilled her. They had come into her mind, persuasive and illuminating, during this fresh golden afternoon.

Together; they would work together! She nodded gravely but her lips broke into her characteristic half-smile.

'As soon as we can, we'll take up our work . . .' she declared with a graceful movement of her head, her stormy eyes meeting his.

'Right now,' he inhaled deeply and closed his eyes. 'To continue with Creation, I have to give form to Man and Woman. The Man is Swayambhu Manu and the Woman I shall name Shatarupa after you,' he stated, his rich voice filling the room, her mind. She closed her eyes.

'Henceforth, humans shall descend from Manu—the manavs.'

He sat meditating, when suddenly, he saw a nebulous image: of him in the throes of a wild shudder, his massive body contracting. From his body, his right side to be exact, there emerged a creature who looked a lot like him . . .

'Man,' he murmured. 'Manu.'

There was a small silence.

'He will be born on his own, thus he is Swayambhu— the First Man, Swayambhu Manu, who shall be born with the *kaya*—the body—of his father Brahma,' said Sarasvati.

'With Manu, there shall also be the feminine principle in the form of Shatarupa,' nodded Brahma.

'Since both will emerge on their own from the body of Brahma, thus, there will be equality of the sexes,' she said emphatically, her eyes still shut, but she could see through him.

She was smart enough to guess what he was thinking, he thought with a silent smile.

He continued in his rich baritone, 'Just as Brahma shall be in every Man, Shatarupa will be in every Woman. God in every human, divinity in humanity.'

He paused, thinking. 'And on Prithvi will they live, lording over all beings on Earth.'

Brahma slowly opened his eyes and saw Sarasvati next to him, in the same meditative pose. He looked at her for some seconds, his face expressionless, his eyes brooding.

I don't know what I'd do without you, Sarasvati.

He did not dare say them aloud, but then Brahma, with a start, realized too late how much he cared for her . . .

Her voice; cool, a little hard, not touched by anything, almost amused, cut through his thoughts. 'It's time to begin . . . shall we start?'

3

THE SCANDAL

'For a quiet man, Brahma seems to have created quite a loud furore!'

Brahma could still hear the jeer in Indra's remark he had overheard this morning. It rankled then and echoed now. And he couldn't get it out of his head. He thrust the bundle of sheaves from his desk, rubbing his jaw angrily.

He clenched his hands into big fists. He had not bothered to answer that silly question, nor had he demanded an explanation. But the first nugget of doubt had stuck in his mind: *What were they saying about him? Were they talking about his feelings for Sarasvati? Or their work together as Shatarupa? Had it shocked everyone?*

Brahma flung the pen away angrily. They were all fools. *And so was he*, taunted a voice. Sarasvati *was* different, he told himself firmly. But what was the point? She wasn't for him, so he'd better forget her.

'I made the mistake of making you bewitchingly perfect, only to fall in love with you!' He suddenly drew a long breath and looked cautiously around as if he were afraid of being overheard. 'And now I cannot stop looking at you, keep my eyes off you—is that why the world is laughing at me?' he thrust his fists deep into his eyes to block off her image. 'And now I have become the cause of your extreme embarrassment. I can hear the wicked whispers behind my back. I see you, trying to turn away from me, my gaze, my love. What do I do?' he screamed in silent agony. 'What do I do to appease my love and save you from this humiliation?'

Love went on around him—forbidden and without reproach. As he stared listlessly through his open window, when the stars were bright enough to compete with the bright oil lamps, he was aware of love on every side. From the open woods, now a silver silhouette in the moonlit sky, seeped a sweet fragrance of blossoms and fresh scent of the crisp breeze. He caught another scent, the mysterious thrilling perfume of love. Hands wanting to touch her un-jewelled hands as she strummed the veena, trembling a little, to run his fingers through her silken mane. The cascade of her sweet music, her pristine, bright white silk brushing against him, her soft, low voice—were all part of his dream he did not want to wake up from.

He was hopelessly in love with her.

He suddenly became sober. The fumes that had clouded his brain went away: as if a blade slit through the gauze of his wild imagination.

Brahma suddenly felt tired and depressed as he rested his head against the chair. He couldn't work any more. His notes were an illegible scrawl, his pen broken from being flung down and the inkwell full. But he didn't feel like working. He pushed the sheets away and was struck by what he saw for the first time in his life, a sinking possibility he would probably never see again: a world with her and one without. He imagined himself lifeless, buried there forever in oblivion, his stifled despair, the dumb dreariness of non-existence interred in this beautiful serenity.

Brahma felt a mix of relief and dread: perspiration had broken out under his tight-pressed fingers in the cool moonshine, as his churning mind was consumed with Sarasvati.

She fascinated him by her fresh frankness, the thoughtful expression in her eyes or the flood of angry colour on her cheeks when arguing with him—which was quite often, he recollected with a smile. Even in the way the fabric hung on her, he saw something extraordinarily charming, touching in its simplicity and elegant grace; the quiet dignity about her accentuating her intelligence and mature thoughts far developed beyond her years. He could talk with her about literature, art or anything else he liked; could complain to her of life, of people. Though it sometimes happened in the middle of a serious conversation, she had the irrepressible habit of interposing her opinions and views on the subject. They worked in perfect harmony and when the day's work was over, he awaited her outside, her faithful shadow in whatever light she stood.

Sometimes he cast a troubled glance at her creased clothes and careless topknot that amplified conspicuousness rather than style. But this was no disloyalty; he deprecated the sniggers behind her back. In her contempt for dressing up, he found grace.

'I know they believe I dress shabbily, or that I wear only boring whites,' she smiled with her clear, clever eyes. 'I am trying to pare down my decision and time. Because I have too many other decisions and too little time.'

He was forced to agree, in concurrence with his own singularly ivory range of attire. With a start, he realized both of them had a penchant for pure whites and everything white: their swan, the white lotus and even the kheer! White, the colour of light, knowledge and truth.

He could look nothing like her but every time he saw himself wearing white, he could not but associate himself with her. She had created a replicable style; that was the charm behind dressing simply.

If she was indifferent to dressing up, she gave all her effort and time to reading and music. She was an insatiable reader and spent almost all her time immersed in books and research. In fact, much to his infinite delight, the book always became the perfect pretext to open a conversation.

'What have you been reading this week since I saw you last?' he would ask, broaching their pet conversation.

And she would tell him, while he listened, all enthralled.

And was it in keeping with him—as God—and more importantly, an intelligent, staid man—to be hoping and sighing in unrequited love? But even the bleakest possibility could not wean him away from thinking of Sarasvati. She would only have to stretch out her hand and he would put his in hers willingly. And he knew that she knew it. That frightened him. But what scared him more was her utter indifference to him.

Sarasvati seemed to be apathetic to love. And she clearly did not feel the same: there was a certain coldness about her that he found attractive and yet, disheartening. It was all confusing and wretched. He knew he was playing with an icy flame.

She had never encouraged him to think that she looked at him as anything more than a kind mentor or a helpful friend who was teaching her, or a colleague whose company she valued and enjoyed enormously.

She did nothing to lead or mislead him. She treated him as an associate whom she liked, and he knew she did like him. He could tell that by the way she spoke and the way she looked at him, but that was as far as it went.

It was *his* attitude towards her that bothered him. He knew if she gave him the slightest encouragement, he would not be able to resist her . . .

He became aware of stiff muscles and a throbbing headache and with a silent groan, Brahma opened his eyes. His eyes flickered and he blinked, aware of a new presence in the room: his tired eyes met the questioning ones of Shiva.

Looking at the tall man, lean yet surprisingly broad, giving the appearance of massiveness without flab, one would never conjure him to be the Destroyer: fair in complexion like camphor, Shiva had the kindest eyes and gentlest of demeanours. Perhaps what made him seem intimidating were the wild dreadlocks, the besmeared ash, the rough tiger skin draped at his slim waist, and the three-pronged *trishul* clenched lightly in his big, powerful hands.

'You are a sight,' Shiva said mildly, taking in Brahma's disturbed appearance. 'Has the scandal affected you so badly?'

The question startled him. Like all those who instinctively felt guilty, he had enormous respect and awe for the truth. Something almost exterior to himself dictated a quick, hurt answer.

'Scandal!' he repeated, looking perplexed.

'You blissfully remain locked indoors while the world outside is rocked by the gossip you have created, besides other things!"

Brahma ignored the jibe and watched Shiva pull a chair towards him to sit opposite him.

'What scandal?' Brahma asked forcefully.

'That you are madly in love and chasing poor Sarasvati and she is mighty miffed with you!'

'I am not!' exploded Brahma, his dark eyebrows coming together in a furious frown. 'Nor is she . . .'

'You are unnaturally defensive,' Shiva observed with narrowed eyes.

For a moment, like a commoner in the king's chair, Brahma tasted the pride of the situation. Then as his friend confronted him with conventional admonitions, he realized that in his denial, he was committing an offence— he was lying.

Brahma didn't move, his face drained of colour, making him appear more haggard.

Shiva studied him, a watchful expression on his face.

'You look bothered. What's troubling you?'

'Nothing,' returned Brahma, impassively, reining in his emotions and expressions. 'I am worried about

something else. Not the scandal—whatever it may be,' he
laced his voice with sarcasm. 'The worse is over. The world
has its couples, now full of pairs of all beings.'

'Yes, thanks entirely to Sarasvati,' concurred Shiva.

Brahma stiffened involuntarily at the mention of
her name.

'She was enormously brave, I must say,' Brahma heard
the admiration in Shiva's voice. 'I never thought she would
succeed in this mission!' smiled Shiva, noticing Brahma
clenching his jaw.

'No, she was well aware of the delicacy,' he said shortly,
with unnecessary vehemence.

'And the danger,' added Shiva.

Brahma ignored the insinuation, saying instead,
'Talking about danger, the next one probably would be a
dangerous one.'

'Why, are you planning to seek her help again?' Shiva
asked bluntly, his eyes narrowing.

'Yes,' he said shortly. 'Ganga and Yamuna have already
declined. So, it will be upon Sarasvati to do the needful,'
he added testily. 'Though I am still not keen on her taking
the risk.'

'What is this task?'

'Taking the Fire of Knowledge to the Earth. As the
Goddess of Knowledge, I guess, it will be upon her.'

Shiva raised his brows. 'That is highly daring! But
for that, she'll need to descend to Earth. Have you
told her?'

Brahma shook his head wordlessly but a worried frown
deeply lined his face.

'She will be able to do it,' Shiva assured him. 'Sarasvati *is* exceptional. She must certainly be very remarkable if she can impress *you*.'

Brahma felt himself turn hot. He was poring over some books, his back turned, so he didn't have to look at Shiva. Otherwise, he thought, he might have given himself away.

'That she is,' he tried to make his voice sound casual. By now, Brahma had enough control over himself to look up and meet Shiva's eyes.

Shiva's grey eyes grew solemn, staring at Brahma, quizzing him. 'She is special to you, Brahma, admit it,' he declared softly.

Brahma looked up at his friend for some seconds, his face expressionless, his eyes brooding.

'Yes, she is,' he confessed with a sigh, looking straight in the eye. 'She is my inspiration,' he paused. 'That is why I created her.'

Shiva glanced swiftly at him, his brows raised high. 'I realize that it is quite discernible,' he commented wryly. 'To help you, she emerged as your Sarasvati—the goddess who would assist you in your unfinished task.'

'She is more than that,' Brahma said in a low voice. 'Without her, I cannot make life exist, *I* couldn't exist,' he went on, as he inhaled deeply, lifting his heavy shoulders. 'It is with *her* ideas, *her* thoughts, *her* help that my work becomes more meaningful. This is true of any of her four *roop*s—Vakdevi, Savitri, Gayatri and even Brahmi, in her warrior form.'

'Where knowledge is her weapon,' observed Shiva, with a crooked smile. 'She gives form to your thoughts, meaning to your words, concept to your ideas, is that it?'

Brahma nodded, a faint flush rising up his neck and flooding his bronzed face. 'Not just ideas, but some action too,' he smiled drily. 'She can't resist a challenge and doesn't hesitate to take on dangers.'

Shiva gave a nod, observing the adulation in his friend's words. His calm eyes searched Brahma's troubled face.

'But does *she* know?' Shiva asked instead, his tone soft. He paused, awaiting his friend's response.

'Know what?' Brahma asked blandly.

'That you admire her so much,' Shiva returned the blandness. He filled a sharp pause with: 'That you love her.'

'She should, she is supposed to know everything!' retorted Brahma with a short, nervous laugh.

Brahma realized he had fallen into his friend's well-orchestrated trap. He stopped walking up and down and fixed Shiva with his cold, hard eyes.

'What do you mean?'

Shiva smiled glibly. 'Are you convincing her or yourself now? Do you acknowledge it yourself?' he persisted, softly.

Brahma did not say anything. Shiva's keen eyes followed him as he moved over to the window.

'It's all very well.' Brahma broke off after a long pause, casting a mirthless smile. 'You know I've been silly about her, Shiva. That is what the scandal is all about, isn't it? That poor Brahma is in love!' he rued, his lips twisted in a grimace. 'But I didn't realize what she meant to me until I created her!'

Shiva walked up to his friend. 'From what I know of her, she respects the mind, not the strings of the heart,' he warned. 'And unlike most women, Sarasvati is neither eager for matrimony nor motherhood.'

'Yes, that makes it more admirable but less hopeful for me,' rued Brahma, rubbing his beard in rising agitation. 'And she isn't the easiest person to talk to!'

'She is singularly aloof,' cautioned Shiva. 'Does she reciprocate your feelings? Do you think she will agree?'

'I thought I'd wait and give her time,' Brahma said uncomfortably.

'That means you are not sure,' Shiva observed. 'Rather, you are sure that she will refuse you.'

'I guess I'll have to see her . . .' Brahma muttered, his frown deepening.

Shiva had never seen Brahma look so unsure, almost scared.

'What are you afraid of?' he asked gently. 'Her rejection?'

Brahma nodded, his jaw tightening.

'And self-doubt,' he said awkwardly.

'And some ugly gossip too?' needled Shiva, his eyes probing.

Brahma flushed. 'What is that?'

'What I mentioned earlier. And the ugliest story going around is that since you have created her, she is like your daughter,' said Shiva in a non-committal way.

Colour drained from Brahma's face, his expression carved of stone.

'What!' he exclaimed in horror. 'That's vile!'

He grappled with struggling emotions, his voice hoarse. 'Yes, I created her: but as my vision! I individualized her with all the qualities I have so longed for!' he shook his head helplessly. 'And if that's the warped logic, then do Kama and all the others who were created by me from my mind become my sons?!' he demanded furiously. His voice had a sharp edge to it.

'But you did create ten sons from your mind—the Prajapati Daksha, Narada and Chitragupta, along with the rishis Angiras, Atri, Pulastya, Marichi, Pulaha, Kratu, Bhrigu and Vashist,' replied Shiva smoothly. 'Matter of fact, it is them, your manas putras who are righteously enraged and consider Sarasvati their sister . . .'

'That's ridiculous!' snapped Brahma, curling his fingers into an angry fist. A wave of wild, proud anger rose in him, and he ground his fist into his hand. 'They should instead be revering her as a mother—as a goddess of inspiration and knowledge.'

As the words left his mouth, Brahma knew what he was up against. And the fading indignant eyes of Shiva facing him signalled an unpleasant truth: the more he protested, the fewer would believe him. But some vague necessity for credibility made him want to dispute and debate; the honesty of his imagination had betrayed him.

His heavy shoulders slumped in defeat.

'Kama may not be your son, but by fashioning him as the God of Love, you generated him with love, lust and longing,' stated Shiva softly.

Brahma started looking up quickly.

'And you seem struck by it yourself,' continued Shiva.

Something in his tone puzzled Brahma.

He frowned. 'Because of Kama?' he asked, his tone incredulous. 'He shot his love arrow at me?!'

Shiva gave a faint nod.

A white, hot rage sliced through Brahma.

'The sheer impertinence . . .' he exploded. 'He needs to be taught a lesson!'

'More likely it was his certain sense of adventurism,' said Shiva laconically. 'You gave him that bow and arrow of love and he's busy trying it on all and everyone—clearly even you have not been spared!' laughed Shiva. 'It's ironic that through Kama, you created love in this world and you became a victim of it yourself.'

'I wanted to create a wonderful emotion, a beautiful feeling. Not to make it so crippling . . .' breathed Brahma, his tone wistful.

He regarded Shiva's serene face, his eyes glittering and hard. 'Is that what some are claiming? That I am in love with Sarasvati, the woman of my dreams, my mind?'

Shiva nodded, his eyes narrowed. 'Not such a kind description—they talk of you chasing your daughter!'

Rage grabbed his throat.

'And you agree?!' Brahma demanded; his shuttered eyes now opened in full wrath. 'But how can some claim that she is my daughter?! I have created her as I have the world. I haven't produced her from my body, she is not my biological daughter . . . This is outrageous!' he went on, his voice strident.

'I am voicing the whispers,' Shiva said dispassionately.

Brahma gave him a sharp look.

'Then they are malicious tongues and wicked minds!' Brahma exhaled deeply to cool his fury. 'If I am the Creator, she's my creativity, she is the intellect to my thoughts.

Wherever there is Brahma, Sarasvati is bound to be there, and wherever there is Sarasvati, Brahma must be there!'

'I am cautioning you, that's all,' Shiva said silkily. 'The rumour must have fallen on Sarasvati's ears too.'

Brahma frowned, his face darkening. 'That was what I was afraid of—she won't take this lying down,' he said, as he had a sudden sinking feeling.

'But it is how the others view it. Some are more kind; they call it a creator's egoistic love for his creation,' said Shiva.

A look of vehement astonishment spread over his friend's haggard face.

He glanced at Shiva, his look almost desperate. 'How can I say it and how can I convince her? Creation and comprehension are reciprocal: one cannot live and thrive without the other . . .'

'But is it reciprocal?' questioned Shiva, his voice now grim.

Brahma reddened under his tan. He shuddered, covering his face in despair, feeling the tears of frustration straining his eyes.

He had no answer. But he would have to tell her.

4

THE PROPOSAL

'There is something I must say to you, Sarasvati . . .'

She detected the terseness in his words and noticed how his face appeared more tense than usual. Only then did Sarasvati see a change in Brahma. He looked pale and was breathing fast. The tremor in his breathing affected his hands and lips and head, even as an irreverent lock fell on his wide forehead. Evidently, he avoided looking her in the face, and, trying to mask his emotion, at one moment touched his jawline, at another draped his shawl on the other shoulder. This whole time Sarasvati had noticed something amiss about him: he had grown strangely abstracted as the morning progressed.

Abruptly, he had turned to her, interrupting her in the middle of a sentence, making it obvious that he had not been listening to what she had been saying.

'I want to say something to you . . .' he repeated, his kohl eyes filled with painful anxiety.

'I am listening,' she said tolerantly, her face unsmiling, her eyes questioning.

'It may seem strange to you. You will be surprised, but I don't care,' he said hastily, his pacing getting stronger and restless.

She straightened her shoulders once more and prepared herself to listen.

'You see,' Brahma began, bowing his head and touching his shawl absently. '. . . This is what I wanted to tell you. You'll think it's strange and silly, but I can't bear it any longer.'

She listened and looked at his face; his eyes were distressed and intelligent, and it was evident that he wanted to say something to her. It was unlike Brahma to look and sound so unsure of himself. Sarasvati was now intrigued. Was it another request that he was afraid she would refuse this time?

She rushed to his rescue. 'If it is some task, I assure you I have no objections,' she said airily, hoping to make him feel more at ease.

He smiled wanly. 'No, it's no errand I am sending you on . . .'

His words died away in an indistinct mutter and were suddenly buried in a long pause. He cleared his throat in confusion and looked on hopelessly, not knowing what to say or do.

Being unused to the sight of him being so uncertain, Sarasvati felt her own anxiety rising, her eyes now filled with sudden doubts.

'What is it?' she insisted, her voice compelling.

'Well!' he muttered helplessly. By now, he thought he had enough control over himself to look up and meet her eyes. She was looking at him with those clear, clever eyes.

He got momentarily distracted, or was it an unconscious excuse to procrastinate? She was standing before a full-length marble statue, her hands lifting her loose, raven hair off her shoulders, her head tilted a little on one side. Her feet were bare, tapping impatiently on the polished floor, as was her habit.

Sarasvati drew in an exasperated breath.

'Brahma, what's this for, I would like to know? Are you . . . oh, why are you so disturbed? Or, is there some trouble? Tell me, perhaps I could, so to say, help you?'

Trying to reassure him, she ventured cautiously to place her hands over his.

Brahma started and turned his face towards her. He was deathly pale.

'I . . . love you.'

The words, so simple and ordinary, had the power to drain colour from Sarasvati's face. They had been uttered in all earnestness and yet, in acute embarrassment, Sarasvati turned away from Brahma, and let go of his hand, while his confusion was followed by terror.

'Just one moment!' she said, with a little gasp. 'I'm sure now that this is a mistake. I don't go in for anything like that.'

'I beg your pardon.' He looked at her in bewilderment, unaware that he had taken too much for granted. Then he drew himself up formally. 'I . . . I think I have made an error. If you will excuse me, I shall take my leave.'

As he turned away, his hand was on the banister.

'Don't go, I didn't mean to be obtuse,' she said, pushing a strand of indefinite hair out of her eyes. 'I . . . this is a revelation!' she shrugged helplessly.

Sarasvati felt invaded by a sudden chill, followed by a sad, warm, sentimental mood induced by Brahma's unexpected words. *He loved her,* she frowned in disbelief. The warm, good feeling of his presence suddenly vanished and gave place to an acute and unpleasant feeling of awkwardness. She felt an inward perplexity; she looked sceptically at him, now that by declaring his love for her, he seemed to have shed off the cloak of aloofness which added to his charm. He appeared to her less formidable, plainer, more ordinary.

'What's the meaning of it?' she thought in dismay. 'But why, how . . . how can he be in love?' she bit her lip, baffled. 'And what do I feel for him? That's the question!' she told herself urgently.

Sarasvati was struck with panic. She could neither retain the silence nor the sequence of his torrential words after his declaration. Both overwhelmed her; she could barely register what he had just said. She could only recall the meaning of what he had said, and the sensation his words evoked in her. She remembered his deep velvety voice, so scared and hesitant—yet which had seemed so stifled and husky with emotion, and the extraordinary passion of his intonation.

Brahma allowed himself to breathe easily and freely; now, that the worst and most difficult thing had been said. He hesitated; there was some element in this that he failed to understand.

He knew now this was no ordinary woman and that his persuasive appeal was a blunted weapon. But he wanted her as he had never wanted any other woman. He was shrewd enough to know that he had to give her free rein. Patience, he told himself.

He noticed her bowed head, the way she was weaving her fingers in quiet agitation. He wanted to clasp them and stop the nervous gesture. He almost did but quickly braced himself and, looking Sarasvati straight in the face instead, began talking warmly, irrepressibly. He was saying something in a low quick voice and she was listening tensely.

Encouraged by her silence, he began '. . . And when I see you coming into the hall or I hear your voice from a distance, I feel a glow in my heart!'

She wanted him to stop speaking, his words engulfing her with mounting dread. The lush beauty of the swaying trees outside with the wisps of mist suddenly seemed hushed listening to her agitated breath, whilst something strange and hostile was passing in Sarasvati's heart . . .

'I know I am being a little presumptuous,' he said, his voice still carrying a tinge of hesitancy. 'But what is the use of preliminaries and procrastinations? What is the use of unnecessary fine words? I love you, Sarasvati. And I hope, I beg, I beseech you . . .' Brahma brought out at last, '. . . to be my wife!'

She raised her head, her eyes startled: this was getting worse by the minute. Telling her of his love, Brahma spoke eloquently and passionately, but she oddly felt only a mounting uncomfortable dread, neither flattered nor glad; she felt nothing but a dull emptiness for him, pity and regret that a good man should be so distressed on her account. *That must be because of my habit of looking at things objectively*, she rued; she could not take in the moment of being loved.

But she didn't want this moment!

His declaration and discomfort struck her as exaggerated, something not to be taken earnestly, and, at the same time, she felt a tide of a rebellious defiance which seemed to urge her that all she was hearing and seeing now was from the point of *his* personal happiness, and what was more important was she and her happiness. Those moments seemed to draw endlessly and she found herself in a vortex of missed feelings: she raged, she was distressed and blamed herself, though she did not understand exactly where she was at fault.

To add to her embarrassment, she was tongue-tied, at a loss for what to say, and yet she had to say. To blurt 'I don't love you' bluntly was beyond her, but she could not bring herself to acquiesce and say 'Yes' because however deep she delved in her heart, she could not find one spark of feeling for him besides admiration.

'Didn't you realize I was so much in love with you?'

She could not meet his earnest eyes. *As if it mattered*, she silently ranted to herself.

'I find it more difficult to say things I mean . . .' his voice trailed off uncertainly.

So eloquently confiding your emotions now, she corrected him mentally, *not cold and private any mor*e . . . This must be the most bizarre love proposal—abrupt and almost tragic.

'Well, it seems the world but you knew about it,' he said, laughing self-consciously. He was leaning towards her intently, with a sort of inspired and chaste romance in his eyes—and she drew back.

She frowned, suddenly realizing the impact of his words. *The world knew... ?!* Is that why Ganga threw her that pointed look whenever she happened to mention Brahma's name? The amused look of the devas? That twinkle in Vishnu's eyes when he saw them together? Or those meaningful glances she had caught being exchanged between Lakshmi and Parvati whenever she discussed work she did with him.

Sarasvati felt a surge of annoyance, reading at last, those innuendos and insinuations and the ambiguous looks thrown at her these last few months . . .

'*No!*' she interrupted him abruptly, horror mounting.

He stopped, his flow of words halted, his face showing his surprise.

She gritted her teeth: the more he spoke, the more unreal it seemed to her, something not to be taken seriously.

'I am very grateful to you, though I feel I've done nothing to deserve such feelings,' she started.

Brahma blinked uncomprehendingly.

Then she knew she had to say it firmly but honestly: she could not feel guilty for something she had not done. 'Brahma,' she stressed, with a very grave face, after a moment's deliberation, 'I am very grateful to you for the honour. I admire you, I . . .'

'I think being admired is lonely,' he said drily, his heart racing erratically; fear swamping him as he dreaded what was to come.

'Perhaps,' she agreed, her eyes as clear as her ringing voice. 'But I respect you too much to feel anything else. I *don't* love you and I will never marry you!'

Her words sliced his heart, his face draining of colour.

Aghast at her tactlessness, she tried to make amends— *but I cannot be false to him and myself*, she warned herself.

She softened her tone. 'It is not about you. It is entirely about me, up to me. I don't believe in love. Nor in matrimony or motherhood,' she declared candidly. 'I don't trust any of those things.'

He gave her a quizzical stare and she felt her eyes drawn to his. They had a hurt tenderness, which she had never seen in them before.

But that's what makes me love you more, he thought wildly.

He said, 'But that is you—honest and singularly aloof—and I admire you for it.'

'That word admiration again,' she said bitterly. 'You admire these traits now, but they are possible cause of conflict later. I don't want any of it,' she added obstinately.

'But I was sure, absolutely certain, that you were extraordinary and going to change the world in some way,' he explained, his white cheeks flushed. 'Not just *my* world, *the* world.'

'I would rather make my own world,' she answered coolly. 'And yes, I am not ordinary, I can't do the usual—I don't want to fall in love, I don't want to surrender myself or any part of me or my feelings to anyone. Love is submission; as is marriage and motherhood. I cannot capitulate, I have to be me,' she stated firmly.

He frowned. 'But who is stopping you from being you?'

'Love and marriage will tie me to you. Vishnu has Lakshmi, Shiva has Parvati and so must you have me?' she asked, rising restlessly. 'Why do I as a goddess have to be partnered with another god, why should I have to marry him? I don't want to be known as someone's wife, some god's spouse, I am *me*—I am Sarasvati, the goddess of learning and knowledge and music and the arts. I would certainly *not* like to be identified as just a consort,' she sneered, lips twisted in a derisive grimace.

Brahma replied, 'You think so, but does it matter? I want to marry you because I love *you*! Not because I wish to diminish your status!' he exclaimed, his tone incredulous. 'There's no subjugation or subservience!'

'But that is how it is viewed, that is why the nasty talk, the tongues wagging,' she lifted her shoulders indignantly. 'It is not just subordination; I call it the spousification of the goddesses. Lakshmi is the Goddess of Wealth but she is known to be Vishnu's consort, and Parvati, the very Shakti, as Shiva's wife.'

Brahma shook his head. 'No, they are one—what is Shiva without Shakti?'

'Exactly!' she exclaimed. 'I don't want us to be one.'

'But we are one—what is Creation without Creativity?' demanded Brahma. 'And is that why you won't be my wife?' he asked in open wonderment. He began to feel bewildered by the way she was controlling not only the conversation but also his happiness and future.

'Yes, because I don't want to be known as someone's wife or controlled by any man,' she said defiantly.

'And what if *I* am known as Sarasvati's husband? I would be honoured!' he said roundly.

Sarasvati looked on, momentarily taken aback.

'But *I* do not want to be known as your wife!' she repeated, spiritedly. 'I am too free, too autonomous to share myself with anyone but myself,' she professed. 'Love is a shackle I am not bound to!'

'You don't get it, do you, Sarasvati? You think too much. It's not the mind, it's the heart!'

'Well, my mind and heart say no,' she retorted with asperity. 'It's better to love with your mind, and think with your heart!'

'What would that make me then, a man without love?' he sounded ironic. 'Like you.'

'Possibly, but better for both of us,' she shrugged airily. 'Love is not rational,' she sighed, scrutinizing the hurting man in front of her. 'I suppose it is the absolute height of madness where one loses reason.'

'Yes, you have to be a little mad to be in love,' admitted Brahma.

'And I am not mad!' she said dismissively, sweeping the hair off her shoulder. 'I don't like the feeling of allowing your mind and emotions to go out of control.'

'Love is not controlling; it is, in fact, humbling, even submissive.'

'Exactly! You are agreeing with me,' she smiled triumphantly.

'No, Sarasvati, you worry about being in love,' he corrected mildly. 'You are scared of the passion and pain that go along with it,' he paused, regarding her quizzically. 'Don't you long for it?'

Sarasvati gave a tired smile. 'I do,' she confessed, noticing the glimmer of hope flaring in his eyes. 'But I also fear it. The idea of part of me being controlled by someone else,' she looked dubiously at him.

'But that's the joy, the surrender,' he murmured.

'Joy in surrender?' she looked almost indignant. 'That's weak submission! I can't imagine someone having the power over me, having the power to . . .' she halted, biting her lips.

'Power to hurt you?' he finished softly.

Her lips outlined a grimace.

'The power to promise, pledge, obligate,' she rued. 'I find it frightening!'

'What are you scared of?' he asked, his brow raised. 'That you cannot love, you cannot commit—or that you are too proud and too arrogant to associate yourself with such emotions?'

Irrational rage grabbed her throat. 'That's too aspiring, and I believe in the mind, not emotions. And I would rather be proud than passive!' she said contemptuously. 'Besides, I don't even know you, to . . . er . . . fall in love with you! I don't know you at all!'

'I think I improve on acquaintance,' he said drily.

She bit her lip to halt a sudden smile; his wit was as ironic as him.

She lifted her shoulders helplessly. 'But seriously, I love something else, not somebody else,' she stated. '*You* know I love *thought*—be it art, books or music; I have dedicated my whole life to it. I am an artist, I want the freedom of creativity and nothing of me can be chained. You and your love want me to be bound to you, to go on living a usual life, which will soon become insufferable to me and to you,' she warned, ignoring his movement of protest. 'Instead of belonging to someone, I would rather belong to some belief, some cause, some vision . . .'

'And hopefully, a more ambitious future for yourself?' said Brahma

'And that too,' she nodded, her chin unconsciously raised in quiet defiance.

'It would be more disappointing if you rejected that than you rejected me,' he countered quietly.

She was momentarily startled. *His hopes for me are exceedingly selfless*, she thought feeling an unfamiliar twinge of guilt.

'Brahma,' she faintly smiled as she pronounced his name. 'You are a good, brilliant, honourable man; you are better than anyone else,' she sighed. 'I feel for you with my whole heart, but that's not enough. Besides, as an honest person, I ought to tell you that happiness depends on equality—that is, when both parties are equally in love.'

He flinched, her words lashing him, whipping in him again the stirring of a dull pain. Seeing his face wretched, his eyes so wounded, she was immediately mortified by her harsh, honest words.

Brahma said nothing more, looking up to see through her, staring vacantly at the wide expanse of the trees. She had hurt him and it surprised her that it hurt her to see him so hurt. But now that he had told her, she felt in some mysterious way that his love was something she had never seen or known or met before. She was a little confused, but she was vaguely elated too. She was acutely conscious of his appearance; she had never seen him as a man who would be attracted to her. For the first time, as she stood so close to him, she saw how fiery his eyes were, how cold his face was, how devastating was the passion in his heart.

'You must forgive me,' she muttered, not able to endure the silence. 'I cannot afford to entertain sentiments of the romantic kind. I don't think I am capable of them,' she finished simply. 'I would rather think and create—that I love.'

'If that is so, it's best we avoid meeting each other as much as possible,' an ashen-faced Brahma said in a dead voice.

Her heart sank unreasonably. She struggled. 'Not even as a friend? A co-worker?' she asked, incredulous.

He shrugged his heavy shoulders. His indifference, surprisingly, hurt Sarasvati.

She inhaled sharply. 'I am who I am. I can't give that up.'

His mouth tightened, his eyes glittering on his pale face. 'I am not asking you to give it up,' he said thickly. 'I would never ask you to do that.'

'So, you are giving up me instead?' she said astutely, her lips stiff, feeling a sharp stab of pain. Watching his stony, brooding face, she knew he had closed her off forever. He was all ice again: glacial and impenetrable.

'It would be better, wouldn't it?' he muttered shakily. 'I shan't disturb you any more . . .'

Her heart contracted, her eyes widening, dark in despair. 'What we do best, *us*, together,' she cried in a painful, hoarse whisper. 'You would sacrifice *that* for . . . for . . . some vapid sentiment?' she asked convulsively.

He didn't have her love; he didn't want anything more from her, he didn't wish to have anything to do with her. She should have been sighing in relief but she was weighed down by the oddly aching heaviness in her heart. They would do nothing together from now on, they would be strangers.

He did not stir. His impassivity was vaguely impressive. She felt uncharacteristically helpless, even angered by the unfairness of it all. She raged inwardly, clenched her fists, and cursed his remoteness and her insensitivity. Still, she preferred being honest—to him and to herself. For however much she tried and found his words futile, she could not muster or stir her feelings for him beyond respect and a certain camaraderie. She was not the least in love with him and she did not know why she had hesitated to refuse him at once. She looked at his sombre face, his tall frame, at his dark, wise eyes and his long, purposeful strides. She remembered his passionate words that touched her heart but did not quicken her pulse.

Brahma paused briefly before turning sharply and walking out. She made a move to rise from her seat.

'No, don't!' he said, with a wave of his hand. 'I can well understand your words and sentiments. Pardon my presumptive behaviour and I hope you find it as appalling as I did!' he said, dismissing her faint protest, giving her an almost kindly look. 'Don't come; I can go alone,' his tone once again frigid and formal.

He walked on rapidly, without looking back at her or raising his head. He had shrunk in himself, his head down, his shoulders hunched. It seemed to her that sorrow had made his shoulders thinner and narrower.

He had left and she was left alone. Returning to her chamber, she walked slowly, continually standing still and looking round with an expression that suggested that she could not believe that the enigmatic man whom she liked so much had just declared his love, and that she had so clumsily and bluntly refused him.

Once again, she was assailed with guilt and a certain helplessness. She had just learnt a hard lesson: how little a person does depends on her own will. Yet she had willingly caused a man to suffer, subjecting the feelings of a decent kindly man to such cruel, undeserved anguish.

Her heart tormented her while reason argued otherwise.

'One can't force oneself to love,' she assured herself, and at the same time she thought. 'I like him—I like him a lot—I admire him enormously, but do I love him?'

And yet, strangely, days later, when Brahma disappeared and locked himself in his palace, refusing to meet anyone, she felt as though she had lost something very precious, someone very near and dear whom she could never find again. She felt that with Brahma, part of her had slipped away from her, and that the moments, which they had passed through so fruitlessly, would never be repeated.

He did not want to meet her; he wanted nothing from her.

She recalled his words: '*Love is an unpleasant pursuit, yet we search, chase, hunt and live for it.*'

5

LOVE AND KAMA

Sarasvati sat down cross-legged, her white sari spreading like a blossoming jasmine, with the tilted veena held slightly away from her. She gently strung on the instrument with both hands, one holding the strings while the other controlling the movements. As the minutes rushed, so did the movements of her hands, playing with all her might. The hall filled with her soulful music. Sarasvati was playing a difficult passage that was long and monotonous, yet interesting because of its difficulty, while Brahma, his face impassive, his jaws clenched, listened. Sarasvati—rosy from the violent exercise, strong and vigorous with a soft swathe of hair falling over her forehead—attracted him a lot. He blinked, tearing his eyes away from her, to stare unseeingly outside the long window of the assembly hall.

To sit in this hall, to watch this young, elegant, pure, perfect woman making such beautiful music and to listen to those heavenly notes was so pleasant, yet so painful . . .

'Superb!' gushed Shiva, standing up to applaud. 'Well, Sarasvati, you have played like never before!' he exclaimed when Sarasvati had finished and stood up. 'Brahma, you could not have created anything better.'

Before a dazed Brahma could respond, Sarasvati swiftly said, 'He made me, but I made the music,' she mocked wryly. 'Give this devi her due.'

'Splendid,' echoed Vishnu, intervening to ease the sudden awkwardness. Sarasvati smiled knowingly: Vishnu was the eternal Preserver, trying to preserve peace and harmony everywhere, every time, and with his perfect social tact, was able to keep up a flow of easy conversation. He was immaculately dressed as always, dark and tall, imposing in his handsomeness, as much with his regal resplendence as his thick black hair and deep brown eyes, twinkling in tandem with the generous smile fixed below his strong, aquiline nose. He had an effortless style about him, which even the handsomest deva envied and sought.

Brahma watched, unsmiling, his face inscrutable, not allowing himself to be carried away by the general enthusiasm.

Everyone flocked around Sarasvati, congratulating her. They expressed astonishment, declaring that it was long since they had heard such music, as she listened to them in silence, with a faint smile, her whole figure expressing triumph. Across the long hall, her eyes met Brahma's. He was tall, dark, disinterested. She knew his gaze was on her all the while but the moment she returned his stare, he looked away.

Sarasvati had dreaded coming for this recital, more out of anxiety of meeting Brahma than meeting others.

His conspicuous absence in the beginning troubled her. But then, he appeared; late as always. Her heart soared unreasonably, beating violently. It was odd that this should be happening, she thought. She was eager yet startled, knowing that she was furtively pleased to be able to see him again; they hadn't met since so long. Nor had he handed her any new task they could work on together.

She found Parvati giving her a pronounced look but besides a polite smile, Sarasvati kept away from Parvati and the others. Sarasvati was used to being stared at, but today she felt incommoded by those stares accentuated by something more than curiosity. The news of her refusal to Brahma's proposal seemed to have caused a sensation, and most, if not all, were already gossiping wildly about them.

The furtive looks and teasing barbs were going to be a daily nuisance, providing entertainment for others, she fumed silently as she briskly made her way out. She had initially tried to laugh it off; she had no choice but to tolerate it with a feigned smile. What angered her more was Brahma being made to look like an amorous fool. *Why should it?* Why did she care what the world thought of him?

Weaning herself from the effusive crowd, Sarasvati sought her escape. She came to an abrupt halt, confronted by Ganga and Yamuna, the two river goddesses.

'It is rare meeting you but for a rare performance like this,' Ganga greeted her. 'We hardly see you otherwise!'

Sarasvati smiled stiffly, her eyes watchful.

Yamuna's chirpy voice piped in. 'She is busy escaping Brahma's besotted gaze which follows her every movement, sprouting new heads watching where she goes!'

Yamuna was slight, her skin of a dark amber colour, her movements always agitated, her big, brown eyes looking restless in sharp contrast to the fair, serene and soft-spoken Ganga.

Sarasvati felt the heat of an angry flush rising up her neck at Yamuna's impertinence and Ganga's faintly mocking smile.

'Oh, is that what you deduced?' Sarasvati remarked coolly, restraining her temper. She raised a brow. 'And all this time I believed, as did everyone else, that Brahma's four heads represented the four Vedas!'

'Or when you move in the four directions . . .' chuckled Yamuna. 'Brahma clearly cannot control his love for you and each time he looks around, his four heads face different directions so that he is always able to see you. Isn't that why you became Shatarupa, changing forms to shy away from his gaze? Imagine creating an entire set of birds and beasts that way . . .'

Sarasvati's face stiffened, favouring silence. She bit her lip to stop an angry retort. *It was all because of him*, she burnt with furious resentment. Instead, she turned her remote eyes on the two women.

'We could never have imagined the cold and lofty Lord Brahma to have fallen so hard in love, could we, Ganga?' chattered Yamuna happily. 'Guess that reclusive, touch-me-not personality of yours makes you more attractive to him!'

'Don't take her words to heart, Sarasvati,' interposed Ganga, her face sardonic, her grey eyes laughing. 'Yami here has an exaggerated sense of the absurd. Worse, she's a compulsive matchmaker, an incurable romantic. Lord Brahma has been unattached so long that everyone is visibly excited, if not inquisitive.'

'Oh, the latest I heard was that Brahma and Kama quarrelled because of you, Sarasvati!' blurted Yamuna, unable to stop herself.

Sarasvati looked startled.

'Clearly you don't know of this,' remarked Ganga, noticing Sarasvati's astonishment. 'Brahma is livid that Kama made him fall in love with you with his love arrow and confronted him.'

Sarasvati felt her face go warm. Now what more, she thought raggedly.

Her eyes glittered warningly. 'I shouldn't bother too much, Ganga, stories have a way of getting circulated and more malicious,' she said flatly.

Sarasvati threw both the women a quelling look. The smile left Yamuna's face and she assumed an expression of grimness.

'Let's watch and witness more drama!' Ganga returned, with her mischievous grin. Sarasvati wanted to wipe the smirk off the beautiful face. She clenched her fists in silent frustration. The annoyance within her was palpable and she had felt it even in the music she had played earlier.

'Is it some sort of public entertainment?' Sarasvati snapped. 'Hope you are never at the receiving end of such cruel fun.'

Ganga, taken aback, smiled stiffly and there was a hint of malice in her eyes.

'It's *you* who is being cruel, Sarasvati, by not reciprocating his love,' she bristled, her smile slipping.

'No, it is all of you making fools of yourself by this silly talk,' responded Sarasvati, her voice even. 'You are celestials, meant to divine fine thoughts and words.'

The reproach in her voice was crisply caustic, Ganga was quick to deduce, and notwithstanding her pleasant demeanour, Sarasvati had a certain tolerance for others' social frailties. And it was impossible to look at her polite smile without being sure that she had an enduring sense of forbearance. But there was another quality in Sarasvati which Ganga vaguely felt, but could not put a name to. Behind the cordiality and exquisite manners, which made Ganga feel unexpectedly gauche, Sarasvati seemed to hold both Yamuna and her at a certain distance, with a certain disdain.

Ganga gave a short laugh, quick to thaw the tension. 'We apologize, we were fooling around,' she said hurriedly. 'But we are all friends here and soon we will be sisters . . . I hear you are going to be made a river yourself, Sarasvati . . .'

Sarasvati again gave a start, not swift enough to hide her surprise.

'Brahma hasn't mentioned it yet to you?' Ganga asked, surprised. 'He had approached both of us, but we flatly refused! It's way too risky!'

'Yes, more daring than when Ganga had to descend to Earth on Brahma's orders!' added Yamuna. 'The Vadavagni— the Great Fire—which Brahma wishes us to transport to Earth is decidedly dangerous.'

'Yes it is,' nodded Sarasvati, frowning. 'But why does Brahma wish to transfer it to Earth? It is dangerous because

if this fire escapes, it will consume the current cycle of
Creation while preparing the universe for the next cycle
of Creation.'

Yamuna shrugged. 'That is why we refused! It is
nothing short of suicidal! Nothing like the kind when
Ganga descended to the Earth on King Bhagirath's
pleading with Brahma so as to free his ancestors' souls from
Rishi Kapila's curse. Well, if you agree to this, Sarasvati,
you too shall become a noble river like us.'

'The three sisters,' added Ganga pleasantly.

Why had Brahma not mentioned this to her yet,
Sarasvati wondered furiously, as she strode out of the room
and down the corridor. She had caught him watching her;
his eyes hooded: which had as much expression as the
diamond crown on his head. Was he not going to work
with her because she had refused him?

It was getting difficult for her each passing day.
Sarasvati knew Brahma was evading her as much as he
could: he always spoke to her quite casually, of trifling
things, as though they were friendly acquaintances, and
there was never anything in his manner to suggest that
he harboured love, disappointment, hurt or malice in his
heart. He rarely met her eyes and he never smiled. But he
was scrupulously polite.

She was beginning to feel a trifle impatient with him.
Why could he not realize what suddenly had become so
clear to her, that beside all the mundaneness of reality,
their own affairs were trivial. There were more important
tasks to be done than being in love. What did it matter if
a man was suffering from unrequited love and why should

the woman, face to face with the disagreeable, have to give
it a thought, she sighed exasperatedly. It was so strange
that Brahma, with all his cleverness, would have so little
sense of proportion. Because he had imagined love to be
eminently inspiring and then discovered that it had been
flung back at him, he could neither forgive her nor himself.
His pride was bruised, his sentiments hurt, his hopes
battered and his soul ripped. It was all a fantasy he had
lived on and when the truth shattered it, he believed reality
itself had shattered. Possibly that was why he was angry
with her because he was so angry with himself.

But she had to admit she felt an undecipherable
sadness at the loss of their friendship; she missed their
easy camaraderie, and their learned conversations. Others
found him cold and formidable but there was something
so deeply genuine about him that she could not help liking
him. He was the only friend she had.

Still perplexed, immersed in her thoughts, she almost
collided into a tall figure. She straightened up to find
herself staring into the frightened, green eyes of Kama,
the Deva of Love, whom they had been just talking about.
Her confused eyes met his stricken face, his body taut yet
trembling and, as always, he was wielding a sugarcane bow
and arrows on his shoulder. *The one which had made Brahma
fall in love with her?*

Another look at his ashen pallor made her fear the
worst. Fright and distress had twisted his handsome
features into an agonized mask.

'Kamadeva, are you all right?' she demanded.

He barely saw her, his eyes glazed.

'I was on my way to seeing you, lady,' he muttered. 'Only you can help me now.'

Puzzled, she frowned. 'What is wrong?' she asked politely, recalling Ganga's mention of the quarrel.

He nodded his head vigorously, barely able to speak.

'Brahma . . .' he stammered.

Her heart gave a jolt; she knew what was coming . . .

'Oh, what have I done?' he mumbled.

Kama looked rattled, his voice shaking. 'I made Brahma fall in love!' he burbled.

Sarasvati felt a rush of colour flooding her face.

'Tell me what happened,' she commanded in a low voice.

Kama felt that her eyes held him in a long and alert look of appraisal, calming him down immediately.

'It all started when I was handed my responsibilities by Brahma when he created me as the God of Love. I was ordered to spread love in the world by shooting my flower arrows . . .'

Sarasvati nodded; she had heard of Kama's flower bow of sugarcane with a string of honeybees and the five arrows, each decorated with five fragrant flowers: the white lotus, jasmine, Ashoka tree flowers, mango tree blossoms and the blue lotus.

'They were all given to me by Brahma himself!' cried Kama, his voice shrill. 'It was Brahma who decided that I, as Kama, would exist and live in twelve erogenous zones—a woman's neck, ear, hair, breasts, navel, vagina—and even in a cuckoo's chirping, the moonlight, the rains, pips and during the months of Chaitra and Vaishakh . . .' he rambled in incoherent despair. 'I was to help create new progenies and generations through love and lust. Basking in this boon of Brahma, I started travelling around the three *loka*s and had every gandharva, yaksha, deva spellbound, casting my love magic on all creatures of the world.'

Sarasvati didn't move, listening wordlessly. She looked at Kama, an odd expression in her eyes that Kama did not notice in his agitation.

'And in my enthusiasm, I struck Brahma too with my arrow . . .' he said in an undertone, his breath coming out in a scared whisper.

'And?' she prompted tersely, knowing the answer.

'And Brahma fell in love with you,' he whispered hoarsely. 'He must have been thinking of you when the arrow struck him.'

The words hung in the air, frozen in an endless pause.

'Did he?' she asked frostily. 'He was working and you interrupted his work,' she snapped, annoyed with herself for defending Brahma. Or was she providing an avoidable clarification?

'It was not planned, it was a mad, random aim,' blurted Kama. 'I didn't realize what I had done! But my regrets, oh lady, and I apologized profusely to Brahma too when he confronted me.'

'*You* are in trouble,' she responded. 'And how do you propose I can be of any help?'

'By making Brahma remove the curse he's put on me!' he cried, his face trembling with panic.

'A curse?' she frowned.

'Yes, that since I did not realize the accountability that comes with the responsibility, I shall soon perish in the fire of love I have created,' Kama blabbered in incoherent fear.

'But how can *I* help?' she shrugged; her brows delicately pleated in a slight frown. 'Words—expressly curses—once uttered cannot be revoked, you know that, Kamadeva.'

'Because *you* are the one with whom he's in love,' he breathed, gathering effort and courage, dreading his impoliteness.

'But I don't have the power to eradicate the curse,' she lifted her shoulders again.

'You have the power of persuasion. He will listen to *you*!' stammered Kamadeva in renewed desperation, his eyes beseeching. 'Please, save me!' he babbled. 'If it cannot be removed, please try to reduce his curse!'

Sarasvati thought about it and then nodded. *I can take this to him on the pretext of asking him about the Fire of Knowledge . . .*

'I will try, but don't be too hopeful.'

'You *are* my only hope,' Kama said fervently, his voice strident with relief.

Sarasvati wondered if she should meet Brahma right away and tackle the matter but she hesitated. This new task which Ganga had mentioned had intrigued her too. She had to talk to him. With a determined lift of her chin, she made her way towards Brahma's palace.

That Brahma seemed surprised to see her would be an understatement. *She is here!* He thought his heart would burst. Of all the things in his lost world, Brahma was most aware of this woman's eyes—the beautiful velvet eyes, with lashes that left them reluctantly and curved back as though to meet them once more. Brahma clenched his fists, restraining his unbridled joy at her sudden presence. He found himself go breathless. She was so slim, almost frail, with her white silk that accentuated her fairness by its blanched simplicity. Two wan dark spots on her cheeks marked the flush on her face.

He looked at her with his jaws set grimly and his steady coal eyes gleaming.

'What are you doing here?' he asked summarily before realizing his question had come out rude.

She ignored his tone. 'I came to talk about Kamadeva,' she stated brusquely, coming straight to the point.

Brahma frowned and stared at Sarasvati, who stared back at him.

'What about him?' he said curtly.

'It's up to you, but I thought you would have wanted to settle this business right now,' she returned carefully. 'About us. About the curse on him,' she added as she noticed the confusion on his face.

He flushed a dull red: was it mortification or anger?

'Kama deserves it,' he said flatly. 'The fool has to realize he is answerable for his foolish actions.'

'You seriously believe you love me because of some random arrow he shot at you?' she questioned, widening her eyes in mock incredulity.

Brahma sat still for a long moment, staring at her, his eyes like granite. He looked tall, dark, suave and suddenly dangerous. He said nothing for a while.

'Don't laugh at me,' he broke his silence finally, through clenched teeth.

'I am not,' she said steadily. 'I am trying to prove to you that emotions are generated by an individual and not through love potions or magic or sorcery. You can't blame Kamadeva for what you feel.'

'You are a fine person to defend him,' snapped Brahma. 'And pray, what do *you* know of love?' he said bitingly, crossing his massive hands across his chest. 'So how do you care if it's from the heart or from an erratic arrow?' his lips curled in cold contempt.

'You've got to be reasonable,' Sarasvati replied calmly. 'You can't get away from it.'

He was sitting bolt upright, his clenched fists resting on his knees, his mind still stupid with the surprise of finding her there, talking to him as if she had known him all her life. Which she did, he admitted with a wry grimace.

'I should be angry too as I am also bearing the brunt of this incident, this emotion of yours!' she cried, her tone waspish. 'This speculation about us is doing the rounds, and it is getting increasingly embarrassing!'

'Go on, why don't you say it?' Brahma said, lifting his frosty eyes to hers. 'Why did I have to fall in love with you in the first place? That's what you wanted to say, wasn't it? If I had kept clear of you, you would be out of this predicament.'

'But it's true,' she said, rounding on him, her face fierce. 'By cursing Kama, you are making it worse, not to mention, making yourself an unreasonable man, which you are not!'

'Oh, so now you profess knowing me better than myself?' Brahma glanced at Sarasvati with a hard, mirthless glint in his eyes.

She was looking embarrassed and visibly annoyed.

Brahma pushed back his head and looked at her. 'I didn't mean to humiliate you,' he said, patiently. 'I can't undo what I said, I meant every word I said to Kama, and it's not because of you. Don't you see? It was nothing to do with either of us. It is his carelessness and foolishness. He should not have attempted to disturb my meditation.'

Sarasvati studied Brahma's white, expressionless face.

'You truly believe that that arrow made you fall in love?' she asked at last with a smile, one so engaging that the response to her answer was in no way offensive.

Brahma sat still, his eyes hooded. He had a sudden idea that there was something very wrong behind Sarasvati's visit. He sat back and appraised her with glacial eyes.

'Go ahead, Sarasvati. Do some talking,' he said, his voice hard and quiet.

'What I can't believe is that an arrow or a potion can seduce you into falling in love!' Her velvet eyes shifted away from Brahma's cold face. 'Can Kama make me fall in love?' she challenged, looking him straight in the eye, her own unfaltering.

Brahma uncrossed his arms and raising his brows, drew in a deep breath. 'Well, I'll be double-confounded!' he said softly. 'You think love is a game, some sort of a dare?'

She responded breezily, 'Indeed. I would like to prove the same, but I need Kama for this.'

Brahma was not sure whether she said this in all seriousness or whether there was in her tone a hint of mockery. There was nothing saucy in her manner.

Brahma looked at her, his face expressionless.

'Go ahead.'

He placed his elbows on his desk and brought his fingertips together. He rested his square chin on the arch thus formed and waited.

She nodded and walked out to come back a moment later with Kama alongside her. Kama came in with slightly dragging feet. Brahma let him walk the long length of the room and he kept the spotlight of his gaze on the hapless deva. Kama had a fine-drawn glistening expression.

Kama found he was sweating profusely by the time he reached the desk where Brahma sat languidly. Brahma leaned back in his seat and eyed him over the way he would eye a fly that has fallen in his broth. Brahma smiled suddenly, and the instant after it was as though he had never smiled in his life. He spoke in a dull, ironic voice.

'The game and now the show,' he drawled laconically.

'No, the test,' Sarasvati replied tersely. 'Kama, please shoot your arrow at me,' she ordered.

Kama gaped at her, throwing Brahma a helpless look. Brahma's eyes looked at him lifelessly above his thick stubble.

'Don't mind me, Kama, start the spectacle, you are almost shaking with curiosity!' quipped Brahma, lightly stroking his beard. 'Let's see if you can make her fall in love, is that not so, Sarasvati?'

The defiant glint in her eyes was the sole reply Brahma received. Kama got more anxious noticing Brahma's reciprocal mirthless smile: *this was about them, not him.* There was a gleam in her velvet eyes that made Kama suspect that there was more in her than he had first supposed.

'Kama, please, do it,' she commanded. 'I want to find out if it's possible.' Brahma watched wordlessly, his eyes hard, his lips pursed.

Kama walked a few paces away from her so that he could take the best aim. He picked up his arrow with shaking hands, his eyes uncertain.

She gave him an affirmative nod.

Kama abruptly threw down his bow. 'No, it cannot happen this way! It's meant to be unconditional! It's not some war where you are taking down an enemy. This . . . this is . . . this cannot happen. I can't do it!'

'But you have to, I need to know!' she exclaimed indignantly.

Brahma snorted. 'Now Kama is going to teach her how to love!' he muttered under his breath.

The expression on her face made Kama wince: he would have to do it, she would not have it otherwise. He threw Brahma a desperate glance, his eyes fearful. The Creator-God stood impassive, but his eyes were alert, watching both of them closely.

'I shall,' Kama concurred reluctantly. 'But not now, not here.'

He saw her frown darkly.

'I shall do it later when you are unaware . . .' he explained hastily. Kama looked pale, and there were smudges under his eyes.

Brahma was not surprised, casting them both an ironic look.

'But how will I know you have done it?' she asked sharply.

'That's exactly what you want to prove, don't you?' intervened Brahma smoothly, his tone silky. 'You will come to know yourself . . . soon.'

Kama nodded his head in quick agreement. 'May I leave now?' he asked.

'Yes, you may,' said Brahma, his voice stern. 'But I can't ease my curse on you if that's what you had come here for. I can merely assure you that it will happen,' he reiterated in clipped tones but noticing the terror in Kama's beautiful eyes, he softened his voice. 'But you won't be annihilated, Kama—love can never perish. You shall be reborn.'

Brahma's voice, for all the drawl, was deadly.

Kama had gone pale. 'So, the curse is still upon me,' he whispered hoarsely.

'Yes, if you are careful, it won't work,' reminded Brahma. 'It is meant to be a caution, not a curse, Kama,' he said in a gentler tone.

'To keep you in check, keep that in mind,' assured Sarasvati, taking her cue from Brahma's look. 'As long as you use it wisely!' she paused. 'Remember you have *my* permission to use it on me.'

Kama stiffened. His eyes shifted away from Sarasvati.

'Kama, you were vain—and wrong—about your powers. You conflate love, lust and longing but with me, your role goes beyond this definition and you instead become a desire: a desire for ambition.'

Kama's nervous eyes followed her as she moved to stand in front of him, her eyes looking unnervingly straight at him. 'For knowledge, you need a desire to gain and earn it. That is how I define love, desire and passion, Kama. It is love for your goal, for your very existence, your worthwhile presence in the world. When you are with me, your perceived notion of desire changes, remember that.'

Kama looked shaken. He did not know whom to fear more: Brahma or Sarasvati. *Or both*, he thought bitterly. Kama gave them a last look before leaving. Sarasvati looked equable, her clear eyes almost pitiful, as she fixed him with her cool stare. Why had he presumed she would help him? But she had, in her brutal way. He knew who he was; there was more to him than just being a gorgeous god of erotica. Wishing to get away from both of them, Kama turned and moved briskly to the door as Brahma watched his hurried departure with cold aloofness.

He commented drily. 'Sarasvati, I think you scared him more than I did.'

She glanced up and caught him at it.

'I hope I managed to teach him what love and desire means.' Her tone turned silky. '*My* definition of it.'

'But I am curious, with whom will you fall in love, if you so allow it to happen?' Brahma asked, his eyes grim thinking of the devas around her, responding to her picturesque fragility with adolescent worship.

'But of course, you!' she cried. 'Who else do I know so well or like but you? I think you're the nicest man I have ever met!'

It came out so easily and honestly that Sarasvati too was taken aback by her words. Had she said it? But she knew she meant it too. She noticed his stiff back. The muscles either side of his jaw stood out suddenly.

How could she have been so tactless, she was aghast. But she had got carried away in the heated flow of their argument, enjoying the debate, the way he frowned, the grudging twist of a smile and his habit of raising his brows.

Brahma stiffened. His chance question and her even more spontaneous reply filled him with that heady pain of hope and dread. Was she teasing him; was she being plain heartless?

'You can choose whomsoever you want,' he said stiltedly.

'Whom would I want?'

She turned her head and stared anxiously at the big man as he leaned over, frowning into space, his long fingers tapping on his knee. It was true; she had known him now for a short time but he was the only one whom she could be comfortable with.

'There are all the devas, the gandharvas, one more handsome than the other!' He lifted his broad shoulders in a casual shrug. *He was jealous*, he thought with dismay. There had not been the faintest emphasis or mention of names, yet Brahma was suddenly ashamed.

She wrinkled her delicate nose. 'It's not the pleasure of the looks, but the goodness of the heart and brightness of the mind that matters, doesn't it?'

'Does it? Ask yourself.'

A slight flush mounted to her face. Gathering her silken folds and her scattered wits together, she declared with her chin raised, 'I have and the answer is the same!'

With a graceful swirl, she turned and glided across the room, out into the corridor. She smiled, pleased, till a thought struck her: in all her glory to make her point, she had forgotten to ask him about what had been troubling her since it had been first mentioned to her: Vadavagni.

6

THE APPEAL

He needed her; he needed her help, urgently. At times Brahma felt like rushing to Sarasvati requesting her to help him out. But he knew he could not bear to see the rejection in her eyes, or the faint contempt, which a woman often feels for a man too slavish in love. His mind was on fire, suffering his dilemma for days. Should he talk to her for help, as he used to before?

They had to work together, he told himself over and over. He would just have to be more proficient and less sentimental. All he had to do was to go to her and request her for help. Had she not come to him to help Kama? And with such smug arrogance too, his lips twitched in slender amusement.

Desperate and his mind made up, he found himself striding to her palace, each step long and swift, his heart racing, until he reached the gates. He took the cobbled path inside slowly and then the stairs. But he stopped abruptly, dreading to meet her, swerved and hurried down the steps, before turning back to look up at the palace. The many shiny windows there stared at him like sets of black eyes suspiciously.

He wondered where she was. All day, he had been waiting for this chance to see her again. He had to stop staring up at the castle, hoping she would come up at one of the windows. He sighed and retraced his steps, dawdling down the garden path.

There she was, sitting on a bench, beside the softly rippling lake, absently patting Shweta, her pet white swan, on her lap.

Her clear, clever eyes lit up at the sight of him. She looked him over coolly. 'I gather it must be critical, or you wouldn't have come here.'

He had one end of his shawl in his hand and a stiff smile fixed on his thin lips. She took him in with one quick glance: as usual tall, wiry and tough-looking with a lined, impassive face, opaque, unreadable, coal-black eyes and aggressive jaw.

'I had to come,' he returned smoothly. 'I can never think on my feet.'

'Particularly witty today, are you?' she scoffed, her lips breaking into an ironic smile. 'But it's good you came over. I was about to meet you myself.'

Against the bright sun, he could barely make out the silhouette of her head, tilted to a side, as she looked at him. The bright sun, shining through the tall trees behind her, lit up her profile. She leaned back, staring at him, caressing her black, wavy hair and adjusting the two curls that had fallen loose on her forehead. A pearl hairpin was her only piece of jewellery: only she could make simplicity look so regal.

His eyes narrowed. 'What did you want to see me for?' he asked, trying to keep his tone and tenor in control.

'You,' she replied glibly. 'Or rather to ask you, what is Vadavagni? And why did Ganga and Yamuna refuse to have anything to do with it?'

'I came here to request you for the same,' he started, more relaxed, his taut expression thawing. *It wasn't going to be as rough as he had assumed* . . .

She nodded, her bright eyes shining. She was not sure what made her happier: his presence or they working together again.

His tone changed.

'How do you plan to impart the legacy of knowledge you are endowed with, to the world?' he asked in an enduring voice. There was that distinctive command in his voice that others obeyed but which she acutely resented.

She bristled. Clearly, he was expecting her to answer, she thought resentfully. 'I will bless rishis and scholars and the creative lot who can impart education.'

Brahma stared at her politely. 'Yes but again how?' he persisted.

She flushed. Her hot black eyes looked visibly exasperated.

'I don't see why you are being so oblique,' she snapped. 'And I don't like your manners. You came here to ask for my help. You can be more courteous! If you want me to do something specific, you could be more specific yourself—and polite,' she stated, raising her chin.

'I'm being polite, you are being ill-mannered,' he retaliated bluntly. 'I came to see you, to request you again . . .'

'You don't make it sound like one,' she replied in the cold voice that always came with her anger. 'I didn't ask for your visit. You came for me!' she said glowering. 'I don't mind you judging me or sounding so condescending. I don't mind your showing me your great powers of wit and sarcasm. You are eminently intelligent and it's a pleasure to make your acquaintance. But I shall not tolerate intimidation of any kind—it brings out my worst manners! Though frankly, I don't care if you don't like my manners either. I don't much grieve over them. But please don't waste your time—and mine—questioning me.'

Brahma could not help being faintly amused. He let her ire drift.

'It is not questioning, I just want to know your method,' he said mildly.

'People don't talk like that to me,' she said indignantly, her pale face now red. 'As if I am a child or an imbecile.'

'You clearly are not, you are the Goddess of Knowledge,' he said drily. 'And I want to know how you deign to spread knowledge, that is all.'

'I got it! And again that condescending tone!' she cried. 'I loathe masterful men,' she said. 'I simply loathe them!'

She said it with a passion that surprised him. He was careful not to stare at her, although he wanted to. He kept his eyes on the garden wall, frowning.

'And, I dislike arrogance,' he said quietly. 'That with ignorance is dangerous. And I do not wish you to be one of them.'

'I am the last one you can accuse of being ignorant!' she said haughtily.

Again, there was a cold pause. He could feel her hostility as she stared at him through the bright morning light, her bright eyes darkening quickly, filling up with annoyance. Her nostrils looked pinched. Very slowly she gathered her breath and sat down on the edge of the bench, hugging the swan close to her.

For the first time in her short life, she felt awkward. She was furious with herself and a little angry with him, although she knew that this was unfair. She felt his amused eyes on her and that made her more discomfited. She must say something. She couldn't stand there staring at this big broad-shouldered man like a confused fool.

She gave ground, her dark eyes still annoyed.

'All right, I don't have a plan,' she acceded, shrugging. 'How do I go about it?' she asked in a tense voice, strained with shreds of anger.

'By becoming a river,' he announced. 'I want you to become a river.'

At last, he had come to the point! She did not blink, her face fixed, her gaze unfazed.

'You are to carry Vadavagni—the Fire of Knowledge—to Earth . . .' He frowned hard. 'But will you be able to do it?' he doubted.

Her black eyes frosted. 'This is exasperating: you mention it and immediately retract! Since when did you become so indecisive?' she snapped. 'Or are you trying to tell me I shan't be able to do it?'

He regarded her wordlessly, but it was a pronounced dubious look.

'We paired life and creatures together, I became Shatarupa!' she paused, reddening. 'I can do it, of course,' she insisted, her voice firm. 'Just tell me how.'

He gave a resigned sigh. 'As you know, the problem is about transferring and spreading knowledge from one world to another,' he started. 'What binds them to us, the mortals with the immortals, Heaven with Earth, is knowledge. It is the vital link. And it needs to be transported.'

'You mean relocated, more specifically?' she asked, stroking the swan with her graceful fingers.

'Yes. The rishis took upon themselves the task of creating a channel through which this knowledge could be transported from Heaven to Earth. This channel could only be fire,' he paused deliberately, awaiting her response.

'Humans are knowledge-hungry beings,' she assented. 'They are forever in quest of information for all of mankind.'

Brahma frowned. 'I want to give it to them. But it's a rite through fire . . .'

Her brows cleared: she realized why he had been annoyingly hesitant. He was worried. She considered him with steady velvet eyes.

'Fire has all the properties through which knowledge can be acquired and dispersed,' she agreed, cupping her chin in one hand. 'Fire is ever-shifting: symbolic of knowledge, which can never remain stunted, static or stagnant. Also, fire burns, again representing the combustion of ignorance. Moreover fire ignites, illustrative of the sparks of knowledge in mind and the world. And last, fire cannot be contained, it is free, again symbolic of knowledge, which should have a free flow. Right?'

He nodded, his eyes hooded, concealing his admiration.
She gave him a sardonic look: 'Have I met your expectations?'

'Excellent! It's a very precise description—and exactly
the way we are going to go about it.'

His praise fired a warm glow within her. 'That's why a
river to transport the fire? Water is the best fluid!' she nodded.

She found there was a lilt in her tone. Or, was it plain
happiness that they were back together? Working together,
she reminded herself acridly.

'Correct. The rishis requested Vishnu to send down
the Holy Fire of Knowledge from Heaven to Earth. He
came to me with this request.'

'As you are the sole keeper of all eternal Knowledge,'
she interposed.

'No longer,' he shrugged, his voice less severe, more
earnest. 'Now you are the one too. And I bring this request
to you.'

He raised his brows, the question left unsaid but
apparent in his eyes. His change of tone melted her.

She smiled unexpectedly; her annoyance drained, her
anger spent. Her eyes warmed, a spark in them. 'Oh, that's
why you came to me. But yes, I comply. I can't say no to
you!' she stated simply.

A sharp silence crashed between them. She coloured
as she saw him stiffen, recoiling as if she had slapped him.

What had she said, she groaned inwardly. *She had said no
to him, hadn't she?*

She felt his strained eyes on her and that made her
more embarrassed. *She had refused him once and so gravely!*
She must say something to end the awkwardness.

'Oh, so this is what the Vadavagni is,' she said briskly looking up at him, her eyes suddenly trusting.

Ignoring the short moment of embarrassment, he forced a grin of strained joviality. 'So, are you ready? I shall be there, I promise I won't put you in any danger,' he assured solemnly.

The tenderness in his voice made her flinch.

She nodded her head, avoiding his eyes. 'I know you will,' she said softly, staring at her twisting fingers on her lap.

Hearing the trust in her voice his heart convulsed. He felt a slight thickening in his throat as he looked at her: *should they go ahead? Was he ready to put her in danger?*

'Sure?' he repeated, more to assure himself of her decision than her.

He regarded her, his stare hard. She wasn't looking too happy either, he thought uneasily. He didn't like the way her lips compressed or her eyes muddled. She looked away. She continued to ponder, but her eyes grew wary suddenly.

'Yes, ' she said. Her voice had gone a little flat.

She paused, exhaling sharply. 'But I want to clear something first . . .'

She gave him her fixed look, which he always found difficult to tear away from. 'Are you still upset with me for turning you down?' she asked abruptly.

'No!' he said, surprised at her bluntness.

'You mean that? You mean we can work together without any awkwardness?' she insisted, lips pursed, but he could see her eyes were troubled. 'It happened just a moment ago!'

He just nodded, not trusting himself to speak.

She looked up at him, as he stood silent, her eyes clouded. 'I assented to become your Shatarupa, the first female being to come into your world. I didn't realize it then but . . .' she said, holding a persistent tone, '. . . when you fell in love with me, you looked at me with desire and created a conflict. I agreed to be Shatarupa for only one reason: all that I offer must be used to elevate the spirit, not indulge the senses. But your desire for me filled the world with longing, which will be the seed of unhappiness. You have fettered love in lust, hope in longing. You shackled the soul in flesh.'

Brahma started to say something, then stopped. He had no more words of defence.

'Yes,' he said sorrowfully. 'I realize. I know it now myself. But I cannot function without you.'

The raw pain in his voice made her heart contract. She tore her eyes away from his tortured face. That was it: it was his sustained loyalty of love that had her confused, almost making her feel ashamed. It was making her feel oddly awkward with him now. Yet, she was strangely moved; she was in his thoughts, his mind, his consciousness, even when he was creating her, even as he created every new form and being. She had to be with him. It was almost like the breath to sustain life . . . *that* was his love. The enormity of that emotion he had for her overwhelmed her, drowning her in a whirl of confusion. *Was this powerful, mighty emotion called love?*

'I am, above all, Sarasvati, the Goddess of Knowledge. But I shall help you in every way I can, I promise,' she said quietly. 'But we needed to clear this before we start to work again. I don't want any awkwardness when we are working or otherwise.'

He gave a brief nod, rising to his feet. 'I agree. There won't be. I shan't embarrass you further. Ever,' he promised quietly.

An obstinate look shadowed her eyes. 'Fine, then I want to take up this task,' she declared with a fierce air. 'I realize, whatever our differences and disagreements are, we will have to work together!'

He looked at her, meeting her dark, velvety eyes and then looking away.

'But this task is dangerous, highly,' he muttered, his heart racing erratically in a sudden fear. 'That is why I have my doubts. This knowledge, when converted to a physical form, can create a conflagration, which can spread and encompass all of Heaven and Earth,' he said and she could detect the anxiety in his voice.

'I can do it,' she said simply, but her voice was strong.

Brahma lifted his broad shoulders. He felt his heart contract. *She could burn in the fire, perishing with all the knowledge she contained. He couldn't lose her! Was this to be her destiny? Would he be responsible for her destruction as he was for her creation? Had he made her to see her fatal undoing?*

'How can you doubt your own work?' she asked. 'If you deem it necessary and if you see me fit to do it, it shall be done. And this is not bravado. Or my arrogance speaking,' she added pointedly.

'It's not you; you have the courage and the brains to do it,' he said. 'In plenty!'

His words warmed her unexpectedly. She smiled, pleased. She quickly looked down to hide her confusion: *did his opinion of her really matter?* 'You are the only one whose energies can successfully contain the fire. The Vadavagni, the monumental Fire of Destiny,' he continued, his brows furrowed.

'With the waters of the river, the best cooling element,' she said swiftly.

He gave a brief nod, waiting for her response again. He listened while he watched her as a teacher would a student, encouraging, yet discerning.

'Water it is,' she reiterated. 'I need an element that is fluid, fast and can counteract the immense heat of fire. I need to take the form of a river, which will extend across Heaven and Earth in its sheer magnitude and mightiness. As a river, I shall receive and carry the Fire of Knowledge from you and fall from Heaven above to flow on to Earth. Is that the plan?'

He saw one of her dark eyebrows lift in excited anticipation.

He looked at her for long seconds, then his hard face creased into the resemblance of a smile.

'You seem to like action too,' he murmured.

'There is always adventure in action like thoughts in imagination, becoming creativity,' she smiled vibrantly. 'But seriously, when do I start?'

His face darkened, the sliver of fear slicing into him again. He hesitated, flooded with worry. He began to pace the garden, his brows wrinkling into a frown. 'I still think I should do it,' he muttered under his breath. 'That is why, I guess, Vishnu came to me!' he exclaimed.

'Don't insult me,' she flared up. 'Of course, I shall be able to do it. If you can, so can I,' she looked indignant.

He turned to look at her, struggling, unsurprised by her vehemence. They exchange a tense look for three seconds. He could see in her eyes no one could make her change her mind.

'Yes, you can,' he agreed, albeit reluctantly. 'But I am responsible for you too. '

'Don't go shielding me!' she protested violently and paused, her tapping foot making a staccato sound. 'You can't do it—the world can't afford to lose its Creator,' she teased. 'You are yet to complete it! But seriously, all you need to do is depute the work. It takes both courage and trust to delegate. After all, it's a question of allotting and sharing responsibilities,' she taunted. 'So when do we begin?'

Her use of the word 'we' sounded excitingly warm, like a secret being shared, the feeling of doing things together. She watched him stop pacing, her words hitting him hard. There was an alert look in her eyes that he did not notice.

'We start right away,' he stated. 'It might be a long course. You need to first consecrate knowledge and I shall have Agni be there to collect it. I shall be present too, of course,' he assured her. 'Nothing should go awry. And then, we will start the process of transformation, when you shall be the water, but the moment the fire is handed to you, another, more dangerous process of transformation starts—your eventual evaporation and precipitation as you fall from Heaven on to Earth. You have to make it in time to hand over the Urn of Fire to the waiting rishis.'

'Where will they be?'

'The Himalayas.'

'Yes, there is thick ice to cool me, and slow the evaporation,' she remarked, unperturbed. 'I shall have to plunge into the mighty depths of snow, hand over the Fire to the waiting rishis, and rush forth through the glaciers to cool my burning self.'

'The danger does not end there. You have to be careful that at any stage you are not combusted,' he cautioned her.

'I shall practise here,' she suggested, her face burning with fresh excitement. 'Let me see how long I can hold it.'

He threw her a wary look, the gnawing dread refusing to dislodge from his heart. He was pushing her to definite destruction. Would she survive this? Glancing at her, he was sure she would. He felt a surge of confidence.

'Break through the glacier and continue to flow fast till you finally submerge yourself in the ocean,' he warned, his expression impassive, refusing to let her see the fear in his heart. 'I have a route chalked out. It has to be just right: neither too short to fully flow, nor too long that you are spent.'

'Just a quick question,' she interrupted him. 'Coming down from that height, do I not need to break my fall? The impact might create an earthquake or some tectonic disturbance,' she cautioned.

Brahma paused and looked at her, visibly impressed at the wisdom of her warning. He studied her, surprised. It was his turn to remain quiet and listen to her, and it was a lesson. She used all his ideas, but in a slightly different way, and he saw at once where he had gone wrong.

His way was just that much more tiring. Her way was neat and swift, and saved them time and effort, besides making her a better planner than him.

'Oh, hadn't thought of that,' he muttered, rubbing his jaw thoughtfully to resume his pacing. He ran his fingers through his dark hair and scowled. 'Yes, you need to cushion the fall,' he was still frowning, furrows deepening, deliberating furiously.

He could not put her in further danger, he could not lose her . . . Fear froze his heart.

She calmly watched him pacing. He stared at the grass under his feet and his brows came down. He looked fierce and formidable, quite unlike himself, more like a real ill-tempered hellion at that moment.

'I shall be there,' he stated after a long silence. His brows cleared, his manner still stiff. 'I shall stand at the Himalayas and break your fall. The higher on the glacier, the safer.'

She looked pensive. 'Yes, it should work! I shall be literally breaking your head!' she gave him a quick glance, then flashed her vivid half-smile. 'And all will claim that I descended and broke my fall into the skull of Lord Brahma, who awaited my entry on Earth. Sounds grand!'

Brahma did not return the infectiousness of her sarcasm. He hesitated, frowning.

Soot-black eyes looked into his. Pink lips twisted into half a smile again—radiant, blatantly mocking, but convincing.

'You are still worrying,' she sighed. 'It shall all go fine, need I have to keep reassuring you? I'm more qualified than anybody else,' she said heroically. 'Why can't you trust me?' Her clear, clever eyes tore at his stability—her face showing exquisite displeasure, chin upturned in quiet determination. 'I suppose you think I'm not capable enough, but I'll prove you wrong, Brahma!'

A thousand unspoken words of fear, dread, passion and tenderness fought on his lips. Then a seamless wave of emotion washed over him, carrying off with it a residue of wisdom, agreement, doubt and honour: this was his Sarasvati who was speaking, his vision and his pride.

7

THE RIVER FLOWS

It all went smoothly as she had foreseen. Sarasvati collected the urn containing the Fire of Knowledge from Agni when he arrived at her doorstep early next morning.

'I would have come myself and picked it up on the way,' she said, greeting him with an affability he was not accustomed to. She was so unlike the others: there was a warm exuberance about her that was all welcoming. But he had to admit to himself that he had been wary to meet her because he had also heard of some stories that she could be cold and sullen if that was how her mood swung that particular day.

'But it is my responsibility to come and hand you the urn,' Agni said solemnly.

'Because it is proper for a man to be chivalrous and improper if I do the same?' she twinkled, with an easy laugh but he detected the soft irony in her tone. 'I don't believe in such chauvinist rules, that's why I often break them.'

She looked up at Agni, seeing a square-shouldered man of medium height, with dark wavy hair, pale brown eyes that looked worried and uneasy, a dimpled chin and a straight narrow nose.

Agni looked anxious, her cheerful, easy smile leaving him a little astonished. Her unanticipated vivacity, quite unlike the divine celestials he knew, confounded him.

'And don't mention status or hierarchy either,' she continued casually but there was a gravity in her voice. 'I don't believe in all that. It's the work that counts, and its success lies in teamwork, not commanding around.'

Agni straightened his shoulders involuntarily; Sarasvati might be a non-conformist but she was a perfectionist as well. There was an edge in her voice and manner that she wanted things to get done as flawlessly as possible. Agni was visibly impressed and he knew why. Dressed in white, the only colour on her being the rosy flush on her face, she spoke with imperious liveliness. From her smooth, pale face, one received an immediate impression of the dignity of her bearing, her assurance and the clear articulation of thought and opinion. It was her compelling eyes, under their thin black brows, which gave her face its intense and intelligent character. They were large, deeply dark and though warm, by their calm steadiness, strangely forceful. But the most striking aspect about her was the air of command tempered by consideration; he felt in her the habit of unusual authority. To order was natural to her but she accepted your obedience with humility.

Agni felt unaccountably nervous. Right now, she was a complete mistress of herself and the situation. She assumed unconsciously the air of controlling power which was habitual to her and held Agni in an appraising scrutiny.

'What all is there in this fire?' she asked, looking at him with fixed eyes. He found she was oddly unsettling. Did she want to know or was she questioning him? Of course, she was testing him, he warned himself. 'This fire is, of course, symbolic of all knowledge,' he started cautiously. 'A blazing fire means both heat and light; the living entity when the mind and the heart become "enlightened" with full spiritual knowledge and get slowly detached from the material world. By transporting this knowledge to the mortals, Man will be able to see through the physical layer of the five elements—earth, water, fire, air and sky—and become free from the five attachments: ignorance, egoism, materialism, envy and anger.'

She rewarded him with a quick smile.

'Yes, to be replaced and liberated by the very same Fire of Knowledge and Detachment. This is the process.'

She held the pot in her hands, her hands white and cool, the blaze of the fire adding a burnished glow on her pale face. 'I need to initiate the process of evaporation right away as soon as I begin my fall on to Earth.'

'Yes, or the fire shall burn you as well,' warned Agni. 'I shall keep it contained as much as I can but the flare has to be controlled by you and you alone.'

He could not but admire her: she was extraordinarily brave. But why had she taken on the danger? Because Lord Brahma had requested her? Whatever the reason, Agni knew his fate too was literally in her hands. If she failed to deliver, he too, like her, would die a certain death but not without the possible annihilation of the three worlds.

But Sarasvati did descend; holding on to the Fire across the ethers from Heaven to Earth, as she had promised. It was a slow descent at first, and as she plunged down through the icy mid-course, she initiated her process of vaporization to cool and contain the fire in her hand. *I have to make it in time*, she kept telling herself, numb with the icy sting of the air on her face. *Or, I shall end in a ball of flame, swelling into a vast inferno, which will devour the world.*

She threw Agni a calm look, hiding her own apprehensions, as he held on to her, her fingers cool and firm in his grip. She would not let him go, he knew, the fear slowly dispelling from him, as he felt the warmth of her strength and sureness.

Her eyes were searching: where was Brahma? He was to be there . . . she would touch down any moment now. She felt the heat singeing her, she had to do it right now, she thought urgently, but where was he?!

And then she saw him; intense relief and an odd sense of an undecipherable emotion coursed through her. She had no time to think further as she rushed towards him. He had to halt her now.

Brahma did it so smoothly that she did not realize she had touched Earth, and plunged into the mighty Himalayas. His calm eyes seemed to propel her towards him, the cold gush of air and the heat of the flame mingling as she converged into his open arms. Her last thought was his gentle face, those dark, brooding eyes searing into hers . . .

He heard her catch her breath sharply as she heard the rumbling sound of the Earth tremble. But all Brahma felt again was the sudden thickening in his throat, the warmth of her softness against his body. The impact did not shake him, as he stood steady and strong and stable, rocking gently on his heels as he sought balance and steered her course. Melting against him, she felt his strength in his locked arms, as they stood together on the lofty heights of the snowy peaks of the Himalayas.

As she had reached for him, Brahma had felt his heart beating violently, fear fast replacing relief. It was odd that this should be happening, he thought, as he held her in his arms, her face cold on his, her body hot and feverish against his, her scented hair tumbling on him and enveloping him in delirious darkness: they were coalesced and merging almost as one. He had feared every moment but she was now safe, here in his arms. He felt a sharp jolt as she rushed away from him, filling him with a strange emptiness.

'This is my source,' she whispered, her warm breath fanning his face, her eyes riveted by the inscrutability in his. 'Holy rivers, when they descend from Heaven, need something to contain the plummet to avoid splitting the Earth with the force—and for me, it was you. People will soon call it the *Brahmakapalam*—the forehead of Brahma—where I descended and broke my fall into the skull of Brahma. That is how soon the legend will go.'

She showered him with a faint smile as she spun away from him in a rush of froth and fury, leaving a trail of misty spray.

He felt inexplicably bereft as he watched her lean forward, to leave him, like a flash, streaking down towards the waiting Earth . . .

From her vantage loftiness, over her gathering surf, Sarasvati glimpsed the awaiting rishis. Her force would wash them away; she quickly grasped the situation. Her eyes trailed the dense sylvan forest, and spotted a gigantic, leafy Plaksha tree. She swiftly took the form of a spring seeping into its wide-spread, deeply entrenched roots.

Rishi Markandeya gently placed a hand on one exposed root. He felt the gurgle and within moments, the health-giving waters of the spring gushed forth from the mighty Plaksha tree.

'Here is the holy place where the sacred river has consecrated the Earth,' bowed Rishi Markandeya.

'For which, these waters shall also be called River Markanda,' smiled Sarasvati.

The other rishis bowed to her, as she cascaded in a gentle fall. She eddied around them, holding out the pot of fire as she stretched her arms to hand it over to them.

The rishis accepted it, bowing their heads in awe.

'True to your name, Saras, the fluid you have become, the *Su-rasa*—the good fluid—today, both literally and metaphorically, O goddess,' said Rishi Markandeya, his tone reverential. 'You are not just the representation of a river handing us eternal knowledge, but we revere you as the symbol of intellectual outpouring. You shall not just be a geographical river but an inner, spiritual river of the arts of our times.'

'But as a river, remember, if I can bless with the waters of life, I can cause destruction too with flooding and perhaps drought,' warned Sarasvati. 'If you take care of me, I shall look after you.'

'You are our river, we shall worship you,' chorused the disciples of Rishi Markandeya and Rishi Dadhich.

She shook her head. 'I acknowledge respect more than worship. Can you do that?' she asked enigmatically. 'Time will prove otherwise. If you worship me, I shall remain a goddess; if you respect me, I shall live and flourish.'

'You are the river of knowledge, Sarasvati Devi,' agreed Rishi Dadhich, looking up and fixing his gaze in the clear, cloudless sky. 'The nakshatra star Swati, meaning the "independent one", conjoins to your *Sara* and hence *Sara-Swati* now holds another meaning. Through your bountiful water, you will also be known as the River Mahata Varita—meaning "mighty pitcher bringing large water". You gave us the Urn of the Fire of Knowledge as well as the Pitcher of Water of Pure Thoughts, Goddess Sarasvati. We shall be forever indebted.'

'Yes, you, O Sarasvati, have risen from the Man Sarovar—the Lake of Brahma's Mind—O highly blessed one,' said Rishi Markandeya.

Brahma went still as the revered rishi's words floated up in the frosty air.

'You have blessed us and we will be privileged to be called by the name of Sarasvata!' proclaimed Rishi Dadhich. 'All and everyone will derive blessings with oblations of your pure water!' he paused, bowing deeply.

'We accept part of this fire but we have another request—we beg you to hold the deadly Vadavagni in your river water for us and cast it into the sea.'

Sarasvati frowned, a look of puzzlement making her furrow her brow. 'We know you have been forced to come down to Earth to take the Vadavagni, this terrible devastating fire to the ocean so that it will not destroy the whole world,' rued Rishi Markandeya. 'This fire was generated by Rishi Aurva, who unleashed his fury against the Kshatriyas who had murdered his family, but after being persuaded by his *pitris*—his ancestors—he agreed to cast the fire of his anger into the sea. But he cannot do it; only a river can carry this lethal fire. Even the mighty Ganga declined to carry it. So did Sindhu and Yamuna. Please, we implore you, not to refuse us. We have no one but you!'

Sarasvati gave a start: so that was the reason for Ganga and Yamuna's reluctance, after which Brahma had sought her help. But why had he not told her about this himself; *because she would rebuff like the other rivers?* She felt a frisson of annoyance, not at the duplicity but at the fact that he had not trusted her enough.

Brahma, reading her fermenting mind, tried to placate her.

'There was no subterfuge,' he assured. 'I honoured upon you a task which you could handle: to transfer the Fire of Knowledge to Earth. Your work is done here. You may return now.'

'But the Vadavagni takes different forms—now it is the Fire of Wrath, which needs to be doused. The work is incomplete,' she protested. 'I can't leave it unfinished!'

'But will you go further?' Brahma asked, troubled.

One look at his haggard face, and Sarasvati realized why he had left some things unsaid: he was not ready to put her at any risk.

'I want to do it,' she insisted firmly.

He heard the resoluteness in her voice.

'I knew only *you* could do this brave deed,' he sighed, his reluctance obvious. 'Only you can go over to the west of the briny sea and submerge it or the world will be burnt alive. Once this is done, peace will reign, and the people will be rid of their fear of annihilation. So, save the world, Sarasvati!'

Brahma paused, standing very still, his fists clenched. 'I did not tell you in fear that you would get destroyed in the process,' he confessed, huskily. 'I knew you can never resist a challenge and you would not have refused me.'

He feared for her safety, as she had rightly guessed. But she was not yet mollified: in his act of solicitousness, was he being overprotective? She did *not* need him as her armour, she thought fiercely.

'This Vadava fire sounds very horrific but neither can I leave my task incomplete,' she murmured, her eyes travelling to all present: the rishis. 'I cannot abandon my people, the world—and most importantly, I cannot disappoint myself,' she admitted with her customary candour. 'I have carried the urn of fire so long, from Heaven to Earth and now I am willing to transport this fire right up to the ocean.'

Her tone had gone flat and final: Brahma knew it was the last word. But he knew she was still displeased with him.

Brahma gave her an imperceptible nod, his heart swelling with pride and pleasure: *she* was going to do it. She recognized the look and forced a smile: It wasn't an easy smile, but it made her look very determined and competent. A woman is so much more beautiful when her intellect defines her more than just her looks; he felt his throat constricting.

He saw her gracefully spiralling away and without waiting another moment, she gushed forth strongly amidst a frothy surf, through the craggy cliffs and fields to cool her burning body. She continued to flow, with an unbridled spring in her step, dancing and twirling down the mountains, into the hilly terrains, disappearing and appearing at places along the way, making the lands fertile for miles along her meandering banks, her waters still warm.

As she turned, from the corner of her eyes, she spotted a looming mountain in the distance. Krtasmara, she recognized and swiftly realized she would have to change her course to go around it. She raced with renewed vim, sharply diverting. Krtasmara moved in the same direction when she changed her path, standing in her way. He was acting difficult, she quickly realized, faced with a now-or-never challenge. 'Please can I go through?' she asked politely.

The massive mountain wordlessly shook his head.

'Let me go. I have to cross to the other side and the shortest way is to flow around you but if you keep shifting, you are clearly blocking my path. And my mission,' she added muscle to her soft voice.

Again Krtasmara shook his massive head.

'Pray why?'

'Because I am the mightiest of this land and I shall not bow to some new river that chooses to flow in my land,' he said in a loud drawl, his beady eyes appraising her.

She straightened her shoulders. 'So, what do I do now?' she gave a helpless shrug. 'I request you, please give way.'

'A river in my land means people, human settlement and a new civilization. I don't want them to disturb my peace,' he barked.

'But that's also a natural progression,' she said quickly.

'Man is a plunderer,' boomed Krtasmara, his tone bitter. 'He shall destroy the trees and foliage and the animals living in this kingdom. He has done it before, leaving many hills and tracts wasted and barren in the wake of his destruction.'

'But how will your trees survive without my waters? Where will your animals drink when thirsty?'

He gave her a stubborn look. 'We have survived till now.'

'But not for long; without water, no being can last. I am here for a reason. For their subsistence, I shall not be threatening your existence,' she maintained.

'A river can never be more powerful than a mountain,' Krtasmara gave a dismissive shrug.

'A mountain and a river can exist together,' she said quietly. 'They are meant to.'

He frowned and moments later, his dull, heavy hooded eyes lit up. 'We have to live together, O fair river? I agree. Will you marry me?'

Sarasvati smiled, faintly amused. 'I am honoured, sir. I am alone and single and, if, to enter your region, I have to marry you, I accept. But look at me—I can't be your bride in such a state! Please can you hold this pot of fire in your hands while I freshen up?'

Delighted at her consent, Krtasmara eagerly seized the Vadava handed over by Sarasvati. No sooner had he touched it, Krtasmara felt a hot, agonizing pain scorching him, reducing him instantly to a mound of ash.

Sarasvati looked dispassionately at the huge heap. 'How the mighty crumble. But this ash will do wonders to the soil and the new riverbank will get fertile!'

She collected the Vadava from the pile and holding it once again, she charged forward, sweeping over the erstwhile Krtasmara, the mighty mountain that once was. She did not look back, forging through more hills, snaking around steep valleys and slowly losing pace as she finally reached the plains, meandering wearily, till spent and fatigued, she caught the welcoming sight of the shimmering expanse of the ocean. Standing on the sandy shore, she was ready to submerge herself into the sea when suddenly Arnav, the God of the Ocean, appeared before her face to face.

'Dear lady, you have another grand deed to accomplish . . .'

Sarasvati was more astonished than angry now: what was this—an assignment or a series of secret, undisclosed missions? Why had Brahma not spelt out all the tasks he had planned for her to do, she seethed silently.

'. . . Do you recognize this man?' Arnav asked, gesturing to a frail, emaciated man shivering next to him, his face ashen, cheeks painfully hollow and his lips a bloodless white. Sarasvati gave a start. Was this Chandra or Soma, the Mood God, once famous for his gorgeous looks? Sarasvati forced her exhausted brains to discern the significance of the situation. This god was infamous for his lustful passion and one who made every woman fall in love with him, including the married Tara, who left her husband, Rishi Brihaspati, for him.

Soma bowed to her, his thin arms shaking. 'Please save me, dear goddess,' he whispered, his voice hoarse from the convulsive cough which barely allowed him to speak. 'Give me back my lost looks, my lost life!' he entreated, his timorous pleas dissolving in violent coughing.

Over the agonized racking of his spasmodic wheeze, Sarasvati recalled what had reduced Soma to such a pitiable state. Soma, the most handsome of gods, had a weakness: women, particularly his obsessive passion for Rohini, his favourite wife. This earned him the wrath and curse of his father-in-law, Prajapati Daksha, who had also married his other daughters to Soma and found they were being neglected. Soma ignored Daksha's repeated requests until, in rage, Daksha cursed Soma with the dreaded tuberculosis; *rajayakshma*. A penitent Soma begged forgiveness and Daksha told him that he would retrieve his lost health and looks when he bathed in the waters of a holy river.

Sarasvati touched his trembling hands, her cool fingers brushing against his parched skin, her foamy spray misting over his sunken face.

Soma closed his eyes, absorbing her touch and felt himself shudder.

'I hope now your *yakshma* has vanished,' she said softly, easing the pain with a light touch of her hands.

Soma's eyes flew open, not believing what he saw. The excruciating pain in his chest was gone. And he was his good self again. His skin glowed, his face shone and the bloody cough had disappeared, taking with it his wasted looks and years of suffering. He almost collapsed in relief and gratitude.

'Oh, you *have* saved me!' he whispered in awe, his eyes glistening.

'Yes, but I hope you will be kinder to your other wives,' she said, her voice still benignant but with a note of sternness in it. 'If you wanted to shower all your love and attention on Rohini alone, why did you agree to marry her sisters? Or was flaunting a host of women around you a show of virility? Or to pamper your vanity?' she asked, her brow raised.

Soma swallowed painfully, noting the reprimand in her voice.

'It is difficult to share love; love is often very possessive,' he said wryly. 'Try doing it the other way round—would you like it if one of your wives had chosen another man over you, or if you had to share your wife with other men?'

Soma flushed under his fair, mottled skin.

'Aha, I see you have recovered your good sense—and colour to your cheeks as well,' she mocked. 'Henceforth, your story will be seen as a lesson in vanity and shall account for the monthly waxing and waning of the Moon.'

'I *am* blessed,' mumbled the mortified Soma.

'The fair Full Moon and the dark New Moon shall
be more of a reminder for you and the others as well of
changing beauty, fortune and health,' she responded, her
eyes grim. 'Divine stories often tell tales of divine follies as
well,' she added kindly.

'And then, there's also the astrological significance,' she
continued, regarding him closely. 'Earlier it was Chandra
with Tara—the Moon and the Star,' she saw him flinch
as he recalled his adulterous affair with Tara, the beautiful
wife of Rishi Brihaspati—Jupiter—from whom was born
their son Buddh—Mercury. 'Likewise, you, as Chandra,
with Rohini and your other twenty-six wives shall form the
moon and the constellation—the nakshatras.'

'And so will this place,' stated a rich baritone. 'It will be
called Somnath.'

Sarasvati recognized the voice immediately, without
turning around. She heard movements of his firm tread as
he walked into the sandy riverbank.

'This is where Soma was resuscitated by you, Sarasvati,
and also the place of confluence, where you joined Sindhu
Sagar after traversing thousands of miles through the
country to reach here.'

Something in Brahma's voice made Soma glance
quickly at him and notice how his brooding eyes softened
a little when he regarded the river goddess. A relentless
romantic, Soma swiftly guessed the situation. Brahma's
hooded look spoke volumes: this was the woman
Brahma would be proud to have as a wife: a tough
go-getter not allowing fear or foreboding to assail her
clear, determined will.

'Are you renaming this old town, Prabhas, to Somnath?'
she asked. 'Always easier to give a new name than respecting
the old one.'

Brahma frowned; he could detect a trace of derision in
her voice.

'If Prabhas was dedicated to the Sun God, Somnath
is the new name to celebrate the resurrection of the Moon
God,' he said shortly. 'Let's celebrate both and that you are
now a holy river flowing on Earth,' he added.

Sarasvati bowed, acknowledging his compliment.
'I am grateful,' she said, her gaze fixed on Brahma, almost
accusatory. 'But it would have been easier if I had known
all that this task entailed.'

Brahma stood cold and impassive, his eyes compelling.
Looking into them, Soma could not hide his uneasiness: he
was witnessing a war of words and wordless glances.

'Why did you not tell me about this Shiva Vadavagni?'
she insisted.

Soma broke in quickly, 'But you did save the world
from Shiva's Third Eye and this fire, this Beast of Doom!'

'Did I? Not that I knew about it,' she countered, an
edge to her voice. 'It was not just Rishi Aurva's Fire of
Anger but also Shiva's wrath which I carried with me in
this Vadavagni,' she said. 'Shiva woke from his meditation,
to discover that the world was teetering in chaos and
corruption. As the Destroyer, Shiva opened his Third Eye
to wipe the world out, emitting a deadly fire that threatened
all existence, the Shiva Vadavagni,' she paused. 'Was that
not the true reason for me to become a river?'

Brahma gave an imperceptible nod.

'But I was kept in ignorance! Why?'

'Because sometimes, ignorance *is* bliss,' he stated quietly.

'Never,' she shook her head. 'Knowledge is always supreme. I can take in the worst truth but never dishonesty, however benign. I would have appreciated if you had been more honest with me. I am not scared of danger, you know that,' she said quietly. 'But by keeping me in the dark, you left me more vulnerable, less prepared. Ignorance is not bliss, it is dangerous.'

Before Brahma could word out his protest, she spun around. 'Please don't be protective, it's belittling!' she gave a weary sigh. 'Don't I belong to your world? Then why don't you give me full responsibility, which I am accountable for? All the gods and goddesses do. I demand respect from you; I have earned it! I don't need your protection or your patronization. Oh, it's so humiliating.' A slight flush mounted to her face, her eyes glinting. 'But I shan't leave this task unfinished. I shall return victorious—I promise you!'

Sarasvati bit her lip, turning away from him. She felt his footsteps recede in the distance. Awash with fatigue, Brahma's duplicity confused her tired brain, but now, as she gazed at the sea, she felt the heat simmer and subside. She knew she was at the very end of her journey—her sluggish gait told her she was nearing exhaustion.

She knew that the enormous force of the waters she carried with her would have to split into five distributaries just before entering the ocean. From the corner of her eyes, she spotted four dark silhouettes along the shore. She recognized them immediately. They were the four

sages: Harina, Vajra, Nyaiiku and Kapila. Having heard
of her arrival, they had stationed themselves at Prabhas, to
summon her for blessings in the holy bath. The fire burnt
within her palms but to please the sages, for their faith and
patience, she took the names of each rishi to form a delta
before she joined the sea.

Straightening her weary shoulders, she said, her voice
clear and gracious: 'From now on I shall also be known by
your names—as Harini, Vajrini, Nyariku, Kapila and, of
course, Sarasvati.'

The four sages paid their obeisance by bowing low
with folded hands. Said Rishi Kapila, 'You, O Goddess,
the river Sarasvati shall henceforth flow in five channels
and shall dispel all the five sins of men if they plunge into
it or drink the waters.'

Drained, she pulled herself up and wishing to hand
over the burning ball of fire, positioned herself and invoked
the ocean: 'O Arnav, you are the primordial one among
Devas,' she pronounced, bowing to the thundering waves
of the ocean. 'You will always be the vital element of all
living beings. Please accept the Vadava from my hands at
the behest of Lord Brahma.'

Sarasvati had the set face of exhaustion but she glanced
up, where Brahma had left a trail behind him: she had
successfully accomplished her given tasks: some assigned,
some ascribed craftily but *they* together had been successful
in their mission. She had become a river for him, for
the world, for mankind. Sarasvati smiled as she lowered
herself into the cool surf of the ocean waters. She took a

deep breath, before she took her closing dip, finally able to deposit the Vadava fire into the ocean.

'I took the form of the river to absorb the fire and now I go into the sea with this fire-spitting Vadavagni,' Sarasvati drew in a deep breath, closing her eyes as her words took a portentous overtone. 'But it can actually become the Beast of Doom if not utilized well. So long as the world is unpolluted and Man sensible, this terrible creature will remain at the bottom of the sea. When wisdom is abandoned and Man corrupts the world, this Vadavagni will burst forth as volcanoes from under the oceans, subsequently consuming the land and destroying the universe and the cycle of Creation!'

Her words hung in the air, crashing against the roaring waves, hoping to be heard, wanting to be heeded . . .

8

TRIVENI

Sarasvati climbed up the steps of Indra's court feeling strangely exhilarated. Brahma and she had completed another mission together, she smiled as she walked straight to the long hall. Never mind those hot words exchanged; or the brief physical intimacy in his arms. They had been successful—again. They were a good team; she smirked, soused with a strong euphoria as she sat alone amidst the milling crowd. With a certain gravity of astonishment, she grasped a little-known fact: she had no friends except Brahma. There were Lakshmi and Parvati, Yamuna and Ganga, Sachi and Menaka and other devis and apsaras all circulating around the hall but Sarasvati got the instinctive feeling they found her odd: that outspoken, drab goddess who liked her own company. She sighed, waiting, with bated breath, her eyes surreptitiously glancing at the entrance, yearning to see Brahma enter with his usual decisive steps, his face forbidding, his dark, gravely eyes unfathomable. She couldn't see him and realized how badly she had wanted to see his face and hear his voice.

'Congratulations, many times over! You seem to have done a lot of good work lately,' interrupted a soft feminine voice near her.

Sarasvati whirled around, her eyes wide and uncomprehending.

It was Ganga, a broad smile on her face.

Sarasvati's heart lurched. Ganga had caught her unawares; *did she know*, she thought fearfully?

'I hear you are a now a grand river like me! And, that you tried to make peace between Kama and Brahma? Both brave efforts. Not many have the courage to carry a deadly fire or interfere between two warring gods,' she gushed, throwing an approving look.

Sarasvati smiled politely, her face stiff. 'I did what I could,' she said shortly.

Yamuna's eyes lit up with genuine admiration. 'But you were wonderful. You saved Kama's life and saved the world!'

Ganga's eyes grew serious. 'But it was impudent of Kama to shoot that arrow at Brahma, of all people! Brahma had no intention of love and marriage in his agenda. He is what we all in Brahmalok claimed him to be: the unmarried man married to his work.'

'But then, Sarasvati came on the scene,' chuckled Yamuna, the teasing note back in her voice. 'Rivers are said to have a source—but your source, Sarasvati, is Brahma himself!'

Sarasvati again felt a faint stir of annoyance but before she could retort, Ganga interposed.

'Yami, don't start!' she reprimanded, turning to Sarasvati. 'I am sorry we teased you earlier, it was unkind of us,' she said with a regret in her voice that Sarasvati was quick to detect.

Sarasvati looked at her suspiciously, wondering if she meant what she said. There was sincere regret on Ganga's fresh face, her grey eyes apologetic.

Ganga sighed, 'I often get into troubled waters because of my running tongue.'

She gave Sarasvati a close look. 'Perhaps you can help me,' she giggled with girlish delight. 'They say you are on the tip of everyone's tongue as Vagdevi, as Vani. You could make me say wiser words!'

'Goddesses don't trade their skills and secrets! But perhaps you might improve in better company?' Sarasvati twinkled back.

'Yours, you clearly mean,' nodded Ganga in mock solemnity. 'Yes, I should do that. And this goes for Yami too, she's another mindless gabber!'

'I like to chat,' Yamuna admitted sheepishly, her hands weaving twitchily.

Sarasvati wondered at the goddess's visible edginess, which she tried to cover by talking too fast, too much. Yamuna otherwise appeared to be a calm person, rarely ruffled but it stemmed more from timidity than self-assurance. Sarasvati had noticed Ganga often trying to spur her to shake away some of that diffident jumpiness.

And there was a legend surrounding it: Yamuna was born trembling because her mother Sanjana found her husband—the Sun God—Surya's effulgence too blinding. Sanjana's eyes had treacherously flickered, and their daughter was born trembling. Yamuna, or Yami as her father fondly called her, was the Sun God's favourite child. Possibly his obvious favouritism overrode a certain festering guilt that he was blamable for his daughter's condition.

Yamuna was not pretty but she had an open, pleasant face, with a tiny tilted nose and a wide mouth. She had deep hazel eyes; her hair, simply done, was of a sandy brown. She was very slender and voluble in a forced way. Sarasvati could not make out if she was flippant and loquacious to mask her painfully timorous nature.

By the time the recital ended, Sarasvati realized she had got herself two new friends, both unlike each other; their dissimilarities bringing them closer. If Ganga was bubbly and frank, Yamuna was restless, fidgety in manner but steady in thought. Sarasvati suspected she was a somewhat troubled girl, but decided not to intrude. She had heard that Yamuna's stepmother Chaya, the second wife of Surya, had ill-treated her as a child and it was only when her twin brother Yama complained to their father, had the mistreatment been exposed. Possibly this sustained abuse had a long-lasting impact; the reason for Yamuna's diffidence and agitated nervousness. Sarasvati looked at the slim, dusky girl more kindly.

'Were you disappointed Brahma wasn't there tonight?' asked Ganga, with astute perspicacity.

Sarasvati halted in her stride. *Just when she had not been thinking of him any more!*

'Let's not talk about it, please,' she warned.

'I won't badger you further from now on,' promised Ganga. 'But let me tell you this—from what I can see, you like him too much and you don't like that feeling. That's why you are resentful.'

Sarasvati rolled her eyes in elaborate exasperation but she felt the dull warmth of a flush rising up her neck.

'I know him longer than you,' said Ganga quietly. 'I base my argument solely on that.'

'But you don't know *me*,' said Sarasvati promptly. 'I don't believe in love, simple.'

'It's not simple, take it any way,' Ganga sighed, gloomily. 'Love and loving is not simple.'

Sarasvati wondered at the strain of despondency in Ganga's voice but she refrained from responding.

Ganga gave a slight smile, her eyes serious. 'But I do know Brahma loves you, I know him too well.'

Sarasvati felt that anxiety again, a mix of annoyance and excitement.

'You are actually defending him, Ganga? And I thought you resented him,' Yamuna interposed, her eyes surprised.

'I resented that he once forced me to leave Heaven and descend to Earth,' Ganga explained, her tone light. 'That was a long time ago,' she lifted her slight shoulders. 'I didn't want to leave Brahmalok and I rebelled. Who likes to leave their home?! I have grown up here!'

'But you surely won't mind this time . . .' teased Yamuna with a knowing wink. She stopped short abruptly, sighting the warning frown on Ganga's face.

Sarasvati was immediately intrigued, but did not allow the curiosity to show on her face.

She said with an encouraging smile, 'Love is always more romantic for others!'

'Exactly!' squealed Yamuna in obvious delight. 'First you and now Ganga . . .' she gushed, ignoring Ganga's quelling look. 'But love is in the air, with or without Kama. Sarasvati, did you catch the blush on Ganga's face?'

Sarasvati noticed the soft colour warming Ganga's fair loveliness.

'What?' she prompted, now fully intrigued.

'Not what, who. Ask *who* Ganga is in love with . . .' giggled Yamuna.

Ganga blushed even more.

'With Mahabhisha,' announced Yamuna with dramatic flair.

Sarasvati's brows cleared, swiftly estimating the situation. From all that she heard and knew, Emperor Mahabhisha had joined the ranks of the celestial beings after his earthly demise, a rare honour accorded to him. He was from the famous Ikshvaku royal dynasty, having performed a thousand Ashwamedh yajnas and a hundred Rajasuya yajnas—all commemorations of his conquests of territories, respect and fame, sealing his authority as supreme emperor. The gods were left with no choice but to allow him entry into Svarga as upon his death, the great man had become a heavenly spirit.

'He is currently a guest in Brahmalok, is he not?' ventured Sarasvati, scrutinizing Ganga's still rosy glow.

'Yes, and Ganga is playing the perfect host!' twittered Yamuna.

Ganga flushed. 'I am doing what is expected of me. Brahma told me he is an important guest and I am being the gracious hostess . . .'

Yamuna snorted. 'Say it, Ganga, you like him too much for your own good!'

Kavita Kané

'If Brahma says he is a guest, keep that in mind, Ganga,' warned Sarasvati, a slight frown furrowing her brows. 'Mahabhisha is a visitor, he won't be allowed to stay here too long . . .'

'And Ganga is making the most of it, by being with him all the time!' grinned Yamuna.

Love makes all lose reason, thought Sarasvati in genuine bewilderment as she noticed how her warning had fallen on deaf ears. First Brahma, now Ganga; *but never her*, she thought with quiet resolve.

She tried again. 'Ganga, he is a mortal, you a celestial, and you know you can't share a future with him,' she persisted.

Ganga looked surprised. 'I have done no wrong!'

The cheerfulness had fled from Yamuna's face, giving way to a sudden alarm.

'What are you saying, Sarasvati?' she asked, her face falling.

'It won't be taken kindly in Svargalok,' Sarasvati cautioned, softening her tone. 'Love happened between the apsara Urvashi and the mortal Pururava but she had to leave him eventually and return here.'

'Urvashi is an apsara, I am a goddess!' said Ganga, obstinately.

'That would make things more difficult,' remarked Sarasvati drily.

'If it comes to that, I shan't mind leaving Heaven for him,' rejoined Ganga, a defiant glint in her grey eyes.

'But again, you shan't be allowed to do so! You are divine, meant to stay in Heaven, not Earth,' said Sarasvati, with characteristic calmness.

Ganga was in a mood of love and the manner of a rebel.

'Each time you descended the Earth was because you were told to do so, to rinse away the sins of mankind,' Sarasvati paused, placing her hand on Ganga's shoulder. 'A few minutes ago, you gave me some advice. I know you said it with good intention and as a friend,' she said quietly. 'And now I say the same to you, out of concern, nothing else.'

'Yes, we are friends now,' assured Yamuna, with an uneasy laugh.

'Oddly enough,' muttered Ganga.

'Not odd, we are all rivers after all!' said Yamuna, her face solemn. 'For some reason or the other,' she added, thoughtfully, her brows knotted. 'It's strange, we seem to be so interconnected—as in sisters. Or the Trinity! Ganga is the white river, the river of salvation and purity. And you, Sarasvati, are the river of wisdom, from which flows the river of consciousness and creativity. You may well be the invisible river! While I am known as the dark river; even my waters are green and dark.'

Sarasvati made an impatient gesture. 'This is ridiculous,' she burst out in sudden vehemence. 'I don't know why you are being too harsh on yourself, Yami, dark is beautiful too! Why belittle yourself as "dark river"?'

'I am Kalindi,' Yamuna reminded her.

Just for a moment hardness crept into Sarasvati's velvety eyes, and her mouth pursed. 'That's not because of your dusky complexion. It symbolizes your relationship with Yama, the Lord of Death and hence Kala or Kalindi.'

Yamuna's brows cleared, her eyes brightening. 'Oh, I saw it otherwise!'

'By disparaging oneself, one subjects oneself to inferiority, not humility,' cautioned Sarasvati. 'But Yamuna, you do know that you are Kalindi because you were instrumental in the creation of the night?'

'Who would know better than you, Sarasvati?' countered Yamuna with a ironical smile. 'And Brahma, of course. Both of you were the creators.'

Yamuna—as Yami—was the first woman, along with her twin brother, Yama. It was a well-known fact that the twins Yama and Yami were extremely fond of each other and lived happily on Earth, where the day never ended. Once, on her return, Yami found Yama lying still and stiff under a tree. Reluctant to disturb him, she decided not to wake him up and waited for him to open his eyes. After a long time, when he did not stir, she gently shook him. He lay motionless. It was only then that she realized he was dead. Disbelief swiftly turned to shock. Yami started to weep, tears fast coursing down her anguished face. Hours passed and her unabated tears threatened to deluge the Earth.

The gods came to pacify her but all she could do was sob heart-brokenly: 'Yama is dead . . . Yama died today!'

The panicking devas had rushed to Brahma and Sarasvati.

'Please help us, please help the Universe!' they cried in alarmed unison. 'Yamuna won't stop weeping and in her sorrow, she will deluge the Earth with her tears!'

'Her grief will not lessen, as she is stuck in time,' Sarasvati had observed. 'That's why she keeps saying Yama died today. Her "today" is forever.' She turned to Brahma, her eyes thoughtful. 'You shall have to create a night for the day. The darkness to separate the light of the Sun.'

The Sun God, Surya, her father too was inconsolable. 'I have lost my son, my daughter is numb with grief, I shall shut off my rays!'

Noticing the despairing faces of the gods, Sarasvati assured them. 'So be it, and that is how night shall be created. The calm of the darkness shall settle in and calm her down too.'

Sarasvati was proved right. Soon, Yamuna's sobs subsided, the floods receded and the world was saved.

When the Sun rose the following morning, Yami is said to have whispered, 'Yama died . . . yesterday.'

Time passed and her feeling of loss reduced.

'You saved us, Devi Sarasvati,' chorused the devas.

'We completed our unfinished work,' Sarasvati answered modestly, glancing at Brahma. 'Yama was chosen as the first mortal destined to die and as his sister, Yami was grieving his death. Because of the continual daytime at the start of creation, Yami was unable to understand the lapse of time since Yama's death. It was a lapse on our part: we should have known that with day comes night, with light comes darkness, with grief comes hope.'

'If Yama, through his mortal death, became the Lord of Death, Yami is paradoxically the Lady of Life. Every life has to die some day: life and death coexist,' Sarasvati had commented when the twins reunited.

Brahma had given his enigmatic smile and nodded, 'Without an end, there is no beginning.'

Oh no, I am thinking of him again, Sarasvati thought dismally and blinked, bringing her back to the now. Glancing self-consciously, she said, 'And from then on, Yami became Yamuna, the river goddess, whose tears flowed down to Earth and became sacred as the embodiment of Shakti.'

'Anyway, interconnected we are as rivers, we are each linked with the Trinity,' noticed Yamuna in her breezy, cordial way. 'If Ganga evokes Shiva, you, Sarasvati, you are naturally allied with Brahma as he created you as his inspiration. See, you can't escape us—or him!'

Yamuna's words were a revelation.

'Yes,' Sarasvati nodded her head slowly. 'Without Ganga, Shiva would remain the scorching, brilliant figure of fire; without Shiva, Ganga would flood the Earth,' she said, looking thoughtful. 'And . . .'

'And that leaves you with Brahma,' finished Ganga quietly. 'There can be no creation without creativity, no Brahma without Sarasvati. And no Sarasvati without Brahma.'

Sarasvati looked away but she could not look away from an undeniable certainty.

Yamuna continued, discreetly, noticing Sarasvati's pale face. 'We are the necessary complement to each other. The three of us are one, we are the Triveni, so essential to life on Earth.'

'We are the confluence of knowledge, dispassion and devotion,' agreed Ganga. 'As rivers, we are the life source.'

Sarasvati rose to her feet with an easy dignity, regarding the two women with new insight. They met her steady scrutiny with a freshly realized empathy.

'They don't have to worship us, they don't need to dip themselves in our waters to wash their sins,' said Sarasvati. 'All Man has to do is realize and understand that it is more fulfilling to bathe in the three scared rivers within him— the 'streams'—the *nadi*s: Ida, Pingala and Sushumna. Or the Ganga, Yamuna and Sarasvati within his body—the three energy pathways, through which prana—the life force—circulates as streams,' she explained. 'Ida is the left channel; white, feminine, cold, embodying the moon and associated with you, Ganga.'

Sarasvati turned to Yamuna. 'Pingala is the right channel—red, dark and passionate, hot like the Sun and linked with you, Yamuna. That's another reason for your dusky beauty, so never call yourself dark and ugly again!'

Yamuna chuckled, nodding. 'I shan't! And you, Sarasvati, are Sushumna, the central channel.'

'And within this nadi there are three more sub-channels: Vajra, Chitrini and Brahma nadi,' said Ganga, throwing Sarasvati a pointed look, '. . . through which Kundalini—the divine feminine energy—moves upwards, running up the body to the crown of the head.' She then paused expressively. 'See, that's also possibly why you are linked with Brahma and the mind!'

Sarasvati ignored her insinuation and continued, 'By equalizing the Ida and Pingala—the left and the right, Ganga and Yamuna, humans will be able to strike the right balance, be it health, attitude or aptitude.'

Ganga was quick to concede the point but added, 'Most people live and die in Ida and Pingala, rarely tapping their Sushumna, which remains neglected, almost dormant. But Sushumna is necessary for the very ascent of the Kundalini, the Shakti at the base of the spine. Only when the opposing energies of Ida and Pingala enter into Sushumna, life begins by energizing the seven chakras, the vital energy points along the spine. That Sushumna is you, Sarasvati,' she said, her tone reverential. 'But how many in mankind realize the immense latent potentials within them? How many know they have this power in them?'

'How many in mankind realize *us*?' agreed Sarasvati. 'They know us as rivers, mere water bodies, not as life-giving sources, within and outside. From the combined Yukta Triveni you mentioned, Man has to move to the Mukta Triveni for liberation through us.'

Yamuna looked at them intently and with perplexity, even with alarm.

'Yes, I fear humans, I fear our future, I fear for our very existence,' she professed, her face troubled. 'We are sisters, our tributaries coming from the same source where the waters are pure and fresh. But Man has polluted us. I have become dark and ugly—all green and sluggish now,' she looked at them helplessly.

'So have I,' sighed Ganga with a resigned droop of her fair shoulders. 'While washing mortal sins . . .'

'Man's crimes,' corrected Sarasvati. 'His mindless violence inflicted on us—the rivers, the aquatic life within us, not to forget the surrounding air, the soil, the vegetation, leaving a barren waste in his wake. And they yet have the gall to worship us as the rivers of salvation!'

An uneasy quiet swamped the room.

Ganga, assuming a lighter manner, threw a quick smile, cheering up.

'Rivers are magnificent, sacred spaces!' she exclaimed. 'Hearing the surge of a river, its breathing so joyful and rushing with excitement; the sound can be so powerful, deafening the ugliness of life. Even for a moment, that respite is heavenly!'

Yamuna looked woeful. 'That was how once we were . . .'

'I would rather dry up and disappear from Earth than allow myself this ignominy,' affirmed Sarasvati, her velvety eyes darkening. 'I shall not serve those who cannot respect me.'

Ganga burst into an uneasy chuckle. 'You are as proud as all claim you to be, Sarasvati!'

'And more,' said Sarasvati quietly, with a bleak smile.

'You will rebel?' questioned Yamuna in open wonderment. 'Leaving the Earth would be abandonment, forsaking your duties, which means open dissension and defying the natural order of things . . .'

'But that's Man's lapse too—he has been disobeying the natural order of things despite warnings! These are precious gifts which humans need to respect and cherish,' she reminded, tartly. 'By polluting us, they are causing not just our passing, but eventually their own death and that of their planet. And I shall not stay in such a callous, heedless world, if it comes to that!'

Yamuna clutched her hand. 'Don't, Sarasvati, don't say such things, please! It is ominous! Here, Ganga is ready to leave Heaven, you are threatening to leave Earth, what is wrong with the two of you?' Yamuna said unhappily. 'We are rivers, we are the Triveni, we are friends, we are sisters, meant to be together!'

Sarasvati suddenly did not feel lonely any more. Yamuna was right: they were connected to each other in some odd way. They were more than friends now. Although they each had their faults, they were good together.

Ganga took her hand, 'And even if you threaten to disappear from here and the Earth in some fit of anger, your power and significance will be in the persistent symbolic presence at the confluence of rivers all over the country. Even if you are, as you say "materially missing", you will always be our third river, who will philosophically emerge to join us in the meeting of rivers, thereby making the waters thrice holy!'

Sarasvati flushed a little under the level gaze of the trusting, grey eyes.

'With that logic, all of us, for whatever reason, have had to descend to Earth,' smiled Sarasvati. 'We are no goddesses who can remain in the luxury of Heaven.'

Ganga smiled back, but it was not a pleasant smile. She did not move, the fixed smile did not leave the corners of her lips, her eyes dull. She made a dim sound with her breath.

'I agree, we are no goddesses who can remain in the luxury of Heaven,' she said slowly. 'You were sent because of Brahma. So was I. But this time, if need be—I shall go for myself, for Mahabhisha.'

Yamuna shook her head in mute dismay.

'If you do, it will be as a penalty, not as a life-giving river,' Sarasvati warned.

Ganga raised her defiant eyes to Sarasvati's. 'I shall go, whatever the consequence.'

'The outcome might be divine punishment,' Sarasvati reminded her gently.

'By Brahma?' shrugged Ganga. 'I am ready to face his wrath too. It is better to live in penalty than with the pain of a broken heart,' she retorted. 'Brahma should know,' she said, her lips twisted. 'He is experiencing all that he created—love, pain, frustration. Till now, he created without knowing the value of his creation and he's paying the price. So shall I, I know. Love does not make a fool out of you, as you believe it to be, Sarasvati. Love makes one stronger, if not wiser.'

Ganga stopped talking and stared down at her hands. Sarasvati didn't hurry her, and after a while, Ganga went on.

'But love seems to have made Brahma more rigid,' she commented, giving Sarasvati a liquid stare. 'As he suffers in its throes, he knows now what love and heartbreak are,' she paused. 'And I hope he understands how he made others suffer.'

She said it without viciousness, her tone flat, but there was hopeful vengeance in her words. Was she exulting that Sarasvati had broken Brahma's heart, did the others see it likewise: that Brahma was being punished?

9

CREATING MUSIC

'And I then played the first sound of music,' she said. 'Together we discovered the melody of mantras in the cacophony of chaos.'

Again, she was assailed by the strange sense of togetherness that she kept pushing away.

She could see Brahma very clearly. She could see his big and powerful shoulders, his narrow, dark head and his closely pursed lips. She could almost feel the power in him.

A small commotion broke her reverie.

'The devas wish to seek your presence,' informed the emissary.

Sarasvati frowned. Why had they come to her directly?

Sarasvati entered the morning chamber. She stood for an instant on the threshold, a grave smile hovered upon her lips as she looked at the group of devas with their uniformly troubled faces. Then she came forward and addressed Indra.

'The day has started early today, has it?' she smiled and gave a bow but her velvety dark eyes had a cool glitter in them.

Indra made a deep bow in return, his face pinched.

'We need your help, O Devi,' he began tactlessly.

With a dignified cordiality, she motioned for her visitors to take their seats and herself sat down, her eyes still on Indra.

Indra felt that her eyes held him in a long and unembarrassed look of appraisal. It was so frank that it made Indra feel distinctly uncomfortable. There was no expression on her face, yet she was appraising him clinically. Fidgeting nervously, Indra was aware that here was a woman whose business was to form an opinion of others and to whom it never occurred that subterfuge or subtlety was necessary.

'Evidently you are in dire need,' she said drily, watching the flush on his handsome face deepen in further distress and discomfiture.

'It is urgent and, worse, we need to be discreet!' he blurted out.

'What is the matter?'

'There has been a theft in Heaven!' he said, his words incoherent.

'Clearly, no one knows of this as none of them— Brahma, Vishnu or Shiva—has informed me,' she said sedately, her brow raised questioningly.

Indra looked at her: even the curve of her brow was intimidating.

'We don't dare go to them,' Indra looked helpless. 'Matters might just flare up . . .' his voice trailed off uncertainly.

'You mean you need a woman's guile and tact,' she mocked.

But Indra was too disturbed to catch her sardonic wit.

'In Indralok right now, there is complete pandemonium!' he cried. 'The devas discovered this theft . . .'

'Who stole what, Indra?' she asked, her tone gentle but the firmness in her voice cleared his befuddled thoughts.

'Vishwavasu, the gandharva, has stolen soma, which he was meant to guard,' said Indra, his tone more composed now and his long, sharp face white and weary.

Sarasvati gave a sigh, in quick comprehension. Apart from the amrit for which the devas and the asuras had so long fought, there was also another potion that the gods treasured: the *somras*, the elixir of life, perceived to be the drink of the gods—a potion that was consumed by all the devas and was definitely Indra's favourite tipple. The soma plant held sap that was life-giving, besides being intoxicating and invigorating. But more importantly, soma had rare properties: to heal illness and to usher in great riches. The devas had gained their immortality by drinking this precious soma and as expected, they kept it hidden in a pitcher and under the guard of the divine demigods, the gandharvas, who were said to have themselves emerged from the scent of flowers. Vishwavasu, the chief of the gandharvas, had been given the charge of safekeeping and had performed his duty well; till now. Much to the chagrin of the devas, he had glibly stolen the urn from under their very nose.

'Probably curiosity made him take it,' murmured Sarasvati while wondering why Vishwavasu had stolen the elixir.

'No, greed!' barked Indra. 'He wants to become more powerful than me . . . us, the devas!'

Sarasvati regarded Indra with her incisive look. Indra and Vishwavasu had a history. Indra was still peeved that Menaka, his favourite apsara, had married Vishwavasu. The grouse gnawed and prickled, hurting his pride more than his heart. Indra had his little flirtations but not all of them were serious. He was much too cunning and self-absorbed to let them cause him any inconvenience— though they often caused trouble for others, she thought wryly. Indra, she knew, was a not clever man; just vain who loved admiration, his throne and himself more than anything else.

'Indra, I have no intention of getting involved in some domestic issue.'

Indra flushed again because he could not help it. He was able to give a laugh that sounded merry enough.

'It is not,' he assured hastily. 'The devas have lost the somras to the gandharvas and with what face do we tell the Trimurti this?' he seethed. 'We are angry, but more helpless than furious. We cannot accuse or attack the gandharvas; they are, after all, our friends, we are family,' he winced as he uttered the words. 'We need to find a peaceful way to retrieve the potion.'

'And so, the great gods are flummoxed! You can't think of a way out of the crisis,' Sarasvati replied. 'Can't you steal it back?' she asked with all seriousness.

Agni hid a smile but her humour was lost on the worried Indra.

'We would have, but we frankly don't know where it is and how to go about it,' replied Indra solemnly. 'That's why we have come to you.'

Sarasvati glanced at the other devas who had stood silent, allowing Indra to do all the talking. From their bowed heads, lowered eyes and wordless presence, Sarasvati fathomed they were too nervous to intervene. Was she so formidable or that fearful?

'This is like the great war between the asuras and the devas over amrit during the *samudramanthan*,' she said. 'As important and as treacherous.'

Indra nodded anxiously; the other devas looked on pale and perplexed.

'That time Mohini—Vishnu's female avatar—came to our help, this time we need you to aid us,' implored Indra, the entreaty strong in his voice.

'Each time a woman to the rescue when the men are in distress,' she remarked, her lips twitching.

She gave the group of devas a hard stare. Then suddenly, she rose to her feet and produced an autumnal smile, a few degrees less chilly than her wintry one.

'You expect me to try my charms on the gandharvas?' she asked imperiously. 'They are expert seducers themselves. Why not send some apsara to get back the pitcher, say Rambha? Or Menaka?' she suggested wickedly.

Indra almost threw an apoplectic fit, a brick red suffusing his face.

'Menaka is Vishwavasu's wife, she is more loyal to him than she is to me now!' he fumed, his handsome face darkening.

'Have you asked her? She can mediate and might thaw this needless tension,' she advised.

Indra shook his head vigorously. 'No! She won't!'

'Or you won't?' she asked bluntly. 'Does it hurt your ego to ask a favour from her?'

Indra flushed furiously.

'I know her, she will refuse,' he said stubbornly through stiff lips. 'You are our only hope.'

Sarasvati was looking past him, a sudden thoughtful expression in her eyes.

'Yes, let me think it over,' she said shortly.

His face fell.

'Let me think how I can do it,' she corrected, her tone assuring.

Indra gave a brief smile, grinning loosely. 'I know you shall.'

His parting words amused her and even after they left, she never stopped smiling. The corners of her mouth just tucked in a little deeper.

Through her smiling eyes, she saw the answer to the quandary . . .

The next morning saw Sarasvati strolling towards Vishwavasu's miniature paradise in Indralok. She had decided she would not go as the goddess Sarasvati but as Vak, that ordinary woman whom the gandharvas would sure be pleased to meet.

But Brahma had revealed to her a different cosmic truth even in that name. 'It is through *vak*—speech or the syllable—that the surrounding world is revealed to the knowing mind,' he had once told her. 'I needed a medium to reveal to my creations and that was vak, whom I transferred into you, rendering the Universe with the word and hence communication.'

'And expression,' she had modified gently. 'Because through the syllable, I represent word, speech and language?' she had asked in her customary interrogatory manner.

'Already on Earth, they are singing hymns about how important speech, language and words are, as they exist in an oral culture where education is verbally transmitted from one generation to another, one tribe to another, one race to another, laying great value on speech, intonations, etymology, grammar and metre, all which define speech. This goddess eventually comes to be associated with you. Yes, you are Vak, who is at the tip of everyone's tongue, to be used prudently.'

She was that Vak today, in the guise of an ordinary woman and suitably so, a walk would do her good than taking her flamboyant peacock as a vehicle, she decided, as she ambled along the fortified walls, absorbing the magnificence of the palace. It was the first time she had seen this part of the heavenly empire.

'Beautiful people in their beautiful land,' she murmured, captivated by the opulence of the garden cosying in the expansive greens bordered by a neat row of flower-splendoured slender, tall trees.

She walked through the arched gateway and walked up the path paved with polished, engraved inlays all the way up to the long palace steps. On either side of the path were dormant rose trees. The neat flower beds were packed with bright hibiscus, tuberoses and a variety of jasmines, the air redolent with their combined heady fragrance. It was intoxicating. She settled down at the edge of the rose garden, cushioned comfortably by the unbridled grass under her as she adjusted the veena on her lap.

'My only one weapon in this war,' she smiled to herself, running an affectionate hand over the smooth curve. 'My veena.'

'Veena is the symbol of music; the start of sound and melody,' Brahma had told her when he had placed the lute in her hands. 'It's like the throat of our body's musical instrument.'

She strung the first hesitant notes in the stillness. The air faintly pulsed with the sweet sound. Sarasvati then started playing and the air filled with wondrous tunes of ragas and raginis, the strings vibrating as fast as the movements of her hands, as she played softly, then strongly, seducing, mesmerizing . . . She strung on various notes, and it sounded as if she would not let go, allowing her music to pass from her mind to her fingers to the strings and then, through her veena into the pregnant air that suddenly filled with soulful music; stimulating everything all around: the birds stopped chirping, the leaves rustled into silence, the flowers raised their faces to sway softly . . .

'What is that you are playing?' asked a rich voice, full of awe and wonderment.

Sarasvati stopped, removing her fingers from the quivering strings. She looked up to see a tall, fair, slim-shouldered man, his raven mane framing a sharply chiselled face with a sensual mouth below a straight narrow nose and golden amber eyes that looked surprised. His head was clustered with wavy dark hair and his smile was swift and smooth.

'It's the veena,' she said, a faint smile on her face. 'It is a lute, a stringed musical instrument that represents the perfection of all arts and sciences.'

'May I know your name, lady?'

'I am Vak.'

'Vak?' he looked puzzled, staring at the lady in ivory. Draped in dull white fabric, her skin as creamy as milk, her whole body as if it was awash with moonlight. Her music was as mesmerizing as her eyes: they were clear, clever and wide with a discernible thinking space between them. She did not look hard but looked as if she knew all the questions and had heard all the answers.

'Vak?' he repeated, blinking. 'That is a strange name!'

'I am into speech and music,' she explained modestly.

A thought struck him.

'I forgot to introduce myself, I am Vishwavasu,' he beamed, his full, sensual lips widening in a warm smile, his handsome head bowed. 'I am the chief of the gandharvas and your bewitched devotee from now on.'

'You are the one who stole a plant cherished by the devas, the soma plant,' she said succinctly.

Vishwavasu looked astonished, making no effort to deny her accusation. His pale eyes narrowed. 'You have been sent to retrieve it?' he demanded, his voice hardening. 'Are you a spy sent by Indra?'

She returned his suspicious glare with an icy coolness.

He bristled. 'But you won't find it; we have hidden it well. Lady, let me assure you, nothing will make me return that potion!' he declared adamantly, crossing his arms in a deliberately belligerent stance. The gesture reminded her immediately of Brahma. She wondered if it was more a defensive gesture.

Sarasvati ignored the gandharva's bellicosity and absently strung a note on the veena, interjecting the conversation with a burst of soft, mellifluous notes.

The notes of the raga seemed to transfix the gandharva. She saw him close his eyes, his face ecstatic. She continued to strum, the melody slowly, softly encompassing him . . . He seemed to stand still in a strange lull, then his eyes flew open, excited and eager.

'The music you played now was as intoxicating and inebriating as the somras!' he exclaimed breathlessly.

She kept silent, thrumming at the frets.

After taking a long pause, he looked at her, his eyes inquiring.

'You are no ordinary person!' he said slowly, his tawny eyes clouded. 'Who are you with such sensational mind and melody?'

A tiny, enigmatic smile played on her mouth, as she drew her hands away from the veena, staring at them as if she were seeing them for the first time.

The gandharva's light eyes widened in wonder and reverence, as realization slowly dawned upon him.

'You said you are Vak . . . but you must be . . . Sarasvati!' he breathed, his tone deferential. 'I am honoured to be in your presence!' he rushed to bow low at her feet. He looked up, his hands still folded. 'My apologies for my rudeness. You are the goddess of all arts . . . Is this the music you play we have heard so much of but never known?'

'You did just now,' she smiled. 'I play my compositions with *anuraga*—that passion which represents all emotions and feelings expressed in speech or music.'

'It is exquisite!' he inhaled, his eyes mesmerized by her rendition.

'Yes, it is as enchanting!' she nodded, her eyes probing his. 'But you don't seem too offended by my accusation that you are a thief?'

Vishwavasu flashed his beautiful smile again. 'I confess I did it,' he said sheepishly. 'But we gandharvas are very desirous creatures—we are not too good at resisting temptation.'

She smiled, faintly amused. 'I wondered why you did it?'

'I have been very curious about this potion in the pot since the time it was handed to me,' he admitted candidly.

'You were supposed to be its sentinel, not a stealer,' she admonished lightly.

Vishwavasu looked unabashed, his smile fixed and dazzling.

'All of us were inquisitive, we knew it means something very important to the devas.'

'That is why they had handed it to you for safekeeping,' she said, with a slight raise of her eyebrow.

'I admit I capitulated to pressure from the other gandharvas,' he confessed, grinning brazenly. '. . . And we decided to steal it. It was easy. I was, after all, in charge of guarding it.'

'Ironic,' she murmured.

'Well, I was entitled to try some of it,' he argued. 'I simply hid it away, appointing two gandharvas, Svan and Bhraji, as guards.'

'And so, the gandharvas are rejoicing swindling the devas!'

Vishwavasu chuckled unrepentantly but stopped short when he saw her plucking the strings again. He lapsed into silence, falling into a trance. Once again, she created magic, unlike anything the gandharva had ever witnessed. The music floated, lingering softly, enticing the other gandharvas, who walked slowly towards the spot, drawn irresistibly to it, as if in a daze, completely under her spell. Soon, the crowd swelled surrounding her while she continued playing.

She hid a smile and her eyes lowered, aware of her audience.

Abruptly, she stopped, watching the swift disappointment on the face of each gandharva in the crowd. Vishwavasu looked visibly distressed.

'Please play on,' he said in a low voice, hoarsely. 'Why did you halt, O lady?'

'No, I have to go,' she said firmly. 'I confess that I was completely bewitched by this beautiful garden. I had to stop and play my music here to complete the perfect picture.'

'You can, whenever,' insisted Vishwavasu. 'Please stay.'

She pretended to think it over, her brows pleated. Vishwavasu grabbed the opportunity to ask the question which was tearing away at his mind.

'C . . . can . . . wi . . . will . . . you please teach me your music?' he blurted, his gold eyes burning. 'Perhaps, you will be kind enough to tutor us as well? We shall be blessed!'

Sarasvati regarded the gathered crowd with her keen eyes. 'I shall be very happy to teach you music, but I have one condition.'

The gandharvas broke into an excited chatter of jubilation at the very idea of learning to play such music, nodding their heads vigorously in unison.

But she noticed the fleeting look of hesitation on Vishwavasu's face. 'Of course, I know what you want: the somras,' he observed shrewdly.

'Yes, I want that one precious thing that you possess,' she confronted with liquid grace, firmly placing her veena down.

Vishwavasu could not take his eyes off it.

'If we can give it to you, we shall lay it at your feet!' said one of the attending gandharva, his voice distinctly rich and velvety. 'I am Tumburu.'

'What a lovely voice you have!' she gushed.

'It would sound better if I had your music,' implored Tumburu, his hands folded.

'Yes, you would certainly be known as the best singer in the three worlds,' she commented with an artful smile. 'But as I said earlier, I shall exchange this music for the somras.'

Tumburu threw Vishwavasu a desperate glance. The taller gandharva shifted his eyes and said nothing.

Sarasvati eyes grew glacial. 'What I want was not yours anyway in the first place,' she said silkily, her smile fixed but stern. 'You stole it.'

Vishwavasu felt a sudden rush of cold blood up his spine.

'The devas are furious at what you did and rightly so. You tricked them. Do you want a war? You are sure to lose. And worse, all of you will be disgraced and sent away in exile!'

Vishwavasu paled, his lips moved, but no words came out.

'All I want is that you return the stolen urn. If you do, I shall graciously grant you the knowledge of music and teach you how to play the notes and all the musical instruments: for I am Sarasvati, and it is within my power to do so.'

Tumburu nodded his head. Vishwavasu's eyes constricted to glittering gold in growing unease, watching the animated babble amongst the gandharvas.

Tumburu hastily intervened. 'We are ashamed of our actions, we betrayed the devas, we broke their trust. Please don't be angry with us, O Devi,' he entreated. 'Bless us instead with your legacy of music.'

Sarasvati turned her clear gaze on Vishwavasu. The muscles on either side of his jaw stood out suddenly.

'I shall inform Svan to hand over the pitcher to you,' he said stiffly, his face pallid.

'Gratitude,' she acknowledged ironically. 'Yes, once I have it, I shall return it to the devas. And I shall keep my word. Henceforth, you shall be known as celestial musicians and not just messengers between the gods and humans! You shall so excel that your music shall be more intoxicating than the somras that you have parted with.'

If she had made the gandharvas happy, she found the devas too visibly elated at having their potion back.

'So, Indra eventually did let all of you know of the theft,' she remarked casually as she placed the pot carefully in Indra's shaking hands in the presence of the Trinity.

Vishnu's eyebrows shot up in mock chagrin. 'We are omnipresent, omnipotent and omniscient, are we not?' he said severely.

'But it was wise of Indra to first go to you than us . . .' said Shiva grimly, his voice deliberately hanging in suspended intimidation.

Indra hastily intervened.

'As I had guessed rightly, only you could have got it back for us without shedding blood,' he started, gushing, his eyes gleaming. He leaned forward, his face became a honeyed smile, his voice dripping.

'I don't believe in war or violence,' Sarasvati reminded him shortly.

'Is that why you don't carry any weapons like other gods and goddesses?' asked Indra, glancing at the veena in her hands.

Her fair, lucent face told him nothing, but her dark eyes were alert as she carefully said, 'Words and wise action can be sharper than swords. I don't need any weapons.'

Indra flushed as Vishnu interceded tactfully. 'Your words and wisdom are your weapons, Sarasvati, which you endow to others. If as a river you are the "water that purifies" then through vak—words and speech—you become that "knowledge which purifies" whose flow refines the essence, the self of a person.'

Brahma again nodded his approval. She was proficient like him, he thought. All she needed was a little nudge to steer and she reacted immediately in the right way. 'By becoming a river, you replaced the conventional modes of rituals and replaced it with your own brand of knowledge: literature, art and now music, flowing with harmony and imagination. Even if the waters of your river dry up, Sarasvati, you will always be the patron of learning through art, music and the letters, making humanity attain salvation and spiritualism through you. You represent not just the creativity but the science of life, assisting in unravelling the mystery, the magnificence and the essentials of existence in the universe.'

Sarasvati lifted her shoulders delicately. 'I was glad to help,' she murmured, a trifle embarrassed.

Shiva threw her a smiling glance, amused at her discomfiture: Sarasvati was superbly uncomfortable with compliments. 'Now since you have blessed not just the gandharvas but the world with music and muse, you have evolved as the Goddess of Harmony, Enlightenment and Cosmic Speech. You are part of the great feminine trinity now, Sarasvati—the secret yoga shakti of rhyme and rhythm: the manifestations of divine mantras. By filling this planet with music, you are now the Veena Vadini.'

Sarasvati smiled, secretly pleased, but covered her awkwardness with asperity. 'Music will be that free expression of thought and imagination and hopefully a great unifier,' she paused, a thoughtful look on her face.

'. . . Bonding all kinds, joining the world and the Universe together into one sound of peace, bliss and enlightenment: Om,' she said, closing her eyes, feeling it seep through her.

'Om,' she repeated softly, opening her eyes, full of wonderment. 'How just one syllable can hold the entire Universe! And what heightened reality it is then to return to that single syllable.'

Shiva was moved by the reverence in her tone.

'Om refers to the atman and the Brahman. That is, the Self within and the Supreme Knowledge,' said Shiva. 'That is why it is revered and this syllable shall be used at the beginning and the end of the chapters in the Vedas, the Upanishads, and any other text. It shall be the sacred spiritual incantation made before and during the recitation of spiritual texts, during yajna and yoga, during pooja and prayers and at rites and rituals.'

Agni stepped forward, the urn now in his hand. 'Last time you had held the Vadavagni, this time the somras. Again it was through the power of your wisdom that we were saved! You are our Anshumati, our saviour. You, O Sarasvati Devi, through devotion and discipline, teach us all the vision of the worldly and spiritual to be meditated upon. You allow one to exist in the material world while striving for the plane of Brahman. Hence, whoever forms that sacred connection with you, through words or music, art or craft of creation, is with the very source of the cosmos and Supreme Knowledge, the Brahman. You are thus, our Brahmi,' he bowed, muttering a chant, softly filling the air to echo through the open skies . . .

'Sarasvati moves among the Gods,
She holds them, sustains them . . .
Whosoever breathes, sees, hears or eats does so because of Her . . .
She creates powerful creators and embed them with wisdom
    and sight . . .
Her powers overflow the universe . . .'

10

GANGA

The high-domed hall of Brahma's palace saw a giant gathering—the full family of celestials: the devas, nakshatras, gandharvas (now the new heavenly musicians), and apsaras as well as the revered rishis from Earth—welcoming King Mahabhisha. Mahabhisha was clearly no ordinary mortal himself. He, who had once been a great king among men, had now joined the sanctified status of the celestial beings. This was not an honour accorded to every great king. Mahabhisha was a rare exception to whom Brahma had accorded this grand welcome, deigning to meet him among the ranks of those he considered important enough.

Sarasvati certainly was not interested in this show of power and privilege. She grimaced as her slim feet moved on the carpet to a long gallery overlooking the sea. She witnessed the occasion with dispassionate eyes and had it not been for Ganga's pleadings, she would not have been sitting here in this magnificently sombre hall, fenced by her two friends.

'I can well understand why you are here, Ganga, but why me?' she muttered in apparent dismay.

'Yes I am here because of Mahabhisha but you, you had to be here . . . for Brahma!' Ganga grinned mischievously. 'I have heard Brahma is going to thank you publicly for saving the world from the Vadavagni and blessing the gandharvas with music. Today is their debut performance. You got music to Heaven!'

Sarasvati went cold, then hot with embarrassment. 'I don't need public acknowledgement,' she mumbled. 'And as messengers between the celestials and the mortals, I hope the gandharvas spread the music beyond Heaven.'

All had gathered at his court, but Brahma had not yet arrived. He was late again, Sarasvati thought crossly; he knew it annoyed her. Typically late at work, he would try to mend her mood with his coal eyes apologizing mutely, as if to say, after all, he had done no more than being late. And she would return that look with an unsmiling face, her lips pursed severely. His habit of not being punctual exasperated her and when she was in this mood, even his slightest action irritated her beyond measure.

Sarasvati knew the true reason why she was unduly piqued: there had been no personal appreciation from his side and that rankled her disappointed heart. She sat looking at the empty chair beside Vishnu and Shiva, feeling unusually agitated, her heart sinking unreasonably. It was odd that this should be happening, she thought. There are foundational elements in our life: people who are so deeply embedded in our life; at times we take their existence for granted, until suddenly they are not there for us or do not express themselves like before, she thought sourly as she rose to her feet.

Yamuna pulled her down. 'No, you can't leave!' she whispered strongly.

Sarasvati sat waiting, with bated breath, her eyes glancing at the doorway, expecting him to enter. She felt oddly restless. To distract herself, she threw a long look at the man who had won over her friend's finicky heart. Mahabhisha was tall, very tall for a mortal. Seated straight on an ornate couch was a dark giant of a man, whose thick, lumpy shoulders dwarfed the back of his seat. His sartorial choice was starkly different from celestial finery: it was more ostentatious, decked with gems and flashing gold. An emperor indeed, she thought with an inward smile. He was not very young, with a thick mane threaded with silver strands, framing a broad forehead, tapering down to a square jaw, a thin nose, deep-set eyes and an almost lipless mouth. His lined, granite-hard face was swarthy, contrasting with his pale grey eyes: the colour of ice. And they were riveted on Ganga, sure and steady.

'Well, I have graced the court with my appearance, it's time I should leave,' sighed Sarasvati, making a move to get up again.

Ganga held her wrist. 'Please don't go. I want you to be here with me.'

Ganga looked nervous, her anxiety heightening her loveliness as she stood out, looking exquisite, almost ethereal in her gossamer silk that teasingly revealed much of what it was meant to conceal, woven with what appeared like the spray of her waters, now froth and now droplets.

But the gods dared not stare, nor did anyone, for she was Ganga.

Sarasvati cast a sardonic look around. Ganga was creating a sensation. Her untrammelled beauty, incomparable to even the fairest of Indra's apsaras, seemed daring, almost dangerous today. The gods and celestial beings were finding it difficult to avoid gazing at her, making an effort to keep their eyes peeled to the ground. She had clearly dressed up for Mahabhisha. And he stared, hopelessly smitten. He gazed at her to his eyes' fill and heart's content. In fact, his contemplation was so adoring that he had not noticed Brahma enter the hall.

What happened next, Sarasvati was not sure if it was chance or a considered act. Was it the presence of Vayu, the God of Wind, which had made Ganga's *angavastra* flutter down to her slim waist, exposing the full creamy curve of her cleavage. Or was it her act of subtle seduction, Sarasvati would never know, but the consequences were swift and devastating. The gods were stunned, hurriedly bowing their heads and lowering their eyes, Brahma included, allowing Ganga to lazily rearrange her fallen stole over her fair shoulders again. All this while her eyes never left Mahabhisha's transfixed face, gazing back at her, eyeing her in fully brazen wantonness, his eyes darkening as they flickered over her magnificent voluptuousness. Their game of gazing seemed to stretch endlessly, till the stony timbre of Brahma's voice broke the ominous silence in the hall.

What he said next sent a tremor of shock through the crowded room, disbelief and distress writ strong on everyone's face.

His cold, angry eyes ran over those present and stopped at the couple.

'You may be amongst celestials, but you proved to be a mortal after all,' barked Brahma, his baritone deepening in anger. 'May you be recast in the mould you don't seem to have outgrown, Mahabhisha,' Brahma pronounced in a sharp rustling voice. 'Return doomed to live, suffer and die as a mortal upon Earth! Wretch, as you have forgotten yourself at the sight of Ganga, you shall be reborn on Earth. But you shall try to attain salvation again.'

The crowd's noise hushed into a deathly silence: the curse seemed to resound loudly. Sarasvati could not believe her ears.

Brahma, his face ivory-white, turned his furious eyes on Ganga, who seemed to have come to her senses, her face shocked and shaken. 'And you too, Ganga, you shall be born in the world of men to hurt him and break his heart grievously.' He turned to Mahabhisha and said, 'And only when you are provoked enough to show your fury at the heartbreak, you and Ganga will then be freed from my curse.'

It was an odd condition to break a curse, Sarasvati wondered wildly as she observed the stillness as his ominous words hung in the hall, washing over Ganga and Mahabhisha. No one dared utter a sound of protest and before Sarasvati could intervene, Mahabhisha spoke, his voice grave.

'If you think I have committed a wrong to look at the woman I love, then I accept your curse,' he said, his voice even. 'But don't make Ganga suffer for my indiscretion.'

Brahma sat still, straight and suddenly dangerous. It wasn't until Mahabhisha encountered the full force that dwelt in his eyes that he realized he was in the presence of a powerful man.

'Ganga was the instigator, the reason why you did it!' growled Brahma, his tone affectedly uncivil. 'She shall be punished and her punishment lies in punishing you!'

Mahabhisha looked unfazed.

'Then I accept my punishment as a blessing,' he said simply.

Ganga rose, looking magnificent. 'I gladly accept the penalty if it means living with Mahabhisha on Earth as a mortal,' she pronounced, the defiance unmistakeable. 'A curse is not a curse any more, when wished for!' she added, her tone triumphant.

She was seeing this curse as a blessing, an opportunity to be with him, Sarasvati thought in disbelief. Love, did it give people the strength to overcome odds? Or did it make some angry and bitter, she thought, as she looked at Brahma with new eyes. She could not recognize this man, whom she believed to be different, *who is now so savage.* Anger grabbed her throat and she got up to speak, but was restrained by Yamuna's warning grip on her hand.

'Don't! You will make matters worse,' she whispered, her voice low but firm.

Sarasvati gave her a bewildered look. 'Why? Someone needs to tell him he's wrong, it's unjust! He can't do this!'

'He has done it,' said Yamuna calmly.

But it must be for a reason, she thought wildly. He could not be so heartless; he was not an unreasonable person.

Yamuna continued, 'You won't be able to persuade him to retract his words. Instead, it's more likely you might aggravate matters. Remain silent,' she begged.

Sarasvati loosed a wild glance of frustration at the throne he sat on.

'Oh God!' she cried to herself, 'why can't I do something?'

Her eyes, straying here and there in desperation, suddenly got fixed on him with renewed fury. She drew a sharp breath, recalling Yamuna's warning.

Mahabhisha spoke up, robbing Sarasvati of further argument. 'I have just one request, if I may,' he said, his voice deep, head bowed. Ganga, who had rushed to stand defiantly beside him, heard his remark, her lips coming together sharply. Taking her hand in his, he continued, 'Please give me the right to choose the family where I shall be reborn.'

Sarasvati was surprised at the strange request. It was as if the two lovers had a secret communication between them, inexorably bringing them closer and stronger. Mahabhisha had got emboldened enough to ask Brahma to choose his place of curse, possibly deriving his boldness from the same prospect as Ganga saw it—that they would soon be together. She was watching Brahma; there was a wary, alert expression in his eyes, but the anger had mysteriously vanished.

'So be it,' Brahma assented with a slight nod, getting up to stand to his full height, as if to remind all of his stature. For a moment, Sarasvati's angry and accusing eyes met his, calm and devoid of the grief he had just caused.

As she saw him striding away from the hall, she found herself frantically following him with furious steps.

Once inside his chamber, she stopped short, her face stiff with rage. He flicked a knowing glance at her.

She stared wordlessly at him, her lips pursed, waiting for him to speak first. A thick silence ensued.

'Do you really want to know the truth?' he asked, breaking the silence that had brooded over them since they had returned from the court.

'Why?' she demanded, having got the opportunity. 'Why did you curse the poor man? He was as guiltless as Ganga—they are in love!'

'Oh, so you believe in love; do you?' he gave a grim smile.

'I do, for others if not for myself!' she retorted. 'And for the one who believes and claims he's in love . . .' she lashed out, having the satisfaction to see him flinch, '. . .you acted like a heartless despot!'

Brahma raised his brows, annoying her further.

'You have destroyed them!' she continued hotly. '*Why?*'

'At the moment, you seem to be destroying your sense of reason,' he returned calmly. 'You are the wise one, lady, the Goddess of Wisdom,' he cast her an ironic glance. 'Think.'

'What?' she broke off.

His hand, palm upwards, was extended towards her. 'Hear me out. I am coming to it. But try to reason it out.'

He was right: she was angry, she wasn't thinking. Something in his resonant voice made her curb her rage. She was about to retort hotly; furious this time because he had forced her to recognize her own shortcomings.

His tone was almost taunting. 'You would know the importance of words, speech and language. You are Vakdevi, the Goddess of Speech, remember? Mind what you say, what you allege . . .' his voice had dropped to a velvety softness, a sardonic purr.

She recalled her own previous thought: *he must have a reason*.

Her brows cleared, as did her mercurial mood. She looked at Brahma, her shadowy eyes probing.

'Tell me,' she commanded with wide-eyed indignation.

Brahma did not bother to look surprised at her tone. He hid a smile.

'This curse on Mahabhisha follows a previous one,' he explained. 'Once, at the earthly ashram of Rishi Vashist, the revered sage cursed the eight *vasus*, the elements of Nature, the causal spirits of cosmic and climatic occurrences. And there was a reason for that curse.

'In order to fulfil his wife's petulant demand for Kamadhenu, the wish-fulfilling cow, the chief vasu, Prabhas, with the help of his seven brothers, stole the sage's pet when he was away. Upon returning to his hermitage and seeing his beloved cow missing, Vashist used his sagely vision to see the truth, following which he cursed the eight vasus to be born on Earth as mortals. They pleaded mercy and Vashist responded by promising that seven of them would be free of their earthly lives within a year of being born. The most stringent punishment was reserved for Prabhas and only he would pay the full penalty as he was the one who had stolen the cow.'

'And they approached Ganga for help to release them from his curse . . .' guessed Sarasvati, her mind working fast. ' . . . To be their mother. Ganga agreed and will be incarnated to be the mother of these eight vasus,' she paused. 'Is that why you agreed to Mahabhisha's strange request to choose the family he'd be born into?'

Brahma smiled faintly. 'You are ending your statement with a question, as you always do . . . that means you are fine now!' he continued, his eyes solemn. 'Yes, Mahabhisha will be reborn as Shantanu, the Kuru prince of the Bharat race, and will fall in love with Ganga and marry her.'

'Which otherwise she would not have been able to do as he is a mortal and she is celestial,' said Sarasvati, a thoughtful frown on her face. 'Is that why you did this, brought them together, even if for a short and bitter period?'

'I hope I am not as despotic as you believe I am,' Brahma responded laconically, but she detected the hurt in his voice.

Sarasvati flushed a little under the level gaze of his black, opaque eyes: *she had assumed the worst of him again.* She remained silent and stiff; her lashes lowered to hide her embarrassment.

'Well, the other vasus will be delivered of their curse, reborn as Ganga's sons on Earth. As their mother, she will drown her newborn babies in her waters . . .'

'No!' Sarasvati could not stop her horrified gasp.

' . . . In their death, they will be released from the curse. All, except Prabhas, of course. He will have to live his curse as the mortal Devavrat,' Brahma said. 'Shantanu will remain the unrequited lover pining for his wife once she returns to Heaven with the baby Devavrat.'

'But a mother killing her children!' she cried. 'Oh, what all are you going to make poor Ganga suffer?'

'She is Ganga, the Mother, the Goddess of Generosity and Plenty. She understands and knows all that she has to go through.'

The interminable pause was stretched, Sarasvati subdued in contemplation, sweeping her hair off her bare shoulders. He found the gesture oddly provocative, as always.

'But Ganga preferred this brief chance at mortal happiness to celestial immortality,' she remarked in open wonderment. 'She saw this as a blessing, not a curse. It presented her with an opportunity to be with her lover, to be his wife and the mother of his children. That's why she agreed.'

'To be a wife and a mother,' nodded Brahma. 'What she could not have sought in Heaven.'

There was silence—Sarasvati knew it was the silence of awe—that the power of love had driven Ganga senseless.

Sarasvati looked blank. 'Is that so important in a woman's life, to be a wife and a mother?' she sighed, her brows furrowed, tone puzzled.

'For most women, yes.'

'But not for me,' she returned archly, absently tucking an errant tendril behind her ear.

'I know,' he sighed, fascinated by the sight. She was lovelier that afternoon than he had ever seen her: delicate, resonant and, for him, desirable, though she kept an aloof distance. But sometimes he wondered if that detached objectivity wasn't for him alone, wasn't a side that, perhaps purposely, she turned towards him.

He sighed. 'We create other things instead, don't we?'

Those words made an odd conspiracy out of their association. They gave her a queer, bittersweet sensation.

'I was talking about Ganga being happy,' she said glibly.

'I did not create the world as a place to be happy in, even as some like to be happy in the belief that it is the reason for life,' Brahma returned smoothly. 'Ganga knows this. Happy is not the right word, it does not depend on us.'

'Happiness does depend on us,' she protested. 'Ganga has chosen her happiness, however short-lived. We are born to fight, not just the odds, but also our right to happiness. There are sad moments, unfortunate and regrettable moments, but happiness is drawn from that very life, which presents us people with moments worth living for. Ganga chose hers—from intimate to lonely.'

'That's also love,' he noted, crisply.

'That has proved itself to be not very sensible!'

'Agreed, love is not always sensible,' he said tightly. He sat perfectly quiet, but his nerves in wild clamour.

She stopped him with a snort, raising her chin as her loose mane rippled, creating a similar wave in his heart, 'Love is more of an acquired emotion.'

Her tone implied that he was already guilty of it.

He hesitated and then slowly nodded his head, his tortured eyes fixed on hers. 'Ah, yes, I agree, love *is* acquired . . . and once is quite enough!' said Brahma with a sad smile. He turned away from her, staring at the sea outside. 'Yet we live for it,' he muttered under his breath.

The torment in his words hit her. His heart constricted. She knew it was all about her, *who else could she be?* It had to be her. It couldn't have been anyone else. Her heart wouldn't be pounding like this.

She found herself walking slowly towards him, stopping right behind him. He was looking the other way: she could see bunched muscles and clenched tension in his neck. For perhaps five long moments, she gazed at him, soaking in the faint male smell and hearing his quick, laboured breathing. And in those five seconds, she forgot to think, only hearing the irrational pounding of her heart . . .

She unclenched her fists and turned to walk away quietly out of the room abruptly, leaving him alone with his misery.

11

THE CHALLENGE

Kama got up impatiently. With quick steps, he went inside again to request Sarasvati for a meeting. She was still in the library, absorbed in a thick tome. There was absolute silence in the huge room, at times broken with the sound of Sarasvati turning the pages of the book. He dared not disturb her. He waited outside, studying Sarasvati from afar. She seemed as if she had not moved since he last saw her in the morning. She was still there as dusk fell. Kama was struck by her evident power of concentration. She had neither noticed him coming in nor going out of the library.

She was so much like the mansion she lived in. The imposing house was set on two acres amid wild woodland and unbridled grass over a steep cliff, overlooking a beach; a narrow pathway led up to the high and long steps of the porch. It was one of the few houses that had complete seclusion.

He made a noise, shuffling his feet. She did not notice.

He cleared his throat.

She looked up, recognizing Kama but made no effort to move.

'Oh, I didn't realize you were here,' she murmured abstractedly.

'I have been here almost all day. I came in twice,' he said hurriedly.

'I come here in the library a good deal. Generally, I have the place to myself . . .'

Away from prying visitors like me, Kama thought facetiously.

'I did not want to disturb you . . .' he started nervously.

'You have clearly come here to tell me something important; you would not waste a day otherwise!' she said with her characteristic half-smile.

All his irritation flew from his face. It occurred to Kama that she had a sweet smile that lit up her face with an inner light.

Heartened, he said hastily, 'I have come to invite you personally for the inauguration of the grand gallery where an art show will also be held.'

She did not respond immediately and Kama began to find the silence awkward. He was on the point of getting up when she threw him a look with her peculiarly opaque eyes. She looked strangely unhappy, grave and intense, staring at the vacant space as if she was meditating. He waited.

'Yes, of course.' The answer was both reticent and impersonal. It discouraged him.

'We are obliged that you can grace the occasion,' he broke out in sudden embarrassment as he watched her push back the book on the shelf. 'Also because you had summoned me . . .' He broke off uncertainly.

'Ah. Oh yes,' she nodded suddenly as if there was no silence in between. 'I wanted an update,' she commanded, turning towards him.

He looked back with frightened eyes.

'About what, Lady?' he asked politely, his tone bewildered.

'That challenge decided the last time we met. You were to make me fall in love?' she prompted, raising one of her dark eyebrows.

Kama flushed deep.

'I dare not commit the same outrage,' he murmured.

She glared at him with wide, indignant eyes. 'But you can, can't you?'

He gave a helpless shrug.

'You are supposed to be in love,' he said diffidently. 'That was your challenge,' he added quickly.

'Yes, as I said, it's a test,' she said impatiently. 'How long does it take for your arrow to affect one?'

'Almost immediately,' he affirmed.

'Have you done it?'

'I am not supposed to reveal,' he said obliquely. 'The target shall start feeling the effect slowly but surely.'

'You seem sure,' she frowned.

'I am,' he admitted. 'As the way you are, you won't succumb to my arrow,' he observed shrewdly.

Her brows cleared. '*That* is the challenge,' she said softly.

It was his turn to become enquiring.

'You are testing my powers or the power of love?' he asked, emboldened.

'Rather your capability of making people fall in love,' she retorted. 'Neither do I believe in it! Love is not logical—neither is what you are doing.' Her tone was flat and final, more to convince herself.

'Because you think with your mind and not feel with your heart,' said Kama quietly.

She nodded, not taking offence at his bluntness. 'You were created for the heart, I have been made for the mind,' she remarked with her customary half-smile, cryptic and mocking. 'The mind is not supposed to fall in love.'

'Not like this, yes,' he conceded. 'But you relished the challenge.'

'Feeling nothing is easy,' she observed. 'Emotions were never a problem for me. But as it goes, now the test is between the mind and the heart; let's see if your arrow works on me?'

Kama stiffened.

'I am confident, it will work!' he said. 'If I could make Brahma . . .' he cut off abruptly. 'I am sorry if you doubt my ability,' he said tautly. 'But, if you ask me, you are either obstinate or don't want to admit it,' he said in a gush, smiling and hoping it would cushion the truth in his words. His smile expanded engagingly. 'No one can be immune to it! Even Ganga believes in me.'

'And she's suffering for it!' she scoffed.

'Ganga is suffering not because she is in love but because of . . .' Kama bristled, halting abruptly.

'Yes?' she prompted.

'Because of Brahma,' he finished stiltedly.

Sarasvati narrowed her eyes. 'You don't like Brahma, do you?' she asked.

'I don't approve of how he punished Ganga,' said Kama shortly.

'And yet you insist I return his feelings,' she returned, tapping her chin thoughtfully.

'No, that is what you are challenging,' he corrected. 'I would rather make him know what the pain and pangs of love are!' he succeeded in making it sound offhand. 'To make him a less tough person.'

'You presume you succeeded by making him fall in love?' she asked, her eyes going remote.

Kama nodded his head and looked at her, unsurprised at the sharpness of her tone. 'Yes. But the more you resist him, the more he will writhe in the throes of love!'

Sarasvati bit her lip, appalled at the vicious glee in his voice.

'You are resentful of Brahma outing a curse on you, but Kama, one day, you shall pay for your thoughtless deeds,' she warned severely. 'You are recklessly playing with everyone's emotions!'

'Brahma did the same, or the lack of it, rather,' retorted Kama. 'Should he too not pay for what he did?'

'Is this your revenge?'

'It is justice,' Kama said stubbornly.

'Revenge can never be justice,' she said quietly. 'And justice for whom?'

'For Ganga and all those he created, forgetting that through me, he created love too,' said Kama with a rush of anger.

'Is it your resentment speaking or your dislike for him?'
she asked astutely. 'I repeat, I have a strong suspicion that
you don't like Brahma very much.'

'I respect him,' returned Kama shortly. 'He has brains
and character and that is a very unusual combination. It is
just that, he's not, er, very amiable . . . He hasn't been nice
to me at all!'

'Nor have you been to him,' she found herself strangely
defending Brahma. 'You fooled him, and not unsurprisingly,
he did not take it too kindly. And in retrospect, I haven't
been very nice to you either,' she added tolerantly.

Kama shook his head vigorously. 'You have been, you
have helped me! You are not unkind.'

Glancing at her, Kama got the impression she was far
from being petty, largely from the dignity of her bearing
and the friendly matter-of-factness on her pleasant face.
This was a woman whose intelligence and grace had grown
with insight and perception, earning her a rare sagacity.
The most striking thing about her was her sense of fairness,
equalled by the air of authority, tempered by her innate
compassion. To be obeyed was natural to her, but she
accepted obedience with humility; sometimes impatience,
but never arrogance. He knew that she was deeply conscious
of the authority of Brahma.

Kama concluded that notwithstanding her austere
demeanour, Sarasvati had a certain kind frailty, an
empathetic tolerance. But today, she seemed strange.
There was a lost look on her smooth, pale face, her eyes
seemed smudged.

'You presume to know us well,' she commented drily.

'I am not presuming; I am being frank about my observations, if I have your permission to express so,' he said politely.

Curious, she gave a brief nod.

'Both of you intrigue me, especially when together,' he stated with a quick smile, his green eyes contracting as he studied her. 'I wonder how the two of you behave when you are alone . . . oh, and I am not being flippant,' he assured quickly. 'But when the others are there, both of you are seen acting—and acting quite badly, I must say . . .'

'What do you mean?' she said tightly, her smile static, trying to keep up a pretence of frivolity.

'Both of you are in love—yet you have a different way of showing it, or rather, concealing it. Both of you don't look at each other, yet steal glances. When he speaks to you, it sounds as though it were not his voice but somebody else's!'

For a moment, she looked away. She did not mean to let Kama see that anything he said affected her.

'That's not a very reasonable observation,' she said lightly.

'Yes, but it is the right one.'

She waited for him to go on, fearful of what he was about to say, for she had a fair idea of his shrewdness and that he never hesitated to speak his mind.

'I don't think for a moment that you are not in love with Brahma . . .' he said, his emerald eyes warming. ' . . . Or, he is not with you, though he isn't expansive with you these days. You pretend to be indifferent to him, but I am quite sure the feelings you have are much stronger than friendship, the preferred explanation you have for your relationship with him. It *is love!*'

'You are wrong,' she said in a low, hard voice.

Kama raised a brow. 'I am not. I am being frank. I have asked myself if you're both playing the game of pretence. I don't know if you fill him with such strong emotions that he avoids being near you or if you are burning with a love that for some reason you will not allow yourself to show!'

Sarasvati rose, her face ashen, her shoulders straight, her chin raised.

'I think you are attaching too much importance to yourself and . . . love,' she disdained him. 'As I said earlier, you sadly see yourself myopically,' she paused to softly quote:

> '*In the beginning there was Kama*
> *Desire that was first seed of Mind.*'

'That's from the Rig Veda's *Nasadiya Sukta*, the Hymn of Creation, where Brahma defines the *ekam* spirit, the essence of oneness,' observed Kama, comprehending another reason for his existence.

'So you are not all love, but mind too,' she reminded him gently. 'That is why I involved you in the making of this art gallery—the invitation for the launch of which you just handed to me,' she tapped the invite in her hand. 'I hope you take this more seriously than your more amorous image which you so love!' she cautioned, turning pointedly to her books again.

Kama knew it was a sign for him to leave, as he gazed at her reflectively with his sarcasm-filled bright, green eyes, with a shadow of an expression of singular respect.

'I realize what I need to do,' he nodded gravely. 'If I am mind as well as love, then, Lady, if I may say so, you too are not all mind, but love as well,' he quipped, watching the flush mount on her face and with a deep bow and a twinkle in his emerald eyes, he walked out of the library, a spring in his step.

Long after Kama left, his words followed her through the day and the next. She did not know how long she tossed in the screaming silence Kama had left behind. His departing words had been troubling. She wished Ganga was here to help her sort out the confusion, the tumble of emotions clashing with her thoughts, sense conflicting with sensibility and reason with reasoning . . . She felt herself flushing her gaze blank, hands clasped tightly, her heart and mind had never felt so heavy and breathless . . .

'You are looking unusually lost!' laughed a deep voice behind her.

She jumped, her eyes widening in recognition: he always caught her unawares. Brahma nonchalantly leaned against the doorway, observing her looking listlessly away from her books.

'Ganga was your close friend, you are going to miss her,' he remarked, observing her white, unhappy face, small and stark against the dark crowning glory of her flowing mane.

He thought she was missing Ganga, she thought with relief. But his unyielding voice irrationally irked her, her eyes flaring. It was because of *him* that Ganga had gone away, it was because of *him* that she was so dismal; it was because of *him* that she was so lost . . .

'. . . And don't blame it on me,' he added blandly, reading her thoughts. 'She is in a happier place. Unlike you. You seem unhappy,' he said silkily.

Kama's words came back to her in a rush and Sarasvati forced a smile: she was being unfairly sullen, unfair to him too.

'Yes, you are right, I am missing her more than I realized and it's no use being churlish about it,' she said edgily, tugging at a loose wisp of hair to coil it around her finger. He was immediately captivated.

'But I have Yamuna.'

His tone softened. 'So I noticed. The three of you seem to have become thick friends!'

He crossed his muscular arms across his chest, a gesture he employed when he wanted to deliberate vocally. 'Ganga, Yamuna and Sarasvati are sisters as well. You are prayed, worshipped and uttered in one breath,' he chuckled, a swathe of hair falling on his wide forehead. It was oddly distracting.

'You seem to be in a very good mood, oddly,' she remarked drily.

He laughed. He laughed rarely but he had the most infectious laugh she had ever heard. And she delighted in it. She was relieved and thankful they were friends again; it mattered so much to her. Her heart began to beat fast.

'*You love him, but are too proud and a fool not to admit it*,' she recalled Ganga's words, resounding loudly over her thumping heart.

'. . . *You are burning with a love that for some reason you will not allow yourself to acknowledge or accept or show!*' Kama's words taunted her again.

Was being happy in his company being in love with him? Was feeling the hot blood move when he looked at her so tenderly, being in love with him? Was feeling the blush of shyness at his words of praise being in love? Was seeing the glint of respect and admiration in his eyes being in love? Was sharing intense moments with him being in love?

During these recent evenings with him, she found herself oddly conflicted again; her confusion over her mixed feelings for him growing to a degree that she had to exert a great deal of control not to show her emotions.

He hid his feelings well and did nothing to encourage her. He treated her as a friend whom he liked, nothing more, expressing less.

She looked up and saw he was watching her. She smiled uneasily, unsure of her emotions. She kept telling herself that she should stop having such treacherous thoughts before they got out of hand. Kama's warning was not helping her either, she thought crossly. She tried to convince herself fiercely that as long as she wasn't falling in love with him, there surely could be no harm in continuing their work and friendship. But . . .

Brahma strolled towards the window, glancing at the sailing clouds outside. 'Yes, I am very happy today. I just completed the concept of Maya in the process of creation . . .'

'Reality and illusion,' she murmured.

He nodded. 'But why are you so glum, does not the new gallery excite you enough?' he quizzed, frowning in concern. 'It was your concept, after all. And, Vishwakarma has been the most deferential architect, adhering to all your advice and instructions in building a unique structure to house paintings, sculpture and other designs.'

'Yes, Kama mentioned . . .' she muttered.

'He was here?' he demanded snappily, his tone making her look sharply at him. His smile slipped, eyes grave again. *The animosity seems to be mutual.*

'He had come here a few days ago to formally invite me to the inauguration,' she said coolly, trying to change his mood and subject, noticing his dark scowl. 'I am sure the gallery will be the most elaborate piece of architecture we have ever seen! Vishwakarma is a known genius.'

'Yes, that's what this fancy invitation informs us,' he said, waving the scroll at her. 'Vishwakarma likes doing things in style: and if the invite is anything to go by, I expect more with the actual gallery,' he nodded, with a wry shake of his handsome head. 'Each time he surpasses himself!'

She smiled, relieved seeing his mood improved. 'We should go and see it, shouldn't we?'

Just for a brief second, he thought he had not heard her correctly. There was something in her voice that suddenly stirred his blood. It sounded so marvellous, he thought he was in Heaven.

12

THE BATTLE

Sarasvati felt unusually elated when Brahma came to pick her up on the day of the grand opening of the art museum.

Dot at the scheduled hour that late afternoon, she saw him pulling up outside her tall gates. He was on time for once, she smiled in genuine amusement. He was standing in the shadows of the tall trees, waiting for her. As he came out of the shade and into the hard light of the sun, she saw the spark of appreciation lighting up his eyes on his impassive face. Her sari looked like sea water sifted over with gold dust, her long hair was taken back by a narrow chain of pearls, sinuously coiling down her back in a soft swirl. She had taken his breath away and she felt improbably ecstatic with her new power over him.

Brahma escorted her to the art gallery. It was as magnificent as she had imagined: all white and elegant in glistening marble, it was an imposing, domed mansion perched on a sprawling knoll. It had tall, fat white columns and dormer windows lining the extensive inside hall, which was intercepted by pieces of sculpture and art along the way. They went along almost a mile of hallway. At the end, it broadened into a huge sunroom. The far side of the sunroom opened into a wide doorway and they stepped past it into an oval room with polished, endless floors and a high-domed, open skylight.

'I like art. But I love the artists,' remarked Sarasvati as they strolled down the aisle, inspecting each piece closely. 'I love the stories behind their work. The characters. The imagination. Their power of invention. The courage to create.'

'Especially when they are defying rules, upsetting established norms and even the establishment?' Brahma commented wryly. 'I know you like the rebels.'

'Yes, there is bravery in free thought; art is the artists' weapon,' she nodded. 'Dissent is not being disloyal. An artist's mission should be to speak and speak out. Art is his canvas of expression, often boldly revealing, exposing themselves to our keen observation and insight. Our scrutiny.'

He glanced down at her. 'Hmm, yes, it is a marvellous feat,' he said in concurrence, taking her elbows in his hands and drawing her a little closer to him. She did not resist. 'But not when it is self-indulgent or petulant; like a tantrum from a child. It becomes immature, childish in its belief and vain in character.'

'What is it that you feel so compelled to say?' she asked, surprised, sensing in him a certain cynicism.

'Wisdom is wasted on the old,' he sighed. 'All you can do is part with it but very few will take it; least of all, the people closest to you. They want no part of it.'

She frowned, wondering whom he meant but before she could voice her question, she was distracted by a row of portraits placed along the long, broad corridor, with miniatures of gods and goddesses on each side. The first portrait that greeted them was one of the Trimurti—Brahma, Vishnu and Shiva. 'The Tridev,' she murmured, leaning forward to take a closer look.

He looked down at the bent, glossy head, inhaling the scent of her hair.

'And hopefully, one day there shall be a painting of the Tridevi too: You with Lakshmi and Parvati, the consorts of the Trinity,' interrupted a jolly voice.

Sarasvati gasped, whirling around at the impertinence, her hair swishing around in tousled confusion. Kama bowed but there was a knowing smirk on his face. Maybe there was something in her gasp that startled Brahma into quick anger. Brahma looked quickly at her, his face flushing against his dark skin and then glanced at the smiling deva and a painting of his which hung on the second row. He reached up to take it down and carefully placed it in the last row of the miniatures.

'That is where you are meant to be,' remarked Brahma, his thin lips curling in contempt. 'A deva who thinks he is way above his stature and manners.'

The smile slipped from Kama's frozen face, the colour seeping and draining away.

There was a dull silence, the other visitors halting at the ringing words echoing through the columned corridor.

'That is an insult,' Kama whispered hoarsely.

'It was meant to be,' said Brahma curtly. 'You should be apologizing, not complaining.'

'I was simply expanding on what the Devi commented. And that challenge she imposed . . .' reminded Kama sneakily, his green eyes bright with anger. 'She would need my help,' he added nastily.

Sarasvati inhaled a deep breath. 'This has gone far enough, Kama!' she said sharply.

Kama gave an elaborate bow. 'I was merely jesting, pardon me! I presumed you would return the jest with similar wit.'

'It is not a matter of mirth, Kama,' warned Brahma, his eyes smouldering. 'I have cautioned you before.'

'And I know my duties,' returned Kama silkily. 'I am merely obeying *your* instructions—of spreading love.'

Brahma made a sudden movement. Kama flinched but Brahma had stretched forward to reach up and pull down Kama's painting and throwing it down. The miniature clattered unceremoniously on the cold, marble floor.

'I think we have seen and heard everything we need to,' said Brahma, his voice hard. 'Shall we leave, Sarasvati?'

Kama's face was as pale as the white marble. 'But not before I meant what I said,' he announced and, with a swift, smooth movement, he brandished an arrow from his bow. 'I have done my work as you had commanded me to do!' mocked Kama with an unsteady laugh. 'The spell is bound to work, courtesy of your blessings, O Brahma! In your own land, in your Brahmalok, I, with my five-flowered arrow, my Kama-bana, have already created an untimely spring to awaken love and longing!'

Sarasvati felt the hot wave of colour sweeping over her; more of annoyance at Kama's impudence.

Brahma's face suffused with hot anger. *No, no*, he was going to curse the foolish deva, she thought in quick panic and she suddenly put her hands on his arms and gripped his muscles tightly. Her strong fingers hurt. Feeling his flesh on hers made her feel light-headed, swamped by a sudden hot flood of inexplicable emotion.

She saw him hesitate for a brief moment. At the back of her churning mind, she knew this could be dangerous. He looked down at her restraining grasp, his own hands balled in fists, the knuckles white. He stood there, breathing unevenly and quickly, watching her, his eyes burning.

Kama's words hung as menacingly as the angry deva himself, as he stormed out of the gallery.

Brahma stood motionless, his hands damp and clenched, his heart beating fast while he stared at the vast expanse of sand, sea and trees across the marbled entrance. In the hard light of the sun, the beach was lit up for miles. The sudden stillness was so deep that it seemed there was no sign of anyone: no celestial visitors, no devas, nothing. They might have been the only two people left in the world.

'Do you want to risk it?' he asked, his voice suddenly harsh.

'Risk what?' she said shakily, collecting her angavastra closer to her and with the other hand sweeping her hair off her shoulder to expose the slim curve of her neck. He felt his throat constrict.

'Risk your heart, your reputation, your everything like you did now?' he said thickly. 'Would you mind, if everyone found out?'

She felt an unfamiliar pang: was it fear or something else? The sunlight was directly on her face. She showed her surprise.

He stood like a stone man, his hands gripping hard.

'I don't understand,' she leaned forward and stared at him. 'You are still angry with Kama, I don't like it!'

'Why don't you like it?' he barked, suddenly furious. 'What's the matter with facing facts? You're a mature, clever woman, aren't you? You're not naive. You must know what I feel about you and more importantly, what you feel about me! Or do you still delude yourself that you don't know?'

She flinched back, her expression changing to shocked anger.

He leaned forward to stare at her.

'Are you in love with me, Sarasvati?'

She stiffened, that same knot of tension slowly uncoiling. 'In love with you? Why, no. You know I am not! I told you so. What are you saying—and here?!' she looked around her, suddenly conscious of where they were. Mercifully, most had drifted away in fear of Brahma's wrath. 'Let's go home, we can talk . . .'

The black bile of disappointment made him a little wild.

'Then why do you keep coming back to me?'

'Please don't,' she said, in a desperate sort of way. 'I couldn't bear to quarrel with you again,' she faltered.

'You don't understand. You don't know how unsure I am,' she muttered under her breath.

'Why do you keep denying? For how long?'

'You assume too easily!' she snapped, looking up at him in cold anger.

'But I want you to understand,' he began, but she turned sharply away from him.

'You've done quite enough already,' she said stonily, her back stiff and straight, her thick hair forming a curtain, hiding her face from him.

Brahma suddenly felt a hot surge of anger. He put his hand on her arm and jerked her round, the curls tumbling over her face. He felt a mad urge to touch them. 'You've got to listen to me,' he said, angrily. 'You've always thought the worst of me, of us. Well, it's time you knew better!'

'And you know better?' her lips curled, her voice dripping ice.

Brahma stood very still, looking at her. He smiled suddenly; it wasn't a pleasant smile.

'What the hell does it matter?' he said. 'Think what you like. I was foolish enough to fall for you. You know it, you feel it. It doesn't hurt you as it hurts me. It is destroying me. But does it make you feel good each time I confess? You're the one woman that has ever meant anything to me. Don't ask me why. I don't know. We've fought ever since we met, but I'm still mad over you and I'll always be consumed about you. But you've always played it cool and you think you like being safe and distant, fearing and fearful all the time . . .'

'You don't know me at all!' she said fiercely, her face white and eyes blazing.

He felt the flare of anger dying and he flung her hands away in self-contempt. 'I can't go on like this,' he said, his eyes tortured. 'I've been waiting and waiting and I never seem to get anywhere. You either love me or you don't. If you don't, then perhaps we'd better not meet any more. *Ever.*'

Fury fled as fear clutched her. *No, not again!* She couldn't *not* meet him any more.

'Of course, I love you,' she cried violently, her hands spread wide in silent appeal. 'I do but I can't . . .' she stopped abruptly, her voice softening. She wanted to laugh now, to make some light cool remark that would bring the situation back into the safe waters of a casual flirtation. But it was too late now.

He stood still, his face ashen.

Words and sentiment rushed out in a stream of passion. 'I think you're a kind, brilliant person and please don't talk about not meeting any more!' she chattered incoherently.

'You love me?' he said carrying an incredulous look. 'You are tossing it so wildly?' he persisted, frowning at her.

'Don't look like this! In another minute, we'll be strangers.' She put her cool hand in his and held it tightly. His blood on fire, Brahma gripped her hand.

'Oh, I do love you, but don't rush me,' she cried. 'I'm so unsure. I don't know where I am going and I don't ever want to hurt you. Don't you see? It's because I don't ever want to hurt you that I hesitate . . . oh, leave it!'

She drew her hand away, standing very still, holding on to the banister rail and not looking at him. She felt weak and her heart hammered against her ribs. 'I don't want to talk about it,' she said, stubbornly.

Brahma lifted his heavy shoulders in a despairing shrug. He wanted to make her see some sense, but he knew her pride and her denial of her own emotions had been partly the cause of their current tension. He had turned her into a muddle of confusion and shrill fury, venting her bewilderment on him. He guessed he was not helping either: he was losing his patience, exasperation setting in.

'That won't get us anywhere,' he returned, watching her and feeling the thickness in his throat again. 'You hesitate, you waver, or are you forever going to be unsure?'

Colour rushed to her face. 'It suits you to talk like that, doesn't it?' she said, ferociously, tucking an errant wisp. 'Why don't you leave me alone? You trouble me, and you'll get yourself into more trouble. I've seen this coming from the start! I don't belong to your world.'

'Nonsense! You are my world, you are part of the world we created together!' he sputtered in indignation.

'Oh, not that world, the world of the two of us—we are perfectly imperfect for each other! I don't want to be your wife; I would hate to be known as Brahma's wife. I am *me*, Sarasvati!' she cried.

'Yes, you are Sarasvati, more in love with herself than others, proud and vain!' His face went cold. 'So, is that it? Just a tussle of ego?' his tone was stony.

'Don't you dare call me an egotist. You're hard and insensitive and you don't care what happens. Oh, I hate you for getting me into this!' she cried, lifting her thick hair off her shoulders with a movement that hinted oddly of despair.

He was so surprised by the suddenness of this attack; he remained motionless, staring at her. White-faced, he stepped up to her and held her, clasping her arms in his hands.

'You're a stubborn little fool,' he said, curtly. 'You won't see that this has nothing to do with me, but it's all about *you*!'

She struggled away, her face on fire. 'Fool? *You* have been foolish all this while! And don't dare speak to me like that—patronizing as always!' she said. 'Oh, go away!'

'Then, why do you force yourself on me?' he demanded, his voice rising. 'What do you imagine I am? Do you think I'm made of stone?!' he shouted, shaking her.

'Stop this, Brahma!' a voice cracked through the tense air.

It was Shiva, his face as dark as the thunderous look on Brahma's face.

'I'm not made of stone, I have feelings!' Brahma repeated, roaring, the blood hammering in his temples.

'And this is no way to address a lady—or the issue,' snapped Shiva. 'Go home, Brahma.'

Shiva bowed to Sarasvati. She looked stunned. Shiva saw her, standing pale and trembling. She wasn't looking too happy, he thought uneasily. He didn't like the way her quivering lips compressed and how her face looked so pallid. Shiva had never seen her in a mood like this before.

It made him perturbed. Usually, she was so self-possessed and confident.

Shiva said, his tone polite but firm. 'I shall take you home . . .'

'No, you won't!' Brahma broke in furiously. 'I got her here and I shall see to it that she safely returns to her palace.'

'You are in no state to handle this,' warned Shiva. 'Step back, Brahma, let's not make a scene.'

'We were having a conversation, a discussion,' said Brahma. '*You* intervened.'

'Your voice was raised, you were shouting! You were harassing her, Brahma! This is a public place.'

'And we had selected a quiet corner,' Brahma reminded Shiva stiffly, lifting frosty eyes.

'It's not a quiet corner any more!' growled Shiva. 'Everyone can see you are having an argument with the lady. You are pursuing her!'

'I am not! And if I was, I think this lady particularly can let me know herself,' said Brahma, his tone rudely dismissive.

Shiva's face darkened to a dull red. '*I* am saying it, you *are* pestering her!'

Brahma glanced at Sarasvati with a hard, ironic smile, his lips twisted. She was looking embarrassed and angry.

'Don't interfere, Shiva! This is between the two of us. Leave us!'

'No, Brahma, I shall not allow you to bother her further. You have chased her enough—you are a laughing stock, you have well made a complete fool of yourself and worse, harried the lady! You are nothing but a nuisance!'

And that was when Sarasvati realized to what level his desperation had brought Brahma down to this situation of shame. Yes, Kama had had his revenge: he had completely stripped Brahma of his pride, dignity and deference.

Sarasvati felt a sliver of agony slice through her: had she brought him down to such a level? Watching the two angry men glowering at each other, she saw two friends turned into two opponents, battling each other. Shiva, she dismally realized, was taking the form of Rudra, the feared, fierce warrior in full fury whose energy could reduce the opponent to ashes in a matter of seconds. Brahma stood facing him, still and stolid, his eyes flashing, getting more tenacious by the moment. And then Shiva attacked him, the full form of his Rudra avatar striking . . . *But Brahma is unarmed*, screamed her mind in alarm.

She watched transfixed: the two men were desperately grappling figures now. The entrance pathway was deserted, and except for their short, tired gasps and the padded sound when one of them slipped on the dusty hard ground, they fought in silence, clearly defined to each other by the waning sunlight as well as by the amber glow that shone out of the open doorway of the gallery. Several times, they both slipped down together, and then for a while the conflict threshed about wildly on the gravel of the courtyard. For stretched, endless minutes, they fought there senselessly in the darkening light. Both were torn and bleeding and so exhausted that they could stand only when by their position they mutually supported each other—the impact, the mere effort of a blow, would send them both to their hands and knees.

Stop. She screamed, her lips moved but no sound issued.

Absorbed in the great fight, she brooded, she must be out of her mind to allow herself to witness this madness. Against the clatter of their scuffle again and again, she saw Brahma's hurt look of startled surprise when he had asked her if she loved him, and each time, she heard her reply: the refusal kept hammering in her mind.

Sarasvati shook her head in confused despair, lifting her shoulders wearily, her face crumpling. And then, a terrible cry tore the sky. It had come from Shiva's throat. She watched him in horror. He was now Bhairav, a figure of terror, his eyes flaming scarlet, he howled as he leaped upon Brahma and with his sharp claws, pulled off Brahma's head. She again screamed without any sound coming from her throat.

One of Brahma's severed heads hung from Shiva's bloodied hand: it seemed to burn him. As it seared through his flesh and clung to his hand, it sapped him of all his strength, driving him mad. Shiva, writhing in agony, ranted wildly.

'*Stop!!!* I say halt this madness!' she charged, sharp and loud, her command forcing the warring men to break apart, a menacing silence hanging taut between them.

Sarasvati rushed towards Shiva, who was fast losing control of his senses. She placed her hands on his scorching skin, slowly cooling him, nursing him back to sanity.

She turned to look at Brahma. His face was haggard, reeling under the shock, but sobered by his encounter with Bhairav, the Lord of Terror.

Shiva said weakly. 'Brahma, you have now escaped from the maze of your own desire. Sarasvati here revealed to you your own liberation.'

Sarasvati clenched her fists and her mouth set in a hard line. 'Allow me to let both of you know this: both of you erred,' she said without raising her voice. 'If Brahma is besotted, you, Shiva, instead of showing him reason, you lost control too in your fit of rage, striking a weaponless man!'

Shiva swallowed convulsively. It was true: in his ferocity, he had resorted to mindless rage, morphing to his dreaded form of Rudra and then to Bhairav, ready to burn, willing to kill . . . he looked horrified at the dawning realization: what was he thinking of, what had he done?

Shiva looked at Sarasvati in dismay.

'Meditate to the Supreme Mother, Adi Parashakti, to rescue both of you,' she commanded softly, throwing both the distinctly uncomfortable men a withering look. 'She will appear in form of Kshama, forgiving Brahma to spare his senses and his four heads, the fifth head of lust, which Shiva you just destroyed in your terrible wrath.'

Brahma looked startled, as did Shiva. In their combat, Shiva had decapitated one head.

She turned to Shiva.

'You didn't even realize it, did you?' she asked in her characteristic enquiring manner. 'That is what anger makes you do; lose sense, reason and recollection. Shiva, like Brahma, you too shall have to pay for this altercation,' she warned quietly. 'Every act has a consequence.'

Shiva bowed. 'In my wrath, I tried to kill Brahma, that is my offence.'

'Your Bhairav roop needs to be tamed,' she said, her tone softening. 'Bhikshatana shall be the gentler form of the gruesome Bhairav, who decapitated Brahma's fifth head.'

'I shall atone,' decided Shiva willingly.

Brahma swiftly intervened. 'It was not his fault, Sarasvati. It was me who went berserk with my passion . . .'

'Yes, you did and *you* will need to penance through the harshest meditation,' she reminded him cuttingly.

But the way she said it and the manner in which she was looking at Brahma, Shiva knew something was amiss.

The thought at last entered his head that Brahma meant something to her. Shiva remembered how quiet she had been all through: it was not unease; it was her struggle with her emotions she was forcing herself to acknowledge. He remembered her embarrassment each time anyone baited her about him. He remembered her look of disappointment at Brahma's absence at the gandharva concert. And remembering all these little points and knowing the strength of Brahma, Shiva's mind opened to a new fact. When he came to think of it, he could see Sarasvati with Brahma. They would look right. They were both determined, both original, both unconventional, both exceptional at their work, both ambitious, both in love.

Her words had affected Brahma deeply, as expected.

Brahma exhaled sharply. 'Yes, I shall atone too. I shall first practise austere meditation and then perform the divine *mahayajna* to purify myself. Only then can I continue with works of creation,' he shook his handsome head ruefully, bowing in remorse.

Sarasvati appeared resolute.

Shiva gave a cryptic smile. 'Brahma, to perform the mahayajna, you shall need a partner . . . er, a wife to sit with you,' he said, his words clearly leading.

Brahma looked baffled, his eyes uncertain.

Sarasvati was quick to comprehend. 'Shiva, if he so wishes he can execute the yajna all by himself, he does not need a wife or a partner to perform it,' she said pleasantly.

Shiva shook his head, his face serene. 'I hope *you* have learnt your lesson too, Sarasvati. Brahma is the Creator God. He created the world. When he created it, he looked around and found himself alone and looking for answers. In his quest for answers, he created you, Sarasvati. But then he got so attracted to you, the creator with his creation. But there is a metaphysical element to it. It symbolizes the male half—that is the inner reality—conjoined with the female half or the *prakriti*, the outside world. Brahma is the creator, Sarasvati the creation. A creator often gets proud and possessive of his creation. That is his love and pride speaking. But he has to get the better of his desire and realize the purpose of creation. So, now me as Rudra had to pin down Brahma to guide him likewise.'

Sarasvati folded her hands to Shiva. 'You are the mindfulness who alone could control the wandering mind.'

'Yet, killing is no solution,' she affirmed, her dark, velvety eyes fixed on him. 'So, your penance will be more severe, Shiva. You will have to undertake the Kapali vow, to roam about the three worlds, with a beggar's bowl in hand, till you are rid of the sin of rage.'

Brahma made a movement of protest, shaking his head weakly. His pained eyes moved from his friend's to

Sarasvati's: she stood grim, the unsmiling twist didn't leave the corners of her lips. Her eyes didn't change.

Shiva bestowed a serene smile. 'So be it.'

Sarasvati thawed, returning the smile. 'And I thank you for bringing Brahma to his senses. And coming to my aid,' she added wryly. 'But I did not need to be rescued, for which you committed this crime in your zeal.'

Shiva nodded. 'Yes, I can see that now,' he said amiably. 'I reacted and in my ungovernable rage, I chopped off Brahma's head. It is this head I shall use as a pot for begging for alms to remind me and others of my offence.'

'Therefore, you shall be known as Kapali—skull carrier—because you change the unworthy to worthy, the evil to good,' said Sarasvati. 'The skull in your hands, Shiva, shall be full of nectar, sustaining life.'

Shiva bowed again. 'I shall leave as soon as matters are done here,' he said cryptically, throwing his friend a knowing, but a faintly amused glance. Turning on his heels, Shiva strode out of the courtyard. Watching his receding figure, Sarasvati suddenly felt drained, the enormity of the event hitting her.

'Please, I want to go home,' she said wearily. 'I feel so low I don't know what to do. Take me home, Brahma.'

Brahma stood stiff and dangerously still, like a tall tree about to be felled. He stood hesitating, feeling that he wanted to take her in his arms and comfort her, but scared that he might make things worse.

She gave a little shiver as she climbed the chariot. 'Let's go now, please Brahma.'

'You're tired. I'll take you home. A good sleep's what you want.' He wanted to put his arm around her, but he still wasn't sure.

She looked up at him as he climbed and sat by her side, her eyes smudged with an undecipherable emotion.

'I am responsible for this battle between the two of you. How can the Creator and the Destroyer ever be in combat?' she cried in obvious distress.

Brahma moved, a swathe falling forward as he gently took her clenched fists in his hands. 'No, it was because of me, not you,' he said slowly, shaking his head. 'My love made me lose reason, confining consciousness and exciting the ego. It disturbed the serenity of the cosmos which roused the supreme ascetic—Shiva—from his meditation, forcing him to open his eyes in wrath,' he gave a rueful sigh. 'Sensing your discomfort, he flew into a fit of rage and turned into the terrible Bhairav. *I* made him do that!' he cried hoarsely with raw remorse in his tone.

The abject misery on his face made her melt.

'It *was* terrifying what occurred just now,' she whispered, pushing back the errant lock of hair from his forehead. It was an oddly tender gesture. 'His eyes had gone red, his growl was menacing, I couldn't move!' she recalled with a slight shudder. 'When he lunged towards you with his sharp claws and wrenched off your head . . . I . . . it was horrific! I thought I had lost you!'

His hand clenched in his lap. 'Never,' he vowed.

A short silence fell between them. She twisted in the seat, so that her shoulder and head were against him. They sat together in the chariot, overcome by each other's presence, beyond all except fragmentary thoughts. Brahma felt that the first happiness of the meeting, the joy he had recognized so surely in her velvety, dark eyes back at the gallery, to be quickly dissipated by the violent intrusion of this battle, something that he had looked forward to, had been brutally lost, and he was brooding on this as he sat stiff next to her. Then his remorse faded as Sarasvati drew his hands in hers into a familiar hold under the dim light. Her emotion reassured him, promised his anxious heart that everything would be all right.

He gave a weak grin. 'I have been a fool. But Shiva's violence subdued my passion!'

'Hope it's not gone cold,' she said primly. 'Will you forgive me for . . . er, spoiling our evening?' Her dancing eyes twinkling up at him.

He lazily leaned back to give her his companionable smile, the lock again falling forward to make him look strangely vulnerable. 'You haven't. You've made me happy. Haven't you told me that you love me, though I still can't believe my ears!'

He looked suddenly unsure. 'You really do?' he questioned, almost fearfully.

She nodded.

He gave a sigh of exasperation, running his fingers through his hair. 'See, so cool and unruffled even after the storm! Characteristically, you declared it almost offhand . . .' He saw her bristle, adding quickly with a crooked smile. '. . . But frankly, I don't mind!'

Her clear, clever eyes clouded. 'You do believe me, don't you?'

'Of course, I do. But I don't know when you'll retract! I'm beginning to think you're a bit of a mercurial riddle I created!'

She gave a self-conscious laugh.

'No, I suppose I should not complain,' he sighed. 'Life would be very dull if I could get everything I wanted. But I want you, dearest, when you feel less low, I'm going to begin a siege. Now that I know how you feel about me, I'm going to pester you until you do marry me.'

'You won't need to take much effort on that,' she smiled pertly.

There was something in her voice that suddenly stirred his blood.

He put his hand on hers. 'You don't really mean that, do you?' he said, feeling his heart beating unevenly. 'Are you sure?'

'Again, you doubt! Of course!' she sighed, her eyes came up and looked into his. Hers had sparks in them.

'I shan't change my mind—or my opinion of you! You are arrogant, conceited and patronizing but I think I like you enough to love you,' she teased. 'You've been supremely patient,' she paused, lightly touching his face, gently pushing back his dark lock, her voice a warm whisper. For the first time he had known her and desired her, the velvety dark eyes were no longer remote. There was that sensual warmth that made his heartbeat quicken and turned his mouth dry.

'Will you marry me, Brahma?'

13

THE REQUEST

'Will you marry me, Brahma . . . ?'

Brahma looked genuinely startled, something he had never considered she would say. The words whirled in his spinning mind, disbelief and hope flaring in his eyes. He had always wanted to marry her, but she had been so determined to stay free: out of love, out of marriage. To be two separate entities side by side, not to be 'devoured', or 'overshadowed' or 'simply swallowed up by each other', as she had once harshly told him. She was as matter-of-fact and sure about this proposal as her earlier refusal. He knew her to be tremendously independent and she was capable of anything, any wild decision she had come to on her own and then decided must be important. But this, he thought frantically, his heart racing, was a shock.

'You *what?*' he breathed, his undertone hoarsely incredulous. 'After all the arguments and pleadings . . .' he shrugged helplessly. 'Are you sure?' he whispered, his baritone now husky.

'Is that going to be your favoured refrain?' Sarasvati pouted, shrugging her hair from her creamy shoulders. His eyes fixed on hers.

'Don't do that!' he said thickly, his hands trembling as they reached to touch her hair. She waited with bated breath. She felt his fingers twining in their thick softness, tingling and searching. They touched the nape of her neck.

'I am,' she whispered as he pulled her face close so he could see her, gazing straight at him. 'I just decided you might be right and it might be time.'

She had thought about it a lot and it was hard to admit to him that somewhere deep inside of her, there was suddenly a yearning to be his, to be part of him forever. She had thought that she was immune to love until Brahma had taken her hand. She knew she was not as hopelessly in love with him as he was, but at the same time, she knew that no other man mattered or would do for her.

'But are *you* sure?' she asked quietly, her eyes steady and so close to his that she could see her reflection in his.

'No,' she restrained his hand, clasping his broad wrist, as he started to protest. 'I know you love me but marriage goes beyond love,' she said gently. 'It's easier to love than stay married, is it not?'

'I don't know, I have never really tried it before!' he grinned broadly, giddy with happiness.

She rolled her eyes in mock exasperation.

He touched her cheek. 'But seriously, for a woman who did not believe in love, marriage is a big decision. Whatever made you think that?'

The question did not surprise her. Her dark velvety eyes stared at him.

'Just that I want to—now,' she looked non-committal and he smiled sketchily.

'No, I want to know,' he insisted, his eyes getting solemn. 'Why do you want to get married if you don't believe in it?'

She moved restlessly. 'I didn't. But I want to be more with you,' she said simply. 'Though to be together, does one need to wed?'

'Yes, it's a vow of commitment,' he said, sombrely.

She looked at him dubiously. 'But vows are shackling.'

'I know freedom and independence are cornerstones of your ideals,' he sighed.

'But in marriage?' she shook her dark head, the curls heaving around her small face.

The question was both reticent and impersonally sad. But this time, it did not depress him.

'You are afraid it might fetter you but it is possible to find and expand your freedom in marriage,' he affirmed. He was watching her narrowly, and was sure that she winced a little, that her eyes closed and then opened wide again. 'When we talk about freedom, we're talking about the ability to pursue happiness and our goals, to not be hindered by each other, by rules, by some undue pressure, and to together have a hopeful outlook for the future. So, in terms of our marriage, this kind of freedom is absolutely attainable,' he explained, his face equable.

'I know we will,' she answered, trying to put cheery faith into her voice. 'And in strong marriages—like

Shiva–Parvati   or   Lakshmi–Narayan—both   in   the
relationship offer each other support, to be the best person
they can be, and encourage one another to find and pursue
the things that lead to a fulfilling life. I frankly don't think
of freedom as something that has to happen individually,
that's why I am sceptical about marriage as it involves two
people—it is a dual relationship. With the support of a
loving partner, one can, ideally speaking, actually enjoy more
freedom, simply because you have another person watching
out for you, helping you overcome challenges, and there
to keep you steady when you stumble,' she threw him an
uncharacteristic affectionate look. 'I think you do that to
me—and we will be good together!'

His heart jumped. He knew what she meant—and
coming from her, it was huge. She was emotionally
scared that the prospect of marrying into a life of pledge
and commitment was putting too much strain upon
her love.

'There's a tremendous joy in providing that kind of
unwavering support for the person you love!' he said tenderly,
with a rush of emotion. 'There's nothing "shackling"
about vows and marriage. The pursuit of "freedom" is not
about lack of responsibilities or commitments. Instead,
it's about finding the things that resonate with you
personally, and having the time and ability to dedicate
yourself to the things most important to you. I will help
you do just that, and I know you will do the same for me!'

Her lips outlined a furtive smile. 'Hmm, yes, I do truly
connect with you, and the freedom I feel to be myself—case
in point, right now—to expose my vulnerable side, and to

share my biggest hopes and dreams is well . . . er, amazing!'
she declared with a self-conscious laugh.

Brahma broke into a hearty guffaw.

'You are either crazy. Or just too proud to admit it,' he
said, taking her in his arms. 'But I love you. I love you very,
very much, whether you marry me or not. Do you want
some more time to think?'

'You have been a patient man and you better not give
me much time,' she chuckled against his broad chest.
'I might change my mind!'

She felt him shake with laughter. 'I think it's because
women change their minds so often that they've got cleaner
ones than us men.'

She turned in his arms to pummel him lightly on his
chest. 'Chauvinist, but you are probably right!' she said and
laughed. 'We had better get it over with quickly!'

'No one could have made their own wedding sound so
painful and difficult!' he sighed with mock exaggeration.
'I promise I'll make it as easy as I can!' he returned her
banter with a wide grin, wildly ecstatic. 'Oh, I've never
been so happy in my life!' he breathed, inhaling deeply,
lifting her face to his. 'I hope we make each other happy.'

He sensed her stiffen against him. 'I am in love, yet I
still don't trust love,' she said simply, her eyes unfaltering.
'Nor marriage: or rather, the expectations from both.
I believe in being together with no impositions on each
other. Is that love? That is exactly what I want to clarify
before we commit ourselves.'

'I know.' *Your fears*, he thought and his tone was
soothing. 'I know your mind will always control your heart,

that's why you are sceptical about love. But love can come from the mind too. That's why and how I love you. And you me.'

She looked away. 'Would that be enough for you?'

'More than enough, I am not a greedy man,' he smiled engagingly. His eyes were serious. 'Sarasvati is bound to be wherever Brahma will be, and Brahma will be where Sarasvati will be: that's how we are married to each other,' he said solemnly, as if wording a vow. 'That's how Destiny defines us. We are inseparable from the beginning. You cannot leave me, nor can I ever live without you.'

He would have preferred a more private space than the chariot for this conversation, but he was in a sensitive mood and involuntarily, he plunged into the specific world he had intended but wanted to avoid.

She was silent a long time before she answered, not thinking—for she had seen the end—but only waiting, because she knew that every word would seem more honest than the last. Finally, she spoke, 'Brahma, I love you with all my heart, and I don't see how I can ever love anyone but you. The power and strength that people gain from happy, healthy relationships is virtually unparalleled, and represents a whole new kind of "independence"—it makes you feel like you've always got a reinforcement, a person in your corner, a supporter, and a place to turn for help. I see it in you, that's why I wish to marry you.'

She took a deep breath. 'But before I commit, I want to be completely honest with you.'

'You always have been,' he interrupted.

'I have never seen myself ever as a person in love, as a wife, but you made me lose my doubts and cynicism,' she said, staring down at her hands neatly folded in her lap. 'Looking after hearth and home are life skills, not gender roles. I don't think, honestly, that I can make a good wife—it is on your trust I faithfully follow,' she paused, biting her lips. 'But being a mother is not what I see for myself either. In fact, I don't want to have a child ever!'

She looked up to stare directly into his opaque eyes. He did not appear shocked as she had supposed.

All at once, her nerves gave way and she sprang to her feet.

'Oh Brahma, motherhood is a lifetime's commitment with no reprieve!' Her eyes turned earnest. 'There's nothing more profound and of long-lasting consequence than the decision and accountability of having a child.'

Brahma nodded. 'It is a responsibility you are not willing to accept. I understand and I agree,' he said solemnly. 'But parenthood is Nature—you shouldn't ask too many questions,' he said, his tone warm. 'Make it easier for yourself by accepting it, not escaping it.'

'*I* am accepting it: I don't want it! I am just not "womanly" enough to measure up to patriarchal hopes!' she said fiercely. She sank down on the seat as suddenly as she had risen. Brahma pulled her close and drawing her head down to his shoulder, began stroking her hair. The feel of her head against his shoulder, of her familiar body, sent a shock of emotion over him. His arms holding her had a tendency to tighten around her, so he leaned back and began to talk thoughtfully against the soft scent of her hair.

He murmured pacifyingly, 'But you, Sarasvati, you *are* nurturing, you are the mother of knowledge, music and the arts.'

She moved impatiently against him. 'You know what I mean, Brahma! The perversion and exploitation of that decision to have a child is complex and oh-so exacting. I do not aspire to beget a child! Nor do I want to be greedy and irresponsible for wanting to have one but not having the courage to carry out the responsibilities entailed,' she protested, jerking up suddenly. 'Why is everyone so anxious that a woman should have a baby? Is that how you made a woman by giving her the baby-bearing womb? Is that how you made Nature, Brahma?' she challenged.

He gave a short laugh but his face was grave. 'No. Nature gives every being a choice to live, exist and coexist—and eventually, it rests on the individual decision,' he said quietly.

'But with choices come decisions and then, complications,' she muttered wryly. 'With a burden of expectations and obligations; *that* is hard to fight. Why are women pressured into marriage and motherhood?'

'It's certainly not essential to rear kids in order to be happy together!' he shrugged. 'Just as it's certainly not essential to marry either in order to be happy together!'

She looked at him, suspicious at his sardonic tone.

'Or because Nature gave me a womb and breasts, do I need to create a child in that womb, and hold a baby to my breast?' she exhaled sharply. 'I don't want to be that woman who accepts motherhood as an obligation rather than a personal choice. I cannot be those who are too afraid and who live in the consolation that it was not the "right" thing to do as everyone but yourself expect so, and so, they would have children anyway and resent them—and themselves— all through their lives.'

Brahma put his hand on her arm. 'Oh my dear, this is what I meant when I said that in any strong relationship, both respect the other's wants and wishes, offering each other the support to be the best person they can be and encourage one another to find and pursue the things for a rewarding life!' he gave her a look that turned her heart over. 'In all the years that I have known you, I know you have not desired either marriage or motherhood.'

She made no comment and sat without moving, her eyes fixed on him with an expression that might have meant everything or nothing.

Eventually, she said softly, 'All that we create is our family too.'

He gave a brief nod. 'Yes, the world is our children. Most are not as clear and courageous as you are, Sarasvati; or so brutally self-honest. Because you are a person of certainty and convictions, you know you don't want children and you have built yourself and your life in such a way that it makes you happy and fulfilled. For most, marriage and motherhood mean fulfilment; but not for you,' he shrugged.

'But I had to clarify this before I committed to you,' she murmured. 'It's about us, not just me.'

'Again, that's your fairness speaking,' he said.

She looked quickly at him, but was reassured by his smile.

'It could be termed as selfishness?'

His face unperturbed, he shifted closer to her, his hand on her waist. 'No, it's choosing differently. I know and I know why,' he repeated, his tone strong. 'That is why I love you. I would never want to change you: you are my idea of perfection, why would I want to alter you or expect more than what I imagine you to be? You are my everything, Sarasvati, my thought, my desire, my vision. You are too free a spirit to be tied down with functions like wife and mother. It is not fair to you—and to me. I don't believe in misinterpretations, however grand.'

He leaned forward. 'I am being honest with you,' he said slowly. 'As you are now with me. I know you are contemptuous of people who limit themselves. And you hate, almost fear, the possibility that you may ever limit yourself, be leashed into a responsibility. That is why you are so scared of love and commitment. Of marriage and children and home. The world is your home, not the palace you live in. Your creativity and creations are the children you have begotten and you love them with that passionate, selfless love a mother has for her child. So, yes, Sarasvati, you are a mother,' he smiled gently. 'You are the mother of imagination, of music, of art, of the Vedas. And you are a wife, the keeper of my creative intelligence.'

Overwhelmed, she sat still, feeling exposed.

'You put it very admirably,' she murmured. 'I see myself simply as a person of faith and all that I do is an act of inventiveness—of what is possible for a person, for the whole world. If people can imagine something, there will come a day when they will achieve something.'

'Achieve what?'

'Whatever they propose to do—even love, kindness, ambition, work, goodness . . . keeping the dream alive: without paralysis of the will and thought by impositions and rules. You said I despise people limiting themselves. Yes, I do. This is why I dislike rules and rigidity: both constrain ideas, hardening beliefs to disallow further viewpoints. Both demand a certain obedience, almost subservient. But the cruelty and ugliness are too strong, mind you! So, it is not about me at all.'

'Just the stand you take,' he said helpfully.

'One must have faith—in oneself!' she concluded robustly.

'And for us now, what is there?'

'For now, I'd like to be married,' she returned jauntily. 'Oh, without the fanfare!'

He sighed, his fingers stroking the length of her bare arm, tingling every nerve of her exposed skin. 'But yes,' he said drily.

'You are Brahma, the world's Creator, and when you wed, you would have to invite all that you created—that means one and all!' she said in mock horror. 'I would rather have no one but you, and yes, a very, very close few.'

'Much obliged,' he exhaled, bowing his head, a dark swathe falling endearingly on his wide forehead.

She laughed, promptly pushing it aside, her fingers lingering. 'I know you don't want a big wedding either, though it's expected of you.'

He felt his blood move. 'No one expected me to fall in love either,' he chuckled throatily, his hands on her uncovered shoulder, the heat permeating swiftly through her porcelain skin. 'And now I am getting married! So, where will it be?'

'Our favourite place,' she said dreamily, her voice breathless. 'The woods.'

'Where we first met?' he muttered. She felt his large hands cupping her face.

She nodded, basking in the warmth of his touch. 'Under the open skies, embraced by the redolence of the perfume of flowers, swaying trees and chirping birds and the benign presence of animals as witness. You can throw some gods in too,' she added, with a twinkle in her dancing eyes.

'So be it,' he said gravely. 'Let's get married.'

He paused, lightly outlining the shape of her lips. 'I never imagined I would say these words . . . or rather hear *you* say them.'

'Believe it!' she ordered huskily. His trailing finger brushed her lips.

There was something utterly disarming about the fact that they were on the same sentimental plane. It made her helpless before the fate that had destined them together. With a long sigh, she leaned against him and he was conscious of a faint illusive perfume as they swayed gently together.

'I always believed luck to be a function of intent,' he chuckled.

She retorted with asperity. 'In this case, mine!'

He bent his head forward suddenly, and she drew herself to him in the same moment, her lips half open in a smile.

'Yes,' he whispered into her smile. 'Love and luck; my love, your luck and the world is ours . . .'

The world is ours—his life and hers, he thought as he pressed her close, sinking his face into the soft curve of her neck, till the muscles knotted on his arms, holding on to her as if she was something desirable and rare that he had fought for and made his own. But for an instant, as he drowned in the fragrance of her hair, in the heady sweetness of the moment, Brahma knew like the intangible whisper in the dusk, he had searched and finally sought her through eternity . . .

14

THE WEDDING

True to his word, Brahma had handled everything at their wedding. All Sarasvati had to do was don the vermilion red silk sari laid out by Yamuna. But that was easier said than done.

'This?!' Sarasvati looked aghast.

'It's a happy colour,' said Yamuna. 'You are a bride, Sarasvati, look like one. Just for today, it's your day after all,' she begged, noting the growing consternation on her friend's face.

'No!' Sarasvati was so disconcerted by the prospect of draping the scarlet sari with the gold and the gems that she almost walked out of the chamber, much to her friend's horror.

'You *have* to dress up!' wailed Yamuna after her. She caught hold of Sarasvati's wrist and thrust an extra gold bangle.

Watching her friend's mutinous expression, Yamuna grumbled, 'You are the most difficult bride to please—and pose!'

'If it's my day, as you claim, let me have the choice to wear what I want!' retorted Sarasvati.

Yamuna rolled her eyes. 'That would be either white or yellow.'

'What's wrong with those colours?' Sarasvati frowned.

'Brides don't frown,' Yamuna scolded. 'Fine, let's do it your way. Definitely not white, so yellow it is,' she sighed dolefully.

Sarasvati gave her a quick smile. 'Happy colour!' she twinkled. 'How about a sunny yellow?'

'I give up!' Yamuna snorted crossly. She gave a sharp cry of exasperation. Three maids came running. The room suddenly filled with vibrations of wild, startled din.

'Suhasini, the necklace!' ordered Yamuna. 'Mudra, the yellow and gold silk with the pure gold slippers. The big pearls too—all the pearls, the egg-diamond and the girdle with the topaz to match. Pradnya, send for a hairdresser on the run. Run a bath again—warm milk but with ice-cold almond cream. Suhasini, rush like lightening to Vishwakarma for more gold bangles and a heavier armlet before he leaves for the day! Find me a brooch, a pendant, a tiara or anything—it doesn't matter—with the wings of a swan . . . !

Before Sarasvati could protest, Yamuna was fumbling at the strings of the *kayabandh*, the sash to hold the shawl, *uttariya*, in place.

'Marigold!' Yamuna called after the maid, '. . . And yellow jasmine, for the love of heaven! Four dozen, so I can choose four.'

'For me?' Sarasvati asked hopefully. 'And since the wedding is in the woods, how about using flowers

rather than these hideous jewels?' she suggested weakly.
'Please!'

'No,' asserted Yamuna firmly. 'Marigolds are for dressing up the venue, which, again, Vishwakarma has arranged, not you! Some flowers you may prettify yourself with, but you have to wear some of these jewels . . . .'

'Some? These are heaps!' Sarasvati exclaimed in dismay.

Under Yamuna's orders, the maids flew about the room like frightened birds. 'Perfume, Mudra. Open the perfume trunk and get that golden-brocaded uttariya, and the diamond nose stud, and the sweet oil for the bride's hands! Here, take these things! This too—and this—ouch!—and this!'

With becoming grace, Sarasvati resigned herself to her fate, in various stages and postures—fatigue, ennui, resignation and despair. In the end, Yamuna managed to gild the bride appropriately: a deep marigold yellow silk *antariya*, held at the waist by a red kayabandh and a gold girdle tied below the navel, emphasizing her soft curves. The long gold pleats of the antariya in the front fell low at her ankles, with the other loose end pleated like a fan. A gold-and-white uttariya, draped across the back, rested on her bare shoulders and left to fall freely on the forearms, and the scarlet, richly embroidered *stanmasuka*, the chest band, clinging voluptuously to the rising bosom.

Yamuna squealed in delight as she looked amply satisfied with the effect.

'You do look like a goddess!' she giggled.

Sarasvati made a face. 'I thought I was a bride!'

She peered into the mirror, scrutinizing her reflection. For the day, the coiffeuse, under Yamuna's supervision, had done Sarasvati's hair up from her face with tiny, white flowers and pearls woven into it, with soft tendrils allowed to escape. Sarasvati's hair was left loose at her loud insistence and crimped with her favourite flowers— champa, the fragrant magnolia, and the yellow palash.

Sarasvati smiled awkwardly in the mirror. It was a gesture of rare self-possession. Into this smile she insinuated a vast impersonality, as if she were unconscious of Yamuna's attempt to play upon her loveliness—but amused nevertheless. She was no longer a 'woman', she was a bride; Sarasvati stripped her attitude to a sheer consciousness of her own impervious beauty, stood there sparkling, ethereal in the cascade of flowers and the perfume swirling around her. The moment was divine.

'I agree, the flowers make you look more exotic than the jewels!' breathed Yamuna, herself bewitched. She gave a start, very pleased with her work.

And when Sarasvati, at the side of Brahma at the yajna, drew a lot of compliments, Yamuna gleefully gave herself a mental pat on the back. She gazed at her friend: Sarasvati shone with an inner glow, looking quietly ecstatic, her face serene but her eyes sparkling like molten diamonds.

Brahma was lost in admiration. His bride was breathtaking: curls, flowers and fragrance tumbled over her slender nape; her little figure so graceful and so dignified. It was true that her strongly intelligent face, with her flashing dark eyes and turned up nose, which he found enchantingly piquant, could be stern and formidable for most. Brahma, who had created thousands of beauties in his life, saw her as inimitable perfection. He loved her, and blind love finds ideal beauty everywhere.

Just like this wedding in the woods, he thought with satisfaction; the whole forest was bathed in temperate sunshine that did not hurt the eyes, covering the wooded canopy in a golden luminescence. As requested, it was witness to their minimal wedding, attended only by Vishnu and Shiva with their consorts and her friend Yamuna by her side, with Agni and Rishi Brihaspati performing the rites.

'I wish Ganga could have been here,' Sarasvati had earlier mentioned, wistfully twirling the ends of her angavastra between restless fingers.

'Celestials can see beyond the beyond, you know,' informed Brahma, hoping he could lift the smudge of sadness in her eyes. It did. She cast him a brilliant smile. 'She can see you.'

'Yes, I can feel her presence too. She's here.'

It was a lovely cloudy morning. The sun, rising against a golden halo lightly flecked with purple, stood above the western horizon on the point of climbing over the faraway hillock. In the woods that Sarasvati so treasured, shadows and half-shadows had vanished, and the air had grown damp, but the golden light was still playing on the treetops, drenched freshly by a spray of rain, making the fresh, transparent fragrant air even fresher. It was delectably cool, fanned by the warmth of the holy fire of the yajna, the flickering flames raising a hot flush of hope and promise . . .

Now and again, their glances rested on each other, and Parvati, who was observing them closely, could glimpse in their exchanged glances not only love but affection. Their eyes met and there was in his eyes a tenderness that was beautiful to see. There is nothing more touching than the sight of love, sighed Parvati. There should be no further impediment to their happiness; their situation and circumstances seemed easy now and there was no reason they should not live happily ever after . . .

Yet, as she studied them, Parvati could not help feel a pang of unease as her troubled eyes rested on Sarasvati. She was sparkling and vivacious as always and was just as vocal, Parvati thought drily. Her radiance, her playful gaiety, her sharp opinions, her enjoyment of life and her intellectual exuberance were exhilarating and in spite of her acerbity and whimsical comportment, Sarasvati was enormously popular. There is a large class of men whose egotism cannot endure humour in a woman, but Brahma wasn't that sort. Parvati couldn't understand the attraction of her 'sincerity'—that was what Brahma insisted he admired most about Sarasvati with his keen and somewhat sardonic mind. Parvati frankly wondered if the grave Brahma would be able to keep pace with her. Sarasvati was so naturally brilliant that she made Brahma, for all his distinguished elegance, look rather sober. Her freshness made him—with his serious, lined face—look weary and ancient. Nevertheless, they did fall in love . . .

The wedding had been simple and swift, presided over by Rishi Brihaspati, and to Sarasvati's great surprise, followed by a feast for everyone at Brahmalok.

'Don't look so shocked, it was I who planned it,' remarked Lakshmi, in her customary mild-mannered way. Vishnu's lively wittiness was in contrast to her quiet, restrained spirit, though they matched perfectly in flamboyance. Dressed in vermilion and gold, Lakshmi glittered in her regal raiment in contrast to the serene gentleness of her tranquil, round face. What immediately struck Sarasvati about her was that Lakshmi had the most gentle, friendly eyes, which made others warm up to her immediately. Her long, light brown hair was tied in a thick plait, covered in gilded jewellery, the burnished gold ornaments shone brightly against her honey skin. Overall, her fragile beauty seemed to be daunted by the dazzle of gold and gems she was encased in. One simply could not take their eyes off her.

'I know you wanted the wedding to be small, but we needed some sort of celebration,' she smiled tentatively at Sarasvati's look of open astonishment. 'That's why Parvati and I arranged for this banquet.'

Sarasvati struggled to smile back. 'I guess I can't complain, you are the perfect hostess,' she said drily, eyeing the rows of tables laden with food and wine.

Vishnu and Lakshmi were the most stylish, social couple, suitably representing the cultural elements of their world, thanks essentially to Vishnu's colourful personality. He liked all things fine, enjoyed music and loved to dress up.

'These are simple traditions to be followed, you can skip or follow them—I got married in the cold mountains of the Kailash, a more austere version of what my mother had imagined!' laughed Parvati, tall and lissome in olive-green silk and purple brocade, which went well with her height and broad shoulders, curving along her narrow hips to fall in gentle pleats at her ankles encased in delicate gold anklets. Her brown hair was silky and piled high on top of her small head. She had smooth, dark skin and rather severe eyebrows. Her big almond-shaped eyes were deep night-sky blue and glitteringly alive with bright intelligence.

Again, Shiva and Parvati were a study in contrasts: he, with his dreadlocks and tiger skin, and she, svelte in the smart silks—the ascetic and the princess; the goddess who made an ascetic into a householder. But in spite of the disparity of age and looks, they were the perfect pair, the ideal couple.

Lakshmi beamed. 'Weddings, however grand, do have their private moments—so deliciously personal,' she gave a small, fleecy smile. 'I knew from the very first moment whom I had to garland during my *swayamwar* held during the chaos of the samudramanthan! Even though I saw all the assembled devas and asuras, I had eyes only for him,' she said shyly.

Parvati chuckled. 'There, you knew your chosen one was him! Was it his twinkling eyes or his mischievous smile that wooed you over or was it the fact that Vishnu was the hero of the hour when he retrieved the amrit from the asuras and gave it to the devas?' she teased and Sarasvati was amused to observe Lakshmi blush delectably.

'Along with the amrit, you arose from the very manthan Vishnu had validated as the divine deification of wealth,' said Sarasvati.

'And dressed suitably so!' laughed Lakshmi. 'All brilliant in gems and gold, robed in the splendour of a thousand bolts of lightning, illuminating the universe!'

'What a beautiful bride you were!' recalled Parvati. 'The moment you appeared from the sea, men, gods and demons fell at your feet, hoping to receive not just mountains of gold and fortune, but also your hand in marriage. You were meant to be a distraction from their task but you had eyes only for Vishnu!'

Lakshmi chuckled. 'And he didn't even look at me!' she exclaimed in feigned affront. 'It was only when I patted him on his shoulder that he turned around, deigning to look at me and that's when I sought my chance to propose to him, which of course, he could not refuse!'

'And here Sarasvati kept refusing poor Brahma!' remarked Parvati, turning to Sarasvati to give her a long look. 'You—and this wedding—surprised us all today.'

'I like surprising those who are surprised easily,' Sarasvati replied coolly but she stiffened, bracing herself. 'He is a patient man. And I am a persistent woman.'

Parvati saw the woman standing in front of her with new eyes. Lakshmi, oblivious to the sudden tension, nodded with a laugh. 'Love needs both patience and persistence, and who should know this better than you, Parvati? You had to be reborn to have him all over again. As Parvati, you waited aeons till Shiva realized you were the reincarnation of his first wife, Sati. So, I reckon Sarasvati too was testing both him and herself when she took her time to reciprocate his feelings, yes?' she turned to Sarasvati, her eyes smiling questioningly.

Sarasvati felt that same discomfiture again: she could not discuss her emotions and experiences so easily.

'Just . . .' she vacillated evasively.

Sarasvati did not speak, her silence non-committal, her face giving nothing away, keeping her smile fixed and gracious.

Parvati continued in her usual self-assured tone. 'You took your time but both of you are meant for each other. He is the mind, you are the essence; his other half.'

'But then, if so, how do *I* need him?' Sarasvati asked brusquely.

Both the women were taken aback at her offhandedness, momentarily speechless.

'Arrogance does not suit intelligence,' Parvati cautioned.

'I was speaking out of curiosity, not arrogance,' replied Sarasvati in good humour. 'Honestly, *how* do I need him? Is there a need at all?'

Lakshmi nodded. 'Yes, there is a need. You need to have an emotional responsibility.'

'To myself or to him?' asked Sarasvati swiftly. 'I think I owe myself that responsibility, not him. When I take responsibility for my own feelings, I should not expect him to be responsible for my or our happiness. As partners, our happiness, that emotional sanctuary, comes from how we treat ourselves, rather than from how the other in the relationship treats us. That is self-worth, the essence.'

She is defining herself and how one should be, thought Parvati as she stared at the petite, purposive bride in front of her. *Sarasvati means 'the essence of the self'; as 'sara' means 'essence' and 'sva' means 'self'.*

Sarasvati continued in her soft, firm tone. 'So, when we abandon ourselves in love and relationships, instead of valuing ourselves, what we are left with is unhappiness and insecurity, corroding pride, worth and dignity. I cannot blame him for *my* feelings; that's what I meant when I said: *how do I need him?*'

Lakshmi lightly shook her head.

'Sarasvati, it takes two to be together,' she reminded her quietly. 'Partners have to trust and support each other in what brings each person joy, and they feel joy in witnessing each other's joy, not threatened by each other's success or happiness. If you are Sarasvati, the essence of the self, do not forget that Brahma, for all his humility and self-effacement, is the greatest manifestation of the all-pervasive mind, the omnipresent,' she warned. 'He was the one who started it all, even you! When you are worshipped as the goddess with four arms, those hands symbolically mirror your husband Brahma's four heads; the mind—*manas*—and the sense with *buddhi*—the intellect and reasoning. As also, *citta*—the imagination—and *ahamkara*—the ego and self-consciousness. While Brahma represents the abstract, you embody action and reality. You are Brahma's partner in every way. So yes, you do need each other.'

Sarasvati was taken aback at Lakshmi's unexpected advice and before she could respond, the massive door swung open behind Lakshmi, and Sarasvati saw two tall men—Vishnu and Shiva—come out chuckling. Brahma held the way for them and helped them laugh clearly with some ironic joke of his. They all seemed to be sharing a secret jest, smiling heartily as they strolled towards them.

At the sight of them, Brahma's smile dropped off his face, a mask coming down his face, taut and blank as always.

'Now that we have got the groom delivered back to you, Devi, I think it is best we start the feast,' said Vishnu, his light eyes smiling wickedly, oblivious to the frisson of tension between the women.

'It truly is a magnificent feast and you are the most lavish host, Lakshmi!' gushed Parvati, eyeing the rows of tables with an array of silver trays and gold bowls displaying the most elaborate cuisine.

Turning to the couple, Shiva bowed to both Brahma and Sarasvati. 'Let me formally officiate the banquet. Salutations to both of you,' he said, handing them each a lotus. 'This is my gift, my blessings: The lotus, which symbolizes knowledge and supreme reality. He is Brahma and you are Brahmani.'

Vishnu bowed, his eyes twinkling. 'They say there is no marriage for gods,' he stated and after the initial amusement had died down, his eyes grew solemn as he continued, 'What we regard as Brahma and Sarasvati are symbols that help one understand lofty concepts difficult to comprehend. The marriage of Brahma and Sarasvati is the manifestation of the universe in different shapes and space. And as such, the couple shall be revered as the fountain of wisdom, skill and talent.'

'For which we need expression,' interposed Sarasvati, smiling.

'Oh yes, be it through art or, yes, the tongue!' grinned Vishnu. 'It is an important organ that performs two functions—tasting and speaking. Man is the only being on Earth who knows language for articulation of his thoughts. And we can well claim that Devi Sarasvati sits on the tongue of Lord Brahma, stressing the importance of speech and expression!'

Over the loud chuckles, Shiva smiled faintly, 'Jokes apart, I would like to expand further. Through words and thoughts, beliefs and opinions, through music and arts, Sarasvati, you are the unifier of people and nations, you are the Sangamani. You create nations through philosophy, ideas and thinking. As Chikitushi, you shall relentlessly protect the sacred bond between Humankind and Nature.'

'You are no conventional goddess, Sarasvati. You are that feminine force that weds the mind,' Parvati looked from Sarasvati to Brahma. '. . . Not through power or play, but through intellectual bonding: *sakhyatva*. Once this bond of friendship and loyalty is formed between art and the artist, the artist and his audience, like the fair woman that you are, Sarasvati, you shall faithfully reveal her all and the best equally both to her followers as well as her partner.'

'So, I shall have competition,' joked Brahma, his eyes creased in easy mirth.

'But always,' warned Parvati. 'That is her gift to her devotees.'

Brahma looked momentarily taken aback at the grave tone in her voice.

Shiva laughed, 'Both of you are headstrong yet vulnerable, confident but cautious. You should get along great!' he assured, patting Brahma on the back.

As the gathering broke into a thunderous applause, Sarasvati was aware of Parvati's brown, thoughtful eyes boring into her. Sarasvati was certain she had not cast a sufficiently good impression on the other two ladies. She sighed: *not a favourable beginning.*

Sarasvati saw Kamadeva coming towards her, his green eyes lighting up at the sight of her.

'So it happened,' he began gleefully. 'Congratulations!' A sneering smile showed his white teeth.

Sarasvati nodded graciously, not deigning to respond: she knew what he was talking about.

'I need to be congratulated too,' he expanded helpfully, hoping for a response. 'I won your challenge!'

Kama looking self-satisfied.

'I realize I was flippant,' she said evenly. 'I should not have made you do it.'

'But I did!' he said triumphantly. 'I am the matchmaker.'

He paused, adding testily. 'But I agree to what you once said: there is a depth of a difference between falling in love and being in love. You never fell in love, you would rather be in love as you have too much intelligence and logic to mind your heart. Yes, you shall always heed your mind.'

She thought he regarded her with a sneering pity that tempted her to unleash her displeasure on him.

Sarasvati looked at him with complete amazement. 'I can't believe you have the temerity to say that!' she said so softly that only Kama could hear the ferocity in her voice.

She stared fixedly at him and then said in a voice tight with displeasure: 'How dare you? How dare you, after all you did at the gallery?' she hissed, feeling blood rush to her face. 'How dare you still meddle and make assumptions about our life and our future?'

Her eyes blazed as, from the distance, Brahma watched her. His face darkened.

Watching the cold fury on her face, Kama was struck by terror. His vanity had set his tongue loose. Would she curse him too?

Face pale, he folded his hands; his hands were shaking. 'My apologies,' he mumbled, hoping desperately she would accept his frightened apology. 'I was trying to be helpful, giving you needless advice as usual. I am afraid I got carried away. But I meant no harm, no malice. It was my stupidity speaking! Please accept my apologies—and congratulations again. I mean it,' he said fervently.

His voice was strident with relief.

His stricken face and the raw fear in his eyes brought her to her senses, her volatile rage cooling down as quickly as she had erupted.

She nodded wordlessly, not trusting herself to speak.

Kama fled, feeling her glare pierce holes in his back, as he walked rapidly out of the canopy, across the pond and out of the floral archway.

She had barely expelled a deep breath of relief when she saw Brahma striding in her direction.

'You fine?' he whispered in a voice as gritty as gravel, his face taut. 'Is he troubling you?'

'No. I think I gave him a hard time for a moment,' she said with forced gaiety, her face still flushed with helpless annoyance. 'No one can spoil this day, it's our moment,' she added cheerfully, linking his hand in hers.

Brahma nodded, though he looked mildly displeased. But as she rightly said, he was not going to allow anything or anyone to seriously upset him on this special day he had waited for so long. They stood looking into each other's eyes, alone for a moment, in the swirl of friends and guests around them.

'Didn't you like the meal?' Brahma whispered as they sat together at the wedding feast, noticing her untouched morsel. 'There's your favourite *boondi*. And there is the kheer with lots of saffron, another of your favourites. Lakshmi made it a point to add it to the menu.'

'No, it's delicious,' she said graciously, throwing a thankful look at both the goddesses sitting opposite them. Lakshmi acknowledged with a small nod, her gentle smile, meant to reassure her, expressing more than she could read: that things would be fine.

'See, it wasn't so bad,' Brahma muttered into her ear, as they stood slightly apart, watching their friends have a good time.

She raised her fine eyebrow. 'Apart from the fact that I am to be known as Brahmi, Brahma's wife,' she murmured mockingly.

'Brahmi; the one who is very, very dear to Brahma,' he whispered thickly, his voice soft with tenderness.

'And so, are you Sarasvat, Sarasvati's husband?'

'Yes, certainly, if very, very dear to Sarasvati!' He smiled, unperturbed by her sardonic tone: she was teasing him in her irreverent way. Hopefully, their tempestuous days were over, he sighed. There seemed now a silent, peaceful bond between them. They had an understanding that surpassed everything for the past tumultuous moments: conflict and hostility and fear and strain and anxiety and lonesomeness and animosity. Theirs was the calm after the storm, serene and placid, the bond of love that brought them together and kept them there, safe and self-assured, against life's winds, sheltered in their new haven.

'Did you do it for me or for them?' he asked gently.

'Funnily, for myself,' she said quietly. 'I did it for myself, in the end.' She had not meant to tell him that, but it seemed right now. 'All of a sudden, I just needed to be with you, to be married to you, and I knew it.'

'That's the nicest thing you have said to me,' he said quietly, but there was a smile in his eyes. 'I needed to be married to you too. For a long, long time . . . and now I am!'

'You've been so patient and good to me about that,' she smiled tremulously. 'It means a lot to me. I guess I just needed time.'

'This is the right time,' he whispered back. 'This is when it was meant to be.'

15

MARRIAGE OF EQUALS

'The newlyweds were certainly not lost for words even on their wedding day!' smiled Parvati, in genuine amusement.

Shiva grinned. 'Come to think of it, who else would they have married but each other? They are both creative as well as combative; perfect, made for each other!'

'Literally,' nodded Parvati, a thoughtful look in her eyes. 'But her character is more aggressive than his. She can give him just what he lacks.'

Shiva grew wary, giving her a knowing little smile. 'Brahma does not lack anything; in fact, he feels more than most men. Sarasvati, being better than everyone at everything, doesn't stop Brahma from being what he is. Sarasvati is smart—she knows she has met and married her true equal in Brahma. He respects her hugely, yet he won't hesitate to be frank and have the courage to tell her when she errs and when she excels, and vice versa. They give each other a hard time because of their closeness and constantly test each other—sometimes harshly—but they strive to bring out their best. And you know, they will go on to create a wonderful world together. He sees her as his equal and more,' assured Shiva, hoping to ease his wife's concerns. 'And don't worry, they are not confrontational; that's their way of expressing emotions—and love,' he added lightly. 'Theirs is a union of equals—two individuals, headstrong yet vulnerable, assertive but circumspect. Both of them should get along great!' he assured her. 'Their married life will have a mind and momentum of its own. That's the reality they know and we need to accept.'

'She is a free spirit, living her true life while he is more controlled and conforms to his own principles,' pointed out Parvati.

'Yes, but not when it comes to his wife. He accepts and wants her to define herself on her own terms. That is how he sees his Sarasvati. Their very differences draw them closer. So, whatever the reasons, their marriage *is* wonderful,' maintained Shiva.

'. . . Isn't love why you marry!' claimed his wife.

'They do love each other,' Shiva insisted. 'It's just that they don't know yet how to fit in with the other's way of life. You see, they haven't learnt to settle down.'

'I can't imagine either settling down!'

'They have,' said Shiva gently. 'And they will love and learn.'

'When you are tempestuous, your emotions are violent, not often durable . . .' Parvati looked at him dubiously. 'They are creators; perhaps that's their creativity speaking?'

'In the end, Brahma and Sarasvati are importantly true friends—a fantastic preamble to a successful partnership.'

Parvati was still sceptical. After the marriage, Brahma no longer joined them at the informal get-togethers at Kailash. If and when the couple was seen together at public gatherings, they were engaged in long, serious discussions which, Parvati presumed, came out of enormous seriousness and ineffectual humour that they found entertaining. But often, their debates flared into unbridled arguments, leaving the onlookers shocked but providing each other a sense of unity in feeling and thought.

Back at Brahma's palace, neither was aware they were being so earnestly scrutinized. After an extended argument over which would be their place of residence, it was mutually decided that Sarasvati's palace would remain her personal space of retreat and Brahma's citadel their new home. She discovered his house, as expected, was as impersonal as him. Built entirely in white marble, it was massive: three storeys high with vast windows, terraces, a white-tiled roof and white walls covered with perfectly pruned flowering climbers. The rear of the house appeared to hang over the cliff face. It had a magnificent view of the two arms of the bay.

As they rode on, huddled together, their hands entwined, Sarasvati looked at her new residence with a fresh perspective: *this would be her home now*, she thought as they drove through a neat, trimmed woodland, and then past the ornate gardens with acres of close-mown lawns, beds of flowers, sunken rose gardens and fountains—unlike the wild woods at her palace.

The gardeners were at work on one of the big beds, planting out *mogra*s: taking their time as skilled workers do, but making a good job of it. Each plant was equidistant from the other and planted at the same level—*a task that no other gardener in the world can perform as well as the artist in Brahma's garden*, she thought. Brahma, my perfectionist husband: her lips twitching in silent amusement, as she leaned against the smooth strength of his arm.

She allowed herself to be held close and led by him across the hall, out into the sunshine that blazed down on a patio, through wide doors and along a passage to a chamber containing lounging chairs, a carpet so thick and soft that it made her think she was walking though flowerbeds, and a couple of sculpted paintings on the wall. This, she guessed, was where he formally met the favoured few.

'This room is left open for visitors to come in and wait—if I have any visitors and they feel like waiting,' he chuckled wryly.

Her new home overlooked the ocean. From their verandah, shaded by a green canopy of a well-groomed shrub, she could look down at the sea below. It was early evening, and the breeze was cool. Away to her right, they could see low emerald islands in a shimmering, painted sea beneath high-piled lavender clouds.

They were sitting on the wide verandah. Brahma sprawled in an armchair, relaxing in the heat and staring at the sea with his narrowed, impatient eyes. Rid of all bridal finery, Sarasvati sat close by his side, one arm flung around him, in a cheery yellow sari that clung to her curves. A huge book lay on her lap.

Looking at her, Brahma thought how very different she was from the others. For one, she was not dressed like a goddess—or a newly-wed bride—he thought with amusement. She had rushed to remove her bridal finery the moment they had stepped into the palace. Yet he found her more arresting, and thought she showed more character. He felt she pleased his eyes more than any other woman he had ever met.

Sarasvati looked up from her book and returned his look. Her eyes lit up and she smiled. The bored, resigned expression vanished.

'I hope you are enjoying your new home,' he drawled, hunching his massive shoulders as he leaned across to remove the book from her lap, placing it on the nearby table. She scrutinized him, amused.

She turned on her side so she could watch him, her hand resting lightly on his arm. 'I like mine better,' she confessed candidly, noticing how tanned his arm was. 'It'll take me some time to settle down in the new house—and the new life.'

She threw him a marked look. He had beautiful eyes, deep and molten, framed by thick, curling lashes that furled open like a feathered fan. Of all the things in her new world Sarasvati was so lost in, she was most aware of Brahma's eyes—beautiful, black and with lashes that left them reluctantly and curved back as though to meet them once more.

'As my wife . . .' he grinned, easing her gently against him, savouring her softness. 'You are not going to stop going to your old home. In fact, I will need to think twice before stepping into *your* palace,' he chuckled, noticing how her soft, raven-coloured hair fell about her shoulders.

'Why do you always wear your hair loose?' he asked abruptly, touching it, almost reverentially.

She looked surprised, throwing him an amused look. 'Why tie it up when I can be free!' she declared, tossing her curls wildly about her in exaggerated explanation. With a tiny, teasing smile, she provocatively wound one of her loose curls up on the back of her neck as she looked at him.

'Why do I bother to ask!' he murmured, burying his face in the soft curve of her nape, inhaling the fragrance of her silky hair. What surprised him the most about their love now was that it no longer seemed to have the undesirable passion of regret and despair but instead promised the kind of happiness that he hadn't known before. Was this love in its fullness and perfection? Was what he was experiencing now—this dream-like, desirous mingling of ecstasy and peace—be captured forever?

'You *are* free; you have your freedom,' he chuckled against her white throat.

'Freedom is deceptive; you think you are free but you might be bound nevertheless,' she remarked with her teasing half-smile. 'This arrangement of ours leaves you with your freedom too. You only need to be in my presence occasionally.'

He stroked her bare arm.

'No mistake about that; I think freedom can be a misconception too,' he nodded solemnly, but there was a languid humour in his coal eyes. 'But everything about us is a series of misconceptions otherwise—the misplaced belief in creating you, the misfortune of falling in love . . .'

'The error of listening to you and regrettably agreeing to marry you,' she joined in the jesting, lacing his wandering hand with her fingers, clasping it warmly. 'All misconceptions,' she murmured huskily.

He looked down at their hands, joined together, his thumb moving sensuously against the inside of her wrist. Her skin prickled.

'. . . On the mistaken assumption that we shall live happily ever after,' he twinkled, kissing the soft, upturned palm in his clasp.

Her skin burnt. His touch was as scorching as the way he was looking at her.

'So much for not being in love,' she murmured as she leaned to rest her head on his chest, his skin warm against her face. She felt oddly happy, content with the world, with herself and with him. He had all the qualities she appreciated and found lacking in most men: warmth, intimacy and a tender capacity for expressing his affection—the attributes often associated with women but ones she admired and hoped men could acquire in a rational, egalitarian world.

He looked down at her, putting his arm around her and pulling her towards himself.

'Thank you,' he said suddenly.

'For what?' she looked up, amused.

'For being together.'

Days dawned as usual as both settled down to serious work.

'It's good to see you busy compiling music while I am struggling here with my work!' Brahma complained, throwing his wife a look of exasperation as she fiddled with the veena, tweaking its strings. 'I am trying to get things in place . . .'

The arguments did not cease; the debates continued. They read, discussed, wrote, criticized and counselled: inexorably in tandem, the sharpness of the interchanges not restricted within the gilded walls of their palace but resounding loudly in public. If their quick, continuous repartee were respected as wit by admirers, some found their verbal battles disconcerting and some took it as a sign of distinct malfunction. A few understood it, while some even envied them for their unconventional love and loving.

'Brahma used to be this silent, impassive man. Is that what marriage did to him?' sighed Rambha, the queen of the apsaras, settling deeper inside the warm water of the leisure pool. She surveyed the apsaras around her: this was their chat session in the pool, away from prying eyes and eager ears.

'Undid him, you mean . . .' giggled Tilottama, splashing noisily. 'They are an odd couple: they seem to have a special connection yet very different from each other. She is so volatile, he so stable, almost rigid. Wonder how long their romance will last.'

'They are leaders in their own fields. They are bound to compete and clash,' shrugged Menaka, discarding her garment as she stepped tentatively into the scented water.

'I seriously believe they do it for effect!' observed Urvashi. 'If Lakshmi–Narayan is the Golden couple, Shiva–Parvati the Ideal one, I think these two want to be identified as the Thinkers,' she added waspishly.

'That's uncharitable; they don't need designations,' Menaka commented, her violet eyes mocking.

'This rally for her defence is courtesy of Vishwavasu, is it?' Urvashi turned churlish. 'Your husband was foolish enough to give away the magic somras to Sarasvati!'

Menaka smiled, 'We got music because of her,' she replied affably. She cast Urvashi a closer look. 'Why the nastiness, Urvashi, or did you get a taste of Sarasvati's sharp tongue?'

Urvashi caught her breath sharply, her lips turning down.

'How right you are! Urvashi was roundly reprimanded by Sarasvati to mind her steps with the music,' chortled Tilottama, recalling with evident glee.

'Sarasvati, as usual, was trying to show herself as superior,' snapped Urvashi, sulking.

'She told you to pay more attention and not insult Guru Bhringeshwar or your intelligence,' corrected Rambha. 'I keep telling you that too!'

Urvashi stiffened, her hands turning into fists as she gazed blankly at her.

'If only she had said it in a nicer way,' pouted Urvashi. 'Her tone and that look in her eyes . . . She's rude and arrogant, even with the holy Trinity of the Supreme Gods. She constantly challenges their authority and decisions.'

'That she is not; she simply speaks her mind,' Menaka protested. 'Guess that's why she is so easily disliked—and feared,' she added, throwing her friend an amused look. 'Let's not reduce a sublime consciousness as Sarasvati to a conversation of spite.'

'That's a strange word,' frowned Rambha. 'But true. Brahma was unobtrusively commanding; quietly keeping himself locked in his palace, locked out from the world, lost in work. But now all's changed. They are the new power couple.'

'Are they?' Urvashi remarked with an unpleasant smile. 'Brahma seems all adoration and admiration. He has gladly given up his all to surrender to her. I think it is she who is getting more influential,' she sighed with a dramatic roll of her eyes. 'Brahma is going to first regret and then resent it some day—like all husbands do—when the wife gets more popular or powerful,' she added with a wicked grin. 'Or is more intelligent . . .'

'He is not that insecure,' retorted Menaka. 'And it requires acknowledgment of the male privilege to overcome that! It is an education for both of them, as marriage should be. Don't be so quick to judge him,' she said. '. . . Or her. We are all victims of our image issues caused by a culture that does not treat us as an individual, rather as typecasts. Brahma never did that. He is the rare one who always treats women—probably because he created them—for their qualities and talent. And Sarasvati is his ideal. The more he is with her, the more aspects of his life and of the man–woman relationship they both together have begun to question.'

She stopped abruptly at the sight of Yamuna, the sole friend Sarasvati could boast of since Ganga left Brahmalok. Yamuna noticed the furtive glances and suppressed giggles and suspected they had been gossiping about her friend, who, though greatly admired, was strangely unpopular. She would have thought their marriage would have put the ugly speculations to rest but instead, a new sort had sprouted. Yamuna frowned: tales turned to rumours as more stories were milled out about them. But she knew it was more a clash of views than personal differences. They were known to be discrete: individually separate yet distinct, dear yet detached, each going their way. Ironically, it was this freedom to be distant, their very discreteness, that made them clash and come together. They might not enjoy the marital harmony of Shiva–Parvati or Lakshmi–Narayan but that was more because of not conforming to traditional norms of marriage and love. She suspected the rumours arose from petty jealousies and resentment: if Brahma was known to be cold and taciturn, Sarasvati was his opposite: too fiery and fierce for the likes of the conservative devas and devis, who found her confrontational and outspoken— an attribute not taken kindly to, especially by the male gods.

Yamuna walked out of the quarters, feeling anxious. Then she saw two sets of footprints in the sand, heading towards the sea. She stood still, feeling the sun beating down on her head and she peered along the distant beach until she saw them.

Brahma and Sarasvati were walking side by side, paddling in the surf, close together: he towering above her, his head bent as if listening to what she was saying. She was barefoot, picking up her antariya higher, swinging the pleats as she walked, kicking at the little waves that broke around her ankles. They looked as if they didn't have a care in the world.

Yamuna smiled to herself, a smile of relief. They were fine.

But vicious tongues refused to leave them alone; they were now 'sorry' for the 'only sadness' in their life: that Sarasvati could not bear children.

'Reports insist that she refuses to have one,' remarked Tilottama.

Urvashi laughed shortly 'I told you she *is* odd! She wilfully ignored so many suitors and when deigned to marry Brahma, she refuses to bear children! Even we apsaras have given birth to children and here the Goddess of Knowledge does not wish to have one! What wisdom is that?'

'They are happy, that's what matters,' said Rambha in a tone that brooked no further gossip.

But if anything, the absence of children brought them closer together. Sarasvati insisted her devotees were her children; and she the kind mother and the strict matron.

'No kids means thankfully we are spared another conflict,' Brahma joked, sinking into his favourite chair and pulling her down on his knees. She curled up on his lap, slipping her arm around his neck and resting her face against his.

'Isn't it a blessing? We can't ever fight over children like other couples!' she said, leaning back against him.

'One less fight,' he chuckled, touching the back of her neck gently.

As the three worlds shook with the outbreak of another war between the devas and the asuras, there was a private war of words between the creators of the world.

'These wars will never end, as long as good and evil exist in the world, both created by you,' accused Sarasvati.

'That's why I gave each of them wisdom too, to be blessed by you,' he countered disarmingly.

'Both are fools and you know I can't suffer fools!' she said, her tone impatient.

'Well, then, there will be no truce!'

She gnawed on her underlip, looking at him.

'I think fighting is a beastly business,' she returned with a grimace. 'I don't believe in war and weapons. That's why both of us don't carry any,' she paused, shrugging. '. . . But sometimes I do wish I at least had a cudgel to beat some sense into these fools. Worse, now even the manavs are following their footsteps!'

'Now what did the humans do?' he sighed.

She drew in a deep breath.

'Don't make me start!' she fumed. 'You mentioned mistakes, well, *that* was your biggest mistake: creating Man.'

'I disagree. Man is the most wondrous creation, intelligent and aware that it can appreciate my creation,' Brahma said formally, in a voice that wanted to say more. He straightened his bulky shoulders, drawing up to his full height, towering over her. She seemed unflustered.

'How long?' she shrugged. 'There will come a time when it will be debated if God created Man or Man created God!' she said in that cryptic manner which he found annoying.

'*Dharma, the means for achievement of everything, born of me, assumed the form of Man at my bidding,*' he quoted himself. 'Man, indeed, is this All, what has been and what is to be, the Lord of the immortal spheres which he surpasses. Such is the measure of his might, and greater still than this is Man. This is how the gods define Man.'

'Keep working at your theories, but I warn you, there will come a day when you will regret it,' she said, lowering her head to tinker with the chords. 'Man will think he is God.'

'So be it. And if that happens, he'll thank you for it,' Brahma retorted. 'Without you, without knowledge, he cannot think himself God. So the onus is on you, Sarasvati. Man will forsake God but you, Sarasvati, cannot forsake Man, because if you do, Man will become God!'

For once, she seemed disconcerted, her brows furrowed in a frown, thinking.

'I just might if that's the only way to stop him and save the world!' she said slowly, her words oddly sounding like an ominous warning as she continued tuning her veena.

'Oh for God's sake,' he snapped irritably. 'How many more notes do you intend to create? Talk about cacophony...'

'This din is less deafening than the dissonance of war and violence,' she quipped. 'Is it just me or is the human race you created now armed with religion, poisoned by prejudice and absolutely frantic with hatred and fear galloping headlong back to darkness?'

'Is it all right to leave your wise comments and just keep my temper?' he asked crossly.

She chuckled; his withering wit often saved the moment.

'If we go on like this, we might forget our dinner tonight,' she suggested, smiling.

His sharp black eyes had a cool glitter in them: She didn't seem as annoyed as he expected her to look. She was mocking him and he was getting riled, as always.

'Yes, I know. I can read the invitation sent by Vishnu and Lakshmi,' he said, still churlish.

She went over to him, put her hands on his waist, her arms warmly encircling him. She slipped her hands in his. His fingers were stiff. 'Don't let our little debate get to you!'

The evening at Vishnulok was an elaborate affair as always, the hot debate between the guests more sumptuous than the feast, while the hosts looked on in amused indulgence.

'What do you think of Sarasvati?' whispered Lakshmi to her husband as they walked back to the palace after seeing their guests out.

'I have seen her as much as you have. She seems tremendously intelligent.'

'Is that all you have to say?'

There was a note of keenness in her voice.

Vishnu smiled. But it was only a gleam. He looked at her steadily and his eyes were serious. 'We invited them to get to know them better. What do *you* think of her?'

'No, not quite, I can't assess her still . . .' Lakshmi confessed. 'It's hard for me to say; you see, I know her so little. Of course, she's attractive—in a very refreshing way. She's more arresting than beautiful, more clever than lovely,' she described. 'And yet, there's something modest, friendly and gentle about her that is very appealing—despite her blunt tongue and mercurial mood!'

Vishnu gave a slow nod. 'She has got a lot of self-possession; quite unlike any other women I have met before.'

Lakshmi raised a brow. Brown eyes twinkled back at her.

'Oh, I am just fumbling, trying to put into words an impression that was not distinct in my own mind!' Vishnu flashed an impish smile at his wife.

'I am often surprised at your power of observation,' she remarked drily.

'I can think of a quality that would be more valuable,' observed Vishnu, his smile crooked. 'Talent, for instance.'

'Which Sarasvati has in plenty!' Lakshmi retorted. 'That neatly closes our debate.'

'They are really terrific hosts,' said Sarasvati sleepily, her head on Brahma's broad shoulder as they headed back home in the chariot.

She struggled to sit upright as a thought struck her fuzzy brain. She looked keen and alert.

'What did Vishnu mean when he said to me that he need not know what you were up to?' she asked, puzzled. 'Was he being roguish as usual?'

She felt him shake with silent laughter. 'Probably the same as what he told me—that he does know what I was doing as long as he knows what you were doing!'

'Oh, you!' she shrugged and rested her head back on his shoulder. 'The peace is finding our balance—of man and woman, you and me.'

He answered prudently. 'It was a compliment, my dear, that we *are* one.'

16

TRIDEVI

She stepped into the darkened chamber, and the door closed behind her. Brahma stepped out from the shadows and she turned, smiling, as he caught her in his arms.

'What a bit of luck, you are actually here!' Brahma muttered against her face and she could hear the wry smile in his voice. 'I was resigning myself to a dull evening. I thought you were again going to spend another night at your palace.'

She put her arms around his neck and pressed her face against his. 'Indra turned up at the last moment,' she said. 'Oh, it seems such a long day!'

'Indra?' He held her close to him while his heart hammered against his chest.

'Let's not talk about it now,' she said tiredly, pulling back and looking up at him with a grimace.

She slipped out of her shawl, going ahead of him in the comfortable chamber, where a blazing lamp greeted her. The room, lit by the warm orange flames, cast shadows and firelight, giving it an intimate atmosphere she had grown to love.

Brahma closed the door and leaned against it, watching her. It fascinated him to see how efficiently she changed her mood and manner. Only this time, he did not have any presentiment of trouble.

'You are most precious to me,' he said suddenly with a catch in his voice.

'Only you can say that and make me believe it!' she smiled as he came over to her, slipped his arm around her, turning her and drawing her against him.

'These are the only moments I live for,' he murmured against her scented skin. 'It's as if the world has stood still and only you and I are left alive.'

'That's strange coming from the one who has created the world!' she quipped with a smile, her palms flat against his chest, feeling a wild thudding.

'I quite like being here with you,' she purred huskily. 'I think I quite like being your wife!'

'Even as Brahma's wife?' he teased.

'I have resigned myself,' she said demurely, in mock sufferance.

She turned in his arms, looking up, her eyes serious. 'I need to talk.'

He remained silent for a moment. He felt deflated as he stared bleakly across the room at the flames of the oil lamps that cast dancing shadows on the carved ceiling.

'I thought you didn't want to talk, that you were too tired . . . ?' he said, flatly.

'I know,' she hesitated, then speaking rapidly as if to force out the words, she said, '. . . but there's something troubling me . . . And I don't seem to get the time and the opportunity to clarify it,' she halted and continued. 'Now as Brahma's wife, I shall be part of the Trinity—the Tridevi: Sarasvati, Lakshmi and Parvati, the consorts of Brahma, Vishnu and Shiva, respectively,' she stated, sounding piqued.

'It displeases you?'

She nodded. 'To create, maintain, regenerate and recycle the Universe,' she added, quoting his definition.

Brahma sighed. 'You say it so critically, like a reluctant queen!'

'Honestly, yes,' confessed Sarasvati, a bored, resigned expression on her face. 'The title weighs too heavily on me.'

He looked at her quizzically. She was an enigma: she was powerful, but she resented power. She was attractive, articulate and astute, but she had contempt for the measurable; she loathed rules and restrictions, rebelling openly against them. Brahma knew Sarasvati's verve. Her spontaneous vivacity arose from her very individuality, her reality a constant conflict, within herself and with others.

She did not wish to be a goddess, possibly because she was not like any of them. She knew it and cared less of what others thought of her; that was probably why she preferred keeping to herself. She favoured her own company while reading or playing music. Even her daily walk in the woods was an intensely private affair as she fiercely cherished her personal space. Her habit of disappearing for days together as she explored the skies and the three worlds, deep in her kind of meditation—her 'mystical adventure' as she called it—was termed as peculiar by many and added to her unwarranted reputation as an argumentative loner. Exceptional. Exclusive. Elusive. With her assumed loftiness, she was more fond of roaming on her winged peacock, armed with her veena, her books and her *japmala* rather than mingling with glitter and gold. The blithe, free soul that she was, Sarasvati could be charming as she was sharp-tongued, fearless and ever ready to give back as good as she got. For someone so assured and assertive, her present state of conflict was perplexing.

'Why?' he asked gently. 'Why are you troubled? You have accomplished more difficult tasks than this . . .'

She lifted her shoulders in an elaborate shrug. 'I would like to earn a title: not receive it as a gift, reward, privilege or entitlement,' she pouted.

'You *have* earned it,' he assured her, frowning in puzzlement. 'Modesty is unbecoming of you, so why this hesitancy?'

Sarasvati gave her half-smile. Brahma's face was expressive of nothing but tolerance and concern.

'I am not afraid of the responsibilities of the title imposed upon me,' she grimaced, as she stared at light playing on his clear olive skin. 'It is the expectations that I dread.'

He went over to her, putting his hands on her shoulders. 'When did you allow yourself to be governed by expectations?'

'I don't and I won't!' she said forcefully. 'But it is a responsibility I will have to accept just *because* of my position as your wife,' she looked morosely. 'I wonder if I shall have the freedom to be a Tridevi as I would like to?

I see the concept of the Tridevi as a rediscovery of a positive creative force empowering men and women alike. If there are gods, there have to be goddesses too, but not as mere wives of the male gods. It is the actions of the female—Prakriti—towards the male—Purush. The female of the pair has to save the male, virtually becoming her spouse's guru. This Prakriti shall help transform herself to reveal the true Purush, in the process destroying the overreaching ego of the deluded Purush. Will Man revere such a goddess?' she challenged.

Brahma nodded, stroking his close-cropped beard. 'The Tridevi is a perception joining the three of you, as a triad of eminent goddesses; as feminine energies.'

'But the popular perception is us as a feminine version of the Trimurti or as consorts of a masculine Trimurti,' she countered, her tone ironic. 'I prefer to see ourselves as triune goddesses who are the manifestations of the Devi, the Adi Parashakti or the Divine Feminine—not relegated as spouses of the Trimurti,' she added, pointedly. 'As the cosmic intelligence, cosmic consciousness and cosmic knowledge, we are the Shakti, the power essential to create, sustain and destroy.'

Brahma watched her pace the room. There was a wary, alert expression in his eyes that Sarasvati did not notice.

'Like the Trimurti, the Tridevi is the Trinity of the Creator, Preserver and the Destroyer,' he agreed. 'And just as energy can never be created nor destroyed but changes from one form to another, this Shakti too can take forms—avatars—to accomplish different tasks. As you did when you formed into a river, or when you became

Vak—the expression of imagination as the multiple streams of fluid thought,' he said. 'That is to say, God is both male and female. But all different forms of energy are with the Tridevi in the form of Mahasarasvati, Mahalakshmi and Mahakali: through the Srishti–Shakti—Sound and Knowledge; Sthiti–Shakti—Light or Resources; and Samhara–Shakti—Heat or Strength, respectively. All of you are those attributes—having the power to do everything as the Supreme Being.'

She pressed her fingers lightly against her temples, thinking, and then slowly nodded her head.

'That is why Sri—Lakshmi—is Vishnu's divine strength, that is why without Shakti, Shiva cannot exist, that is why without me, Sarasvati, you, Brahma cannot create,' she stated. 'Without the feminine energy, he cannot destroy society and nature: the goddesses' power is significant and co-existent. Or put more bluntly, despite man's claims he is superior, but in terms of context and acumen, women surpass men.'

Brahma's smile widened at his wife's characteristically radical remark, to be abruptly cut off with the announcement of the arrival of Parvati at the palace.

'What is the matter? Why is she here?' he demanded, his face puckered, an expression of dismay visible.

'Nothing,' assured Sarasvati with her serene half-smile, patting his arm with a cool hand. 'It is about us, the Tridevi.'

As she entered the outer chamber to greet her unexpected guest, Sarasvati was not surprised to see Lakshmi alongside a visibly peeved Parvati.

'Welcome,' she said with a shadow of a bow. 'It is
the first time you have visited my home,' she continued
pleasantly. 'It is a great pleasure to witness the presence of
both of you at once.'

She knew they did not much care for her; they
considered her both too frank and unconventional. But now
after marriage, her status had clearly altered. She was now
Brahma's wife and since their husbands were congenial and
spent time together, the women would have to keep up an
elaborate pretence of warm amity.

Lakshmi felt Sarasvati's remote eyes held in a long and
unembarrassed look of appraisal. It was so frank and open
that it was not uncivil. Lakshmi felt that here was a woman
whose business was to form an opinion of others and yet to
whom it never occurred that discretion was necessary.

Sarasvati motioned her unexpected visitors to take
seats and she sat down, immediately defining the manner
and mood of the moment.

'But I must make my excuses. I did not expect this
visit—so late in the evening,' Sarasvati observed briskly.

'I shall swiftly explain why.'

Parvati's response was correspondingly succinct, her
tone frosty, her tall frame stiff with displeasure. It just took
her a moment to comprehend the reason for the other
woman's obvious animosity.

'Are you angry with me for what I did to Shiva?' asked
Sarasvati directly, with customary candor.

Parvati glared at her level-eyed, her jaws tight. Her
hazel eyes had an opaque look. 'Yes, I just got to know

about it now or I would not have been courteous enough to even attend your wedding!' she began unceremoniously.

'Much gratitude,' said Sarasvati, smoothly.

Parvati mouth tightened. 'Shiva came to your rescue and you turned on him instead! You forced him to take the form of Bhikshtana murti, who now shall roam the world as the terrible, maimed beggar!' she fumed. 'What an ingrate you are, Sarasvati!'

Not an emotion flickered in Sarasvati's cool, serene eyes, watching the other woman tremble with rage. 'I am sorry for the hurt I have caused,' she said quietly. 'You see Bhikshtana murti as a vagrant, but remember, Shiva is the eternal mendicant,' she enunciated, her tone cryptic.

Parvati's voice was tight and cold when she spoke, her face pale with anger. 'All I know is that you did not return his good deed,' she said bitterly. 'And that you have separated us!'

She was standing very still, her hands clasped tight at her sides, glowering at Sarasvati. A couple of red spots burnt in her cheeks, her eyes bleak and bitter.

Sarasvati started to explain but Parvati cut in hotly. 'All he did was mediate in your public quarrel with Brahma but instead, you turned around making him a culprit! Oh, how heartless are you, how could such a learned person as yourself lay a curse on your well-wisher? While you enjoy being a bride in your newly found nuptial bliss, you separated me from my husband, inflicting this needless grief...'

Her voice broke, her eyes glistening with angry, unshed tears.

'Hear Sarasvati out. That's why we are here!' exclaimed Lakshmi hastily, hoping to ease the escalating tension. She looked eager and earnest but not quite sure of herself, of how exactly to cool down the row.

Sarasvati had always had a trying relationship with her sister goddesses: they were meant to be naturally inseparable, as together they formed another Trinity, the Shakti, the very energy of this universe. But Lakshmi knew in her frightened heart that they had more admiration than affection for her. Most were a little afraid of her. They had found her odd and vague: either lost in her private world or confronting them with her outspokenness. Some secretly laughed at her curious dressing manner, perpetually in lifeless white or a dull mustard yellow, devoid of any ornamentation, but for that soft, smug smile of hers. Right now, Lakshmi was again swamped with the familiar discomfiting feeling when in her presence; Sarasvati's unflustered face and that small smile, pleasant, yet taunting as if challenging them with her own question: what would be a life without meaning, what would be all the power and the wealth without wisdom?

'The battle was between Shiva and Brahma,' returned Sarasvati calmly. 'Not me.'

Rage again flared in Parvati's stormy eyes. '*You* were the reason! *You* pronounced this curse on my husband!' stormed Parvati, her eyes glittering.

'I punished both,' Sarasvati corrected her.

Parvati gave a derisive snort.

'What does Brahma receive as penalty—a propitiating yajna?!' she seethed. '*And*, he got to marry you after all!

While Shiva suffers the indignity! You were grossly unfair, Sarasvati. Just as you were protecting Brahma! I will do the same for Shiva. As his wife, I shall fight for him with all my power . . .'

'Shiva needs no protection from me,' Sarasvati said drily. 'But there is a prelude to this incident,' she stated, her tone more gentle, hoping to simmer Parvati's wrath. 'The reason for their battle was Brahma's obsession of his creation . . .' Sarasvati paused meaningfully.

'You mean yourself!' snapped Parvati.

'But only Shiva had the power to destroy Brahma's obsession.'

Parvati furiously turned on her again 'I don't care. The fact remains that *you* are responsible for his suffering!'

'The fact remains that we are fighting right now over the deeds of our husbands,' stated Sarasvati, her eyes ironic. 'It is their battle. Why are *we* quarrelling?'

The ensuing pause was swift and sharp.

Parvati immediately softened, the vehemence dimming.

Lakshmi looked aghast. 'We can't fight amongst us. We are the Tridevi!' she exclaimed timorously.

'We are fighting for the men we love!' Parvati defended herself as the anger drained from her eyes.

'If it's a clash of our own egos, a conflict of our individualism as goddesses, then the disagreement can be justified,' Sarasvati lifted her chin, unconsciously assuming defiance. 'Or has gender hierarchy pervaded us, the goddesses too? I had presumed that in our world, individual independence is founded on a profound unity at the core. Amongst us, at least.'

'To enable us, to unite us,' nodded Parvati, looking mollified. 'Only when our united power and strength is reinforced from within can it be exercised most responsibly and favourably for us as well as the world.'

'It should also be a resource for rediscovering oneself,' Sarasvati reminded grimly.

Parvati nodded, her steady brown eyes serious. 'I recall the day when the divine Devi brought me in touch with unfathomable depths within myself and from Sati, I became Parvati. Now when I see us, I find the significance of Adi Shakti, the Divine Mother. But our struggle continues in the various forms of the Devi while battling personal and social constraints of the worldly female role.'

Lakshmi showed her surprise as she nodded her head. 'Which make us particularly relevant as symbols of equality and social change. Not through worship and veneration alone.'

Sarasvati suppressed a grimace of exasperation.

'This blind worship is laughable; it does not see the irony. Only if veneration is inferred and instilled as respect for the womenfolk, it will mean true worship. Otherwise, it becomes a mockery, a collective hypocrisy. So, we need to ask the good question: if as goddesses we are worshipped as symbols of power and independence, then how encouraging are we to female enablement? Glorifying us as goddesses while subjugating the womenfolk—isn't that wicked irony? The social paradox of exalting us as idols of worship deprives our representation of its very context to make ourselves meaningful in the social fabric. It might appear inspiring yet it fails to usher in women's enablement at a mass level.'

'If it affects even a single man or woman, change has happened, challenging the legacy of conformist thought,' insisted Parvati.

Sarasvati peered down from the window into the darkness, as if looking into a dark corner of the Earth. 'Did an ingrained misogyny predate human patriarchy or the vice versa?' she murmured, her voice low but vehement. 'We will have to fight both.'

Parvati gave a short, loud laugh. 'We will! We will offer alternative paths for building fundamental thought, however radical. They say we as Shakti are a symbol of all that man fears the most in a woman.'

Sarasvati turned around, her lips twisted in a wry smile. 'Sacrificing anything individual, particularly male power, is always non-negotiable—for the man, of course! However, because we, as the great goddesses of the fearsome Cosmic Energy, offer possibilities men are not familiar with, will they consider it worthwhile listening to our voice at all?' she frowned. 'Worship is easier than education; that's why faith is blind. Worse, it's a radical reality, that the world we created, the world we live in is chauvinist, and we cannot work if we allow androcentric designations to define us, demoting us as consorts and auxiliary divinities to the more eminently masculine Trimurti. Rather, our Shakti has given the feminine Tridevi goddesses the divine roles to "create" as Mahasarasvati, to "preserve" as Mahalakshmi and to "destroy" as Mahakali.'

' . . . Where the masculine Trimurti will be relegated as representatives of the feminine Tridevi,' observed Lakshmi thoughtfully. 'But as you rightly questioned: will anyone truly comprehend the goddess's voice at all?'

'That is what we need to do, the question *we* have to answer—and somehow make all attend and respond to.'

That is the question Brahma, too, will need to answer some day, thought Parvati as she cast a covert glance at Lakshmi. Both had the same sinking doubt: would Sarasvati surpass Brahma some day? And then what would happen?

17

THE WAR OF THE SAGES

From the loftiness of the skies, Sarasvati glimpsed the shimmering blue streak, affording a good view of the river. Was that a part of her on the mortals' Earth? She gave a small sigh of contentment as she tapped her full-plumed peacock, Mayur, who promptly paused in his flight—knowing this spot was her favourite haunt, where she allowed herself to soak in the mesmerizing sight. The long, meandering bank of River Sarasvati in all its emerald lushness, that unbelievable green, against the sparkling blue mirrored in the frothy waters. The sight pleased her immensely as she heard the water and smelt the earth. She looked past the sun rays playing on the water's surface and seeing what the waters really were: a deep jade-blue fluid with the living and the dying submerged in it. *The past is continuously reinterpreted from the vantage point of the present to decide the future . . .*

It's not vanity, she told herself scrupulously, but a reverent curiosity to know all that was happening along her riverbank. She watched the flowing streak from every conceivable dominant position, every possible season: warm and sluggish in summer, cold and icy in winter, the water a dull, flinty grey, the banks dark and stark, distinct unlike the lavish leafiness along the swollen, thickening banks in the monsoons. Pleased, she affectionately patted Mayur. He ruffled his wet plumage in all his flamboyance. 'No, it's not going to be your celebration of dance, oh devourer of snakes. I chose you not for your obvious beauty. I picked you over other beings for your magical ability to transmute the serpent poison of self into the radiant plumage of enlightenment.'

Mayur cocked his head on one side, as if in agreement.

On one such drizzly day, she spotted Vashist, the revered rishi, in deep meditation. His selection of this site surprised her. The renowned sage was a scholar, a guru who moved across River Sindhu to establish his many schools and ashrams. And his preferred place of residence was on the banks of the Ganga in the loftier parts of the Himalayas. Why then had he chosen this spot on the banks of her river, Sarasvati wondered.

'But to glean knowledge from you, Devi,' she heard his voice.

He had not spoken, his lips pursed in a long silence. He did not open his eyes, which were serenely shut in meditating thought. Lean and frail, his face, though heavily lined, cold and translucent, glowed with luminous intensity.

His silent words reached her. 'By crossing your bank, I have passed over from the world of ignorance and bondage to the far shore—the world of enlightenment and freedom.

You, O Devi, as the sacred river, represents not just fluidity of thought and imagination but the state of transition too: right from the period of birth in which the spiritual traveller undergoes that crucial transformation. You are the great purifying power in which a pilgrim drowns his old self and is born anew, free and enlightened. When I die, I wish to die in your waters.'

'I would prefer you flourishing on the riverbank than you drowning in my waters,' she replied cheerily. 'Please continue with your meditation. I had no intention of disturbing you.'

With a parting smile, she rose higher, surveying the winding blue as it plunged over cliffs, winding through the mountains, hugging foothills and valleys, rolling leisurely in the flat land before she stopped short. A long way down, at a far distance, across the bank, standing on the shingly shore, she spied the lone figure of a man. She recognized him instantly. It was Rishi Vishwamitra, another legendary seer, whose feud with the older rishi, unfortunately, made more news than his scholarship. As the powerful king Kaushik, he had attempted to steal Vashist's wish-fulfilling cow, Nandini, but a livid Vashist had destroyed his army within moments through his deep power of meditation. Humiliated and now spurred into vengeance and a new vision of becoming a powerful rishi himself, the king, through severe penance to Shiva and Brahma, had acquired the deadly Brahmastra to incinerate Vashist's ashram. Vashist had destroyed all of the king's celestial weapons by using a mere stick—the Brahmadanda.

Last Sarasvati had heard, Kaushik had, after relentless penance for years, become a maharishi, renamed 'Vishwamitra' by Brahma himself. She had supposed he had reconciled with Vashist by now . . . But what was he doing here, pursuing his 'former' rival?

She saw him approach her: a lanky, swarthy man with a pronounced hooked nose and piercing, tawny eyes, both of which lent him a certain rugged ruthlessness. He greeted her with a customary bow.

'I can't believe my good fortune, two famous rishis on my banks today,' she started laconically, but her eyes narrowed, scrutinizing him. 'What is the reason, I wonder.'

'It was my prayers that got you down here at this very spot,' announced Vishwamitra, not without his unmistakeable air of smugness.

She chose to ignore his apparent conceit, returning wryly. 'And for what purpose, I wonder again,' her eyes following his as they fixed on the elderly rishi, his eyes and mind closed in meditation.

'You guessed right,' said Vishwamitra. 'Flow on and bring Vashist floating on your waves.'

Sarasvati vacillated, folding her arms, frowning. He assumed her hesitation for compliance.

'You are a learned man now, not a king to command,' she reminded him gently, but Vishwamitra was too self-absorbed to notice the soft sharpness in her tone.

Vishwamitra straightened his heavy shoulders to his full height. 'Consider it a request then, Devi,' he said.

Sarasvati studied him, her eyes grim. 'Are you sure?'

But she knew very well that impatience drove his inherent arrogance, depriving him of the last remnants of reason.

Anger crept quickly into his eyes. 'You are a river, Devi. Would you be able to stop your flow?'

Sarasvati knew it was futile reasoning with an unreasonable man. It was like tussling with a pig in the muck: he would enjoy the wrestle and she would muddy herself instead.

She gave a slight shrug and then squirting his angry face with water, she gushed downwards towards Rishi Vashist. She knew the power of her waters as she broke through her banks, where Vashist sat meditating. She glanced back; Vishwamitra looked pleased.

With a small smile, she raced forth, not halting her stream, rushing down eastwards, with Vashist riding on the crest of her waves.

She again glanced back. Vishwamitra now looked visibly incensed, realizing she had foiled his plan: he had used her to attack the rival rishi but she was instead shielding his enemy from him.

'O lady, you who flows with her mighty waters, I will turn it into blood!' he pronounced, his voice rising furiously.

It was like a thunderclap. The other hermits who had come for their morning oblations gasped in horror. 'No sir, you cannot curse Sarasvati and turn her into a river of blood! How will we survive? How will Nature and animals and civilization survive without the waters of the Sarasvati?'

'She should have thought of this before she disobeyed me!' scoffed Vishwamitra, a pulse throbbing at his temple, unmoved by the sages' pleadings.

Sarasvati smiled. 'Who disobeyed whom, rishi?' she asked, her tone deceptively dulcet. 'Did you obey your finer feelings and not succumb to arrogance and evil thought of harming your colleague?'

The words were spoken slowly and distinctly. There was no possibility of mistaking them. She regarded him as she walked closer to them: no smile, no frown. A lift of delicate eyebrows, the eyes going over him with a scrutiny that made him feel he would shrivel in his skin.

Vishwamitra flushed.

'I was a river of pure water, pure intent. Unlike you, o rishi,' she stated. 'You ordered me to bring your rival, the good sage Vashist, floating to you. I sensed malice and mischief, and decided to play your game. So, I carried Vashist away from you to a safer place. That is why you are furious,' she said scornfully. 'Did you think I was afraid of your ire? You think you have cursed me by transforming me into a stream of blood, to humiliate me and make me feel unclean.'

'O Devi, forgive him,' implored one hermit. 'Through our prayers and our good deeds, we shall cleanse your water and restore your purity to make you again a river flowing with water.'

'I am pure!' declared Sarasvati. 'I have given no man,' she paused to taunt Vishwamitra, ' . . . or rishi the power to corrupt me, to make me impure.'

Vishwamitra stood still for a long moment, staring at her, his eyes like granite. He had a sudden, sinking idea that there was something very menacing behind Sarasvati's words.

She bestowed him a smile, but not a very pleasant smile. 'I see it differently, Vishwamitra,' she said, her voice dangerously soft. 'You have turned my waters to blood, and I take it as a blessing, not a curse. This is the blood of all women and womanhood; this flowing blood river I see as a manifestation of the period blood flow of all women— not impure, not unclean, not a taboo,' she paused, looking searchingly at each one of the frightened faces of the men. 'This blood is as fertile as the soil, as bountiful as the water in the river, as natural as the air we breathe, as life-giving as the sunshine warming this Earth . . . If any of these turn against you and mankind, Vishwamitra, what would happen?'

'There would be annihilation!' whispered a hermit in open horror.

He threw himself at her feet. 'Yes, you are the life-giving river; the blood that flows shall purify and fertilize the Earth!'

A gentle cough broke the strained silence.

'You are Shonapunya, the one purified of blood,' muttered Vashist, opening his eyes.

'But why should *I* be purified?' demanded Sarasvati, trying to match his quiet tone but aware that her voice was harsh. '*He* is the one with polluted thought,' she declared, pointing roundly at Vishwamitra.

He looked at her, his heart suddenly beginning to thump.

She continued, speaking slowly and carefully, her tone measured. 'I turned his malice to good, his curse to blessing. The blood is neither dirty nor impure to be "purified": the purity of mind is all that matters. How did something as pure become so "unclean"? When religious patriarchs inappropriately twisted into taboos in their attempt to denigrate women and the female ecology. How can a woman's blood be tainted as "impure" when it derives from the very womb essential for the creation of any human being? The mother's blood is fundamental to life. O learned rishi, do you not know that even the hunter-gatherer cultures respect menstrual observances as a Nature-blessed process, positive and empowering without any connotation of uncleanness? Learn from them, o learned ones, that our blood is unsullied, more sublime than the blood in your veins as it is meant for creation and birthing. So there is no reason for me or any other woman to be "purified",' she added savagely, her glance derisive.

The others looked visibly startled.

Vishwamitra stepped forward, straightening his shoulders, his small dark eyes shifting away from Sarasvati's scornful face. 'The Sarasvati we know wears white, or some un-dyed fabric, blanched of colour. She wears no jewellery and seeks no ornaments. O Devi, when did you associate yourself with the colour red and fertility?'

Sarasvati, unsmiling now, a reflective look on her face, shook her head.

'Since you made me bleed into my waters,' retorted Sarasvati. 'In your blind ignorance, or should I say arrogance, you refuse to see that the arts I represent have always been associated with all colours, be it joy, despair, peace, pain or passion. If red is the colour of desire and passion, is it not vibrant and alive—just like blood?' she enquired, her voice dripping ice. 'I represent the arts, which is gandharva-vidya: it's meant to be sensuous and sensual, arousing the senses from which are derived the sixty-four variants of arts of the apsaras, the gandharvas, the writers, the singers, the musicians, all the artistes gifted with it. They celebrate passion and desire; the passion to pursue, the desire to excel. You have that in you, Vishwamitra, but it has been blunted with your pride and jealousy!'

Vishwamitra did not move. He felt his muscles stiffen. Slowly, he looked up at her, a hard expression in his eyes and his hands damp.

'You are in love with your "self", by what you have achieved, constantly measuring with the success of others and hence, for all your knowledge, you lack wisdom!' she studied Vishwamitra's swarthy face. 'You are trapped in your arrogance, imprisoned in your ignorance. You are more anxious about your rival than your own competence and in doing so, you have wasted your education on envy and frustration. Till you outgrow this twisted need to compete, not for yourself but for your rival, you, Vishwamitra, shall always remain what you are now—a disappointment. To me, to everyone and worse, to yourself.'

Vishwamitra started to say something, then caught the look in Sarasvati's eyes. He lifted his shoulders in a despairing shrug, staring at her in wretched silence.

Sarasvati smiled; her face softened, 'But I still have hope—for you,' her voice was so soft, he could barely hear it. 'We shall meet again, Vishwamitra, on a better day, probably, in a better mood?'

Vishwamitra could not easily meet the eyes that rested on him with detached scrutiny, but he could see an ironical kindliness in her soft, velvet eyes. 'I hope so too,' he whispered hoarsely. 'And I hope I am forgiven. May you bless me someday,' he muttered, his head bowed. His voice didn't sound like his own.

Once more, Sarasvati gave Vishwamitra a searching, sagacious look. 'You know, dear sir, that one cannot find peace in work or even in meditation in this world. It only lies in one's soul. That alone is yours to own, to be won.'

She nodded, smiled cryptically and, bowing to all, disappeared within the scarlet waters.

All of them stood silent, staring at the swirling bloody river.

'See what you did!' remonstrated Vashist, his thin face alarmed. 'But your curse, as she rightly said, is a blessing in disguise. It has empowered her and all womankind. In Sarasvati's temple of love and service, all will be welcome—men, women and children—anyone who wishes to be blessed with knowledge and enlightenment. You forget, Vishwamitra, that in her four hands she also holds the water pot, besides the *pustaka*, the mala and the veena. That pot of water represents the purifying power to separate right from wrong, the clean from the unclean, and essence from the inessential. It also carries the somras—the divine drink that liberates and leads to knowledge. You turned that water to blood!' Vashist choked with mounting rage.

'She even blessed the blood, liberating it from discrimination, shame and stigma.'

'Sarasvati is all-forgiving; she never holds grudges,' said Vishwamitra, throwing up his hands helplessly. 'The book—the pustaka she holds—symbolizes the Vedas representing the universal, divine, eternal and true knowledge as well as all forms of learning. Her mala of crystal rosary signifies the power of meditation, inner reflection and spirituality. From now on, I shall persevere in atoning for what I have done and seeking her forgiveness through her blessings,' he whispered in a troubled voice. 'I shall dedicate a hymn to her name, the One Supreme Creator—the Gayatri mantra—in tune which resonates with all, just as her veena rings in eternal harmony, expressing knowledge that creates harmony.'

'Exactly, knowledge for concord, not discord!' roared Vashist. 'But you, Vishwamitra, you failed in all accounts!' he muttered with a violent shake of his silver head. 'You will have to work at it all over again. Penance and meditation do not please her. For she is a different kind of goddess; she is elusive. You have to earn her respect. She has to respect you enough to give you her blessings. She neither needs blind worship nor adulation, fame nor fortune, rituals nor rites to reaffirm her understanding of herself or of her followers. Beautiful temples do not impress her. For her, the open sky is the roof of free thought. She will not be affected by penance or pleading, praise or veneration. You can pursue her; never possess her. For she can never be trapped by the wishes of her followers. Only if she believes in her believer, only if she has faith in her faithful, will she bless. *That* is her condition; *that* is her benediction. That is her gift but *that* is her curse too.'

Vishwamitra felt a prickle of fear, shutting his eyes to a new horror: had he, in his unwarranted arrogance, sought Sarasvati's curse instead?

18

THE BROTHERS

The very sight of Indra in the long hall was enough for Sarasvati to know something again was amiss in Heaven.

His thin, handsome face broke into an ingratiating smile as he bowed to her.

Sarasvati gave him a hard look and sat down.

'What now?' she asked peremptorily, more impatient than imperious.

'It is Kumbhakarna,' he provided shortly.

She didn't bat an eyelid. She sat looking up at him, an odd expression in her eyes that he did not like.

'You have been made the King of Gods, which is a powerful enough position to fight one's battles,' she responded coldly. 'Pray, then, why do you seek my help?'

Indra stiffened, his eyes squirming away from hers: she had an uncanny knack of making the other feel small and deficient.

'I would have done so had it been in my hands,' he muttered awkwardly. 'But he is favoured by Lord Brahma,' he left his words unsaid, throwing her a sly look, knowing well that the unspoken would be more effective.

Sarasvati suppressed a sigh of frustration: *why does Brahma grant boons to the unworthy?*

She had heard of Kumbhakarna and his elder brother Ravan, the sons of Rishi Vishrawas and Kaikeshi, the ambitious daitya princess. These brothers, more impressively, were the worthy grandsons of Rishi Pulastya, one of the hallowed saptarishis (seven great sages) as well as one of the ten Prajapatis—the mind-born sons of Brahma. Like their father and grandfather, the two boys were highly intelligent and gifted. Unlike his more ruthless brother, Kumbhakarna was considered pious, kind-hearted and benevolent, and with his unusual intelligence and as an unchallenged warrior in battle, he was fondly known as the 'godly rakshasa'. Reasons enough to make Indra insecure, she thought drily.

'As you must know, by now the three rakshasa brothers—Ravan, Vibhishan and Kumbhakarna—are performing a major yajna and penance to please Lord Brahma . . .' Indra faltered as he noticed Sarasvati tightening her jaw.

'Yes, they are singularly brilliant young men like their grandfather,' she remarked. 'And possibly, they are trying to woo their great-grandfather, Brahma, and are engaged in severe penance to please the God of Creation.'

Indra scowled and stared at Sarasvati, who stared back at him equably.

'But, of course,' Indra replied hastily, noting her expression. 'They have been endowed with Rishi Pulastya's intellect but they have also unfortunately inherited their mother Kaikeshi's deep sense of grievance against the devas.'

Sarasvati narrowed her eyes. 'And that makes them rakshasa? Each man is made of his past as well as his genes.'

Indra again hesitated, his scowl deepening. 'But it is going to affect the future if we don't stop them now,' he blurted. 'Or they will get more powerful so as to vanquish the devas . . .'

'And you,' said Sarasvati, with a small smile.

Indra's head dipped in anxious agreement. 'Yes! To take over Indralok, they are having this yajna to appease Brahma and each one of them is bound to ask for immortality and more.'

'Can't you stop mortal ambition with some of your divine intervention?' she asked innocuously, her smile expanding.

Indra flushed. 'They have practised many austerities to appease Lord Brahma and they seek to conquer the three worlds. Ravan has undergone severe penance and meditation, hoping to seek immortality from Lord Brahma,' cried Indra. 'All the gods fear that now Kumbhakarna too may ask a boon that would make him invincible. Please stop him from asking the impossible! Only you can outwit him!' he implored, his voice rising in mounting agitation.

Sarasvati sat still for a long moment, staring at Indra, her eyes thoughtful.

'If it's a fair game, I don't mind but I loathe trickery,' she warned after a long pause, in an effort to placate the visibly frantic deva.

'Do something!' Indra sputtered, almost prostrating himself before her. 'Please! Quickly! Brahma is likely to bless them sometime soon . . .'

She pressed her fingers lightly to her temple.

'I cannot stop Brahma from granting him a boon, if that's what you are implying and intend me to do,' she said slowly. 'Words, once said, cannot be taken back . . .'

She stopped abruptly, letting her words sink in and slowly her lips broke into a little smile . . .

Brahma was impressed with the three boys standing before him in the misty peaks of Mount Gokarna: they were his great-grandsons. He looked them over without any overt expression of paternal affection. Ravan was a handsome young man, tall and powerfully built, with long swinging arms and a ruthless, jutting jaw. The other two paled in comparison, though Kumbhakarna was monstrous in girth and height, a huge, strapping, ungainly bulk of a man with sad, gentle eyes. Vibhishan was clearly the youngest and the mildest, with his lean, lanky frame, earnest face and wide, awestruck eyes.

But it was Ravan that impressed Brahma the most. He was a devout Shiva devotee and a great scholar, having had mastered the Vedas and the holy books and all the martial arts of war and weaponry. He was well versed in the shastras and the Upanishads, political science, philosophy, science, literature and art. He was a maestro of the veena, Sarasvati's favourite chordophone musical instrument. He wished Sarasvati would have met his grandson, he rued with an odd family pride. Ravan was currently authoring the *Ravana Samhita*, a book on astrology, after having written another book on Siddha medicine and Ayurveda treatment—*Arka Prakasham*. Sarasvati would have been equally impressed with this outstanding young man, Brahma beamed silently.

Ravan had just finished asking for his boon. 'I, Ravan, wish for the boon of immortality,' said the young man.

The smile was wiped off Brahma's face.

'But that's impossible!' he shook his head, frowning. 'You are a learned man, Ravan. You surely know that neither I nor anyone else can grant immortality to you.'

Ravan's amber eyes gleamed. 'I have proved myself to you,' he said softly. 'I have chopped off my head ten times to get this wish granted and each time, Lord Shiva replaced the decapitated head with a new one for me to continue my *tapasya*—penance. I have proved myself to you ten times now, O Brahma!'

'Yes, you have,' nodded Brahma, his tone a shade deprecating. 'That's why I am here and so are you.'

'Then please grant me my wish,' Ravan repeated, his head bowed and his hands folded but Brahma detected stubborn petulance in his voice.

He studied Ravan's handsome, expectant face.

'I cannot offer you immortality,' he exhaled sharply.

Ravan flushed a dull red. 'Please, you have to!' he pleaded, scrutinizing the Creator's face, his probing eyes shrewd. 'Or a near equivalent,' he hinted slyly, his hands folded humbly.

Brahma sighed and Sarasvati could hear the angst in his breath. But she made no move to stop what was to come.

'But I can give you a nectar of immortality ensuring your invincibility as long as it lasts,' stated Brahma as she had expected him to say.

Ravan bowed his head. 'Just as you say. I shall keep this nectar within me, in a protected place, stored safely in my navel. Also, grant me the blessing that I should not be killed by gods, serpents, animals, demons and birds.'

Brahma nodded without hesitation. 'Yes.'

Ravan's face lit up.

Brahma proceeded, getting carried away with his generous mood, 'And for your severe penance for so many years, I grant you weapons and a special chariot as well.'

'Your Pushpak Viman?' requested Ravan, hopefully.

Brahma was taken aback at the mention of his flying craft.

'But I have already gifted my Pushpak Viman to Kuber,' deferred Brahma mildly.

'My half-brother,' muttered Ravan resentfully.

He looked straight into Brahma's surprised eyes.

'The Pushpak Viman was gifted to you by Vishwakarma, the divine engineer and architect, so that you could move around the three worlds fast and easy,' Ravan paused, making Brahma shift uneasily as the young man looked hard at him. 'How is it that you gift away a gift given to you?'

'I really didn't have much use for it as I prefer staying put in my palace,' Brahma smiled briefly. 'Kuber, as you know well, finds it difficult to move around because of his . . . er, weight and consequent limp. I thought it best to give this magnificent machine to someone who needed it more than me,' he regarded the tall, young man warily. 'I can't give you the Pushpak but don't you want the other chariots—and the weapons, Ravan?'

Ravan nodded slowly, the tilt of his head reluctant, almost abject. Sarasvati's words came back to Brahma: *give your boon to the worthy* . . .

'Yes, I am thankful to all you have given me,' said Ravan carefully, his baritone deepening in gratitude and reverence. 'Please grant the same to my brother Kumbhakarna too.'

The enormous, lumbering lad stepped forward with folded hands, his voice sonorously soft and respectful. 'Please grant me your blessing of everlasting strength and courage.'

'That you already have, Kumbhakarna,' smiled Brahma. 'There is no warrior as brave and strong as you.'

Kumbhakarna turned a dull red, looking charmingly embarrassed, clearly uncomfortable with the compliment. His small eyes, set deep in the fat-veined face, showed suspicion and surprise.

Ravan made an impatient movement and Kumbhakarna cleared his throat, momentarily tongue-tied.

'Please then, I ask for. . . er, Nidraasan,' he requested, his voice hoarse, the words rushing out in a swift blurt. 'As also Nidravatvam.'

'Yes,' granted Brahma readily, more shocked than intrigued by the strange request.

The stunned silence that followed was broken by an inarticulate cry of fury from Ravan. He strode furiously towards a dazed, speechless Kumbhakarna, clutching at his mouth in dawning despair.

'What did you do, Kumbha?' Ravan exploded, his amber eyes ablaze, his face contorted in hot fury. 'You asked for all the wrong blessings. Instead of asking Indraasana—the seat of Indra—you asked for Nidraasana—the bed for sleeping! You were supposed to ask for Nirdevatvam—

the annihilation of the devas—but instead requested Nidravatvam *or* sleep! How can this be?'

Brahma drew in a short, sharp breath, his eyes widening in quick comprehension. *Sarasvati! She had done this!*

Ravan had swung back to look at Brahma. 'This can't be!' His face became twisted, turning to the colour of old ivory. 'This is not a blessing; this is a curse! Please take it back!' he shouted.

'I cannot,' said Brahma quietly. 'I can't take back the boon, just as Kumbhakarna cannot take back his request. I gave him what he asked for.'

Kumbhakarna seemed paralysed. He stood stunned, swaying in disbelief. Only his eyes were alive and they regarded Brahma confusedly.

Ravan seemed suddenly to lose control of himself. He leaned forward, his eyes snapping fire and his great face turning mauve with vicious rage. 'This wasn't what he wanted,' he muttered through clenched teeth, his voice coming in a hiss. 'We have been cheated and you know this too, o lord. You have to change your boon!'

'Ravan, calm down!' begged Vibhishan, alarmed.

Ravan took no notice of him. His face was set in a furious, vindictive mask shaking with rage. He shook a quivering finger at Brahma. 'How could you do this?'

Brahma forced his face to remain expressionless, keeping his eyes fixed on an enraged Ravan, refusing to meet Sarasvati's amused eyes, as she remained invisible standing right behind the dumbfounded Kumbhakarna.

Watching Brahma's inscrutable face, Ravan grappled for a moment, struggling to calm down. He stood staring at him. His amber eyes were flecked with red. A look of frantic desperation sprang into them. 'Wait,' he muttered gruffly. 'You have to help, lord, please!'

'Do I?' Brahma looked surprised. 'How more can I help?'

'You have to amend this curse,' Ravan said thickly and Brahma could see the snarling anger lurking in his flat, amber eyes. 'Or my brother is doomed!'

Brahma frowned as if in deep thought and, over Kumbhakarna's shoulder, he saw Sarasvati nodding at him. 'I can only mitigate the request, not obliterate it. Instead of sleeping forever, Kumbhakarna will sleep six months a year and stay awake for the remaining six with all his preserved strength and courage.'

Ravan stared at Brahma for a brief moment, surprise and alarm in his eyes, then he bowed low to him but unexpectedly turned to his right, still bowing and said in a low voice. 'Accept my greetings, O Sarasvati, and bless me with your good wishes.'

Sarasvati made herself visible. She acknowledged Ravan with a little smile. It was neither friendly nor hostile: a goddess welcoming a faithful, a show of civil manners; no more, no less.

'You have my good wishes and that's why you are the scholar you are renowned for,' she said softly.

'Gratitude, o Devi, I am indeed blessed,' he said, his voice still low but his amber eyes blazed with quiet fury. 'I have a question I wish to ask. May I?'

Sarasvati gave a brief nod.

'You are the Goddess of Learning. You are fair and just. Then, why are you selective in offering knowledge to the world; why are there some "gifted", a few clever, the rest mediocre and some plain stupid?' he asked, with a sardonic smile. 'How fair are you as you were just now with Kumbhakarna?'

Her mouth tightened, but otherwise, her expression didn't change.

'In fact, all you three brothers are gifted . . .' she smiled politely. 'But you have a sister too, don't you?'

Ravan looked surprised. 'Yes, Surpanakha.'

'The lovely Meenakshi,' Sarasvati corrected him gently. 'Where is she? Why is she too not here to be blessed by Brahma with . . . er, his boons?'

'She is simply not accomplished enough to even stand in front of him!' dismissed Ravan with deep condescension.

She was now looking straight at him and her dark eyes had a disconcerting directness.

'Why? Did she not receive the education given to you and your brothers?'

Vibhishan rushed to explain. 'Not fully, she's yet to finish her schooling. She's the youngest and so . . .' his voice trailed off, withering under her unwavering look.

'You mean, she's a girl and thus, not qualified for the highest education which your learned father, Rishi Vishravas, reserved only for his sons,' she said in a chilly tone.

'She was, er . . . too distracted, just too naughty . . .' Vibhishan said lamely.

She stiffened a little and frowned, looking severe. 'All the more reason for the teacher to attend to such a student,' she stated. 'Wouldn't that be just a pretext for shirking one's responsibility as a guru—and as a father? Or was it reluctance to teach a daughter? Rishi Vishrawas knows well that knowledge is the most potent weapon, one that can change the world—and oneself. Clearly, he—and all of you here—did not give her the right to education which she was entitled to . . . Again, because she was just a girl, a person of no consequence?' she paused, her eyes frostily scrutinizing each one of the three young men. 'Isn't that how and why a beautiful Meenakshi has turned into a bitter Surpanakha?'

None of them could meet her cold, steady gaze.

'You have answered your own question which you asked me before, Ravan,' she said in a flat, final tone. 'I bless all who wish to learn with knowledge. I do not distinguish; I do not discriminate. *You* do. *You* denied your sister this knowledge. By imparting education to only a select few, you create an unjust world, and you dare to accuse me of being unfair?'

She glared up at them, her face white and her eyes glittering. She looked formidable, a tough and dangerous adversary. Even Brahma could feel the air thick with ominous apprehension and was warily thankful when the three brothers finally left Mount Gokarna.

'That was quite a performance,' he said, running his fingers through his grey-streaked hair and scowled.

She looked surprised. 'I thought you would welcome it.'

'You made your point,' he said flatly.

'And you gave your blessings unconditionally to the undeserving, as always!'

He turned on her, his eyes blazing down at her shocked ones. 'To make your point, do you realize you were unfair to Kumbhakarna?' he snapped in a tight, controlled voice. 'It was a nasty, unforgivable trick! I didn't anticipate this from you, Sarasvati.'

Sarasvati gauged he was angry with her. She stood still for a long moment, watching him containing his rage. He turned around and walked back to his waiting vehicle.

He waited. She strolled slowly towards him.

'Kumbhakarna was going to ask for the impossible,' she said.

'I know, I could have dealt with him,' he gave her a look he reserved strictly for erring subjects. 'I did not expect you, of all the people, to be so . . . so devious!'

She flinched but held her ground.

'There was nothing else to do.' He could see she was desperately anxious to explain it all to him. 'And you would have willingly acceded to their demands—which you did!'

'Is that right?' He was ready to explode. 'I would still prefer if you did not intervene, explicitly . . . or furtively!'

'I tried to help matters,' she said, for once defensive. A fleeting thought struck her: had she crossed the line in trying to bring peace?

He forced himself to stay calm.

'You think so?' He sat forward, the blood rising to his face. 'You might have. It's not that I am angry or averse to your help, but I am disappointed with how you did it!'

She looked shocked for a moment and then stared directly at him. She nodded, her face flaming. Her hands turned into fists. She looked very unsure and unsettled.

'You are disappointed in me,' she said in a small, quick voice. His disillusionment troubled her; she sensed the anguished disappointment in his voice and that affected her more strongly than his apparent anger.

Her crumpled face brought him up short. His anger died. He hesitated, then lifted his hands helplessly.

'Yes, you are always so fiercely fair and honest, so why this subterfuge . . . ?'

That was it, and she detested herself for having had to acknowledge she was guilty as accused.

He stroked his jaw edgily. 'I just didn't expect you would agree to do something like this, so beneath you . . . Did Indra put you up to it?' he exhaled sharply.

Her silence was voluble and her clenched lips were enough to let him know the truth.

He sighed, crossing his arms to lean his heavy shoulders against the rough bark of a tree. 'I'm sorry. I didn't mean to lose my temper . . . But this is important to me. It's important to you too.'

She abruptly turned her face away: he was making her feel miserable.

'I guess I know now how it is to feel bad to do good,' she bit her lip. 'There was no way out. I had to do it, despite your disapproval.'

He looked around for a way to ease the tension. 'Have time to stay awhile? This place is lovely.'

She nodded, her troubled eyes sweeping over the charming landscape, barely processing the beauty, the displeasure in his voice still ringing in her ears. He waited. She was sitting on a rock, staring unseeingly across at the snowy peaks. Her hand was unsteady. He padded across to her, taking her trembling hand in his. She gripped them hard, the knuckles as white as the snowflakes on the trees. But the tension had eased.

He smiled at her, bending forward to touch her hair, she lifting her face to his. They lingered over some moments. They had been married long, and they were much more in love than that implied. It was seldom that they were indifferent to each other with their violent passions, for both of them were still actively sensitive to each other, disagreements included.

'Why did you not intervene when Ravan asked for his boon as you did so wonderfully with poor Kumbhakarna?' he asked with a chuckle.

'I didn't need to,' she smiled back, slowly. 'Ravan did the needful; he signed his own death.'

Brahma stopped, his hands still. He looked at her, a surprised expression on his face. 'I just granted him near-immortality.'

'That is what you think you granted him, and that's what he thinks he has,' said Sarasvati complacently.

He studied her, his eyes interested.

'What did you *do*, Sarasvati?'

She heard the fond exasperation in his well-modulated voice.

'I didn't do anything,' she said in mock defence. 'He did it to himself,' she returned pertly.

Brahma lifted curious eyes to hers. 'What's the idea?' he asked. 'Are you trying to suggest that Ravan can't look after himself? He asked for eternal glory and nothing can destroy him.'

'But himself,' she said enigmatically, linking her arm cautiously through his. 'No one can kill him—no animal, bird or being. He named all except Man . . .' she paused. 'It will be a Man who will kill him one fine day.'

'How did he miss mentioning Man?' Brahma demanded, smacking his hand on his thigh and then grinned with obvious delight.

With their arms about each other, they started walking to the carriage taking them home.

'His arrogance, his inflated ego,' stated Sarasvati, nimbly climbing the Hamsa, the white swan, their shared divine vehicle. Guess he found Man too insignificant to be able to kill him someday. But what Ravan in his conceit forgot is that one does not get destroyed by the all-powerful, but the strong-willed.'

Brahma followed, settling himself comfortably, pulling her close against him. 'So you proved your point,' he exhaled slowly. 'For all his profound knowledge, Ravan will bring about his own fall through his ego,' he remarked, almost sadly.

She smiled, pleased, propped securely against him as the bird took flight.

'Arrogance is democratic; it affects the foolish and the learned too,' she replied equably, the cold air stinging her face, her hair whipping around her. 'That is why arrogance is unwise; it suits nothing, it is unbecoming to all. With pride, it becomes ego; with vanity, it becomes conceit; with confidence, it becomes pomposity. It is a needless, excessive pretentiousness afflicting many, if not most!'

'He is an extraordinarily bright boy; it's unfortunate that he's fuelled by anger and ego,' Brahma gave a regretful sigh, lifting his broad shoulders. 'He chopped off his head ten times to pursue his penance and he stands now as Dashaanan, the man with ten heads, referencing him of possessing an extensive knowledge of the four Vedas and six Upanishads, which made him as powerful as ten scholars.'

Sarasvati leaned against his broad chest. 'His supernatural number of heads can well be seen as a metaphor to symbolize power and knowledge. He could be a complete man with his nine heads representing nine human emotions and attributes—anger, pride, jealousy, happiness, sadness, fear, selfishness, passion, ambition and intellect. Let's see which he uses—wisely—to survive.'

Brahma nodded, a hard little smile on his face. He looked down at her glossy dark head, his arms snug around her.

'You outwitted them,' he declared, a look of admiration coming to his eyes. 'The scholar-king who wanted to be immortal will die because of his own foolish ego. And the man who wanted to conquer the three worlds, you quietly put to sleep!'

'I can fight wars too—without weapons,' she said, feeling the power of his arms around her, her hands reflexively gripping his.

'You do it each time,' he said warmly, his hands tightening at her waist. 'Right from the time you saved the world from the Vadavagni. The world is indebted to you, and, in its gratitude, there are many stories of how you brought the Vadavagni under control.'

'Each time, the definition of the fire of the Vadavagni changes,' she remarked pointedly. 'One can say it started with Man and his bloodlust for wars. Of how the warring clans of the Bhargavas and the Hehayas wreaked havoc and destruction everywhere with the all-consuming fire called Vadavagni. It was a man-made fire of hate and violence and bloodshed, which could have spread to end empires.'

'But you doused it with the waters of sanity, bringing them all to their senses,' he remarked.

'Rishi Uttank, the great disciple of Rishi Gautam, helped me . . .'

He gave her a quick glance, then grinned.

'Rather you helped Uttank in spreading peace through wise words of truce!'

They flew over a vast swathe of sylvan stretches of thick forest cover on the mountain slopes.

Sarasvati hesitated, frowning.

'But it wasn't easy dousing those hate flames of the Vadavagni. I had to take the form of the Plaksha tree, where I merged with a peepal tree to absorb and cool the Vadavagni and then diffuse it as a life-giving vapour.'

She felt Brahma shrug behind her. 'That was also how you made Man understand the importance of the green world he lives in!' he said thoughtfully. 'Plaksha also reflects the idea of education: the tree from which a river of learning flows. That is how the image of the Tree of Life or world tree came about, with trees having deep and sacred meaning . . .'

'Primarily, as a way of protecting them,' maintained Sarasvati. 'Making them sacred was the only way to ensure that Man revered and, more importantly, preserved the natural bounty of this green wealth gifted to him—a gift he has no value for,' she added cuttingly.

'You made him appreciate it through the Plaksha tree,' Brahma nodded his head sagely. 'Or the sacred groves protected so fiercely. Man celebrates autumn and spring by making trees powerful symbols of growth, death and rebirth. Just as evergreen trees are emblematic of fertility or the eternal and immortal.'

But Sarasvati looked strangely distracted, the wind in her hair. She said in a flat, tired voice, 'All these tales and fables to make Man understand . . .' she moved restlessly against him. 'Why is that after all the knowledge we give them, Brahma, they can't understand any of what we are trying to tell them?! The problem is not being uneducated; but being educated just enough to believe but not understand what they have been taught.'

'Not educated enough to think and question, you mean,' Brahma murmured, her scented hair brushing against his face. His eyes followed hers as they flew over another green sweep, gazing unseeingly in the distance below. 'Arrogance makes them believe that the stupider you are, the smarter you think you are, and the other way round! It keeps happening. An accomplished rishi like Vishwamitra, a self-made king like Ravan, both brilliant scholars yet foolish egotists! Impressed by their intellect and penance, you bestow your boons on your devotees, but they misuse the power of knowledge given to them each time. It happened with another set of asura brothers—Sumbha and Nisumbha—and again with Mahishasura . . .'

'They were all killed by a woman—as you later wisely advised me to do,' Brahma interrupted quietly, his voice soft against her nape.

'They were vain enough to think that they were indestructible and sought to conquer the three worlds by subjecting themselves to severe penance and prayers to you so that no man or demon could destroy them. But a woman could!' he could hear the laugh in her voice, her velvety eyes dancing up at him. 'The brothers Sumbha and Nisumbha even travelled to Pushkar, your favourite city on Earth, to make you grant your boons!'

Brahma looked down at her, tightening his arms, drawing her closer against him.

'They all wished for immortality, which I, of course, could not grant them, but I could grant them their wish of invincibility . . .'

'*Of not being killed by any male form—man or demon,*' she quoted with an exasperated sigh. 'Was it presumptuousness or plain chauvinism on their part to not consider a woman as their destined destroyer?' she smiled grimly, her lips curling in withering contempt. 'It took a devi to kill these brothers and Mahishasura; the Shakti, the unified symbol of all feminine force, manifested when evil forces threatened the very existence of the gods.'

A hint of a smile came into his coal-black eyes. 'No one can escape the Devi's supremacy.'

'These are also stories warning against the dangers of distributing generous boons!' she returned, her voice wafting in the crisp air. 'Knowledge and Education do not always make Wisdom.'

19

MOTHERHOOD

'Ganesh is the most well-behaved boy I have ever met!' murmured Sarasvati, giving the little cherubic boy a speculative look as he collected the books from her and left the room. 'He's adorable! And smart.'

Parvati beamed a smile of maternal pride. But what had surprised her was when Sarasvati looked at Ganesh, she had a rare affectionate smile on her face. It was sweet and yet so profound: like a sunbeam on a wet day. Parvati had never suspected from Sarasvati's reticence about babies and children that she was capable of showing Ganesh a charming and playful tenderness without any awkwardness.

'Both of you seem to get along famously,' observed Parvati. 'I didn't know you liked kids, Sarasvati.'

She said it without thinking much and instantly looked apologetic.

Sarasvati's steady eyes had gone cold suddenly. Then she relaxed, giving a small smile.

'You don't need to look so remorseful!' she chuckled. 'Though I am used to such slip-ups and those pitying glances.'

Parvati sighed, standing up to rearrange her son's books, the cobalt silk falling gracefully along her tall frame, the strings of pearls, turquoise and corals perfectly toning her sleek elegance and her slender feet tapping impatiently as was her manner, Sarasvati noted.

Sarasvati could see that Parvati was wearing make-up but couldn't see where it began or stopped. The make-up, even at this early hour, was a masterpiece. She could not help admiring how Parvati always managed to look so smart and svelte.

'I *am* sorry,' Parvati reiterated. 'It was an unfeeling remark.'

She glanced at Sarasvati, but was reassured by her smile.

Sarasvati shrugged lightly. 'There is no need for an explanation: either from you or me. I explained it just once—to the person who matters to me the most—and Brahma took it surprisingly well,' she said.

'Brahma has many mind-born sons, the world is his children,' Parvati gave a short laugh and stopped abruptly. 'Oh, I am being tactless again!' she sighed with dismay.

Sarasvati pressed her hand reassuringly. 'It does not matter,' she said quietly. 'I think everyone is more worried than I am about not being a mother!'

Parvati could not help persisting. 'It is how women are equipped: they want babies,' she murmured. 'What *you* are doing is unusual.'

'It *is* usual for me,' amended Sarasvati, her tone mild. 'It is not defiance, you know, but a decision. My decision,' she added quietly.

She got up to collect a glass of sherbet. 'And it is not always how women are equipped; they are made to think likewise. The idea that you are a real woman only if you bear a child has been borrowed from a man's mind,' she said, sipping the sherbet delicately. '*That* is true slavery. But by freeing herself from this expectation, by being an individualist, she doesn't become less feminine, does she? Nor is she denying anything to the woman in her. A woman's existence is more complex, more compelling than procreating—but again, that's something only she can decide!' she sighed, sweeping her hair off her shoulders. 'A certain conditioning has every woman feeling like her primary role is to have a child. It is not. I *don't* want children. It is not unusual.'

Parvati probed. 'If you don't want children, then what else do you want?'

'I wanted a calling. And I found one in an occupation I love.'

'But you don't have to give up one for the other!' exclaimed Parvati with a conviction that was at once dignified and affable.

'No, but then, I would have two full-time occupations. I want one—and it's not being a mother. And there is no regret, no guilt, nothing. You don't miss what you don't want.'

Parvati sighed in quiet exasperation.

Sarasvati remained unmoved. Nor was she unduly offended.

'I don't wish to be a mother, but I do recognize a mother is the source of existence, the beginning of every life on Earth,' Sarasvati contemplated with a thin smile. 'And that is why she will always be respected, loved and worshipped. Not just as one who gives birth, her role in raising a child, who would later be part of the collective fabric, but as one who is crucial in other ways as well. She is the first teacher, the first school for the child: she teaches and tutors, instilling the seed of birth and worth in her child.'

'*Since God couldn't be present everywhere; mothers were created,*' Parvati murmured softly, almost to herself.

'Parvati, you are the Mother of the Universe—the Ambika and the Amba, the gentle, nurturing aspect of Shakti, the Mother Goddess of Love, Fertility and Devotion, the source of power and beauty. And, of course, the mother of Kartikeya and Ganesh. So, yes, you would find my disinterest most unusual.'

'Though both my sons were born not from my womb,' Parvati reminded her tartly. 'That is unusual too!'

'Courtesy of the curse of Rati,' nodded Sarasvati, her face bland. She knew the full story of Parvati and Rati, Kama's wife. It all started when Kama was sent by the devas to Shiva—still mourning over the violent death of Sati, his first wife—to make him fall in love with Parvati. Enraged, Shiva had reduced Kama to ashes. A grieving Rati blamed Parvati for her husband's death and cursed her that as this charade had been orchestrated for the sake of having a child (their offspring was destined to kill the invincible Tarkasura), Parvati would never have a child from her womb.

'But you *are* a mother; nothing else matters,' Sarasvati assured gently, holding out her hand to Parvati. While she held it, Parvati was conscious of those cool, thoughtful eyes which rested on her with detachment and yet with something that Parvati reckoned was profound understanding.

But in that moving moment, a shadow—insistent and plain—disconcerted Parvati. She felt Sarasvati was aloof and it bothered her. She and Sarasvati were friendly and even cordial, but at the same time, she felt Sarasvati held something back to make her conscious of the fact that though welcome, she was still a stranger. There was a barrier between Sarasvati and her and the others. Sarasvati spoke a different language, not only of the mind but of the heart.

Parvati sighed. 'I am being quite prickly. I wonder how you deal with all the curious comments, often uncharitable, I am sure.'

'Actually, no one dares to mention it to my face,' Sarasvati said cheerfully. 'I am more amused than annoyed! Most seem to believe that my decision about how I use my body has something to do with them, so they feel the need to comment on how I'm doing it wrong.'

Parvati didn't move. She sat looking up at Sarasvati, an amazed expression in her eyes that Sarasvati found amusing: she was used to such scrutiny. Sarasvati knew they considered her odd, building an invisible, yet formidable wall between her and them.

'Since we have been discussing this so long, let me further clarify,' Sarasvati expanded, settling herself more deeply into the couch. 'Being constantly told that they know me better than I know myself and how I'll feel about this later in life isn't even the worst part. It gets more annoying when some insist I will never experience that "true joy of motherhood" without children. Would they be callous enough to say the same to those who desperately want children and can't have them?' she demanded, frowning hard. 'All because motherhood has been made out to be a woman's fate, her future; but it neither defines nor completes her as supposed. Choosing to be child-free was my conscious decision.'

Parvati sat still for a long moment, staring at Sarasvati, her eyes concerned. 'I am sure it was a mutual decision,' she said carefully. 'You must have taken this parenthood decision very seriously.'

'Non-parenthood decision,' amended Sarasvati with a laugh. 'My decision to not bear and rear was clear from the very start, for I just never thought of myself as a mother. We knew before we got married that we did not want children.'

'You didn't want marriage either,' Parvati reminded her. 'Yet you changed your decision and married Brahma. Perhaps it can happen again too?'

Sarasvati shook her head violently. 'Never!'

'When did you know?' asked Parvati curiously.

'I've just always known,' Sarasvati said simply. 'I've never wanted children, for as long as I can remember. I told myself that I was making the decision then and there: no new facts to consider, no guilt to deal with. So, I just went with my gut instinct—I suffered no maternal twinges ever. It's not that I went through any angst over it, wondering how I could look at a baby and feel nothing inside or trying to talk myself into having a child eventually. As you know well, I didn't want to get married either!' she added drily.

'So I never ever dreamt of a beautiful home with a husband, full of kids, the whole golden gift! Rather a home with books, my music and my pets!'

'And Brahma, what did *he* want?' probed Parvati.

'He is as unconventional as I am, I guess,' smiled Sarasvati.

Sarasvati saw one of her dark eyebrows lift in surprise.

'But seriously, he has been a surprise ever since he met you—first he fell in love, then chased you, then eventually made you marry him and even agreed not to have children . . .'

'He agreed and supported my views. But then, he is a rare man with a rare understanding,' said Sarasvati quietly. 'And that's why I love him,' she paused, looking past her, distantly into the woods beyond the window. 'In an ideal world, that's what you hope for—that you find someone you can be yourself with?' Sarasvati's voice was soused in a tenderness Parvati had never heard before, her velvety eyes softening. 'Some smart, witty man, honest and kind and full of fire who looks great even when all grey and dishevelled and can obviously see straight through you!'

Parvati was momentarily moved by her words.

Sarasvati broke the thickening silence with a sigh. 'Brahma has the rare ability to think outside of his own experiences; it is to see how other people—including his wife—experience the world. It is his simple ability to sit back and listen that is most admirable,' she murmured, her voice warm, rich with emotion. 'I had talked with him about how I did not want parenthood to be part of my life. Brahma comprehended and assented. Perhaps he too did not have a strong desire to become a parent, so going along with me was not much of an issue,' she lifted her elegant shoulders. 'But yes, it was a joint verdict; we did not make this decision quickly. We took the time to take a hard look at how much we wanted our lives to revolve around the raising of children. When we got to the heart of it, our desire to have kids just did not counterweigh concerns we had about allowing parenthood into our marriage.'

Parvati listened while Sarasvati watched her. She thought about this, then nodded, but all she could hear was the noisy racket of her sons playing in the garden or the hearty laugh of Shiva . . . she found it difficult to picture herself without him and her two sons, all together . . .

Sarasvati noticed the swift scepticism creeping into the other goddess's eyes. 'We had no concerns about how our non-parenthood would affect the marriage,' she assured lightly. 'As a child-free couple, I believe we have a happy marriage, and the absence of raising kids does not impact it. Having a fulfilling marriage definitely came first. What mattered more was about how parenthood would affect us, our goals. Pursuing our passions outweighed any need to raise children. It was a mutually responsible choice.'

'For whom?' Parvati countered wryly.

'Better for both: the world, and us,' quipped Sarasvati. 'Fewer children would make the world a better, and definitely less-crowded place.'

Parvati gave a snort. 'Is this selfishness in the guise of altruism?'

Sarasvati tucked her stray curl behind her ears and said carefully, 'I find this accusation of being selfish particularly ironic as it is often followed by "Oh, you are missing out on a loving family! Who will look after you later?!"'

She caught the awkward look in Parvati's large, luminous eyes. ' . . . Assuming your children will become your caregivers someday is selfish, and naïve, I think,' Sarasvati gave a sardonic smile. 'Besides, it's not always selfish to want what you want; it's being honest.'

Parvati flushed. She had not meant anything in particular, and at the implication that she had, she became more uneasy. 'I was discussing, not criticizing. You would make such a wonderful mother—you are affectionate, generous and patient.'

'Would I?' Sarasvati looked dubiously at her, lifting her shoulders. 'I am not sure what I would be like in that role. But such fleeting thoughts are just that—thoughts. Not fear, not a regret that needs to be eased: they don't run my life. It never was a defining factor. To this day, kids and babies make me very uncomfortable. Playing with your sons occasionally, Parvati, is different. As distinctive as bearing kids and bearing with kids!' she twinkled.

Parvati shook her head. 'There's still time,' she said. 'You might change your mind.'

'Oh no, I am certain I shan't have a baby ever!' grinned Sarasvati, with a wave of her hands. 'Do you think, after all that I have told you, I shall wait until I'm more tired and less tolerant to introduce an invasive, demanding, bawling baby into my very established life?' she asked with a hearty laugh. 'The concept of making marriage enticing is based on the notion that a family is beautiful and having children is beautiful. But there are many unspoken things that actually happen to a woman physically and mentally. This is why I say leave the choice to the woman. It is she who is going to be a wife or mother, not the man.'

'But you are a goddess, you have to act on behalf of other women and womanhood!' argued Parvati.

'But does motherhood—or say, even marriage—alone define a woman and womanhood?' asked Sarasvati quietly. 'As a goddess, I would rather attempt to redefine fundamentals along more egalitarian lines in the world which worships us. Like . . .' she paused to wave her hand vaguely. '. . . The very genesis of voicing gender assumptions against a set of expectations like marriage and motherhood.'

Parvati had a faint idea of what Sarasvati was talking about, and she slowly nodded and Sarasvati nodded back at her as they returned to their conversation.

'If I have to talk about rejecting marriage and motherhood, it is purely due to personal convictions,' maintained Sarasvati. 'Like there are those who seem to be willing to choose to mother, but not to get married . . .'

'I can well understand a woman to be more comfortable being a single mother than banking on the support of a husband first and then becoming a mother,' smiled Parvati. 'Rishi Vishwamitra's and Menaka's daughter Shakuntala proved it beautifully, didn't she? She was the first single mother who brought up her son from King Dushyant on her own in the forest! You don't need a man to raise your child or, as in my case, a man to even have a child!' she gave a self-conscious chuckle.

She meant the birth of Ganesh, Sarasvati reflected. Ganesh was born out of the clay-and-sandal paste from Parvati's body, out of which she created a statue of a boy to whom she lent life to become her second son.

Sarasvati tilted her head in quiet agreement. 'It is crucial to understand this choice of motherhood, rendering marriage unnecessary!'

'Or when she reckons that someone is not the "right" man, who wouldn't make a good husband or father,' commented Parvati wryly.

Sarasvati again gave a slow nod. 'So as I said, it all comes down to the personal decision of the woman—whether she wants marriage, motherhood, motherhood without marriage, marriage without motherhood or if she wants neither or both!'

Sarasvati paused, observing Parvati's sceptical expression. 'This traditional role enforced on women right from birth already makes them subservient enough: as wives, as progeny-givers.'

Parvati shot a quick look at Sarasvati. Her bright eyes softened a little when she regarded the other unadorned goddess clad in her customary white silk. This was the kind of woman she would have been proud to have as a daughter: a hard, tough go-getter without any man's hold hanging over her. Brahma had created the perfect woman in an imperfect world, she thought.

'Did you ever complain to Brahma about this "natural disparity" and how he needs to improvise on his creation?' she grinned.

'Always!' Sarasvati grinned back.

'Well, next time tell him, I had mine without the womb, so he can pick some ideas!' jested Parvati.

Sarasvati put her hand on her arm. 'You are their mother, nothing else matters. And not just theirs, you are the Mother of the world.'

'As are you, Sarasvati,' returned Parvati, quietly. 'You are the Mother of the Vedas, bestowing knowledge and art, music and muse on her children. We often question everything about the "naturalness" of motherhood, ascribed only to mothers specifically and to women in general. It is furthered by the concept of selflessness, a distinctive representation of maternal love. You need not be a mother to bear a child or become a father by begetting one. Brahma has fathered many mind-born sons, he is an exemplary father to Narad, Daksha and the four Kumars . . .' she cut short, realizing dismally she had trod on another forbidden topic.

'It's fine. Brahma is no longer angry with the four Kumars. They are his sons, after all,' Sarasvati drew in a deep breath, thinking of the four rishis who roamed the universe as children, respectively named Sanak, Sanatan, Sanandan and Sanatkumar. Their collective decision of lifelong celibacy—*brahmacharya*—against Brahma's wishes had long been resolved. Between their wanderings through the spiritual universe, they visited their father asking him for tips on teaching. All the four brothers had studied the Vedas from her and now travelled together, touring the world, without any desire of matrimony but just the zealous purpose to teach and educate.

'If Brahma has his sons, you have your daughters too,' remarked Parvati with an enigmatic smile.

Furrowing her brows, Sarasvati studied Parvati, her eyes interested, her mind conjecturing.

'Vani, Kavya and Sahitya,' she deduced swiftly, with a quick flash of a smile, her eyes growing incandescently soft.

'As the presiding goddess of all knowledge, you have birthed all three!' commented Parvati, leaning back in her chair. 'First was born Vani—language—sweet and alluring, born through the sound of Om. It was with Vani that the vigorous tradition of speech and recitation was employed resourcefully for oral communication. Vani made language rich in vocabulary, phonology, grammar and syntax, undiluted in its purity, making it the perfect language for word formation and pronunciation.'

Sarasvati listened, hunching her shoulders, leaning forward on her couch, her face intense.

'With Kavya was born the first person to bring poetry to this world, expressing in perfect rhythmic and structured metres,' continued Parvati, tapping her fingers lightly on the arm of the chair to replicate rhythm. 'Her utterance was the earliest poetry, embodying all that poetry represents. She was told about Vani—the language prose born before her, her elder sister. This is how Vani and Kavya together became profound with their expressive quality, bringing out the best,' she continued. 'And then came Sahitya, who followed her sisters wherever they went, trying different modes of expression, residing in the minds of all writers and poets. Your daughters are the fountainhead of knowledge, Sarasvati.'

Sarasvati sat motionless. She was intent, her pale face flushed with pride, her eyes luminous with love.

'That's when, as the divine authority on academics and arts, you decided to give them away to the scholars and enlightened rishis,' said Parvati, admiration flaring up in her eyes. 'I recall how you took them to Ganga for a holy dip . . .'

'Ganga is my closest friend. I needed her to bless my children.'

'A rishi heard them and took them in. He was so entranced by them that he swiftly composed a poem in praise of you in the Rig Veda and many followed suit. Your girls helped them, being immensely proud daughters of their mother. Since then, they have moved from one ashram to another, from one house to another of poets and writers. They were recently seen at Rishi Valmiki's ashram . . . I think they are helping him compose a lengthy poem?'

Sarasvati nodded, beaming. 'An epic poem.'

Parvati's eyes widened in sincere appreciation.

'Rishi Parashar's young son, Vyas, too is seeking their blessings. He wishes to pen the longest epic poem in the world,' she pondered, then she looked at Sarasvati, her clear eyes inquiring. 'I hear they are also helping compile the Puranas?'

'Yes, it is a vast genre of literature, almost encyclopaedic, with intricate layers of symbolism depicted within their stories,' explained Sarasvati with her customary nod.

'So your daughters are responsible for producing the earliest works of the Rig Veda hymns and poets like Valmiki and Vyas in the history of rhythmic poetry!'

'They are still there, constantly mingling with other scholars and poets,' beamed Sarasvati, her velvety eyes darkening with maternal pride. 'Searching for another Valmiki and Vyas perhaps?'

'They have been groomed well by you,' responded Parvati, 'despite the fact that you could not always be by their side, busy here resolving disputes in the three worlds!'

Sarasvati gave a short laugh. 'Rather, smoothening ruffled feathers of the egomaniacs! Be it the devas, danavs, manavs or the rishis, ego, not enlightenment, seems to rule their minds,' she added, with a slight curl of her lips. 'Yes, we have our children: all that we created, big and small.'

Parvati crossed her arms in front of her, leaning back, her face thoughtful, wondering what a huge difference a woman could make to a man. Years back, Brahma would not have been what he was now: a husband and a father and a wiser creator.

'Possibly, both of you as creators, ironically, do not conform to traditional parenthood, not always reaffirming the guardianship myth. I think you have shattered all the conventional notions: the "naturalness" of parenting, the "curse" of childlessness, the dread of "barrenness" yet filling your lives with purpose and pleasure. Yours is not about a life of lacking, with a loss of what might have been: it is a life of love with a gift to treasure.'

Sarasvati smiled and looked at her searchingly.

'Creators are the original parents, the makers of their progeny.'

20

BOONS AND CURSES

Minutes went past. Brahma was sitting on his chair on the side of the desk, away from the window. He moved slightly to reach for the sheaves.

'Work,' he explained, leaning back with a resigned shrug.

She patted his hand as he picked up his pen, her fingers making his skin tingle. He stopped looking questioningly.

She nodded and sighed. 'Perhaps this isn't the right time, but I have to ask; but should I allow our work to come between us now?'

Brahma looked up from his books at his wife's short tone. He started to say something, and then caught the look in her eyes.

'All our arguments, dear, often, if not always, arise at work and because of work,' he said amiably.

'Why is that each time you grant a boon to your devotee, it is I who have to rein them in?' she asked suddenly.

He lifted his heavy shoulders in a resigned shrug, mentally preparing himself to face a potentially long debate with his annoyed wife. 'Are we at it again?' he muttered under his breath. 'But I try not to interfere in the affairs of the other devas and even more rarely in mortal affairs,' he responded mildly.

But his placid tone seemed to irk Sarasvati more. 'Do you? You did force Soma to give Tara back to her husband, Rishi Brihaspati,' she reminded him sharply.

'That was to bring peace to the warring couple,' he sighed.

'But Tara wasn't too keen to return to her husband!' she quipped. 'It was not about the war between two men, it was the choice of one woman: whom to love and whom to live with!'

'All's well with them now, Soma fell in love again and got married to Rohini and you even rescued poor Soma from his curse!' he reminded her, leaning back and stroking his beard.

'Yes, precisely, the curse . . . and the boons, which I was talking about and which you so generously distribute!'

'I didn't give Soma a boon or a curse. Come to the point,' he said resignedly. 'But first let me explain why, as you say I "generously distribute" boons. My boons are not godsend blessings as you seem to believe,' he corrected her gently. 'I offer them to make those blessed realize their own potential. I am not handing out boons to devas, manavs or asuras but ideas created by my creative Brahma force. From ideas to action, there are seven stages: Indra who symbolizes dream; Shakti, the strength of illusion; third is Brahma's creativity; then Vishnu's stability; followed by Shiva's determination; and finally, there is

Shani's compulsion and Yama—that is, death. In these seven stages, Vishnu comes after Brahma, which means he kills the demons blessed by me. It means Vishnu gets rid of the demonic ideas created by My creative force,' Brahma threw her a careful look. 'I thought you would understand, Sarasvati. As Brahma, I symbolize a force that can make ideas positive and prolific as well as demonic and bizarre. It is up to the blessed how he uses the boon.'

He gave her a quick glance. She was looking away from him, remote and thoughtful, her face as expressionless and as smooth as an ivory mask.

'Exactly, that they don't use it constructively proves they are unworthy!' she contended.

She reminded him of Ravan, Sumbha and Nisumbha, and Vishwamitra. She told him a lot of things in detail slowly and carefully. And Brahma began in some vague way to look jaded. His eyes flickered at her, away, back again, restlessly.

'. . . Each time, they became more powerful because of your boons!' she accused. 'Vishwamitra, in his arrogance, even had the temerity to create an alternate Universe, a replica of yours—the Trishanku Milky Way—just to spite Vashist and yet, thanks to you, he was made a Brahmarishi!'

'Not thanks to me,' Brahma said mildly. 'Thanks to his own achievements.'

'I am well aware of that,' she said vehemently. 'Before giving a particular boon to a person, should you not ensure whether that person deserves it? Whether he is capable of preserving the boon without misusing it?'

'Vishwamitra was entitled to it, he had earned it,' explained Brahma, unperturbed.

'And did he earn the deadly Brahmastra too?' she asked. 'The most lethal weapon of war, capable of destroying the world, made by the Creator himself!'

Her voice was harsh and full of emotion.

Brahma turned to look at her, surprised by her vehemence. They stared at each other. He could see by the expression in her eyes no one would make her change her mind: *he stood accused*.

'It can be used only by a select few, to be employed solely to uphold dharma and satya when both are in danger of being lost,' said Brahma evenly. 'Yes, Brahmastra is the weapon of Brahma. Like other celestial weapons, it is invoked by a special mantra and can be used to destroy anything created by Me—Brahma. The Brahmastra is an ordinary weapon made extraordinary by the user.'

'Once discharged, it cannot be retrieved. Nor does it have a counter-attack, so it needs to be used extremely discreetly. And discretion often is not the best weapon used by man,' she said emphatically.

He looked up sharply. There was a note in her voice that brought him up short. 'Yes. But there is the Brahmadanda, which is deadlier than the Brahmastra as it manifests with the fifth head of Brahma—your deadly, violent self,' retorted Sarasvati heatedly. 'And then there is the Brahmashira Astra, manifested from your four heads and four times stronger than the normal Brahmastra. All of them can annihilate the world. The spot where it eventually crashes remains barren forever, making all beings and soil infertile. Life ceases, greenery vanishes, rains dry up, drought flourishes, people either die or live deformed. How can a creator create such a terrible weapon of destruction? Is that your great legacy of violence and destruction you have bestowed to the world *you* created, Brahma?'

Her pale face was suffused with colour as she was agitated. He didn't say anything. After a long pause, she turned to look intently at him.

'It is another wrong assumption that Vishnu, the Preserver, only protects; Brahma, the Creator, only creates; and Shiva, the Destructor, only destroys,' he said gently. 'All three of us—Brahma, Vishnu and Shiva—are capable of creation, protection and destruction, according to our wish and requirement,' he added, but had a sudden notion that she was not going to let it go. *There was something very insistent in her words.*

'And what does this say?' she demanded.

'That the faithful are devotees essentially, and only those who want such high level of actualization with God take that path,' he returned mildly. 'For instance, Shiva never judges a person before giving a boon. He is Ashutosha, one who can be easily pleased, who is just and fair. Shiva has the ability to deal with the worst of the worse humans. He gives his blessings and knowledge to all. He is beyond good and evil.'

'But not the followers; they use your boons for evil and their own good!' she snapped. 'Coming back to the same argument: You should know better, you dispense boons so charitably,' she added, casting him one of her painfully direct stares, which Brahma was now unaffected by.

'How am I supposed to control that?' he asked placidly. 'I give a gift, and the receiver should know how to treasure it. We give knowledge, Sarasvati; wisdom has to be learnt, not taught.'

She gave him a long, thoughtful look, her fingers lightly pressing her temple. 'Brahma, by being the Creator you are also the god of creative thinking . . . thereby giving the blessed the power and ability to think and modify what I have given.'

'But they modify it to unrealistic, often demonic and horrific proportions! Your Brahma force may be the ideal force for experiments and creative thinking, but it is seen in its most violent interpretations!'

Brahma shook his head. 'Sadly that is how they misconstrue it. I symbolize an idea, independent of all other ideas of life.'

'Your ideas create crisis and you don't want to own the responsibility of those ideas or boons!' she retorted, tossing her hair tetchily. 'You are not a god of action like Vishnu; you seem more like a crisis maker! Since You, Brahma, have no upper or lower limits, these ideas can easily reach demonic proportions, as seen and witnessed so often! Blessed with them, these favoured few have less goodness and more arrogance. The wise who is arrogant is . . .'

'No, it is wise not to be arrogant,' amended Brahma suavely.

Sarasvati flicked her hair off her shoulder impatiently. 'Either way, the wise men that you bless are not blessed with humility: that's my point,' she remarked drily. 'I can understand a person proud of his abilities, but arrogance is inexcusable. It is an inflated, often overestimated opinion of those very abilities he has been blessed with! Pride is usual and sufficiently justifiable, arrogance is not.'

'Humility, like arrogance, is an attitude, not an ability,' he moved his arms in the lazy beginning of a shrug. 'Then what? We bless by granting aptitudes, not attitudes.'

She thought about this, then nodded. 'Yet your blessing of aptitude becomes a terrible attitude!' she conceded with a lift of her delicate eyebrows. 'Those you have blessed, do not give their blessings to others. Dronacharya was unconquerable in the Kurukshetra war because he held your sword Asi, another deadly weapon. This was the great guru, who, despite being an acharya, was an unjust teacher. He refused to accept *sutaputra* Karna because the boy was not a Kshatriya,' she said, her voice dipping dangerously low in anger. 'Instead of accepting the child as his student, as a teacher should, he drove him out. He did worse with Eklavya, the young prince of the Nishadha tribe. The tribal boy wanted to become a disciple of Dronacharya, but was rejected by him. Disappointed, but not discouraged, Eklavya made a statue of his famed teacher with the mud Drona walked upon, and worshipped it as his guru. For many years, he practised himself to excel in archery. Instead of saluting such an extraordinary student, Drona extracted a most terrible *gurudakshina*. He asked for Eklavya's right thumb, which the young boy readily agreed to give, severing his thumb and offering it to his guru, knowing well he could never string a bow any more.'

Sarasvati paused, chewed her lower lip, frowning, with her eyes giving a stern look.

'And for this crime, you cursed him . . .' said Brahma. '. . . With an ungallant death.'

'What about the living death he inflicted on those two blameless boys?' she countered bitterly. 'Knowledge belongs to all, and, as a teacher, it was the acharya's duty to impart it to all.'

'Drona was possibly compelled by the refuge the kingdom of Hastinapur had given him,' commented Brahma.

'Loyalty or plain pride?' she scoffed. 'Drona wanted to put his obligation to Hastinapur over dharma so that no one questioned his honour. Whatever his reasons may be, Drona criminally cheated Eklavya and Karna, depriving them of his knowledge and instead achieved something for himself. All to protect his promise to Arjun that he would make him the world's greatest archer, and his oath of loyalty to his patron, the throne of Hastinapur.'

He watched with an empty stare that meant nothing.

'You cursed Dronacharya, yet you forgave his mentor, the murderous Parashuram, as he dipped in your purifying waters of River Sarasvati after ridding the world of Kshatriyas twenty-one times as revenge for the killing of his father by the mighty King Kartavirya Arjuna . . .'

'. . . After cleansing the earth of the scourge of tyranny,' she corrected.

'You forgave Vishwamitra too,' he pointed out. 'You generously blessed him with the Gayatri mantra.'

'That was when I saw his devotion and contrition, when he conquered his lust, anger, attachment, arrogance and envy. Only then did he become the first master of the Gayatri Sadhana. Rishi Vishwamitra created the Gayatri mantra from his mind, as a Universal prayer, which asks for a clear intellect so that the truth is reflected without distortion. It was he who harmonized the mantra for the common man, to be chanted by man and woman alike with humility and reverence.'

'But you did pardon him,' he repeated.

'He felt remorse, and remorse is repentance, retribution,' she said. 'The ones whom you grant it to are not remorseful but misuse your boons for power, glory and greed.'

'That is their way of retribution, that is their salvation,' Brahma quipped cryptically. 'Boons are given, but blessed are those who take them as blessings.'

He paused before adding, 'Or they become a curse.'

'You're late, Brahma, as usual,' Sarasvati said in a mock stern tone, smiling at him. He cut a fine figure with his sheer white silk, enhancing his severe, chiselled features and grey temples. 'I was beginning to wonder if you were coming at all.'

'Sorry,' he returned, a faint smile drifted across his face. 'But I was held up . . .' he threw her a quick look, surmising her mood. 'I'm here for you now.'

It was one of his favourite days, Brahma thought, as Sarasvati readjusted the white shawl over his broad shoulders. He proudly looked at his wife, diminutive and intent as she smoothened the wrinkles of his angavastra. It was her day. Sarasvati would be holding a music performance in full attendance: the maharishis, devarishis, rajarishis and brahmarishis, seated on the left, and asuras, yakshas, garudas, gandharvas, kinnaras and kimpurushas on the opposite aisle.

He's clearly very pleased—and proud, Sarasvati observed him standing tall, grandly greeting his guests. His pride and love for her was touching and today again, as every other day, she was moved by his sensitivity. It was with a rare sense of gratitude that she settled down on the cushioned seat, fine-tuning her veena on her lap. By the elaborate doorway stood the master of the mansion, the Creator of the world, resplendent in ivory silk, matching with his silver crown and stubble. He held a lamp to show the guests the way inside, smiling cordially and nodding his head.

She raised the veena and the hall immediately fell into deep silence. Sarasvati struck a chord, then began playing and singing softly. Playing two pieces, her face glowed in an exquisite expression, suffusing the room with music and emotion; its warmth and insight producing a pure and lofty feeling.

She was playing a difficult, long and monotonous, but interesting passage. Brahma listened to her music, completely rapt, unaware of the squat figure who had slipped in unnoticed.

The stranger stood watching the performance; his deep-set eyes moving swiftly from the slim, white figure playing the veena to the grey-haired man sitting on the gold throne watching her. He noticed an empty chair and sat down.

It took a lot to startle him, but this hall brought him to an abrupt halt, his face clearly showing his astonishment as well as disdain. It was a huge hall. He first became aware of the space when a vast stretch of polished marble spread out

before him. It seemed to go on till the long red silk drapes
that covered the windows. Rows of white cushioned divans
and two white thrones cringed in the empty space. A slim and
elegant sitar stood in an alcove by the window. On either side
of the thrones were lit six-foot-tall white candles. A life-size
painting, supposedly Sarasvati's latest masterpiece, adorned
one of the red walls of the room. Other walls were covered
with red silk drapes, but his eyes kept moving back to the
startlingly white and beautiful painting.

So, this was just a glimpse of Brahmalok, thought the
guest warily, as he settled more comfortably in his chair,
inhaling the faint smell of incense in the room. Before the
music came to an end, the man started to get up, rising
rudely from his chair.

Brahma looked up in quick anger, but noticing the
man, his ire melted into surprise.

'Bhrigu!' he exclaimed.

Sarasvati stopped, her hands halting midway at the
strings, swivelling her clear, clever eyes to the man in
question. Maharishi Bhrigu was Brahma's manas putra,
born of his mind, a small, dour man. He was one of the
seven great sages, the saptarishis, and was also among the
many Prajapatis—the facilitators of Creation by Brahma.

From the grim expression on the rishi's florid face, she
had a sudden notion that there was something very wrong
with Bhrigu's visit. This man had not come to exchange
pleasantries with his father.

The maharishi, upon being acknowledged, sat back
on his chair abruptly, without even greeting Brahma
and others.

Brahma frowned.

'First you interrupt a performance and then you do not greet or meet the host. Why this impertinence, Bhrigu?'

Bhrigu didn't move, staying quiet. He sat regarding Brahma, an odd expression in his eyes that the host didn't like.

'What's on your mind?' Brahma asked curtly.

'That's for you to say,' Bhrigu returned peremptorily. 'You were clearly deeply engrossed in your wife,' he added with a laconic leer.

Brahma flushed.

'Sarasvati was playing music,' he said tightly, his lips compressed into a thin, unhappy line.

Bhrigu pulled his chair forward, still not getting up, but looking at Brahma, and said, 'I don't have to tell you how discourteous it is that I enter this room and you do not notice my presence, on the contrary, I see you lost in her . . . er, in her music!'

Brahma sat still for a long time, staring at Bhrigu, his eyes like granite and a pulse throbbing on his temple. 'You are being uncivil. This is an insult, son!'

Bhrigu ran his thumbnail along his thick, starkly black moustache before adding insolently, '*You* insulted me by ignoring me, Father.'

Brahma went white, his eyes cold with rage. 'What sort of intolerable behaviour is this?' he demanded fiercely, keeping his voice down. 'Bhrigu, you are my son; you belong to an evolved race of the most intelligent people and you have acquired many powers because of your great meditation; I could have never anticipated such boorish behaviour from you. Do you think that you are greater than any of the maharishis here? Are you greater than Anasuya? Or Rishi Gautam, who cursed Devendra here? Are you more powerful than Rishi Jamadagni?'

'I may be, I may not be,' stated the rishi succinctly. 'But that does not validate your bad manners either!'

Brahma opened his mouth to speak, ready to explode. He started to say something but then caught the look in Sarasvati's eyes. He glowered and sat down, his fingers curling into angry fists. He stared at her, his right fist grinding into the palm of his left hand.

There was distinctly something in Bhrigu's manner that Sarasvati did not like. His whole demeanour seemed suspicious.

'Why are you telling us all this, Bhrigu?' Sarasvati asked at last, her eyes narrowing on the man still seated on the chair. 'You have clearly come here to create a scene. You should be thankful for I just stopped a father from cursing his son,' she said, her eyes unsmiling and smile frosty.

Facing her, Bhrigu shrugged. 'Don't you agree with me that ideally as the Creator, Lord Brahma should have both the sattva and rajasguna—spiritual qualities, along with physical passion?'

'Stop it, Bhrigu!' interrupted Brahma, his voice soft and dangerous.

Sarasvati said, 'I know of your intentions, Bhrigu. On my very banks, many great sages have gathered to participate in a mahayajna, where all of you could not decide who of the Trinity is the most eminent to be the Pradhanta, the master of the yajna. It has been agreed that you, Maharishi Bhrigu, will test the Trinity and choose the foremost. You first went to Kailash, but on being halted by Nandi, the guarding bull, as Shiva and Parvati were in their private chamber, you cursed the Lord. Likewise, you went to test Vishnu at Vaikunth, entered his chamber without permission, and on seeing the Lord resting, you shook him awake by kicking his chest . . .'

The hall broke into a collective gasp of incredulity.

Sarasvati continued, her velvety eyes hard, 'Instead of being angry, Vishnu, with his usual generosity of spirit, enquired in all politeness, "Maharishi, are you hurt? My strong chest might have injured you!"'

Hearing her words, there was a marked titter in the hall. His anger dispelled, Brahma gave a sudden snort, bursting out in loud laughter, his heavy chest rumbling with obvious amusement. 'Vishnu outwitted you, did he? And, what did you do, Bhrigu? Declare him the winner?' he said, grinning broadly.

Bhrigu's fleshy complexion turned a dark red.

'Yes!' he shouted, leaning forward to glare at Brahma. 'I was testing who was the best amongst the three of you.'

'And how, pray, does it concern you?' interjected Brahma smoothly, a hard little smile lighting his face.

The mood in the room changed rapidly.

'Who are you to test the Trimurtis?' demanded Rishi Vashist. 'And what sort of a silly test is that? How could you rudely intrude into their privacy and then expect them to be polite to you?'

Rishi Atri added, his face grave, 'Do you realize that you would be a dead man for such impertinence! You curse those who have blessed you, made you famous and who can turn you to ash with a mere glance? Brahma is your father, and you did not spare even him in your fervour for mad glory!'

Sarasvati cut in, her voice dripping ice. 'Bhrigu, *you* are the last person to cast aspersions, you are a vain egoist yourself!' she countered, her eyes glacial. 'You reckon you can get away with anything. You, Bhrigu . . .'

'Please no, don't lay a curse on me!' begged Bhrigu. 'You stopped my father from cursing me; please don't curse me yourself! Devi Lakshmi, enraged with my misconduct, cursed me as well as my ilk, that henceforth she would never bless us with wealth. After I explained my behaviour, she said that her curse would haunt us till we are blessed by you, Devi Sarasvati.'

'Am I to bless an arrogant person like you?' she asked silkily. 'This is not the first time you have erred . . .' she said. 'Once, when the three worlds existed in peace, Brahma created the saptarishis who would spread knowledge among the inhabitants. *You* were one of them, Bhrigu . . .'

Bhrigu blinked and sat back.

'All of you travelled around the three worlds and continued your divine work of narrating the Vedas that was revealed to you by Brahma. The other six sons invoked me and gained enlightenment. But you, the seventh son, Bhrigu, refused, arguing you were in the quest for what hunger means, for which you would invoke Lakshmi, one who nourishes the body and not the one who nourishes the mind. But little did you know that in this quest, you were actually searching for knowledge. Did you learn, o learned rishi, that everything in this universe is ultimately about hunger—hunger for food, wealth and knowledge? Man is a greedy being.' She murmured, her slow smile warming her glacial face.

Bhrigu's eyes bulged, apprehension slowly creeping in.

'For a balanced and happy life—it is you, Goddess Sarasvati, who nourishes the mind, and Goddess Lakshmi who nourishes the body, and both are equally important,' blurted Bhrigu, panic in his voice.

'You realize that now?' she raised a brow. 'In your unwarranted arrogance, you tried to pit the Trinity against each other, just as you had done with Lakshmi and me. So how can you receive both wisdom and wealth while nourishing both mind and body?' she asked pleasantly.

'Just as you say,' Bhrigu implored, getting hurriedly to his feet. 'Sadly and surely, I have realized that the best of merits is to remain free of vain pride and conceit. I beg pardon from the gods who have displayed great forbearance and kindness towards me. . .'

'Qualities you cannot boast of, Bhrigu,' Sarasvati chided. 'Yet, they will be generous and glad to bless you, seeing that you have understood your folly,' she said, bestowing him with a sharp look. Turning to the crowded hall, she announced, 'From this day, the Trimurti shall be the supreme owners of the *purnahuti* and the faithful will be able to offer the *aahuti*, the oblations, to the god of their choice and devotion.'

In the applause that followed, Bhrigu managed to sneak off, gone unnoticed the way he had come.

Brahma was the first to notice his absence. 'He scurried away!' he exclaimed indignantly. 'He should be thankful that he was so easily spared!'

Sarasvati looked at him, a thoughtful expression on her face. 'He is more than thankful; hopefully he is penitent. And it is his repentance that shall make him more prolific: he will be the first compiler of predictive astrology and begin to write his most famous work, the *Bhrigu Samhita*—a tome on *jyotish vidya*—to help rishis earn their living so that they never remain poor—with mind or money.'

'Removing Lakshmi's curse with your blessings,' murmured Brahma.

'He learnt his lesson,' chuckled Sarasvati. She paused, throwing him a saucy look. 'Did *you*?'

Brahma patted her arm and stood up.

'You mean me being too generous with my boons?' he laughed softly and looked at her through his long lashes. She lightly touched his smooth grey hair, peeking under his crown at the nape of his neck.

'. . . Being more careful about giving and to whom,' she corrected elegantly. She stepped closer and stood by his side, slipping her arm through his.

'Like that, is it?' he said, a look of sheepish admiration coming to his eyes as he slipped his arm around her waist.

She had taught her lesson well to both father and son today.

21

THE TWO GODDESSES

Narada appeared at the doorway. He never entered; he invariably appeared, like a well-oiled apparition. Sarasvati groaned; she could not avoid him.

'I have a question for both of you,' announced Narada with a perfunctory bow and settled himself comfortably on a couch near the window.

Lakshmi threw Sarasvati a knowing look. Sarasvati nodded, tilting her head, a polite smile fixed on her lips. Both knew what Narada would say. *Or stir up trouble*, sighed Sarasvati, straightening her shoulders in mental preparation. Narada was a known mischief-maker in his role as the divine messenger of the gods, or in his words, 'I am a journalist! I bring news, carry messages, make stories . . .'

His notorious habit of meddling often made it hard to believe that he was a scholar. As Brahma's manas putra, he was the brilliant son of a brilliant father: he was a master of both the Vedas and the Upanishads, and was just as conversant with history, the Puranas and the six Angas: pronunciation, grammar, prosody, terms, religious rites and astronomy. Eloquent, witty and endowed with sharp memory, he was proficient in the philosophical texts that allowed him to differentiate while applying general principles to particular cases. That's how he consistently outwitted everyone, even Rishi Brihaspati—the guru of the devas. He could swiftly interpret contraries by referring to different situations, his understanding of logic and the *nyay* of moral science coming to quick use. Tenacious and sharp, he knew the science of morals and politics very well, and how and when to play them against or with one another. In short, he was a master of the art of distortion.

Narada was a good talker, if only you could keep him off any subject, taking on a position of being unassailable and exalted. He allowed himself, especially when one was alone with him, to be amusing and boldly blunt. He had a pleasantly malicious tongue and there was no scandal involving any exalted personage that did not reach him and he did not hesitate in sharing it with others. Sarasvati recalled the 'scandal' involving them that had rocked the three worlds. Narada knew more about the inner life of the celestials than the Trimurtis.

Sarasvati glanced guardedly at the slight young man with dark wavy hair. It was not just the fact that he was Brahma's son that made both of them circumspect. There was also a recent history of disagreements. As the Goddess of Knowledge, she had been reluctant to confer on this master of sixty-four vidyas the gift of knowing the past, present and future. She did eventually, but upon realizing that he would misuse it, she smartly added a restraining corollary: that although he would tell the truth and warn people, they would never believe him. He had not taken it too kindly.

A smile on his serene, pale face suggested that he had forgotten about their previous argument. 'What's your question?' she asked politely, throwing Lakshmi a warning look.

'This question keeps arising in my mind: who is it that people as well as Brahma, the Creator, needs more? Lakshmi or Sarasvati? Wealth or Knowledge?'

'We were having a good chat till you came along, Narada,' remarked Sarasvati, her eyes narrowing. 'But now you wish to turn friends into quarrelling sisters?'

'Isn't Brahma the best person to answer the question?' responded Lakshmi, spreading her hands.

Both had spoken at once and each gave the other a guarded look: Narada was succeeding in his ploy.

Narada's smile widened, 'I want to know what *you* have to say,' he chuckled. 'After all, but for winning a draw, Man needs knowledge and skills to earn wealth: he needs Sarasvati to get Lakshmi. Greater your knowledge, better are the chances of wealth accumulation. A carpenter cannot make or sell a table without knowledge, nor can a farmer grow crops if he does not know how to farm . . .' his voice trailed off as he deliberately kept his unsaid words hanging, his eyes shifting craftily between the two goddesses.

He regarded them quizzically: they were a study in contrasts. Sarasvati wore a simple white sari with a golden chain at her waist and a string of pearls around her long,

slender neck. Lakshmi looked resplendent in a radiant
green heavy brocaded silk, glittering from head to toe with
gold and emeralds, her flowing red-gold hair adding just
the right finish to that magnificent look.

'One needs both, of course,' chorused the two goddesses
simultaneously.

Narada feigned surprise, his brows shooting up on his
thin face. 'But how so? One can well argue that knowledge
can enrich the brain but not the man—knowledge doesn't
assuage clawing hunger, can it? For that, you need food you
can buy,' he paused deliberately. 'But then, there's another
argument—wealth keeps man prosperous but gives no
meaning to life.'

'Brahma needs both knowledge and wealth to sustain
the cosmos,' said Sarasvati. 'Without knowledge, he
cannot plan. Without wealth, he cannot implement a
plan.'

'Yes, wealth sustains life; the arts give value to life,'
concurred Lakshmi with her gentle smile. 'So, both
Lakshmi and Sarasvati are needed to live a full life.'

*Ya Brahma Achyuta Shankara—prabhrutibhir devaha
sada poojita, Saa maam paatu Sarasvati Bhagavati nihshessa
jaddya apaha,'* Narada recited softly.

'Is that meant to provoke me, Narada, mentioning
this hymn that people invoke in the name of Sarasvati?'
enquired Lakshmi mildly, her gold bangles clinking.

'Always adored by gods like Brahma, Achyuta—that is
Vishnu—Shankar and many others, O Goddess Sarasvati,
protect, awaken and deliver me from my ignorance,' she
pertly translated.

Narada flushed. He blinked and continued, 'Yes, but it's a fact that you, O Sarasvati Devi, our Goddess of Learning, are hugely revered by the gods.'

'Am I?' enquired an amused Sarasvati. 'I thought I was considered haughty and argumentative.'

'That you are, when you wish to!' laughed Lakshmi, the emerald earrings dangling as she moved her head. 'They think you are odd because you are different—a free soul, Sarasvati, fearless, frank and ready to give back. Poor Narada will soon bear the brunt of that sharp tongue!'

Narada gave a sheepish grin. 'I fear to admit, but yes, even I, the eternal gabber, am left speechless! We revere Sarasvati here, but both manav and danav seem to love Lakshmi more, the goddess of big things and big money,' he paused again, letting his words take effect. 'They worship Lakshmi every day while apart from the obligatory puja every year, they have largely forgotten Sarasvati.'

'Besides the occasional *Mangalacharan* invocation at the beginning of a recital,' assented Sarasvati cheerfully. 'But that says more about Man, not us, Narada!'

'If Man invokes Lakshmi and not Sarasvati, it is the beginning of the end,' said Lakshmi. 'In his mad rush to chase wealth, if he believes that my blessings alone matter, he is surely a poor fool,' she continued with a tinge of irony. 'Perhaps he reckons that once he acquires money, all else will follow,' she shrugged lightly, but her face showed her displeasure. 'This is plain folly, a sign of the dark times to come.'

'Man, thanks to his essentially acquisitive nature, is a highly intelligent tyrant, who wants to conquer and rule all—land, water, the sky, the mind, the beings, the planet and even perhaps knowledge,' Sarasvati sighed deeply. 'Wealth is a means of acquisition of all this and more.'

'Are you saying this because Man prefers Lakshmi to you?' asked Narada bluntly, his face brave.

Lakshmi inhaled sharply. 'You are irreverent, Narada!' She reproved him with a wave of her hands, the emerald bracelets jingling noisily in protest.

'He is simply trying to have some fun at our expense, Lakshmi,' assured Sarasvati, casting him a sardonic smile. 'But I was talking to Lakshmi, not you, Narada, for she will understand what I mean. Man has inflicted damage on us too. Worse, he has managed to project the goddesses on to the human society of how men see their women,' reasoned Sarasvati, a troubled look in her dark, large eyes. 'If a woman brings dowry or other material gifts, she might get respect—but not always. But if she wants her share of education, she is often deprived of it or has to fight for it,' she paused, regarding them steadily, her smoky black eyes remote. 'They worship us, but do they respect their women, grant them their human dignity? The manifestation comes with recognizing and respecting the feminine divine present in all genders. The goddesses are kept on a pedestal in the hallowed sanctum of temples, but their women largely remain shackled in their own homes.'

'Or sexualized as objects of lust and fertility,' said Lakshmi.

'Till they are not seen as equals and given their basic right as the other half of the human race, we goddesses too will not be freed from these fetters and get our rightful place again.'

Narada looked thoughtful. 'I never saw it this way. Probably that's also another reason why Lakshmi is more popular as the docile, devoted consort of Vishnu. She is more relatable.'

'Why? Because a mild, mellow woman can be easily pushed around . . .' demanded Lakshmi. ' . . . And disregarded by everyone around?'

Sarasvati frowned. 'How conveniently have we been defined according to patriarchal constructs; where Man has projected his notions to control their women on to us, the goddesses. That's why, Lakshmi, you are alternatively docile and dutiful while also being "*chanchal*" with fickle, running feet, and there is this notion that if free, you will flee with all that prosperity!'

Lakshmi gave a brief nod, her face grim. 'What they don't realize is that when they chase me, they become rakshasas from manav. They want to grab and usurp wealth.'

Narada frowned as he suddenly thought of something. 'But both of you are part of the Tridevi. Like the Trimurti.'

'But we are seen more as that Tridevi, the respective consorts of the Trimurti, linking our greatness with our spouses,' she remarked drily. 'Or linking their greatness with ours.'

'Not you, Sarasvati. You have an individual identity,' said Lakshmi. 'It is Lakshmi–Narayan and Shiva–Parvati, but does anyone see you through a Brahma–Sarasvati concept?'

'Probably we are not that perfect made-for-each-other-couple,' quipped Sarasvati in good humour.

'No, you are unique, Sarasvati, not tied down by man or matrimony. You are worshipped as an individual entity of feminine value and veneration without an appended mandatory spouse!'

Narada looked at her, a feigned expression of surprise on his face. 'Oh, is that how the mainstreaming of spouses of the Trinity happened? Is that why you as the strongest stand-alone goddess are being pushed aside?' he asked slyly. 'Or perhaps the deceptively conventional image of you as the contemplative Sarasvati—all dressed in serene white and lost in her veena and books—doesn't have the same significance as other fiery, fierce and fearsome figures like, say, Parvati or Durga astride the lion of domination and patriarchy.'

Sarasvati gave a mirthless laugh. 'Good, that's how it should be!'

'But you are fiery and fierce in real life,' laughed Lakshmi, throwing up her hands as her ringed fingers glinted in the sunlight. 'You are the most feisty amongst all of us. It's just that people don't *know* you. You are an enigma to most . . .'

'Possibly,' Narada wondered aloud, doubtfully. 'There was once a time when knowledge, wisdom and scholarly pursuit were respected with the utmost regard. It was not seen as a means to an end but something that people pursued with devotion just for the love of it,' he pointed out, glancing at Sarasvati. 'That's your ideal, isn't it, Devi Sarasvati?'

Sarasvati sat wordlessly, much to the surprise of the other two.

'I repeat it: God help the world if it moves too far away from Sarasvati,' warned Lakshmi, absently moving the diamond ring around her finger. 'We are sisters—Sarasvati, Parvati and Lakshmi. Symbolically, this means you cannot gain wealth and empowerment without first acquiring knowledge.'

'Tell that to the ignorant and the arrogant,' snickered Narada, looking up to note Sarasvati's response.

She sat silently, her long fingers pressed to her temple. Her smoky black eyes opened a trifle wider. She appeared to hesitate, then she nodded. 'I am listening,' she murmured, scrutinizing him with narrowed eyes. He felt a prickle of apprehension.

'If I usher in prosperity into a household, Sarasvati brings wisdom and peace. I would love to go to places where Sarasvati resides!' Lakshmi observed as she absently adjusted the folds of her red brocaded shawl.

Narada refused to give up. He persisted. 'But, O Devi, does your arrival not mark the end of wisdom and peace in a family?' He countered. 'With wealth comes conflict over money. This in itself means that good sense or Sarasvati has flown out of the door, proving what I claim: peace and prosperity, or Lakshmi and Sarasvati, cannot coexist.'

'Wrong,' interrupted Sarasvati, with an imperious wave of her slim hands. 'You need intellect to make and maintain wealth, unless, of course, it's inherited,' she added, deprecatingly. 'Or, if it's earned by gambling!'

Lakshmi flinched. 'That's revolting!'

'Some celebrate you in that fashion,' prompted Narada, bowing to Lakshmi.

'Man worships as per his convenience—or who would conceive gambling as a measure of worshipping wealth and good fortune?' Sarasvati said in mock horror. 'Honestly, I am happy I have fewer temples of worship in my honour,' she smiled with relief. 'I prefer the open skies of free thought and expression.'

'You mean Lakshmi is shackled?' Narada had an indignant look on his face.

Lakshmi gave him a reproving stare. 'Narada, I am not shackled, but those attached to me are—*they* are trapped in their greed and quest for wealth. The same can be said about the learned too if they crave only success and glory but not wisdom.'

'But success can be fame and fortune,' Narada reminded her. 'When the learned and the creative reduce knowledge to a vocation, a means of earning fame and fortune, then is it not the scholar forgetting his vidya and chasing Lakshmi? Is not Lakshmi overshadowing Sarasvati?'

Lakshmi shook her head, the green gems twinkling at her ears. 'That is such a myopic way of looking at us, Narada. Man needs to appreciate Sarasvati's gift or he remains cursed in ignorance and poverty.'

'Besides, wisdom, like wealth, has to be earned with hard work, self-reflection and experience,' chuckled Sarasvati.

'Let me illustrate, Narada,' expanded Lakshmi, her smile brighter than the diamonds in her hair. 'In good times, Sarasvati teaches you how to earn, and, in bad times, how to turn the misfortune into fortune. So, in brief, Lakshmi and Sarasvati have to be hand-in-hand—always!'

Narada's thin shoulders sagged. 'I concede defeat. I agree that where Sarasvati dwells, Lakshmi joins in. But if ignored, Sarasvati will storm out and that also means Lakshmi too shall leave. That is why Lord Vishnu treats both Lakshmi and Sarasvati equally. It is just a myth that Sarasvati and Lakshmi are rivals.'

'A hollow rumour started by some,' corrected Sarasvati, throwing him a pointed look. 'And perpetuated by many . . .'

Narada flushed and nodded solemnly. 'You are soul sisters, so reciprocal and inseparable.'

'Like we are now,' she twinkled. 'Like we were before you came in.'

She suddenly put her head back and laughed. It was a full-throated laugh, a triumphant one filled with challenge and contempt. But it was also an infectious laugh. Before Lakshmi realized the delicacy of the situation, she too had joined in; audible, distinct laughter, not unlike Sarasvati's, partaking of the same overtones.

Narada stared sullenly at them, then moved to the door. As he turned the corner of the corridor, he paused. He could still hear the ring of their laughter . . .

22

SARASVATI'S CURSE

'What's taking you so long to decide what to wear?' asked an exasperated Yamuna. 'Or rather, not to wear?'

Sarasvati gave a slight shrug. 'Anything goes, but it's you who always expects me to be in my best finery!'

'Yes, because it's a mahayajna you are hosting,' returned Yamuna patiently, but her tone turned sharp. 'Will you hurry up? You can't be late for your own function, however much you disapprove of it.'

'I am never late!' Sarasvati muttered. 'I think it's an exercise in vanity and a waste of time!'

'But you have to reach before the *mahurat* . . .' Yamuna said in a frustrated tone. As she watched Sarasvati's disinterested face, her own scrunched up in a frown. Sarasvati paid no attention to what she was saying. There was a look of aloof disinterest on her face—that characteristic expression that hinted she seldom listened to something she was bored with.

'Never mind, I know you don't believe in ceremonies, but it's my job to make sure you arrive there on time!'

Sarasvati scowled. 'Why did Brahma command you to do so?'

Yamuna was suddenly aware that Sarasvati wasn't bored or distracted any more and that she was staring at her with an intent, rather odd, expression in her eyes.

'Yes, he specifically told me to get you there on time.'

'He's a fine one to say that. He's the one who is never punctual!' said Sarasvati with a snort.

Yamuna took a visibly impatient breath. '. . . That's my job for today and besides, I am your friend who wants to see you at your best!'

It was Sarasvati's turn to frown. 'It's just a puja . . .'she started.

'It is *your* event, Sarasvati,' wailed Yamuna indignantly. 'Yours and Brahma's as a couple. You have to perform the yajna together . . .'

'. . . When Brahma knows well I don't believe in it!' grumbled Sarasvati. 'I don't know why he wants to do this—commemorating war and victory!'

Yamuna looked up sharply. There was a note in her friend's voice that had brought her up short. 'Are you still miffed about that?'

It had all started when Brahma had blessed the demon, Vajranabha, after he had performed severe penance. Pleased, Brahma had granted him the city of Vajra: a city so strong and fortified that even air could not enter without Vajranabha's permission. Empowered with Brahma's blessing and ruling from his impregnable city, Vajranabha had set his sights on Indra's heavenly kingdom.

When Brahma had come to know of his dubious intentions, he had strangely decided to teach the demon a lesson himself.

'Why do you want to go to war with him?' Sarasvati had questioned him, catching hold of his arm as he paced angrily in the room. 'Indra had come to you. You could have sent him to Vishnu. You don't believe in war, *we* don't believe in war—or weapons and bloodshed,' she had reminded him gently.

'I believed Vajranabha was my friend but he betrayed me,' Brahma had said shortly. 'I have to fight him myself.'

He had felt her stiffen and there was a note of keenness in her voice when she said, 'Why, what are you saying? Let's not discuss the topic of war again. You know it never gets us anywhere.'

His face was chiselled in a cold mask. She had put her hands on his and stared at them as if she was seeing them for the first time.

'Please, Brahma,' she had said, gripping his hands. 'Don't be like that. You are going into darkness and destruction, not light and creation.'

'You mustn't worry,' he had said, running his fingers through his hair. 'I know what I'm going to do. I like to finish what I start. It's the way I'm made.'

'No, it isn't,' she had said. 'No one's made like that.'
'I am.'

'Please don't do this.' Her hands trembled in his. 'Let it go, Vajranabha will meet his end—either Vishnu or Shiva will look into it. Please, just this once.'

He had shaken his head slightly. 'It's my responsibility this time!' he had said grimly.

She took her hands away. 'You and your pride,' she had said, her voice suddenly hard. 'You don't care about this. You don't care about us, our values.' She drew in a deep breath and burst out, 'You've seen too many wars—that's what's wrong with you. You want to be part of it, participate in the violence and become a hero or some saviour!'

'It's not like that,' he had said, his tone taut.

'Yes, it is,' she had replied, her voice now elaborately controlled. 'You want revenge. You think Vajranabha has crowded you, deceived you, abused your patronage and you have to shake your reputation in his face. You can't resist doing that. You like long chances. You think it's big and clever and gallant to fight that asura—who stops at nothing—alone. Just because Vishnu and Shiva do it, you have to do it too.'

'That's absurd!' he barked in a voice thick with rage. 'If you don't agree, that's your choice. I shan't force you to see my way, nor can you force me to see yours!'

Sarasvati stood still, regarding Brahma with glittering, furious eyes. Both of them were angry now, and their voices had risen—though on his face there still remained the semblance of a cold, haughty smile.

There was a long silence, and then he heard her get up. She came and stood in front of him, stiff and straight. He could feel the anger coming from her. 'That was what I meant when I said you wouldn't fit in with my kind of life!' she had said bitterly.

'Yes, so do I,' he said intensely. 'I'm not made to be pushed around. I'm sorry if I have disappointed you, but I'm going to confront him. I said I'd fix Vajranabha, and

I'm going to fix him. If you find it dishonourable, so be it. But I have to live with myself, and I'd never forgive myself if I let that rogue slip through my fingers.'

'All right,' she said. 'I see how it is. But there is one condition,' she shook her head. 'Otherwise I won't be here when you come back. I mean it.'

'And what is that condition?' asked Brahma.

'You're not to kill Vajranabha. Until now, you have defended yourself. If you kill him, it will be murder. That mustn't happen. Will you promise?'

'I can't promise that,' Brahma protested swiftly. 'He might get me in a spot . . .'

'That's different, but you're not going to hound him and kill him as you have been planning to do.'

'Kill in self-defence, you mean,' he nodded. 'All right, I promise. I shan't kill him in cold blood.'

The pleased, satisfied expression in his eyes had jarred her to the heels. The quarrel was averted, but there was a strange tenseness between them since then.

And as vowed, Brahma confronted his enemy. It was only when Vajranabha showered his arrows that Brahma retaliated by releasing his lotus. As the petals fell on the fortified city, the demon got crushed under its weight. The petals landed on three different spots, creating craters. Brahma later filled those craters with water to form lakes: Jyestha Pushkar, Madhya Pushkar and Kanishta Pushkar. It was in this Pushkar forest, near the Jyestha Pushkar lake, that Brahma decided to perform the mahayajna, creating a chain of hills around the site to protect it from attacking demons.

Yamuna's voice cut through Sarasvati's thoughts. 'Will you stop dreaming and please get ready?' said Yamuna.

Yamuna's dusky face wore a weary grimace. She was glad Brahma was not here as the couple would have started a heated debate: Sarasvati was still displeased about the asura's killing and the yajna to commemorate it. Yamuna suspected that was probably why he had handed her the responsibility to get his wife dressed and ready on time at the assembly hall.

Yamuna could not let go of the strong feeling of unease. Brahma and Sarasvati were known as the most combative pair: there had been quarrels which at first didn't seem to amount to much—just natural disappointment in marriage and a clash of wills and egos of two strong-headed people. It was understandable, Yamuna had told herself, but she wished they were more reasonable and calm. She hated confrontations of any kind and she knew how deeply each argument affected both of them, although her friend feigned being unaffected. Often, Sarasvati would throw a fit and, in a show of annoyance, would rush out of the palace and roam away in the wilds from Heaven and would only return after such a long lapse that Brahma would be beside himself, worrying about his missing wife.

Each prided themselves on their own self-importance, but that was something they both had to put up with. But very often, Yamuna's fiery friend wouldn't put up with it. Which meant, Yamuna rued with a silent sigh, the quarrels developed into rows, and rows into scenes and now she was getting concerned about them. Today seemed to be one of those days and probably sensing it and his wife's mood,

Brahma had wisely stepped away, letting Yamuna handle the situation.

'Just see to it that she turns up on time,' he warned her.

'She will, she's stubbornly punctual! She dislikes people who are late: says they neither respect themselves nor the other person and worse, through their lethargic brain, fail to realize this,' Yamuna quoted her friend with a grin.

Brahma shook his head. 'She's not too happy about this yajna. She considers it a waste of her time! If she had her way, she would want no part in it!'

Or my success, he grimaced.

Yamuna had been struck by the angry bitterness in his voice. She had given a brief nod. 'I understand. I shall get her ready,' she had assured him.

Today, Yamuna's big task was to get her reluctant friend to the yajna on time, but she was not succeeding. She cast an apprehensive glance between her friend, dressing up leisurely, and the fast-rising sun beyond the tall trees of the forest below.

'Hurry, Sarasvati, we shall be late,' she said weakly.

'The function cannot start without me, however late I am,' said Sarasvati, assuring Yamuna in her usual imperious manner.

Yamuna knew her efforts were futile: Sarasvati was too independent-minded and strong-willed and never one to be ordered around by anyone, even if that happened to be her spouse—an important member of the supreme Trinity with all kinds of godly powers—hosting one of the grandest ceremonial rites. Sarasvati could well afford to engage in mock make-up and dressing.

'And why the hurry, Yamuna? I am sure that the other ladies must not yet have reached?' shrugged Sarasvati airily.

'Because you are the hostess!' hissed Yamuna.

Sarasvati elegantly moved her shoulders in the semblance of a shrug. 'I shan't wait for latecomers—not today!' she insisted stubbornly.

Edgy now, Yamuna grabbed Sarasvati by the wrist and pushed her towards the doorway. 'We have to leave, *now!*' she said in exasperation.

Sarasvati threw her friend a resigned look, conceding with a short laugh. 'Oh all right, I'll admit why I wasn't ready—I got late searching for a book I had misplaced. But now, here I am, toddling alongside you, all prepared and pretty again. Thanks to you, I am giving out a sense of being ready, all equipped!'

Yamuna pursed her lips, giving her a wordless nod: *I hope for her sake we are not late*, she thought, quickening her steps to stifle her panic.

They heard a distant bell ringing sharply to remind them of their tardiness and Sarasvati increased her pace, striding rapidly down the hill. She was wearing her new golden silk forced upon her by her friend: a brocaded, mustard-yellow creation, the bodice of which was covered with deep purple trimmings. Her dark hair was parted and fell in loose but not unstudied waves. Yamuna had made her look her best as if to remind Sarasvati of the grand significance of the occasion, and she was now uneasily aware of the threat of unpunctuality ticking slowly in pace with her quickening steps.

Even as they walked briskly through the woods, Sarasvati could not but observe that it was colourful and scented, humming with the chirping of birds, delighting in the senses of smell and vision. The trees were full of abundant flowers and it appeared as if there was a spring festival with softly blowing wind carrying the fragrance of the flowers, perfuming the forest and the sky. The cuckoos and parrots sang and the peacocks danced as she deftly dodged a few. The charming forest appeared like their own garden in Brahmalok. She was momentarily distracted, her steps faltering to a slow pace.

They finally entered the clearing in the forest reserved for the occasion and were greeted with a hundred pairs of probing eyes and deafening silence. All eyes seemed to be boring into them with either surprise or reproach. *Everyone is here, and we are late*, Yamuna sighed in silent lament.

Sarasvati stopped in mid-stride, her eyes widening in disbelief. She was not looking at the gaping crowd but at the flower-decked arbor where stood a tall, slim woman by the side of Brahma, attired in vermilion silk. *Her rightful side . . .*

'Who is *she*?' demanded Sarasvati in the cold, quiet voice that always came with her anger. Her animated expression turned to a dark frown: a transformation as swift and as final as a storm extinguishing the flame of an oil lamp.

Brahma crossed his arms, his gaze inscrutable: a tall, loose-limbed, powerfully built man, resplendent in white and silver robes, reminding Sarasvati of when they had first met in a similar forest all those years ago. Brahma looked at her for a long moment, his face expressionless, his eyes brooding.

'You are late, Sarasvati,' he said in his lax, drawling voice, the accusation menacingly soft. 'I had hoped you would not be. Not today, of all the days.'

'And so you start the yajna without me and perform it with *her*?!' Sarasvati raised her voice as she walked over to the couple. 'Who is she?'

'Gayatri,' he replied silkily. 'My wife.'

His softly spoken words hurtled into her screaming mind. *Wife? He had got married?!* She looked at him blankly. What he had said was so unexpected that at first she could hardly gather its sense.

'What on earth are you talking about?' she faltered.

Even to herself her reply rang embarrassingly weak, and she saw the mockery gleaming on Brahma's otherwise stern face.

'My wife Gayatri,' he repeated smoothly.

His voice, so cold and hard, had the effect of exciting in her a violent indignation.

'Like you did the last time when you had to perform a yajna and needed a wife! Me!' she reminded him, forcefully, glaring at the two standing close together in the bower, a sudden, unending surge of jealous rage going through her.

Shiva threw an apprehensive look at his friend. Vishnu felt a frisson of alarm: Sarasvati was livid as never before.

Brahma smiled suddenly; it wasn't a pleasant smile.

'Yes,' he said shortly, his steady gaze revealing an unsettling equanimity as his voice boomed against her ear, splitting into the tense gathering. 'This yajna was as important; regardless, you did not consider it so for you to be there by my side . . .'

She glared at him, motioning with her hand for him to be quiet.

'How dare you?' she rasped, clenching her fists and her mouth set in a hard, furious line.

He stood impassive. Her angry eyes swivelled at the woman standing close to him. She could more easily have coped with the situation if he had raved and stormed as well. She could have met violence with violence. His self-control was inhuman and she hated him now as she had never hated him before.

'Where did you find this wife on hire?' she spat contemptuously.

The muscles either side of Brahma's jaw stood out suddenly. The moment she had said this she flushed, for she was ashamed at her pettiness. He did not answer, but in his eyes she read an icy contempt. The shadow of a smile flickered on his lips.

'Gayatri is everywhere,' he commented cryptically. His solid olive sun-tanned face told her nothing, but his dark eyes were hard as he said, 'She was ready to be my consort for the yajna you considered unimportant.'

Gayatri smiled at her in response: a soft, knowing smile, enraging her further.

The thought entered Sarasvati's head that this woman meant something to him. She noticed how quiet Gayatri had been all this while, with Brahma doing all the talking and defending Gayatri against his first wife's wrath. She observed he showed no embarrassment as she confronted him now, almost revelling in her discomfiture, her public humiliation. She perceived how he looked at Gayatri—with the fond admiration he reserved for her. Detecting all these little points and knowing the strength of the harsh truth, her heart sank, her fury soaring.

Sarasvati caught her breath sharply.

'Is this a yajna or a sham of a wedding?'

Brahma nodded his head. His eyes narrowed.

'You made it so, Sarasvati, by showing disrespect and not being here on time for the yajna as my *ardhangani*,' cut in Brahma, his voice like ice.

'You found a quick substitute,' she lashed back wildly.

'Now be calm and let's go home. I shall explain everything.' He fixed her with his cold, hard eyes.

His patronizing tone incensed her even more. 'Home! I shan't stay a moment with you!' she raged. 'You remarried! You dared to insult me and betray me!'

She leaned forward and, with the back of her hand, she swept the ornaments, the plate of flowers and the bowl of fruits off the low table, to crash those on to the ground.

'This wedding, this yajna is nothing but an unacceptable act! It's a disgrace I refuse to be part of!'

'Sarasvati!' Brahma came quickly towards her. 'Now stop that!' He restrained his irritation with some effort.

'Oh, you don't get to tell me anything from now on, it's over for us!' she enunciated in the same cold, quiet voice. She stared at him, her eyes hostile and glittering. 'Go and play your charade of weddings and wives. Never mind about me, but don't expect to find me there when you get back. From now on, I leave you. I am not your wife, your consort, your anything!'

Brahma's mouth tightened. He went across to her, but she turned away from him, as she stood, stiff and straight, with her back to him, facing the guests.

Yamuna shivered, her mouth dry: her friend's face was a frozen mask of cold white fury, her eyes glacial, yet flashing.

'Calm down, Sarasvati, it is not what you think it is . . .' Brahma started. He ran his fingers through his dark hair and scowled.

'Oh, you just announced she is your wife, Gayatri. What else is there to say?' she fumed through clenched teeth. She glowered at him. 'You don't have to worry about me. Go and worry about your silly little new toy. I'll get along fine on my own!' she flared.

She caught sight of Gayatri, standing with Parvati and Lakshmi and the other devis, at the bride's bower, under the canopied banyan tree. A surge of red, hot fury swelled inside her, spilling over to the hapless women. With blazing eyes and a smouldering voice, Sarasvati addressed them. '*You* were there for my wedding too,' she started, her tone scathing. 'Standing just like you are now—either side of me, like companions. But today, it is Gayatri. As women, how could you allow such injustice?'

Without waiting for their reply, her livid eyes swung to the priests engaged in performing the sacred rites.

'All the same people, but a different bride this time,' she remarked bitterly.

A violent rage consumed Sarasvati. Her pale face glistened and her skin was drained of colour as she addressed Brahma. 'By the powers I have obtained by the performance of *tapas*, may you, Brahma, never be worshipped!' Her dangerously soft voice pulsated through the stunned silence. 'You will not be worshipped by Man or any other follower, never to be revered and venerated. Be it in a temple or a sacred place. You will be a god without the faithful!'

There was an audible collective gasp. Brahma stood still, his face immobile, his eyes expressionless, infuriating her more. Nothing seemed to affect him; neither her dishonour nor his disgrace.

Parvati interposed urgently, 'Sarasvati, don't . . . he's the Creator. You deprive him of his glory?'

'He did this yajna for glory,' hissed Sarasvati, her face deathly pale. 'He deserves no glory!'

Her smoky, dark eyes swung back to her husband. Brahma remained stolidly silent.

His eyes flickered. Brahma started to say something, then stopped. When she was in this mood, there was no reasoning with her.

Vishnu stepped forward. 'You have not cursed your husband, Sarasvati. You have cursed Brahma, the fountainhead of conception and creation.'

Parvati tried again. 'What is not created cannot be preserved or destroyed. Without Brahma, nothing exists . . . not even you!' she warned.

Vishnu threw up his hands. 'How can you shame him so ignominiously?'

Shiva interjected, obviously displeased. '. . . And the disgrace of never being worshipped or respected?'

Throwing them an ironical look, Sarasvati spoke over the volley of strong protestations, her voice clear and crisp.

'You employ words like shame and disgrace when defending your friend, but is not the presence of another wife at the yajna a disgrace, a shame for me?' she demanded. 'How could you allow it? Worse, you sanctioned and celebrated it!'

'Please, first listen to what Brahma has to say . . .' implored Lakshmi. 'Don't let your anger destroy the man you love!'

Sarasvati exploded. 'If he loved and honoured me, would he have married another woman for the sake of some yajna?!'

'But Gayatri is . . .'

Lakshmi threw Vishnu an anxious look, begging him to intercede.

'The yajna was to venerate the two of you . . .' Vishnu started.

'The yajna was the cause of all this!' Sarasvati said.

Her inflamed eyes centred on the crackling fire, as she proclaimed to the Fire God, 'Oh Agni, since you are part of this outrage, may you be the devourer of all things, clean and unclean, good and evil!'

To the terror-stricken priests around the holy fire, she pronounced: 'Henceforth you shall perform sacrifices not for knowledge or realization but solely from the desire of obtaining the usual gifts: and from covetousness alone shall you attend temples and holy places; satisfied only shall you be with the food of others, and dissatisfied with that of your own houses; and in quest of riches shall you unduly perform holy rites and ceremonies!'

Parvati made a sudden movement of protest. 'Why is your ire on the holy yajna?'

'It is the holy fire that witnessed an unholy alliance!' thundered Sarasvati.

'No!' cried Parvati. 'It was a commemoration of your husband's win over an evil rakshasa, the first time Brahma ever used a weapon in warfare. It was a tribute to both of you as a couple.'

'But where was I in this?' Sarasvati broke in, furiously. 'He didn't wait for me but installed another wife, with more than a little help from all of you!'

'Where were *you*?' interrupted Shiva.

Sarasvati bristled. 'My reply does not justify his action or answer your question.'

'Your words will have consequences,' Shiva reminded her quietly. 'Unhappy consequences that will have ramifications down the ages . . .'

Vishnu intervened, stepping in front of her. 'Sarasvati, please stop, listen to what Brahma has to say . . .'

Sarasvati looked from Brahma to Vishnu and her eyes snapped furiously. 'Does he have the face to say anything?' she said witheringly. 'And you don't utter another word!' she said violently as she spun around to Vishnu, her eyes narrowed in ferocious fury. 'All of you present here are guilty like him. All of you conspired for this second wedding, his second wife!' her lips curled in cold contempt. 'You are all allies in his crime.'

Her fiery eyes pivoted over all, burning through each one of them with a smouldering, deliberate gaze. 'Each one of you is culpable, each responsible for this unconscionable injustice!'

There was a look of vicious, ungovernable rage on her face. As her stormy eyes swept past each one of them, the gathering was numb with an unspoken terror.

She turned on Vishnu, standing nearest to her. 'Since you gave Gayatri in marriage to Brahma, you shall, in consequence of Bhrigu's curse, be born amongst men, and shall endure the agony of having your wife separated from you by your enemy; and you shall also wander as the heart-broken husband, as the humble keeper of cattle, for long!'

Sarasvati's words hammered through Lakshmi's frozen mind, her heart contracting painfully.

'No!' she cried, her eyes bright with anguished tears. 'How can you?! How can you break us apart?'

'Because all of you just did the same with me!' whispered Sarasvati hoarsely, grief momentarily overriding her wrath. 'Each one of you present here right now!' she said through her stiff lips.

She addressed a pale-faced Indra. 'Since it was *you* who brought this maid to Brahma, you shall lose your all, and these very hands shall be bound in chains by your enemies. You will be held a prisoner in a strange country; your city and kingdom that you so gloat about, will be occupied by your foes.'

Indra threw up his hands in despair, turning imploringly to Shiva.

'You reckon he can help you out?' sneered Sarasvati, glancing into the tranquil face of Shiva. 'I shan't say anything more to you, Shiva, but this I warn you that one day by the curse of the holy sages, you shall be deprived of your manhood!'

Parvati leapt to her feet. 'If you think your husband has erred, it is between the two of you. Why are you venting your anger on us?'

Sarasvati looked up swiftly, her face resentful. 'Because none of you advised my husband when he erred: you all stood by him, aiding him, supporting him with your very actions. It is no longer a matter between the two of us,' she added, her eyes flinty.

'We were supporting our husbands, not just Brahma . . .' Lakshmi intervened but stopped abruptly, observing Parvati's warning glare.

'Exactly,' smiled Sarasvati and it was not a pleasant smile. 'You aided your husbands, who aided their friend,' she grimaced, her lips twisting. 'All a sweet team.'

The tone in her voice sent a shiver down Lakshmi's spine, her eyes large and scared. So Sarasvati had eventually struck back at them.

'You are as guilty as the devas!' Sarasvati was raging. 'All you silent wives, who blindly aided their husbands, may you be barren!'

Sachi, Indra's wife, stepped back in horror.

Parvati went pale, shaking with fear and fury. 'Do you know what you are saying, Sarasvati?' she demanded, her voice trembling, her voice quivering. 'How can you do so being a woman? Or is it because you are childless yourself?'

Sarasvati gave a mirthless chuckle.

'Oh, that same barb again. I meant barren, not as in being infertile, but by leading unproductive, sterile lives. Which you all do anyway—you with your glory of power, Parvati! And Lakshmi, with her show of wealth,' Sarasvati's lips pursed in tight, furious line. 'But, today, in this hour of my humiliation, I, by saying this curse, am reminding you of your unfulfilled loves, your lives dedicated to just power and wealth which is worthless without wisdom, producing nothing! Barren!' she uttered scornfully, straightening her back, her face proud and contemptuous. She turned abruptly on her heels and marched out: a proud, retreating figure walking purposefully out of his life, thought Brahma, his heart sinking. She would go to the hills, he knew, retreating to the highest mount above the skies, to be alone: which is probably where she would have rather been anyway, he sighed bleakly, since he knew well how his loner wife had always been—disinterested in pomp and ceremony of any kind. And in that moment, Brahma knew he had probably lost her . . .

23

REMORSE

It was going to be another hot day. The sun penetrated the thin silk of her sari; Sarasvati felt irritated that she had to stay indoors to avoid the heat. She would have preferred to have a long walk in the woods or roam the skies. With a resigned sigh, she went near the window once more, and leaning against the wall, she gazed at the line of trees outside her garden absently.

As she stood there, her mind half on the garden and half on vague shadowy thoughts of what she should do that day, she heard Yamuna say haltingly, 'Sarasvati's *he's* here. He won't go . . .'

'No, I shan't till I have spoken with you,' announced a voice she loved and despised to distraction.

She turned to stare at him and then quickly turned away, her back straight and stiff, refusing to turn around. She heard the sound of the diminishing steps of Yamuna as she discreetly left the chamber. She glanced over her shoulder and then turned back to the window.

Brahma was breathing hard—he noticed this but he told himself that it was emotion, not just anxiety. He was here; she was here—that was enough. He was not even sure what he had to say to her. But this was the moment of his life that he felt he could least easily have dispensed with. There was no triumph, just surrender: he stood remorseful and defeated, laying his spoils, his faults, at her feet—to hold them for the final arbitrating moment before her eyes.

He recalled the ponderous journey from his house to hers. Assailed with doubt and trepidation, stifled by an unspoken shame, her palace had loomed up suddenly ahead of him, and his first thought was that it had assumed a strange unreality. Like she had for him now: distant and illusory. Nothing had changed there—only everything had changed. It seemed smaller and simpler than before—there was no haze of enchantment hovering over its roof, no music coming out of the open windows of the top floor. He wet his lips nervously and marched to the porch. The guard dared not stop him and as he walked inside, the feeling of unreality increased. This was only a room and not the enchanted chamber where they had once passed those poignant hours. He proceeded, thinking that his imagination had distorted and coloured all these simple, familiar things, to be abruptly stopped by Yamuna who flatly declared he was still unwelcome. It was then that he had burst into her chamber.

She was dressed in pale cream, her dark, straight hair uncoiling from her loose bun. The familiar velvety eyes caught his as he had come through the door, and a spasm of shock went through him because of her beauty's power of inflicting pain. His conscience tormented him. When Sarasvati had disappeared, he had felt as though he had lost something very precious, someone very near and dear whom he could never find again. He felt that with her, a part of his existence had slipped away, and that the moments he had passed through so fruitlessly would never be repeated.

'Will you please hear me out? I shan't leave till then,' he said quietly and something in his tone made her turn around to look at him. His fine-boned face was pale. His best features, his eyes, large and dark with thick eyelashes, were agonized.

He stood in the doorway, looking at her with his hopeful eyes; then he came into her chamber, quietly closing the heavy door behind him.

'Will you tell me what you are doing here instead of being with your bride?' She was getting her nerve back with a steady voice.

He flushed deep. 'It's been more than a month . . . you just disappeared before I could explain,' he ran his impatient fingers through his hair, throwing her a desperate look. 'Let me tell you why I did what I did. You haven't allowed us to talk! That's why I'm here.'

'I don't want you here!' She turned to him dispassionately with cool eyes. 'Nor anyone, for that matter,' she said and shrugged her shoulders.

'Yes I heard Shiva–Parvati and Lakshmi–Narayan were not entertained either,' he muttered.

'I told them what I had to,' she said. 'I owe them an apology.'

'I owe you one,' he replied.

'I don't want it.'

Her calmness scared him.

'But see what you made me do . . . You started this,' she lifted her shoulders, her voice strained. 'If it hadn't been for *you* . . .' she turned away as if the sight of him galled her. The flash of displeasure was gone almost before it started. He sat down stiff and still on the large settee, his twisting hands giving him away.

'If it hadn't been for *me* . . .' he repeated her words with a hint of mockery in his voice.

'We wouldn't be in the situation we are in now,' she finished smoothly.

She wasn't looking too happy, he thought uneasily. Her composure unnerved him. He didn't like the way her lips compressed when she caught the sight of him. Somehow, he felt the success or failure of this evening was going to determine their future.

'What now? Will you let me explain?' he pleaded gently.

He tried to neutralize the tremor in his voice by looking away. The obligation to speak was on him, but unless he immediately began to explain, it seemed that there was nothing to say. There had never been anything casual in their relationship previously—it was tumultuous, just as the ensuing turbulent silence between them.

She said nothing, but he was not surprised to see how her eyes froze him out: she had a reason to be offended. She continued to ignore him, turning her head away, looking out of the window, unseeingly. Her stony face made him nervous. He wished she would scream at him or argue or accuse. Anything would have been better than that set face and icy cold eyes.

He went near her and took her hands in his. She stiffened and pulled away.

'You're intelligent, you will comprehend what I have to say . . .'

'Do you understand me?' she asked coldly.

'You are a stubborn woman,' he said desperately, his eyes tormented. 'You won't see me, hear me out . . . you won't see it that way because it doesn't suit you! There was never anyone but you! Gayatri is not your substitute. Nor is she my second wife, she's *you!*'

Her eyebrows came together in swift puzzlement. 'What!' she began, for once, at a loss for words, her cold eyes confused. Colour rushed back to her pale face. 'That cannot be!'

She stared at him. He could see at once, she believed him. Her white face tightened, her lips trembled. She turned away and dropped back against the settee, her hand covering her eyes. The white column of her throat jerked spasmodically as she struggled with her emotions.

'Oh, believe me!' he cried impetuously, holding out his hands to her.

'Listen, please.' He came close to her. His voice had a sharp edge to it. 'Please, please, let me explain.'

She sat very still, holding on to her clenched fists, not looking at him. She felt weak and her heart hammered against her ribs. 'I don't want to talk about it,' she returned obstinately. 'I can never forgive you!'

'That won't get us anywhere,' he returned, watching her pale face and feeling the thickness in his throat again. 'I'd do anything for you, for us. You have to believe me!' he drew in a long breath. 'When you did not turn up on time, I admit I was furious and to teach you a lesson . . .'

'Teach me a lesson?' she asked, her eyes widening in incredulity. 'For what?'

Brahma had the grace to look ashamed. '. . . That you were taking the yajna so lightly,' he admitted awkwardly. 'You didn't reach on time, considering you are a stickler for punctuality.'

Her brows cleared. 'You thought I was deliberately late . . . to disrespect you!' she looked incredulous. She paused, a veil of sadness coming down her clear eyes. 'Is that what you believed?' she said quietly.

Brahma shook his head helplessly. 'I was livid and, in my hurt anger, I decided to replace you with . . . you. I created Gayatri—Sarasvati in another form—another wife, a new bride. As expected, you assumed the worst. But I didn't realize it would get out of my control . . . ' he flinched in despair. 'I tried to tell you, but by then, you were in no mood to listen. . . you had vanished . . . things had gone just too far . . .' he broke off.

'But you married another woman!' she mumbled, raising her stricken eyes at him. There was no longer any anger, no accusation, which he had expected but the despair in her eyes broke his heart, loathing himself in self-disgust.

'No, no,' he cried wildly. 'It was you, Sarasvati, always you!'

She did not comment, sat still, her eyes fixed on him with an expression that might have meant everything or nothing.

There was a short, awkward pause, and then he said, 'I had to create Gayatri as a form of you, as you were absent. I wanted you by my side for the yajna, but with every passing moment, the mahurat—the auspicious time—was going by. I waited . . .' he paused with a long sigh. 'I waited till the very last moment till Rishi Brihaspati said we had to begin or forsake the yajna. It was then that I thought of you and created Gayatri, another version of you, Sarasvati. The primordial generative force that manifests is Gayatri, the Brahma-Shakti, You.'

Sarasvati regarded him. 'You always have a profound logic to your explanation,' she said unimpressed. 'And where is she now?' she queried, her tone flat.

Brahma did not fail to observe the cynicism in her tone.

'No, she's there, you are there, omnipresent! Gayatri—or as Shiva renamed her, Brahmi or Brahmani—is a creation and transformation of you, created in my time of need. By creating her, with due diligence, and with whose Shakti I was capable of overriding my most difficult hour. Likewise, Gayatri shall contribute to the welfare of all and be a symbol of gratitude.'

Sarasvati struggled to believe him and yet she considered every word he said.

Brahma stole a long look at her: she had not thawed as he had hoped. She had gone stock-still; her stillness terrified him.

She swiftly rose and went over to the open window to push a flapping curtain back in the clasp while he came near her and stood at her side. In the hard light of the chandelier above, he noticed the rosy hue high on her pale cheeks.

She regarded him, her eyes narrowed. 'And that time, you decided to use Gayatri as I, Sarasvati, was not there,' she said crisply, scrutinizing him with ruthless impersonality.

She knew what he was saying. The primordial Shakti has two forms: one phenomenal and physical—*Sarasvati*—and the other inherent, almost mystical, the spiritual—Gayatri—who even energizes the Sun with her power. *Was the spirit in the body or the body in the spirit?*

She stood still, her eyes closed in quiet prayer. It was a moment of great revelation to her. She found then what she meant to him, and he to her, what they had done to each other . . .

She opened her eyes, clear and bright now.

'I am well aware that I have had all of you worried . . .,' she started, her tone formally apologetic. 'I have heard all that you and the others had to say. Now, let me explain, not that I need to, but for the sake of clarification,' continued Sarasvati with her characteristic candour. 'These past few months when I disappeared, as you said, I thought I was devastated. That you had betrayed me.' He flinched at the wealth of emotion in her voice. 'While my broken heart wept, my mind kept taunting me: why had I given you that power to hurt me? And then, I knew. I have had a queer feeling that I was stagnating—in irrational emotion and wasted feelings—but now I realize that I was actually growing, evolving and rebuilding myself. The constant occupation of work and music and travel was not just an escape—it did distract me from my pain and more importantly, my mind. As I travelled the skies, the worlds, I was able to have a glimpse of other lives and outlooks,' she gave a swift, sardonic smile. 'It reawakened my will as well as my imagination. I began to regain my spirits; I felt better and stronger. It had seemed to me that I could do nothing but simmer in resentment and misery, but to my surprise—and some confusion—I caught myself not thinking of you or us at all! It began to seem quite natural to live in the midst of a terrible crisis; I ceased very much to think of it,' she drew in a deep breath.

'And then, there came the day when it occurred to me that I had neither thought of you, Brahma,' she confessed, and Brahma could feel his heart break: it gave a sudden thud against his ribs. 'I was cured! I could think of you now with a certain rationality, call it an indifferent affection. You could hurt me no longer. The relief and the sense of liberation in my blood and mind made me sink in the jubilant irony of it. It was strange to look back and remember how passionate we had been for each other. And now, considering you calmly, I wonder with a little laugh and I know: I am free, free at last . . . '

 . . . *Of him.* Brahma shut his eyes, darkness engulfing him thick and quick. The stillness stretched the interminable pause; none dared to speak aloud. He felt his throat go thick, his tongue swelling, his words choked and unspoken. *No! No!*

She looked white and ill; there was a pinched, drawn look about her that spoke clearer than words how she had suffered all these days. Yet her voice was strongly sanguine.

'In your anger, you insulted me by remarrying and flaunting your new wife, Gayatri,' she ignored his protests. 'But I, in my ungovernable anger, vented it on the innocent. I cursed you, others as well. I have been at fault in my warranted anger. I did what I never imagined: let loose my emotions. I allowed my heart to rule my mind, anger overriding reason. I cursed,' she paused, breathless. 'What did I do?' she murmured in a disturbed whisper. 'I damned everyone!'

She sat, wooden, staring blankly. 'No, no, this is worse than I had ever thought . . . how can I be a goddess?' she cried in sudden self-disparagement. 'How can I be Knowledge when I cannot realize, understand or comprehend, when I cannot control my anger?' she cried, her fists clenched so hard that her knuckles shone in the sunlight. 'How can I ever face them? How can I face myself?' she turned to him again. 'See what you reduced me to—an avenging, angry woman!' she cried.

She made a self-deprecating gesture and got up, moving slowly across the chamber. 'I respected thought over emotion, brain over heart; I prided myself on having the ability to recall without rancour and resentment, but in one stroke, I demeaned myself—and all those present at the yajna. You changed everything, Brahma!'

Brahma was shocked by her vehemence, as he watched her pace the room. There was a wary, alert expression in her eyes that he felt uneasy about.

'They understand; they have already forgiven you,' he said soothingly, moving towards her. She felt him standing close beside her but not daring to touch her. He felt her shuddering and that made him feel worse.

She looked up at him fiercely, 'But I can't forgive myself! Can you?' she demanded. 'Can you forgive yourself, Brahma? We are both doomed, we are both damned—not by anyone, but ourselves!'

She regarded him. The probing stare made him feel uncomfortable.

'You were angry, hurt and humiliated, Sarasvati. But as Gayatri, you reduced each of their curses . . . they won't be potent now,' he added with a diffident smile of reassurance. 'Gayatri stepped in and, much to the relief of all the gods present, altered the curses for a happier ending. She diluted the curse for all, starting with Pushkar and blessing the place to be the king of pilgrimages. To Indra, she promised that though he would be chained and made prisoner by his enemies in a strange land and have all his coveted possessions gone, his sons will bring about his release . . .'

'That means Sachi won't be barren,' Sarasvati interrupted tersely.

'Yes, none of them,' he comforted. 'Gayatri assured the devis would not be barren, but would have children through unorthodox means,' he continued. 'To Vishnu, she blessed that he would take the form of a mortal to finally unite with Lakshmi. And finally, to Shiva, she assured that even though he would be deprived of his manhood, it would be universally worshipped in his place.'

'. . . With Shakti, of course,' Sarasvati reminded him.

Brahma nodded gravely, 'Shiva would thus not be emasculated but worshipped. And, lastly, the priests would become scholars and duly respected,' he smiled.

But she did not return the smile.

'And you? How did Gayatri save you?'

Her tone was stilted. Brahma shook his head. 'That I will be worshipped once a year at Pushkar, even though neither any temple be henceforth built for me, nor my idol be ever seen again.'

'So all's well,' she sighed wearily. 'All have been relieved of my fury. I am at peace now.'

She was peering at him, sunrays falling on her hair and her eyes alive with relief. He liked the feeling of having her close to himself, her faint scent tugging at his senses, and the sight of her delighting his heart.

'But there was a lot of truth in your curse,' he observed quietly. 'I am accused and accursed: why worship such a desirous god who has already fulfilled his role?' he shrugged. 'The Creator need not be worshipped. He does not need a temple, a house to remind people of His existence. It is the creation that needs to be venerated: Nature, the Universe, elements, rivers and the living beings, all that is around you to live in harmony. That is why you, my dear Sarasvati, as Knowledge, you will always be worshipped in your pure, beautiful form, the greatest gift of all to mankind.'

'I cannot imagine a world without Knowledge!' she scoffed. 'I understand. I don't believe in temples either. I can't see myself as a domesticated goddess, housed in some temple with an ornate roof over my head. The only offering is Knowledge—no riches, no fancy structure, no protection.'

'You are an ascetic, not just a goddess,' he gave a wan smile, his cheeks creasing attractively. She was calm, undisturbed by his smile. His smile had won him difficult conquests in the past. He moved restlessly. 'You do think from the material mind, but an intellectual, almost a spiritual one. Like your crystal-clear waters, Sarasvati, you will never be polluted by the desire of power, pride or wealth.'

Her eyes were thoughtful. 'Yes, I would rather remain an abstraction, as the supreme power of the mind . . .' she halted and said in that quiet, controlled voice that he had always admired. '. . . I can't see myself either as a devoted, dutiful consort you wish for Brahma,' she added firmly.

His face went white. She was rejecting him—all over again. He shut his eyes, darkness again swirling over him.

She shook her head. An obstinate look came into her eyes. 'I want to see the end of this. No, let me say it, 'she insisted, her voice even, her eyes steady. 'Let me tell you what's been wrong with us, right from the beginning. It is not the first time you have dishonoured me,' she said slowly. 'You did it when you fell in love with me, treating me not as an inspiration but as a figure of desire. I resisted and eventually I succumbed to the emotion.'

He was so surprised by the suddenness of this attack; he remained motionless, staring at her. She tapped her foot absently on floor, restlessly weaving her fingers. She struggled away, her face on fire. 'You, as the Creator, disrespectfully treated his Creation as if it were an object—not as a subject of inspiration or a vision. As if I belonged to you . . .'

Brahma made a protesting movement, but she waved him away with a sweeping gesture of her hands. 'No, let me speak, Brahma. By actualizing me, you generated a disturbing contradiction. By submitting yourself to desire and possessiveness, you personified me, your objectified Knowledge, as if, I, as your point of desire, had the power of fulfilment—and obedience.'

He still stared at her and shook his head. 'You don't understand . . . I don't believe this is what you think of me . . .' He slid across to her in one movement and pushed his hand in hers. She recoiled.

'For our sake, Sarasvati,' he said roughly. 'Will you listen to me? You have it all wrong!'

His urgency touched her and she said quickly, 'No, I know.' She resisted for a moment, and then began to calm down. 'You had fallen under the spell of the very illusion you created. Blinded, you could not see that you were both the cause and the form of all that is there. You were besotted with me, almost mesmerized, and you longed to possess me as an entity, as a body, as a woman. I cannot be owned! As if I weren't already yours, as if I could bring fulfilment, as if happiness depended upon a thing, something external, which was not already part of the Creation.'

Brahma stepped back, stiffening. 'You are misunderstanding me again . . .' He swung around. 'Don't insult all that we have! I thought we were beyond this!'

Her face was an expressionless mask again, but a nerve throbbed on her temple.

He could scarcely recognize his wife. She seemed beyond hurt and anger, almost reviewing him and this episode with a certain detached outlook. This aloof woman wasn't her. There was an icy flint in her black, remote eyes and her lips were paper-thin.

'No, *you* keep insulting me, and all that I stand for,' she said quietly. 'I assumed you would have learnt by now. But then you slipped again . . .' her lips pursed delicately. 'Each time you slipped, leaving good sense, chaos followed. Be it when you lost your head to Shiva or recently at the Pushkar yajna. You performed that yajna for *your* sake, but again, you treated me—Knowledge—like I was something to be owned or disowned, an object replaceable, dispensable.'

Brahma stiffened. His eyes shifted away from her.

There was a pause, then with a disbelieving shake of his head, Brahma said, 'Tell me more; let's go ahead with this. That's why I'm here.'

Looking at him, Sarasvati was surprised. There was no weakness in that stony white face that stared at her fixedly, prepared for the worst.

'I could possibly say your original mistake was very simply taking me for granted . . .'

Brahma laughed. It was a flat, mirthless noise, the nearest he ever came to showing that he was amused. 'Original mistake!' he exclaimed, and laughed again. 'It was love, Sarasvati, which you still seem to deny!' he sighed wearily.

The statement angered her, her dark eyes blazing like molten diamonds.

'Stop it,' she flared. 'Let's not talk of love! You confuse love with ownership. You can possess me as Knowledge but never as a person. Neither can you discard me when it suits you!'

'Yes, the cure for my disease or my crime, as you say, is Knowledge. When will I get to know and learn about *you*?' he asked bitterly.

She shook her head. 'You still don't get it. In fact, it is self-knowledge: the wisdom, which comes from within. It is contained in self-awareness, introspection of oneself. There is nothing in this Universe that can be acquired, possessed or consumed, that can provide complete fulfilment. The liberation from this endless cycle of desire is this self-knowledge: the happiness that one seeks. And it cannot simply be replaced by a substitute!' she added drily. 'Sarasvati will only become Gayatri when *She* wants to be, not when *You* want Her to be!'

'That won't get us anywhere,' Brahma pleaded, watching her and feeling the thickness in his throat again: that strangulating fear of losing her. 'I'd do anything for you, for us. I cannot exist without you . . . You are my soul; you are the only friend I've got in this world!'

His words tore at her heart, his tormented voice more communicable in expressing his regret: irresistible, persuasive and compelling . . .

'How could you even imagine I would take another woman?' he asked helplessly. 'You are everything, Sarasvati—my mind, my heart, my spirit, my love.'

She was pale, but he had glimpsed a light in her eyes that gave him hope.

She shook her head. She was leaning back, looking into his eyes. 'Oh, I know you better than you know yourself,' she returned. 'We can work together—but beyond that, you wouldn't do any good to me and I wouldn't to you. There's no use going on,' she said firmly. 'You see, Brahma, I've lived too long in your expectations . . . and my disappointments.'

A look of disbelief flitted across his haggard face.

'This is not it,' he insisted stubbornly. 'I hate going on alone. I cannot do it alone! If you come back and take a chance with me, I can make good on anything, but not while I'm agonizing about you down here, loving you to distraction . . .'

She frowned, reining in her impatience. For a while, she was sorry, then merely kind. Now she would have to be heartless as she was meant to be.

'I'm so sick of these unrealistic expectations, such pointless emotions!' she cried. 'I'm so tired of this struggle for validation, the endless search for gratification, this willingness to sacrifice everything for the sake of love, to get what you want. One time, I did fall for you, but not now. I'm the Knowledge you divined,' her lips drooped sneeringly. 'All I want is to be left alone to the little happiness that's left to me.'

Brahma suddenly thought that he was on dangerous ground. He had not intended to let anything spoil this opportunity. He moved closer to her, but she stiffened and stepped back. He shook his head and tried again desperately with words: 'No, Sarasvati, we can't be separated—we are one!' he said, 'You're my everything and I love you . . .'

She placed her hand on his, warningly putting her cool fingers on his wrist.

'Please don't,' she said, in her quiet, sure tone, and there was no doubt or desperation in her clear, steady eyes. 'I couldn't bear to quarrel with you. You know how sure I am. And I love you . . .'

His heart leapt.

'. . . But just not the way you would wish or love.'

Just for a brief second, it had sounded so marvellous, then what she said next, it all turned to ashes.

'Then if you love me, why can't you forgive me?' he persisted, frowning at her, his otherwise inscrutable face twisted in helpless anguish.

Sarasvati hesitated, her face flushed and eyes darting to Brahma's tormented face. Her heart missed a beat. 'I . . . I can't . . . it's different now, both of us have changed . . .' She stopped, her tone weary. The colour on her face was deep. 'I guess I love myself more than I love you,' she finished drily.

'I am more proud than loving?' He looked at her, his eyes twin pools of despair. It seemed to him that he was being very calm and logical and that she was putting him in the wrong deliberately. With every word, they were drawing farther and farther apart—and he was unable to stop himself or keep the hurt and pain from coming out of his mouth.

'Did I hurt your pride more or your heart, Sarasvati?'

'My worth,' she retorted and stopped short. She was silent a long time before she answered, not thinking—for she had seen the end—but only waiting because she knew that every word would seem more cruel than the last. She suddenly grew conscious of the look in his eyes, tender as it always was when fixed on her, but faintly hopeful, infinitely sad. Finally, she spoke: 'Don't look at me like that! In another minute, we'll be strangers . . . and we can never be that! We'll be seeing each other—we still have work to do together . . .' she said urgently. 'But Brahma, don't you see you are asking something of me that I am not fit for, that I am not interested in and don't want to be interested in! I do love you but . . .'

'You say you do, yet you don't . . .' he paused, a faint flush coming to his face. His eyes looked hard and bitter. And defeated. He felt his throat thicken, gathering his shattered emotions. 'I'm sorry. I am so sorry I hurt you.'

Her voice firmed. 'But unfortunately, sometimes one cannot do what one thinks is right without hurting the person you love, without making the person you love unhappy.'

He shook his head, 'No,' he answered, smiling, a sad, defeated smile. 'The only thing that makes me unhappy is that I am making you unhappy.'

In the heat of the darkening day, the moment of separation drew closer. They had each guessed right about each other, but of the two, she was readier to admit the situation. They held each other with their gaze for a long time. Outside, the distant trees were now black silhouettes as the daylight dimmed and dusk cloaked a starless sky.

With ill-concealed agony in his face, Brahma held out his hands towards her. She took an uncertain step, faltered, and then pressed his hand quickly as if she were taking leave of a chance friend.

'But I shall wait for you . . . I am waiting . . .' he whispered, swallowing convulsively, rooted to the ground.

She knew he was talking to himself, so she didn't say anything, but shook her head, her look cold as if her face was carved out of ice.

She briskly walked away from him, feeling his eyes on her. She had not broken down. Nothing seemed to be changed, except that now she would not be with him. She could hardly believe everything was over—it wasn't—they still had a lot to do together, they would continue working together, she was certain. She was surprised, with a slight sense of satisfaction that it was over so easily. She would have given a lot to know exactly what he was feeling: crushed, yes, but his coal-black eyes were a mask that even she, who had known him for so many years, could not penetrate. But she was not going to let him think she felt any resentment towards him and her pride constrained her to act calm and collected.

Brahma stood motionless, his eyes still fixed on her as she disappeared, swallowed into the long corridor. He felt defeated and weak—if he had only come before. If only he had not done what he did . . .

Speechless and almost blind with pain, and in some dazed way, he turned slowly towards the front porch and let himself out, the evening air stinging his distorted face, his eyes burning with unshed tears. Their world—his and hers—stood still; she was something extraordinary and rare that he had created, fought for and loved . . . and lost.

Past the lined trees, swaying in a slow, melancholic step, he walked unhurriedly through wide empty spaces towards the sunset, realizing that he could never recapture those lost times, even if he searched across eternity. This dusk would forever cover the sun, the trees, the flowers and the laughter in his world. Perhaps she too would see the sunset and pause for a moment, turning, remembering him, before he faded away into the past while she slept.

'She'll be back,' he murmured to himself, *'Perhaps one day . . .'*

EPILOGUE

WORLD FORSAKEN

'*Stop, Sarasvati!*'

Sarasvati halted, half turning to regard the Trimurti.

Her hard, velvety eyes met theirs. 'Tell me why I should not leave.'

'And leave the world without Knowledge?' Vishnu looked aghast. He frowned down at her. 'It will drown in the anarchy of darkness and chaos, violence and bloodshed, destruction and death . . . Man will become a barbarian again!'

'It is still happening, though,' mocked Sarasvati, her eyes grim. 'The world does not need me. Man has forsaken Knowledge and good sense; Man has forsaken me; I did not forsake him. It is time I did. I shall simply retreat.'

'You are not defeated for you to retreat!' Vishnu said vehemently.

'If not defeated, then I surrender to human foolishness,' she shrugged. 'Even his wickedness is foolish; his foolishness so wicked. He does not deserve to be blessed with Knowledge: he has used it not to dispel ignorance, but to indulge in mindless violence—against Nature as well as mankind.'

Shiva nodded. 'I agree and it was you who saved the world last time and me too, when I was suffering the same anger and disgust that you are feeling now. I was about to open my third eye and annihilate the world.'

'The Vadavagni Shiva's wrath created plunged the world into panic but it was on your assurance that only the evil and the corrupt would be destroyed,' Vishnu reminded her. 'After which you took the form of a river and with your pure waters picked up the dreaded fire—the beast of doom.'

Sarasvati stared at him, calm and remote.

He persuaded, 'You saved the world many times as you did the wisest of men. You saved Rishi Vashist when he tried to commit suicide by drowning in your waters, Sarasvati, by splitting into hundreds of shallow channels and of course, your kind words of advice.'

'I saved him but I could not save myself. I should have known this was the first sign of the river withering up when I started braiding into distributaries,' she said quietly, with a sad shake of her head. 'I am a mythical river now. River Sarasvati parched up to warn the world against Man's atrocities on Nature and fellow beings. But it was a lesson Man never learnt.'

'You are a river that gave birth to a great human civilization!' Vishnu said quietly. 'You are Sarasvati that gave birth to sublime literature, language and tradition. But your disappearance has made you more holy, kept alive by the Triveni of you, Ganga and Yamuna . . . '

'If unheeded, someday perhaps Ganga and Yamuna will likewise revolt . . .' warned Sarasvati, her tone ominous.

Shiva gaped at her.

'No, please don't say it, the world will die—dry and parched—in everlasting drought and famine,' he pleaded.

'I withered away a long time ago—after the great war of Kurukshetra,' she said quietly. 'Fearing Yamuna would follow me, Balaram altered her course . . .' her words hung gloomily in the cold, crisp air.

Shiva shook his head, the dreadlocks shaking menacingly. 'You dried up the river in your wrath, but your life-giving waters still sustain and nourish humanity and civilization. Through Knowledge.'

'Does it?' Sarasvati looked dispirited. She again gave a slight shrug. 'I had once said that as long as Man is wise, this terrible creature of power, greed and violence will remain at the bottom of the sea. But wisdom has been abandoned and man corrupts the world and the Vadavagni will emerge and destroy the universe,' she lingered and went on, 'Fire is also symbolic of the Fire of Knowledge remember? The time has come,' she said in a flat, final voice.

Vishnu frowned, his eyes grim, and tried to conceal his edginess.

'It's not the end of the world. It is the end of an era, another will start,' he argued.

'How often have you said that and how often have you taken avatars to save Man and the world?' she demanded. 'Has he learnt his lesson? Has he become wiser?'

'No, he has not,' assented Brahma, speaking at last, his deep baritone after overcoming a faint tendency to waver, went on with gracious formality. 'But then that is all the more reason for you not to relinquish your responsibility, Sarasvati. You are meant to guide the people to enlightenment, not destruction. Sarasvati, you are the goddess of the forefathers as well as of the present generation. Right now, you are their future, their hope.'

He succeeded in making this sound offhand. His voice, equable and unmoved, disturbed her, but not as she had expected. They hadn't seen each other for the longest time. Both knew how long it had been—to the day. This was the voice of a stranger, unexcited; pleasantly glad to see her—that was all. Yet, she intuitively knew it was more than that. He was persuading her, imploring her in his dispassionate manner.

'It is Man's biggest misfortune that he never understood you or what you mean to them, Sarasvati,' Brahma continued, his tone regretful. 'He failed to recognize you, as that mighty stream of thought; that holistic river of tradition that has created and recreated man and mankind.'

Sarasvati gave a mirthless smile. 'It's not about me, Brahma. It is about Man.'

He shook his handsome head. 'It is about *you* . . . and you leaving the world of Man. The world where you are the force of the mind and intellect, that river of cultural consciousness that flows to usher progress and prosperity; you are that dawning light, whose rays dispel darkness of ignorance. Without you, there will be only chaos and confusion, anarchy and annihilation.'

'Man is bent on destroying the world and in the process destroying himself too,' Sarasvati commented, her face hardening. 'He is violent—in mind, in spirit, in his actions and right now, the way he's going, he's deprived and depraved of any vision. His progress is nothing but mass destruction—of himself and the world.'

Vishnu interposed, his face bleak. 'Till humanity pays obeisance to Sarasvati, the Fountainhead of Knowledge, for awakening its mind to this reality and help believing in what, at some level, it instinctively knows, is the truth. Don't abandon the world, Sarasvati, may you reconfirm the faith, may you re-attain your lost glory and find your true place in the history of Man and the ancient land on Earth.'

Sarasvati chewed her underlip, her luminous eyes shifting away from Vishnu's entreating face.

Brahma studied her expressionless face. He stated, this time on a softer key, standing in front of her, as if to halt her stride. 'Sarasvati, Man creates his world of happiness and unhappiness, of peace and violence, of knowledge and ignorance. This world I created have both: to see the good, you have to know the bad. Man is bound to fight and battle, clashing the good and the evil within him and outside. Hopefully, the good will—one day—prevail, enriching him, enlightening him. The world is not a place where all or anyone can be happy. I did not create the world for man's happiness, though many may like to reckon that it is the very reason for living and existence.'

'The issue of happiness does not exist for me, knowledge, peace and harmony does,' returned Sarasvati. 'Man wants to be God, creating his own world of hate and power, fuelled by a certain callous obliviousness.'

Brahma shook his head. 'The true measure of Man is his willingness to right the wrong.'

Sarasvati permitted herself to smile, albeit a sad one. 'You always have been an optimist, Brahma. Man thinks wrong is right; there is no wrong in all he is doing. He has ruined his planet and yet hopes to conquer new ones. That is his definition of knowledge and progress,' she scoffed, lifting her shoulders. 'His own world is filled with weapons and war and violence corresponding to the unprecedented escalation in hatred. His own people are dying from man-made war, poverty, disease and forced starvation, yet the rest of his world pretends not to notice. Either way, it is a symptom of where the world is right now—the rage of the many against a few. It's not easy even for Man to have faith in Man. And it is in this state of chaos and desperation that humans are losing their sense of humanity.'

Vishnu and Shiva exchanged a quick glance: they did not deem it necessary to speak further. Only Brahma could persuade Sarasvati. Despite their break-up, Brahma acted as though his position was unchanged. And she did not seem to mind either. The gravity of the situation notwithstanding, they were meeting up as long-lost friends. Brahma was as pleasant, as attentive and soberly observant as usual. He was treating her with the same comradely admiration with which he had always treated her. He did not seem either harassed or upset or fundamentally sorrowful; nor did Sarasvati appear dispirited. Right now in the implacable temper she was in, both knew only Brahma would be able to coax her out of her momentous decision.

'But if Man does not believe in God, then the only alternative is Man to believe in Man!' exclaimed Brahma.

'You have faith in your creation,' she murmured cynically. 'I don't. I don't believe in Man, just as Man does not have faith in me. Even if he did, I'm not sure I'd be the same god that they believe in.'

'Man does not believe in God because he considers why does God allow for all the suffering that goes on...?' suggested Brahma, silkily.

'He is foolish to believe that; not knowing that he has created and caused the suffering himself!' she retorted. 'Man wants control—of everything - be it land, water, space, and now information! He has misused the power of Knowledge. He has amassed so much intelligence that he knows how to employ it to master all—never mind the huge loss and human tragedy he generates in the process. So, that is what I am doing—taking away that information from him forever by walking away from his world, from his cruel mind!'

Brahma pursed his thin lips into a stern line. 'Without the tools of knowledge, you will reduce him again into a savage?!'

'He still is!' she said hotly. 'He makes the same mistakes over and over again, inflicting mindless pain and destruction. In such a dark world, I refuse to preside.'

'But you have to!' he insisted, his tone cutting sharp.

Brahma frowned, studied her lovely, intent face and seemed to draw inspiration from it, for he said, 'Actually, yes you have to stay and help make things right again. You are that sliver of hope and light in this darkness. Humanity witnessed recently the worst of disease and disaster, which brought them and their world to their knees, begging for sense and sanity. If that has not allowed them to see the power of Wisdom, of Mother Nature and how they as a human race have responded to it, then all I can say is that *you* will show them the way!'

Sarasvati brooded off into a silence that lasted some time. She was suddenly aware that he wasn't vague or profound any more, and that he was staring at her with a direct, rather odd expression in his eyes.

'And yes, even in the throes of the worst, the most hopeless doubt, I still do believe in Man,' he said forcefully. 'I believe in Man's innate sense of humanity, his potential for compassion, reason, righteousness of heart. I appeal to you in that hope . . .' He gave her a long, searching look. 'But Man needs you. We all need you, Sarasvati.'

It was an entreaty; she couldn't meet his steady, pleading gaze. His voice was persuasively soft, revealing the tenderness he would always feel for her against her non-committal attitude towards him. Here with the past around them, besides him and her, mounting moment-by-moment, hanging heavier in the air, it seemed intimate and effective.

'You left the Earth as a river; you left me once. I tried in vain to stop you. I do so again. But this time, not for me, for us. For them. For the world; you are, plainly and clearly, the Goddess of the World, the goddess of a divine inspiration. Don't turn against mankind because Brahma is in every human being. Imagination makes him think, knowledge makes him wise. You taught them to think; now teach them to care...'

She felt her heart stir. She slid her eyes away from his, staring at her fingers laced in a clenched grip.

'You are Prakriti and as Nature is the parent, humanity is your child. Can a mother leave her baby?'

Sarasvati looked up and stared fixedly at him, a pulse beating at her throat.

'Imagination leads to consciousness,' he continued softly. 'And this very consciousness makes for his creations and discoveries which he calls progress. But this consciousness shall one day also lead to enlightenment. In this way, it makes you, Sarasvati, both mother and daughter of Man. Either way, you can't abandon him.'

Her velvety, dark eyes were no longer remote.

'Possibly my expectations of you are unreal, even illusory, but you are real. Nature does not love or hate and does not have a preference as all are equal before her. Even Man.'

The benign, kindly expression came back into her eyes. Once more, she was the efficient, dignified goddess.

'Please don't leave, stay . . .' Brahma breathed, not daring to move, or think, or hope, all lulled into numbness by the feeling of dread. Time would pulsate on, past them, past eternity, beyond that he saw only tomorrow and despair. 'Please.'

And then a curious thing happened; she moved. Brahma stepped aside to let her pass, but instead of going through, Sarasvati stood still and stared at him for a minute. It was not so much the look, which was not a smile, as it was the moment of silence. They saw each other's eyes, over faintly accelerated breath, overcome by each other's presence, a convinced acknowledgment of the other.

Shiva held his breath as Vishnu's worried face broke into a slow smile.

Sarasvati had halted her stride, one foot on the step of the threshold: neither in, nor out. That was enough . . . for now.